OUTLAW RANGER

VOLUME THREE

JAMES REASONER

WOLFPACK PUBLISHING
— EST 2013 —

Outlaw Ranger, Volume Three
Paperback Edition
© Copyright 2021 (As Revised) James Reasoner

Wolfpack Publishing
5130 S. Fort Apache Rd. 215-380
Las Vegas, NV 89148

wolfpackpublishing.com

eBook ISBN 978-1-64734-767-3
Paperback ISBN 978-1-63977-205-6

OUTLAW RANGER

GUN DEVILS OF THE RIO GRANDE

1

HELL CAME TO SANTA ROSALIA WHILE THE VILLAGE SLEPT. The raiders charged in on horseback, shouting and shooting, when the eastern sky had barely begun to show streaks of red and gold. Men hurried out of their jacals to see what was going on and were shot down, swiftly and brutally. Their bullet-riddled bodies flopped in the dust and their women ran to them, falling to their knees, weeping and wailing.

The screams grew louder as the raiders dismounted and jerked the women away from their slain loved ones —but only the women young and pretty enough. Then, the killers strode into the *jacals* to search for more women and girls. They kicked aside the boys who put up a fight. The old women who tried to protect their daughters and granddaughters and nieces were gunned down just as the village's men had been.

In the end, the only ones left living in Santa Rosalia were the very young, the very old, the infirm, and the women so ugly no man would ever want them. And since most women grew beautiful when a man guzzled down enough tequila, there were very few of those.

The raiders found a number of carts in the village, normally used in the farming that gave these people their livelihood. They forced the prisoners into those carts, where they huddled together in their nightclothes, stunned and terrified. Then, the men brought donkeys from their pens and hitched them to the carts. The crude vehicles lurched into motion and rolled northwest from Santa Rosalia, following the course of the river that divided Mexico from Texas.

Some of the weeping women looked across the river at the level, brush-dotted terrain. The *Tejanos*, many of them anyway, were regarded as devils who liked nothing better than to kill Mexicans. But, right now, these prisoners would have welcomed the sight of a band of bloody-handed Texans charging across the Rio Grande to kill their captors.

No help waited for them, in Texas or elsewhere. The carts rolled slowly past several men who sat on their horses in the growing light and studied the prisoners. Martin Larrizo's mount stood slightly ahead of the other two. His lieutenants flanked him. He nodded slowly, satisfied with what he saw.

He lifted a hand and pointed at one of the young women. "That one."

Hector Gonsalvo spurred forward and leaned down toward the prisoners. The women cringed from him but couldn't get away. Gonsalvo looped a long, ape-like arm around the captive Larrizo had pointed out and dragged her from the cart as she screamed and punched futilely at him. He rode with her back toward Larrizo, then reined in and dropped her on the ground next to his horse.

4

He held on tight to her nightdress, though, so it ripped away from her as she fell, leaving her slender body nude. She hunkered on the ground, doubling over in an attempt to hide her nakedness.

Larrizo, tall in the saddle, barrel-chested, with a heavy-jawed face and thick mustache, nodded to Gonsalvo. The lieutenant dismounted, wrapped sausage-like fingers in the girl's long black hair, and jerked her to her feet, putting her body on blatant display. Larrizo nodded.

"This one is mine," he said. "No one touches her." He lifted his voice and addressed all his men. "No one touches *any* of them until we know what value they are to us." He looked at Gonsalvo again. "Bring her, Hector."

Gonsalvo lifted the young woman who struggled for a second before going limp as if all her resistance, all her hope, had run out of her like water. He placed her on Larrizo's horse in front of the leader, who looped his left arm around her waist and jerked the reins with his right hand to turn the big black horse. The rowels of his spurs raked the animal's flanks and it leaped forward into a gallop.

Martin Larrizo rode like the wind away from the conquered village with his prize firmly in his grasp.

But this was just the beginning and a much greater prize waited out there for him to seize.

All of Mexico.

BRADDOCK SAT IN THE OPULENT BAR OF THE CAMINO REAL Hotel in El Paso and nursed a beer. His surroundings— gleaming hardwood, polished brass, sparkling crystal— were a far cry from what he was accustomed to in his simple adobe cabin in Esperanza, the Mexican village downriver that had become his home.

The Camino Real boasted all sorts of guests. Mexican *grandees* and *hacendados*, Texas cattlemen, railroad tycoons, successful businessmen of all stripes...and their ladies, gowned and coiffed and perfumed, possessed of all the loveliness money could buy. It wasn't exactly the sort of place where a disgraced former lawman would spend an evening. A man wanted by the authorities on this side of the river.

An outlaw Ranger.

Braddock was tall, lean, deeply tanned, with a scar running up the side of his face into his sandy hair. He wore a brown suit that was nothing fancy, especially compared to the garb of the bar's other patrons but still the best outfit he owned. A cream-colored Stetson with a tightly curled brim sat on the table.

Most folks didn't parade around with guns on their hips anymore, not in the early days of this new, modern century, so Braddock had left his shell belt and Colt at the boarding house where he had rented a room. He had an over/under .41 caliber derringer tucked in his waistband just above the watch pocket where he carried the badge he had once worn as a member of the Texas Rangers, the West's most famous outlaw hunters.

He might not have a legal right to that vaunted emblem anymore but it never left his possession. A bullet had punched a hole right in the center of the badge.

He took another sip of the beer and looked around the room, studying the faces of the people without being too obvious about it. He had come here to meet someone but he didn't know the man by sight.

A letter for Braddock had made its way to Esperanza where mail delivery was an uncertain thing, to begin with. It was no real secret Braddock lived in the village but he didn't think too many people north of the border knew about it.

A man named E.J. Caldwell had sent the letter which asked that Braddock meet him at the Camino Real in El Paso to discuss a business arrangement. Also inside the envelope, Braddock found a fifty dollar greenback.

Braddock could have stuck the bill in his pocket, thrown away the letter, and forgotten the whole thing. It would have been easy enough to do and he'd considered it.

But his friend, the padre, who was there when Braddock read the letter, had smiled and said, "You are curious, my friend. You want to know who this man is, how he knows about you...and what he wants you to do."

"Curiosity's not a sin, is it?"

"No. But it can be a temptation that *leads* one into sin."

"You can't know where a trail goes unless you follow it," Braddock had said and, the next morning, he had gathered a few supplies, saddled his dun horse, and ridden toward El Paso after telling the priest goodbye and adding, "I'll be back."

"I pray to *El Señor Dios* it is so."

Braddock left the fifty bucks with the padre. If he didn't come back, the money might as well stay where it could do some good. Braddock had only a few needs: food, shelter, ammunition.

He couldn't afford to stay at the Camino Real, so he found more suitable accommodations. Then he'd shaken out his suit, brushed his hat, stuck the derringer in his waistband, and come here to meet Mr. E.J. Caldwell.

Who might just be the stocky, florid-faced gent with curling mustaches coming toward Braddock now. He looked like the sort of man who could stick a fifty dollar bill in an envelope without thinking twice about it.

He had a drink in one hand and a derby in the other. Braddock kept an eye on the derby which might have a gun hidden in it, although such a crude subterfuge in a room as fancy as this seemed out of place. The man stopped on the other side of the table and said, "Mr. Braddock? G.W. Braddock?"

"Who's asking the question?"

"E.J. Caldwell, sir. Would you object if I sat down?"

"That depends. How much did you pay for this meeting?"

The man smiled and said, "Ah, testing my bona fides. The amount in question is fifty simoleons, my friend."

Braddock didn't like it when people he didn't know took him for their friend but he let it pass. He gestured with his left hand for Caldwell to sit down. His right hand lay easily in his lap, handy to the derringer.

Caldwell set the glass of whiskey and the derby on the table and took a seat. "I'm very happy you saw fit to meet me," he said. "I didn't know exactly when you'd arrive, so I've been checking here every evening for a week."

"You knew what I look like?"

"I had an excellent description of you."

And where had he gotten that description, Braddock wondered? Off a reward poster? He knew charges had been levied against him and the Rangers, at least some of them, would like to see him in custody but he didn't know if they had circulated posters on him. He could have asked Caldwell and pressed for an answer, he supposed, but he wasn't sure it was worth the trouble just yet.

Instead, he asked, "What can I do for you, Mr. Caldwell?"

"First of all, you should understand the fifty dollars was to pay for your time and trouble coming up here."

Braddock smiled faintly. "That's sort of what I figured."

"I have a business proposition for you and, if you take the job, there'll be further remuneration. A goodly amount, in fact."

"How goodly?"

Caldwell put out a fat-fingered hand and wobbled it a little. "That's a matter for negotiation."

Something bristled inside Braddock. He wasn't a

hired gun. He had been a lawman and, when he'd lost his badge not through any fault of his own but through corrupt political shenanigans, he had continued bringing owlhoots to justice even though that put him on the wrong side of the law as far as some were concerned.

The idea of sitting here and haggling with this man put a bitter taste in his mouth. Had he really come to this? To hell with it. He didn't even care what the job was anymore. He drank the rest of the beer and set the empty glass on the table between them.

"Forget it."

Caldwell's bushy eyebrows rose in surprise. "Excuse me?"

"I said forget it. I don't want the job. I don't care what it pays. I'm not a hired gun."

"Please, Mr. Braddock, don't be hasty. Perhaps I didn't make it clear how urgent this matter is."

"It's not urgent to me," Braddock said. He scraped his chair back and started to stand up.

"I've offended you. That wasn't my intention. I know you're not a gunman for hire. You're a Texas Ranger."

That made Braddock pause and settle back in his chair. His history wasn't that hard to look up. There had even been a few newspaper stories written about him although he wasn't what anybody would call a notorious character.

Caldwell leaned forward and went on, "It really is vital that I talk to you and explain the whole situation but not here."

That raised Braddock's hackles. "Where, then?"

"I have a room upstairs."

Well, that had *trap* written all over it. Could Caldwell be working for Captain Hughes? If he went up to the man's room, would he find it full of Rangers waiting to clap him in irons and haul him off to jail? The Rangers had gone to elaborate lengths to catch outlaws in the past. He wasn't sure they actually wanted him that badly, but on the other hand, he sort of gave the organization a bad name by tackling problems they couldn't take on in their currently hamstrung operation.

Anyway, there was that curiosity again, the temptation the padre had warned him about.

On still one more hand, Braddock was pretty sure he was going to hell no matter what he did, so why not give in? It might just get him there quicker.

"All right," he said, reaching for his hat. "Let's go."

Caldwell looked a little surprised again as if he hadn't really expected Braddock to agree this quickly. But he picked up his derby—turning it so Braddock could see no gun was hidden in it, although Braddock figured such a revelation wasn't the man's intention—and said, "Thank you. I appreciate you indulging me."

The Camino Real had an elevator, the first in this whole part of the country. Braddock didn't like it much as the little cage rattled and shook and lifted them to the hotel's third floor. Like most things about an increasingly modern world, it just didn't seem right to him. He didn't show that on his face, though, as he rode up with Caldwell.

"My suite is right down here," the man said as they walked along a hallway with a thick carpet runner on the floor. Gilt wallpaper covered the corridor's walls and fancy sconces held gas lamps that hissed faintly.

Caldwell paused in front of a door and took a key out of his pocket. He unlocked it, turned the knob, pushed the door open an inch or so, glanced over his shoulder to smile at Braddock.

Braddock planted his left hand in the middle of Cald-

11

well's back and shoved hard. As Caldwell exclaimed in alarm and crashed into the door, Braddock palmed out the derringer. Caldwell stumbled across the room, lost his balance, and planted himself face first. Luckily for him, he landed on a well-upholstered divan. He rolled off it and half-sat, half-lay in the floor looking stunned. His derby had fallen off.

Braddock didn't see anybody else but, somewhere in the room, a woman laughed and said, "Such a dramatic entrance wasn't really necessary, Mr. Braddock, but please, come in."

BRADDOCK'S HAND TIGHTENED ON THE DERRINGER. HE had expected he might find trouble up here but not a woman.

Of course, those two things often went together.

When he didn't move, the unseen woman went on, "This isn't a trap, I assure you, although I admit, I did get you up here on false pretenses. A little anyway."

The man sitting on the floor had recovered enough from his surprise to flush with anger. He looked to his left, glared, and said, "You didn't pay me enough to be manhandled like that, lady. I don't care how pretty you are."

That was intriguing. Braddock hadn't been with a woman in quite a while but he was no more immune to their charms than any other man. The comment just added to his curiosity.

A twenty-dollar gold piece sailed toward the man, bounced off his chest, and landed on the floor beside him. The man still glared but he picked up the coin.

"There's a bonus," the woman said. "You can get out

now since you've outlived your usefulness. I should have known it was better just to be honest and forthright."

The man scrambled to his feet, made some huffing noises, and left the room, stepping quickly to the side as soon as he came through the door so he could give Braddock a wide berth. He stomped off down the hall, glancing back in a mixture of anger and nervousness, as if worried Braddock might come after him.

For the most part, Braddock had already forgotten about the man. He focused his attention on the woman inside the room, who said without moving into view, "Well? Are you coming in or not?"

Braddock stepped across the threshold and swung to his right, toeing the door back farther so he could see the woman. He pointed the derringer at her. She didn't flinch.

She looked like she didn't flinch from much. She leveled cool and intelligent blue eyes at him. Blond hair put up in a stylish bun topped an attractive face. The dark blue dress the woman wore hugged the appealing curves of her body.

"You'd be Miss E.J. Caldwell, I reckon," Braddock said.

"Elizabeth Jane Caldwell, yes. I use the initials professionally."

"What sort of *profession* are we talking about that requires a woman to use her initials?"

She frowned and said, "Don't be crude, Mr. Braddock. It doesn't become you." She gestured toward a silver tray with a pot and a couple of china cups on it. "Coffee? Of course, you'd have to put up that gun in order to drink it."

"If you'll pour, I can manage one-handed, thanks."

She burst out in a laugh. "Oh, come on. Surely you

14

don't think I'm that much of a threat. What am I going to do, bushwhack you?" She moved her hands to indicate her body. "I'm not exactly toting a six-shooter."

"Yeah, well, a fella' never knows. But the way you throw money around, I suppose you've earned a little indulgence."

He slipped the derringer back inside his waistband.

"Thank you," she said. "I've had guns pointed at me before. It's never a pleasant experience."

"I could say the same thing. Only the ones pointed at me usually go off."

"I've had that happen, too," she said as she poured coffee in the china cups.

"Is that so? You don't look like the sort of lady who winds up in gunfights."

"I wind up all sorts of places you wouldn't expect me to be."

She handed Braddock one of the cups. He sipped the coffee, found it to be as good as you'd expect in a place like the Camino Real. He said, "This drawing room banter is amusing as all hell but I'd just as soon get down to business."

"I agree. Have a seat. Take off your hat."

Braddock looked around. The room had a couple of plushly upholstered wing chairs in it, to go along with the divan. All of them would be difficult to get up from in a hurry if a man needed to. A straight-backed wooden chair sat at a writing desk. He picked it up, swung it around, and straddled it. He put his hat on the floor beside him.

"Are you always this careful?" Elizabeth Jane Caldwell asked as she sat on the divan.

"Generally."

"I suppose a man in your position has to be."

"My position?"

"A man with a lot of enemies...on both sides of the law."

She drew her legs up partially underneath her. Braddock couldn't tell if it was a calculated move or if she was just getting comfortable but he thought it made her look like a magazine illustration. One of those, what were they called, Gibson girls, that was it.

"Look, Miss Caldwell, you don't have to try to charm me. You got me here for a business deal. I reckon you hired that fella' to pretend to be you because you thought if you showed up downstairs, I wouldn't talk to you."

"Yes, that's what I meant about false pretenses. That man is a salesman. Smith, Johnson, some sort of plain name, I don't know but I met him here in the hotel and thought he might prove useful. If I've offended you, I apologize."

Braddock shrugged. "I'm not offended. It just wasn't necessary. I don't care if you're a man or a woman. Your money spends the same either way."

"Well, it's not exactly *my* money..."

"It comes from the newspaper you write for, doesn't it?"

"So you know who I am. You probably knew all along, didn't you?"

Braddock didn't say anything. To tell the truth, it had just come to him. When he'd seen the name E.J. Caldwell on the letter, it hadn't meant a damn thing to him. But he supposed a memory had been lurking in the back of his head and it had chosen this moment to come forward.

"I've seen the name on stories you've written. Didn't know you were a lady. You don't write like a woman— and I don't mean just your hand on that letter you sent me."

"They're just words on paper, Mr. Braddock," she said with a faint sharp edge to her voice. "They don't know whether it's a man or a woman writing them."

"I suppose not. But people have ideas about things like that and that's why you use initials."

"That's true. At any rate, I didn't ask you to come here so we could talk about me. I want to talk about you."

"You're writing a story about how I was unjustly dismissed from the Rangers, like plenty of other good lawmen? And how a lot of justified convictions got set aside because of some crooked politicians?"

"Whether a politician is a corrupt scoundrel or a sterling example of public service is usually a matter of whether or not you voted for him."

"Not in this case," Braddock said. "Those sons of bitches who ruined the Rangers are all as crooked as a dog's hind leg. Pardon my French."

"I've heard much worse in newspaper offices, I assure you. But I didn't want to meet you so I could write about that. I'm more interested in what you've been doing since you left the Rangers...and what you might do in the future."

Braddock cocked an eyebrow. "What do you mean, what I've been doing since I left the Rangers?"

Elizabeth Jane Caldwell drank some of the coffee and said, "There are all sorts of rumors about you, Mr. Braddock. They say that even though you have no legal right to do so, you're still carrying a Ranger badge and go around pretending that you're a member of the organization so you can chase outlaws. You don't really follow the law anymore. You just dispense justice as you see fit."

"Those are good stories. Not sure anybody could prove there's any truth to them."

"A number of lawbreakers...very bad men, each and every one of them...have wound up dead in the past year and a man matching your description has been reported to have been in the area each time."

"There are a lot of men who might match my general description."

She reached over to a side table and set the cup on it, then said, "Let's not dance around it. You think you're still a Ranger, or at least you act like one, and you make it your business to go after criminals. That's what I want you to do."

"There some owlhoot in particular you want to sic me onto?"

"I don't have any names. The only thing I know is what happened with the guns."

"What guns?"

Her eyes darkened. "A shipment of a thousand brand-new Springfield rifles, the Krag-Jorgensen model, stolen from a train bound for Fort Bliss, here in El Paso. The holdup took place east of here, between Van Horn and Sierra Blanca."

"Not much out there in those parts."

"Which made it a good place to stop the train, murder the army escort, load those crates full of rifles and ammunition on wagons, and drive off."

"When did this happen?" Braddock asked.

"Two weeks ago."

"I hadn't heard anything about it."

"The railroad and the military are trying to keep it quiet, of course. They don't want people knowing they lost enough rifles to equip a small army."

"A thousand men *is* pretty small when it comes to an army, all right."

"But a thousand well-armed men can do a great deal

of damage before they're stopped," Elizabeth Jane Caldwell said.

"True enough, I suppose. If this is supposed to be a big secret, how'd you find out about it?"

She smiled. "I have my own sources and methods, Mr. Braddock. I was in Dallas when I heard rumors about the theft. I've been investigating it ever since."

"A woman could get in big trouble, asking questions about stolen rifles in the wrong places."

"Unfortunately, that's true. A man might be less likely to be suspected."

Braddock sat up straighter and frowned. "That's what you want me to do? Find those rifles? And then tell you so you can write all about it?"

"I thought—"

"A man can get his throat cut for poking into things that aren't his business almost as easy as a woman can." Braddock picked up his hat, stood, stepped over to the side table, and put his cup next to the one she had set aside a few minutes earlier. "Thanks for the coffee and the fifty bucks. You've wasted your newspaper's money, though. Those rifles are probably scattered all over the Southwest by now. I couldn't track 'em down if I tried."

She looked up at him and said, "According to the information I've turned up, that's not the case. The rifles are all still together, pending some sort of deal. I haven't been able to find out where they're being kept or what the plan is, though. But I have a name...Shadrach Palmer."

Braddock frowned. He knew the name. Shad Palmer wasn't in the Rangers' doomsday book, their listing of the most wanted criminals in Texas, but only because nobody had ever been able to get enough proof against the man to charge him with anything. But he was rumored to have his hands in every crooked operation between San Antonio and El Paso, right up to the elbows. He owned a saloon and bawdy house here in El Paso, down close to the river, and was on a first-name basis with every desperado on both sides of the Rio Grande.

"You think Shad Palmer is brokering the deal for the guns?"

"I've heard whispers to that effect."

"But they haven't been delivered yet."

"That's right."

Braddock stood there, his expression cold and not giving anything away as he considered what she had told him. Shad Palmer was a very dangerous man, according to everything Braddock had heard. He had never had any dealings with the man or even crossed trails with him, so it was unlikely Palmer would recognize him. That was one point in Braddock's favor.

And as the young woman had said, a thousand Krags could wreak havoc along the border. Especially if they were concentrated in the hands of one group rather than being scattered and sold off piecemeal. He'd never handled one of the rifles but he knew the army had carried them during the Spanish-American War and in the Philippines.

Elizabeth Jane Caldwell had been right about something else: this sort of affair interested him. But a couple of questions still bothered him.

"Isn't the army looking for these guns?" he asked.

"I'm sure they are but I haven't been able to find out any specifics." She smiled. "They sort of get quiet out at the fort when I come around."

"And what's your interest in this?"

"Why, I want to write the story, of course—"

"No," Braddock interrupted her. "I saw something else on your face when you explained about that robbery. Something in your eyes, like it hurt you to talk about it. You have a personal connection with this, don't you?"

"I'd prefer not to answer that—"

"And I'd prefer to turn around and walk out of here. All I need is a good reason to do that and, I reckon, you keeping secrets from me would qualify."

She stood up and drew in a deep breath. She had to look up to meet his gaze but there was no give in her. She said, "All right, if you insist. That army escort I mentioned..."

"The troops on the train who were killed in the holdup."

"That's right. They were under the command of a young lieutenant. His name was Peter Caldwell."

BRADDOCK DIDN'T SAY ANYTHING FOR A COUPLE OF heartbeats. Then he asked, "Your husband?"

"My brother."

"I'm sorry."

"I cried for a day when I heard about it but not since. Not even at Peter's funeral. I'm more interested in seeing the men responsible brought to justice than I am in grieving. They should pay for what they've done."

"We're in agreement on that. I expect those other soldiers had sisters and wives and parents, too."

"So in a way you'd be working for all of them as well, I suppose."

"I suppose." Braddock set his hat on the table next to the coffee cups. "What else do you know about Palmer's involvement?"

"One of my sources told me Palmer was going to be handling a large transaction involving some goods being taken across the river."

"That could be anything," Braddock said.

"A lot of things come across the border from Mexico

to the United States. What goes the other way except guns?"

She had a point there.

"And it's not just the guns," she went on. "Something else is coming across the river to pay for them. I don't know what it is. As you said, there are a lot of possibilities. But that's all I've been able to find out."

Braddock frowned for a moment, then said, "I suppose I could go down to Palmer's place and hang around a little. Maybe ask a few questions without being too obvious about it. No guarantees I'd find out anything, though."

Elizabeth Jane Caldwell started to stand up. "We need to discuss your payment—"

Braddock stopped her by picking up his hat. "We can talk about that later. Give me, let's say, fifty bucks in case I need to throw any money around at Palmer's. I wouldn't even ask for that if I wasn't a mite cash-strapped at the moment."

"The money I sent you..."

"I didn't bring it with me," Braddock said without offering any explanation of what he'd done with the greenback.

"There's not a lot of financial profit in what you do, is there?"

A faint smile touched his lips. "I'm not admitting you're right about me. But my needs don't amount to much and I get by. There are other things in life besides money."

"Like justice."

Braddock shrugged, put his hat on, and left.

BRADDOCK HAD HEARD OF THE PALMER HOUSE WHICH HE thought was some fancy hotel in Chicago, much like the Camino Real was here in El Paso.

Casa de Palmer, which translated to Palmer House, was a far cry from either of those places, although it was fancy, too, in its own gaudy, sleazy way. Gas lamps lit up the long boardwalk in front of the saloon. Red curtains hung at the sides of the big windows which offered good views of the cavernous main room. Long mahogany bars ran down both side walls. The back of the room boasted a dance floor and stage where girls in short skirts kicked up their heels. It would have been a stretch to call them dancers but they tried, making up for what they lacked in talent with exposed flesh.

Poker tables, roulette wheels, faro layouts, and other games of chance filled about half of the floor area. The other half had tables where customers could sit and drink. The light from numerous chandeliers competed with a never-ending, blue-gray haze of tobacco smoke.

In one of the rear corners, next to the stage, was a

curving staircase with burgundy carpet on the steps, an ornately carved baluster railing, and a finial on the newel post carved in the shape of a naked woman from the waist up. Those stairs led to the second floor where another major part of Shadrach Palmer's business was carried out.

Braddock had never been on the second floor of Casa de Palmer. In fact, as he leaned on the bar and sipped from a mug of beer, he tried to remember if he had ever set foot in the building during any of his previous visits to El Paso, back when he'd been a Ranger. He didn't think he had.

He'd heard about the second floor, though. This wasn't some squalid frontier whorehouse with paper-thin walls between the rooms that sometimes didn't even go all the way to the ceiling. The girls here worked in proper rooms with decent beds instead of cots covered by bug-infested straw ticking. The rooms even had rugs on the floor.

They probably still had a certain disreputable air about them, considering what went on there, but nice enough Palmer could justify charging higher prices. Palmer's real money came from his criminal enterprises but his saloon and bawdy house turned a nice legal profit, too.

Braddock wore the same dusty range clothes he'd worn on the ride upriver from Esperanza. A gunbelt was snugged around his hips and his Colt with well-worn walnut grips rode in the holster.

El Paso had a modern police department that frowned on men wearing guns openly like in the old, lawless days but this close to the border, with the Rio Grande less than two blocks away, nobody tried to enforce that very stringently.

Braddock wasn't going to venture into this part of town with just the derringer, either.

A craggy-faced bartender, one of several drink jugglers working tonight, ambled down the hardwood and frowned at him. Braddock had been working on the beer for a while and the longer he took drinking it, the less money Shad Palmer made. Braddock figured the bartender was going to tell him to drink up and order another or get out but, before the man could say anything, a commotion erupted on the other side of the room.

"All I'm sayin' is I'd like to know where that third jack came from," a man declared in a loud, angry voice.

"Are you saying that I cheated, sir?"

The room hadn't gone completely quiet after the first outburst but enough so Braddock had no trouble hearing the question phrased in cool, yet taut tones.

The bartender who'd been about to speak to him had lost interest in him, so Braddock turned to see what was going to happen.

Not surprisingly, the two men who had raised their voices faced each other across a baize-covered poker table. One was clearly a professional gambler wearing a frock coat and a fancy vest and shirt. His hair was slicked down and he sported a Van Dyke beard.

The man who had asked about the third jack was dressed like a cowboy, with a brown vest over a cotton shirt and an old Stetson pushed back on fair hair. He was approaching middle age and his face reminded Braddock of a wedge used to split wood.

He was no puncher, despite his clothes. His hands were too soft for that, Braddock noted.

Which meant the holstered gun on the man's hip was probably the tool he used most often.

Braddock took in all those details in the first second after he turned around. By that time the gunman was saying, "I just don't like losin' in a game that ain't on the up and up."

"I deal a fair game," the gambler said, tight-lipped.

"Huh. You couldn't prove it by me."

The gambler stared coldly at him for a moment, then gestured toward the pile of bills and coins in the center of the table.

"Take what you put in the pot and leave," he said. "I want this to be a congenial game and, if you're bent on causing trouble, you're not welcome."

The other man's mouth curved in an ugly grin as he said, "You've got it backwards. I'm the one who tells you to get out. Or have you forgotten who my boss is?"

Anger made the gambler's jaw clench even more. He said, "You don't run this saloon—"

"One word from me is all it's gonna take to get you run out of here, though. Not just this saloon, either. I'll see to it you don't ever set foot in El Paso again."

The gambler put up a bold front but, after a few seconds, he sighed and said to the other players, "Help yourselves to the pot, gentlemen. It appears this game has come to an unfortunately abrupt end."

He scraped back his chair, picked up a flat-crowned hat from the table, and stood. Braddock could tell he was trying to muster up as much dignity as he could while he put on the hat and turned toward the saloon's bat-winged entrance.

The gambler was about halfway to the door when the man at the table laughed and said loudly enough to be heard over the growing buzz of conversation, "That's how we deal with damn cheatin' tinhorns around here."

Braddock saw the gambler stop short, saw the way

the man's body stiffened, and knew what was going to happen next.

The gambler swung around swiftly. His hand darted under the frock coat to come out clutching a small pistol.

6

THE GAMBLER'S COURSE AS HE LEFT THE SALOON HAD brought him closer to Braddock. Close enough that Braddock was able to take two fast steps and bring the beer mug crashing down on the back of the man's head.

The blow made the gambler stumble forward a couple of steps. His arm sagged and, even though the pistol went off, the bullet smacked harmlessly into the sawdust-littered floor right in front of him.

The mug hadn't broken. Braddock hit the gambler again and, this time, the blow laid the man out.

The wedge-faced man was on his feet, gun in hand, but he didn't fire. Instead, he pouched the iron, snapped his fingers, and pointed at the senseless form on the floor.

A couple of rough-looking men came forward, grabbed the gambler's arms, and hauled him to his feet. The gambler groaned and his head wobbled back and forth as he tried to regain his senses.

As the two men started to half-carry, half-drag the gambler toward the door, the man at the table told them,

"Make it clear to him he don't ever show his face around these parts again. Break a finger or two while you're at it, so he won't be so fast to palm those jacks."

"Sure, Dex," one of the men said.

Then the wedge-faced man looked at Braddock and said, "You. C'mere."

Braddock looked down at the beer mug which was nice and thick and still hadn't shattered. The beer had spilled from it, leaving it empty. He set it on a table where several men were drinking and then walked toward the poker table.

The man greeted him with a cocky grin. "I'd say I'm obliged to you but I would have killed the son of a bitch, so there wasn't really any need for you to step in."

"Looked to me like he had you shaded," Braddock said. "Maybe I was wrong."

Anger flared for a second in the man's eyes but then faded as he laughed.

"We'll never know," he said. "My name's Dex Wilcox."

"George." That really was Braddock's first name since the G.W. stood for George Washington.

"First or last?"

"Enough."

"That way, eh? Fine. Let me buy you a drink, George, even though I don't really owe you anything. I'm just the hospitable sort."

"Well, since I lost the rest of my beer trying to keep that tinhorn from shooting you..."

Wilcox jerked his head toward the bar.

As Braddock walked across the room, which was now loud and jovial again, he thought about the man beside him. He had never crossed trail with Dex Wilcox but he knew the name. Wilcox had a reputation as a gunman and hardcase. Rumor said he had been a

30

member of Black Jack Ketchum's gang of train robbers over in New Mexico Territory.

The things he had said to the gambler made it sound like he now worked for Shadrach Palmer. Braddock had taken note of that at the time but he hadn't expected to have the chance to make use of the knowledge quite so soon. It was certainly possible Wilcox was working for Palmer, given the saloon owner's rumored connection to all sorts of crimes.

Wilcox signaled to one of the bartenders, who placed two glasses on the bar and then reached underneath it to take out a bottle.

"Hope you don't mind the good stuff," Wilcox said as the bartender poured.

"Well, I may not know what to do with whiskey that doesn't taste like rattlesnake heads and strychnine but I'll try to manage."

Wilcox laughed. He picked up his drink and raised the glass to Braddock who returned the gesture. Both men threw back the liquor.

It was the good stuff, all right. Braddock couldn't help but lick his lips in appreciation.

"I told you." Wilcox nodded toward the gun on Braddock's hip. "Are you as handy with that as you are with a beer mug?"

"Handier, I'd like to think."

"Looking for work?"

"That's why I drifted this way. It's a far piece from Arizona."

"A mite warm over there, is it?"

"It's always hot in Arizona," Braddock said. "You know of any work in these parts?"

Braddock kept his voice casual as he asked the question. He had come here to Casa de Palmer to poke around a little and see if he could pick up any information on those stolen rifles. However, good fortune had put him in the right place at the right time to maybe find out even more. He couldn't appear too eager, though, or he might waste this opportunity.

Wilcox seemed to be thinking about the question Braddock had asked him. After a moment, he said, "I know somebody who's always looking to hire good men. You want to meet him?"

"I wouldn't mind," Braddock said.

"Put your glass down, then. He's right upstairs."

7

SHADRACH PALMER LOOKED MORE LIKE A SHOPKEEPER than a criminal. A short and pudgy man, he had a few strands of dark hair combed over an otherwise bald pate. He wore a simple dark suit and no gaudy jewelry, just a simple stickpin in his cravat.

The eyes made the difference. Braddock had gazed into a rattlesnake's eyes more than once and Palmer's eyes had that same flat, dead look to them.

He sat at a writing desk on one side of the suite's sitting room, an open ledger book in front of him. On the other side of the room, a woman relaxed among the cushions of a divan with her legs up. Someone less beautiful would have seemed to be sprawled there but, on her, the pose looked elegant.

She was a mulatto, Braddock decided. Just a touch of coffee in the cream of her skin. Waves of dark brown hair framed her lovely face. She wore a silk dressing gown open at the throat just enough to hint at the glories underneath.

It took a man damned dedicated to making money to

be studying a ledger book with a woman like that in the room, Braddock thought.

"Got somebody I'd like for you to meet, boss," Dex Wilcox said. "Fella's name is George. That seems to be his only handle."

Palmer didn't get up but he nodded cordially enough.

"George," he said. "I'm Shadrach Palmer. This is my place."

Braddock returned the nod but didn't take his hat off. He said, "I've heard of you, Mr. Palmer. Pleasure to meet you."

The woman cleared her throat. Palmer smiled, nodded to her, and said, "This is Elise."

Braddock reached for his hat this time. He held it in front of him and said, "It's an honor, ma'am."

"You cowboys are so polite," she said.

"George ain't a cowboy," Wilcox said. "He's in the same line of work I am, from over Arizona Territory way." The gunman paused, then added significantly, "Or at least so he claims."

Braddock's eyes flicked toward him. "Wouldn't be calling me a liar, would you?"

"Nope, just...what do you call it...pleadin' ignorance. After all, George, all we got to go by...is your word."

"You're the one asked me to come up here," Braddock said, not bothering to keep the irritation out of his voice. "Said you wanted me to meet your boss. Why'd you do that if you didn't believe me?"

"Don't get testy, George," Palmer put in. "Dex didn't say he didn't believe you. It's just that sometimes men boast about things they can't back up."

Braddock shook his head slightly and said, "I didn't make any boasts."

Palmer pushed back his chair and stood up. "Let's cut

through all this. Why *did* you bring George up here, Dex?"

"You know that gambler Ballantine? He slipped an extra jack into the game I was sittin' in on. I called him on it, he backed down, so I told him to get out. Then as he was leavin', he tried to spin around and gun me." Wilcox didn't say anything about how his words had goaded Ballantine into drawing. He nodded toward Braddock and went on, "George walloped him with a beer mug before he could pull the trigger."

"Saved your life, eh?"

"I wouldn't go that far," Wilcox said, looking annoyed at the suggestion.

Palmer turned to Braddock. "Did the beer mug break?"

"Nope," Braddock said. "It was good and solid."

"Good. If it had, I might have been forced to take the cost out of Dex's wages since you acted on his behalf and I'm sure he wouldn't have liked that."

"Blast it!" Wilcox said. "I would have killed that tinhorn before he gunned me."

Palmer chuckled and said, "Take it easy, Dex. We all know what a dangerous gunman you are." He faced Braddock again. "So Dex brought you up here to meet me out of a...sense of gratitude? He thought you would enjoy making my acquaintance?"

"He asked me if I was looking for work and I told him I was."

"Ah," Palmer said. "I see. Well, I suppose I could always use another bartender or a man to help unload cases of liquor and sweep out the place—"

Braddock had figured out by now that Palmer was the sort of man who liked to get under people's skin, mostly for the sheer meanness of it. Ignoring Palmer, he turned to Elise, nodded, and interrupted the saloon owner by saying, "It was a real pleasure to meet such a beautiful lady, ma'am. I'll be going now."

He clapped his hat on and turned toward the door of the suite.

"Now wait just a damned minute," Wilcox began. "You can't—"

Palmer silenced him with a lifted hand. "That's all right, Dex. I admire a man with the guts to call my bluff...every now and then." He faced Braddock. "Let's talk plain, shall we?"

"That's the way I like best."

"You do gun work."

"I do."

"And I can always use a man who's quick on the shoot and who isn't overly burdened with, shall we say, moral compunctions."

"Far as I recall, nobody's ever accused me of that. The moral part, I mean. The quick on the shoot part, that's true enough, I reckon."

Palmer put his hands together in front of him, patted them lightly against each other, and said, "There's one good way to find out on both accounts. I want you to kill a man for me."

8

BRADDOCK KEPT HIS FACE IMPASSIVE, BUT INSIDE, HE thought this was more than he'd bargained for when he agreed to help Elizabeth Jane Caldwell avenge her brother.

Of course, there was more to it than that. There were all those other soldiers who'd been killed and the carnage those rifles could wreak if they got into the wrong hands had to be considered, too.

But Palmer seemed to be talking about murder. Braddock might be an outlaw Ranger, but he still tried to uphold the law.

He didn't let any of those thoughts show as they flashed through his mind. Anyway, it wouldn't hurt anything to find out more.

"Who did you have in mind?" he asked coolly.

"There's a man named Larkin. He used to work for me."

Wilcox said, "I've told you, boss, I can take care of Larkin any time you say the word."

"But I haven't said the word, have I?" Palmer snapped

at the gunman. "Maybe I've been holding the problem in reserve for just such an occasion as this."

Braddock asked, "What did this hombre Larkin do?"

"He decided he could go out on his own and compete with me." Palmer spread his hands. "I bring in certain...commodities...from across the border and then have them transported to other distribution points."

"You're talking about smuggling." Braddock made a guess. "Opium?"

The flicker of surprise in Palmer's eyes told him he was right but the man said, "That doesn't matter. What's important is that Larkin betrayed me and I can't have that. Other people can see what he's done and, if he gets away with it, that will only lead to more trouble for me in the future. It's an annoyance and I can't have it. Not right now."

Palmer made it sound as if he had a lot bigger deal on the table than just this business with Larkin. Like moving a thousand Krags across the border, maybe?

"Take care of Larkin for me," Palmer went on, "and I'd say you have a job for as long as you want it."

"Answering to you," Braddock said, "or to Wilcox?"

"Now wait just a damned minute," Wilcox said again, clearly displeased that Braddock seemed to be trying to go around him.

"Dex is my chief lieutenant when it comes to matters like this," Palmer said. "You'd answer to him. Do you have any objection to that?"

"None for now," Braddock said.

That didn't do much to mollify Wilcox. He still glared at Braddock when Palmer went on, "Most nights, you can find Larkin at a place over in Juarez owned by a man called Hernandez. I'm not sure it has a name but Dex can show you where it is. When do you plan to go over there?"

"Nothing wrong with tonight, is there?"

Palmer raised one eyebrow. "So soon?"

"I never believed in wasting time."

"Apparently not." Palmer looked at Wilcox. "Did you have any further plans for the evening, Dex?"

"No, I reckon not." Wilcox's eyes were still narrow with anger as he looked at Braddock.

"Very well, then. Come see me when you get back, George."

"I'll be here," Braddock said.

He turned toward the door. Elise said, "It was nice to meet you, George. Maybe we'll get to know each other better in the future."

Braddock looked back at her and smiled. "Yes, ma'am, maybe."

Palmer frowned a little.

Braddock got out of there. Wilcox followed right behind him.

"You're pretty damned sure of yourself, aren't you?" the gunman said as they walked toward the second-floor landing.

"I've never seen any reason not to be."

"Yeah, well, maybe you will tonight. Larkin's generally not by himself. He's liable to have a couple of men with him."

"I take things as they come."

"You'd better not be thinkin' about the woman like that. Palmer wants Larkin dead for hornin' in on his business. He'd want considerably worse for anybody who tried anything with his woman."

"What's considerably worse than being dead?"

"You don't want to know but trust me...it's out there."

Braddock didn't say anything else as they went down the stairs and crossed the saloon's main room to the entrance. His mind raced.

He had just agreed to go across the river into Mexico and kill one man, maybe more. If Palmer had told the truth about Larkin—and Braddock's gut told him Palmer had—the man smuggled opium across the border, causing a considerable amount of misery among those addicted to the stuff and their families. In all likelihood, Larkin had committed murders as well.

So the world wouldn't miss the man. Braddock often went after that sort, anyway. Considered against the lives in the balance because of those stolen rifles, the deaths of a few criminals didn't mean much.

"You sure you're ready for this?" Wilcox asked when they reached the street.

"I'm ready," Braddock said.

9

THEIR BOOTHEELS MADE ECHOES IN THE NIGHT AS THEY crossed the wooden bridge spanning the Rio Grande. A lot fewer lights burned in Juarez than in El Paso behind them but one building, not far from the river, was well lit, a sprawling, two-story adobe with a balcony along the front that overhung its gallery.

"Hernandez's place," Wilcox said as he nodded toward the building.

"A cantina?"

"And a gambling den and a dance hall and a whore-house." Wilcox laughed. "The boss and Hernandez sort of occupy the same position on each one's side of the river. They ain't partners, exactly, but I guess you could say there's a truce between 'em, for the greater good of both."

"But now Hernandez has thrown in with Larkin?"

"Not yet." Wilcox dug in his left ear with his little finger. "But he might be thinkin' about it. I figure he's waitin' to see what Palmer does about Larkin. In the meantime, he lets Larkin drink and gamble at his place." Wilcox shrugged. "One man's money is as good as another's, I reckon that's the way Hernandez sees it. And I sure as hell can't argue with that idea, either."

They had almost reached the big building. Braddock slowed and looked over at Wilcox.

"You're going to back my play in there?"

Wilcox hooked his thumbs in his gun belt.

"Now, what sort of a test would that be if I was to save your bacon? You're the one who talked big. Now you got to back it up." Wilcox laughed again. "But don't worry, George. If Larkin or one of his boys kills you, that'll give me all the excuse I need to kill them. The boss gets what he wants, either way."

"And that's what's important, right?"

"As long as he's payin' the wages, it is." Wilcox leaned his head toward the river. "It ain't too late to go back across and say the hell with it. Get on your horse and ride out of El Paso. Nobody'll try to stop you."

"I say I'll do a job, I do it," Braddock replied.

That was the reason he carried a Ranger badge with a bullet hole in it, tucked away now in a hidden pocket cunningly concealed on the back of his gunbelt. He had sworn an oath and no damned dirty politicians could ever change that.

He pushed open one of the big double doors at the entrance to Hernandez's.

Music rushed out, guitar and piano blending in a staccato rhythm. With it came talk and laughter and tobacco smoke, along with the sharp tang of highly spiced food cooking.

The smell wasn't exactly the same as that of a saloon north of the border but it had certain similarities. Braddock had been in enough cantinas to recognize it. Here the aromas were just exaggerated because Hernandez's place was bigger.

Braddock and Wilcox moved inside and let the door swing closed behind them. No one seemed to pay any attention to their entrance but Braddock would have bet some of the men in the room noted it. He paused to take a look around for himself.

The long mahogany bar stretched most of the way across the back of the room. At either end, a staircase rose to the second-floor balcony. The side walls were divided into alcoves where tables could be dimly seen through the beaded curtains hanging over the openings. People could meet in those alcoves to talk, eat, and drink —or whatever else they wanted to do—in private.

The musicians, a piano player and two guitarists, were tucked into a rear corner. Near them, a Mexican girl danced, her colorful skirt swirling around slim brown legs that flashed back and forth in intricate patterns as she moved around a small open area.

Some of the customers watched the dancer and tapped their toes in time to the music but most remained caught up in their own affairs to which the music and the lithely sensuous girl served as mere background.

All the tables were occupied and Braddock didn't see many open spaces at the bar.

"Come on," Wilcox said, then added quietly enough that only Braddock could hear him over the hubbub in the room, "I don't see Larkin but his men are here, so he's somewhere close by."

"Which ones are they?"

"Hatchet-faced scarecrow and a redheaded tree stump at a table to your left."

Braddock let his gaze roam around for a second so it seemed to come back naturally to the table and the men

Wilcox indicated. As far as he recalled, he had never seen either of them before but they looked like the sort of hardcases he had dealt with plenty of times in the past.

"Let's get a drink," Wilcox went on. "Hernandez has the best tequila you'll find this side of Mexico City."

Braddock wasn't that fond of tequila but he nodded and walked toward the bar at Wilcox's side.

Three bartenders worked behind the hardwood. One of them, a little man with iron-gray hair, came over to them and said, "Señores, what can I do for you?"

"Tequila for both of us," Wilcox said. "Where's Hernandez tonight?"

"Señor Hernandez pays my wages, señor. I do not inquire as to his comings and goings."

Wilcox grunted and said, "You can say whether or not you've seen him, can't you?"

"I see only my customers, Señor Wilcox," the bartender said as he poured tequila from an unlabeled bottle into two glasses. The glasses appeared to be clean, Braddock noticed. He'd give Hernandez credit for that.

"All right, fine," Wilcox said. He picked up his drink. So did Braddock.

Before either of them could down the tequila, a scream shrilled over the music and talk and laughter and, when Braddock glanced toward the source of the sound, he saw a young woman running along the second-floor balcony, naked as a jaybird.

10

RAUCOUS LAUGHTER ERUPTED FROM THE PLACE'S PATRONS, especially when a man stumbled out of an open door from one of the second-floor rooms, pulling up his pants as he awkwardly gave chase to the girl.

In a place like this, such pursuits might be just part of the play between the soiled doves and their customers. It didn't have to mean anything.

Braddock thought the scream sounded more serious than that, however, and his interest perked up even more when Wilcox said, "That's Larkin."

Braddock knew Wilcox meant the man chasing the whore. Larkin wore trousers and boots but was nude from the waist up, displaying a torso thick with both fat and muscles and covered with coarse black hair like the pelt of a bear. His drooping mustache and the shaggy hair on his head were the same shade.

He got the trousers fastened and loped after the girl. His long legs allowed him to catch her just as she reached the landing of the stairs to Braddock's left. He grabbed her arm and jerked her to a halt, then swung her around and took hold of her other arm as well.

"What the hell's the matter with you?" he roared as he shook her. "I paid for your time. You'll damned well do what I want you to do!"

"N-no, señor!" she gasped. Her head bobbed back and forth from the shaking. "You will injure me! I will die!"

"The hell you will! Even if you do, what's it matter? You're just a whore!"

Braddock saw a couple of hard-faced Mexicans moving toward the stairs. He figured they worked for Hernandez and planned to step in to calm Larkin down and persuade him to leave the girl alone. A whore she might be but she made money for Hernandez and that meant she was valuable to him.

Braddock was closer to the stairs than Hernandez's men were. As he put down his untouched drink and stepped away from the bar, he heard Wilcox say, "Hey, what are you—" but then he didn't pay any more attention.

Instead, he called up the stairs, "Hey, you big shaggy ape! Let go of her."

Larkin had been drinking. The slur in his voice made that obvious. The insult cut through any fog in his brain, though. His head snapped around toward Braddock.

"What the hell did you say to me, mister?"

"I called you a big shaggy ape and told you to let the girl go. Are you deaf as well as stupid?"

From the corner of his eye, Braddock saw the sly grin that appeared on Wilcox's face. The gunman had figured out that he was baiting Larkin into a fight.

The musicians had stopped playing and the room was quiet now. The good-natured violence of a man chasing and probably slapping around a whore, which most of the men in here would have accepted without a second thought, had changed into something else, something that might turn deadly serious. Everyone watched to see what would happen next.

With a growl, Larkin shoved the girl away from him. Seizing the opportunity, she sprinted for the room from which she had fled. The door slammed behind her.

"Come up here and say that to me, you son of a bitch," Larkin challenged.

"I'd be glad to," Braddock said. He started up the stairs.

Larkin stood at the landing, grinning and flexing his long, sausage-like fingers. As Braddock neared the top of the stairs, Larkin backed off a little and said, "I ain't armed."

"That's all right. I don't need a gun to deal with gutter trash like you."

Larkin's mouth twisted in a snarl. As soon as Braddock set foot on the landing, Larkin lunged at him, long arms extended, hands reaching to grab and crush and destroy.

11

BRADDOCK EXPECTED THE ATTACK, OF COURSE, BUT Larkin's speed still surprised him. When Larkin had been chasing the girl, he had seemed clumsy and most men as big as him tended to lumber.

Not Larkin. He barreled at Braddock and crossed the few feet between them like a runaway freight.

Braddock barely had time to twist aside and throw an arm up to block Larkin's intended bear hug. Larkin changed tactics in the blink of an eye, grabbed the arm Braddock used to fend him off and threw him toward the railing along the edge of the balcony.

Most men would have hit the railing, flipped over it, and fallen. Braddock slapped a hand down on the polished wood and closed it with enough strength to catch himself.

Still, he was dangerously off balance and, if Larkin landed a solid punch on him now, he *would* go over.

Larkin intended to do just that. He swung a looping blow at Braddock's head, again moving faster than it seemed like he ought to be able to. Braddock ducked it, pushed off the railing, and lowered his head. He drove forward and rammed a shoulder into Larkin's chest.

Braddock's rangy body contained a considerable amount of heft and power. The collision sent Larkin reeling back across the balcony to crash into the wall. He rebounded from it and Braddock displayed his own quickness by darting in and snapping a punch to the bigger man's face.

Blood spurted from Larkin's lips as Braddock's fist landed on them. Larkin grunted and swung his left arm in a backhanded blow. It caught Braddock on the shoulder and knocked him to the side.

Larkin's right fist looped around and dug hard into Braddock's ribs. Larkin followed it, an instant later, with a straight left that took Braddock just above the heart.

For a moment, Braddock thought he was done for. The blow stunned him and left him unable to move.

Larkin sensed victory, too, and grinned.

"I think I'll squeeze your neck hard enough to pop your head right off your shoulders," he said.

The boast was a mistake. Even those few seconds gave Braddock the chance to recover a little.

He tried to appear defenseless, though, so when Larkin lunged for Braddock's throat again, he wasn't prepared for his foe to spring out of the way.

Larkin stumbled past Braddock, who clubbed both hands together, lifted them high, and smashed them on the back of Larkin's neck. Larkin doubled over. Braddock grabbed his shoulder, jerked him around, and brought a knee up into Larkin's face. More blood flew as the impact flattened Larkin's nose.

Braddock kicked the smuggler's legs out from under him. Larkin landed in a bloody heap on the balcony. Air rasped through his ruined nose as he breathed heavily.

He wasn't dead, though, and that was what Shadrach Palmer wanted. Braddock couldn't just draw his gun and put a bullet in Larkin's brain. That would be cold-blooded murder.

Luckily—if you could call it that—Larkin wasn't through. He looked up at Braddock with sheer hatred blazing like bonfires in his eyes and reached down to his right boot. He came up with a dagger that had been hidden in the boot. He'd been lying about being unarmed, probably because he had believed he could break Braddock apart with his bare hands.

Now, hurt and on the verge of defeat, he just wanted to destroy his enemy any way he could.

Larkin uncoiled from the floor and came at Braddock, slashing back and forth with the dagger. He didn't even seem to consider that Braddock could have gunned him down, probably because he was so full of rage.

Braddock gave ground until he had retreated about halfway along the balcony as it ran across the back of the room. He took a risk then, letting Larkin close in on him. The dagger flashed right in front of his eyes, mere inches away. Braddock's hands shot up, closed around Larkin's wrist, twisted and shoved.

Larkin wasn't expecting the move and couldn't stop the dagger in time. The razor-sharp point went in under his chin. Braddock threw his weight against Larkin's wrist and drove the blade deep. He felt it scrape against the spine in Larkin's neck.

Larkin's eyes widened and bulged out. He tried to speak but only a grotesque gurgle came out. Braddock crowded against him, forcing him back against the railing. Larkin's now nerveless fingers slid loosely off the dagger's handle.

Braddock put both hands against Larkin's chest and pushed.

Larkin went up and over, falling like a stone to land on his back on the bar. Men who had been standing down there craning their necks to watch the fight yelled angry curses and jumped back out of the way. Bottles and glasses and liquor flew. A woman screamed at the sight of Larkin's lifeless body lying there with his arms stretched out on either side of him, the dagger still buried up to the hilt in his throat.

More men scrambled aside but, this time, to get out of the line of fire. Braddock glanced toward the hatchet-faced man and the stumpy redhead and saw their gun barrels coming up at him.

12

B<small>RADDOCK</small> <small>WASN'T</small> <small>IN</small> <small>TOP-NOTCH</small> <small>SHAPE</small> <small>AFTER</small> <small>THE</small> battle and the two gunmen had beaten him to the draw already.

But his hand stabbed down to the gun on his hip and, thankfully, it hadn't fallen out during the fracas with Larkin.

The Colt came out of leather with smooth, blinding speed and started roaring a fraction of a second before the shots from below. The redhead had barely pulled his trigger when Braddock's first bullet hammered into his chest and knocked him back over the chair where he'd been sitting.

Hatchet-face got two shots off. The first whipped past Braddock's right ear. The second missed him wide to the left because the gunman had slewed halfway around from the impact of Braddock's second shot. He staggered and pressed his free hand to his chest but couldn't stop the blood bubbling between his fingers. As he tried to lift his gun again for a third shot, Braddock put a round through his head. That dumped him onto the sawdust, dead before he hit.

The redhead was still alive, though. He grabbed hold of the overturned chair and tried to pull himself up. Braddock shot him in the head, too.

That left him with one round in the Colt in case anybody else wanted trouble but no one seemed to.

The room had cleared out around Larkin's friends. Everybody in the place, customers and employees alike, had pulled back along the walls. Some stared at the carnage, others just seemed annoyed that their night's entertainment had been interrupted.

Braddock heard a little noise to his left and turned. One of the doors stood open a few inches and a brown face peered out anxiously. The girl said, "Señor Larkin is...is..."

"*Muerto*," Braddock said.

She closed her eyes, sighed, and crossed herself, which might have seemed more reverent if her bare breasts hadn't been peeking out through the open door, too.

The two men who had been getting ready to step in and deal with Larkin moved over to the dead gunmen and checked on them. The pools of blood around their heads left no doubt they were dead. The two men then turned toward the stairs.

Braddock opened the Colt's cylinder, reached to his shell belt, and started thumbing fresh rounds into the gun. He didn't think Hernandez's men figured on trying anything but he wanted to be ready if they did.

A glance told him Dex Wilcox was standing off to one side of the room, the glass of tequila still in his hand. He saw Braddock looking at him, grinned, and lifted the glass in a toast of sorts before taking a sip of the fiery liquor.

Down below, the bartenders and a couple of swampers started to gather up the bodies and haul them out. It would take a while to clean up the blood and the other mess but things would be back to normal in the place fairly quickly.

Assuming no more gunplay erupted. Braddock didn't holster the Colt as the two men reached the top of the stairs and approached him.

"No trouble, señor," one of them said as he raised a hand slightly in a placating gesture. "Señor Larkin brought his fate upon himself, as did his men."

"Is that what the law's going to think?"

A faint smile curved the man's lips. "In this part of Juarez, señor, my employer *is* the law."

"Well, that's good to know, I reckon," Braddock said. "You fellas aren't upset that I horned in? I just can't stand to see an hombre mistreating a woman, even a whore."

"If Señor Hernandez had been here, he would have told us to stop Larkin from hurting the señorita. Larkin might have backed down or he might have forced us to kill him, too." The man's shoulders rose and fell in an eloquent shrug. "We will never know. But I am sure Señor Hernandez would like to speak with you when he returns. In the meantime, you can drink or gamble or avail yourselves of the other pleasures we have to offer."

An edge of steel under the polite words made it clear Braddock wasn't free to leave here until Hernandez gave the word. That was all right, he decided. Hernandez was tied in with Shadrach Palmer and Braddock was convinced Palmer had those Krags. Maybe talking to the man was a good idea.

He slid his Colt into its holster and said, "I'll take you up on that, fellas. I—"

"Señor..." a soft voice said behind him.

Braddock looked over his shoulder and saw the girl standing there. She wore a low-on-the-shoulder blouse and long skirt now. Her fingers knotted together nervously in front of her.

"Do not interrupt, Carmen," the man who had been talking to Braddock snapped at her.

"I...I am sorry. I just wanted to thank the señor..."

Acting on impulse, Braddock grinned and said, "I think I know how I want to pass the time until Señor Hernandez gets back."

Again the man shrugged. "As you wish."

"Tell my friend I'll see him later, if he wants to hang around, would you?"

"You mean Señor Wilcox?"

"Yeah."

"You work for Señor Palmer, too?"

"That's right," Braddock said, not bothering to explain that he'd been sent over here on a provisional basis with his assignment being to kill Larkin for double-crossing Palmer. Let them think the deaths of Larkin and his men had been just an unfortunate turn of events.

"Very well. Enjoy your time with Carmen. We will let you know when Señor Hernandez arrives. Would you like a bottle of tequila sent up?"

"I think that's a mighty good idea," Braddock said.

After everything that had happened, poor little Carmen looked like she could use a drink.

13

WHEN THE TWO OF THEM WERE ALONE IN CARMEN'S room, the girl looked down at the threadbare rug on the floor next to the bed and said, "Anything you want to do with me, señor, it is all right. I owe you my life."

"I don't know about that," Braddock said. "Hernandez's men would stepped in and done something about Larkin."

Carmen shook her head. "Even if they made him leave me alone tonight, Señor Larkin would have caught me some other night. He would not have forgotten. He is like a dog. Once he has gotten his jaws on something, he will not let go."

"Yeah, he was a son of a bitch, all right," Braddock said with a smile.

"He has hurt other girls in the past, very badly. I have heard stories about him..."

"Well, he won't hurt anybody else." Braddock put a couple of fingers under her chin. "Why won't you look at me?"

He urged her head up. When she blinked at him, he saw tears shining in her dark eyes.

"I am so...so ashamed!" she burst out. She stepped back, put her hands over her face, and sobbed.

Braddock frowned. Like most men, crying women made him distinctly uncomfortable. He didn't know if it would be better to put his arms around Carmen or keep his distance.

A soft knock sounded on the door. Braddock said, "Why don't you sit down on the bed?" and turned to answer it. He rested his right hand on the butt of the Colt and used his left to open the door.

The gray-haired bartender from downstairs stood there holding a tray with a bottle of tequila and two glasses on it.

"Perhaps this time you will actually get to enjoy your drink, señor," he said. He ignored Carmen crying quietly as she perched on the edge of the bed.

"Here's hoping." Braddock slipped a silver dollar from his pocket, handed it to the bartender, and took the tray.

"Gracias, señor."

"Is my friend still downstairs?"

"Señor Wilcox? Sí. I think he intends to wait for you. He is playing poker with some other men."

That came as no surprise. Wilcox seemed to like gambling.

Braddock closed the door with his foot and set the tray on a small table. He poured a couple of inches of tequila into one of the glasses and carried it over to Carmen.

"Here," he told her. "Drink this."

She took the glass, gulped down the liquor, gagged a little, and shuddered.

"Not used to drinking, are you?"

"I am...not used to...many things," she said. "All of this..." She moved a hand in a vague gesture to indicate the room around them. "This is new to me."

Braddock glanced around the spartanly furnished room. It held a bed, a single chair, a table with a basin of water and a cheap oil lamp on it. He had seen worse, though. The floor had a rug on it and a thin curtain hung over the single window, open to let in a little breeze. As a whore's room, it wasn't that bad.

"You don't have to be ashamed," he said. "Folks do what they have to do in order to survive."

"You do not understand, Señor...?"

"George."

"Señor George. It was not my choice to come here. I was taken from my village and *brought* here. Stolen with all the others by evil men."

"Others?" Braddock repeated.

Carmen nodded. "More than two dozen women and girls, some as young as ten years old." She swallowed hard. "And now we are all doomed."

BRADDOCK HAD TO POUR ANOTHER DRINK FOR HER BEFORE she could go on with the story. She didn't shudder as much as she downed the liquor this time.

She told him about the dawn raid on the village of Santa Rosalia where she had lived with her family.

"So many of the men were killed, including my father," she said in a voice hollow with grief. Braddock saw the shock and horror of that morning on her face as she relived it in her memory. "Then they rounded up the women and put us onto carts like nothing more than...than sheep. We were nothing but livestock to those terrible men."

She was right about that, Braddock thought.

"Then their leader, he...he pointed to me and had one of his men bring me to him. That man, Gonsalvo, tore my clothes from me and left me naked and ashamed."

"This Gonsalvo, he was their leader?" Braddock didn't know the name.

Carmen shook her head. "No, no, Hector Gonsalvo

was the, how do you say it, the segundo...the lieutenant. The leader was Martin Larrizo."

That name rang a faint bell for Braddock. He thought for a moment and dredged up the details from his brain.

The Rangers had suspected Larrizo of being involved with several raids across the border into Texas to steal cattle and loot isolated ranches. As far as they knew, he was just a minor bandido.

Maybe Larrizo had in mind becoming something bigger and the mass kidnapping of the women of Santa Rosalia was a start.

"Go on," he told Carmen.

She frowned at him in confusion. "Why do you ask me these questions? Why do you want to know about me? I thought we would..."

"I can see how upset you are. I just figured you might like to talk a little and tell me about it. I'm a nice hombre, after all."

She peered intently at him for a long moment, then shook her head.

"No. You are not an evil man, I can sense that. But you are hard and dangerous and...and not nice."

Braddock laughed and said, "I'm sure some folks would agree with that last part. But I still want to know about what happened to you."

So far, he didn't have any idea if Carmen's story had anything to do with the mission that had brought him to Juarez but, again, connections existed between Palmer and Hernandez, so that meant Hernandez's other activities might be involved, too.

"It is an ugly thing," Carmen went on. "Larrizo took me as his...his prize. His men were not allowed to touch the other prisoners and, if they did, Larrizo or Gonsalvo would kill them. Gonsalvo told the men this. But Larrizo had his way with me. Until then I...I had never been with a man before. He said he had to...sample the merchandise."

She had handed the empty glass back to Braddock after downing the tequila. His fingers tightened on it in anger until he thought it might break.

He suppressed that fury for the moment and told her, "I'm sorry you had to go through that, Carmen, I really am. Where are the other women now? Are they still together?"

"I do not know. I think...maybe they are. Larrizo and his men, they brought us to a place...They blindfolded us so we could not see where we were going...and when they took the blindfolds off, we were all in a room with stone walls and no windows and only one door which was always guarded. They gave us food and water and kept us there."

"You weren't with Larrizo anymore?"

She shook her head and said in a small voice, "I think he had grown tired of me."

"But he didn't take any of the other women to replace you?"

"No. We were all there."

"How'd you wind up here?"

"Gonsalvo came and got me. He put a...a bag of some kind over my head this time, instead of blindfolding me, and brought me away from there. The next thing I knew, I was here at Señor Hernandez's."

Braddock tugged at his earlobe as he frowned in thought. He said, "Wait a minute. Tell me *everything* you remember about being taken out of that place where the prisoners are kept."

"Why?" she asked. "I do not understand—"

"It might be important," Braddock said. He wasn't quite sure why, either, but his gut told him to find out as much as he could.

Carmen took a deep breath. "There is nothing to remember. Gonsalvo covered my head and then he held my arm so tight it hurt and he took me upstairs and lifted me onto a horse. We rode and rode and then he took me down from the horse and we went up more stairs and then we were here. I have seen little but the inside of this room...and the men who come to me here...since."

The wheels of Braddock's brain turned faster now. Carmen didn't seem to realize it, but she had told him something. When Gonsalvo had left the prison with her, they had gone up some stairs, Carmen had said, and gotten on a horse.

That meant the other women and girls were being kept below ground level, probably in a cellar. That would match the description of no windows and only one door.

But a cellar where? Right now, that was impossible to answer and Braddock still wasn't sure why he needed to know, other than the fact he didn't like the idea of all those women ultimately facing the same fate as Carmen.

Braddock rubbed his chin and asked, "Did Gonsalvo say anything when he brought you here?"

"He...he made a joke or at least acted like he thought it was funny. He said someone else wanted to see what they would be getting for their money. He said for me to get used to it. But I think he was angry, too, that he and the rest of Larrizo's men had been ordered to leave the prisoners alone."

Braddock didn't say anything. A picture had begun to

form in his head, a picture that would explain everything he had come across so far.

It was a damned ugly picture, too.

But before he could ponder that any more, a knock sounded on the door. Braddock glanced toward it, then looked back at Carmen and said, "Take your clothes off."

15

SHE GAVE HIM THAT CONFUSED LOOK AGAIN AND SAID, "I had started to think you did not want—"

"Now," he told her in a quiet but urgent voice.

She stood up, peeled the blouse over her head, pushed the skirt down over flaring hips and kicked out of it.

The covers were already pulled back on the bed. Braddock motioned toward it.

"Don't mention what we talked about to the other women who work for Hernandez," he told her.

"I don't talk to them."

"Good."

He wished he could tell her to have faith, that everything would be all right. He wished he could promise he'd see to it.

But he didn't know any of that for certain and didn't want to give her false hope. She had survived for this long. Maybe she could hold out for a while longer.

Another knock sounded on the door, a sharper rapping this time. Braddock turned toward it and glanced over his shoulder at the bed. Carmen sprawled on top of the covers, knees up and legs slightly spread.

Braddock opened the door. The pair of Hernandez's men stood there, just as he expected.

"Señor Hernandez is back," the talkative one—if you could call him that—said. "He wishes to see you, as I knew he would."

"Fine," Braddock said. He straightened his hat a little as if he had just put it on. He saw the men look past him at Carmen lying on the bed. Their scrutiny probably embarrassed her but that couldn't be helped. He turned slightly and told her, "Vaya con Dios, señorita," then went out and closed the door behind him.

From what he could see of the main room below, things had indeed gone back to normal. Wilcox wasn't in his line of sight but he supposed the gunman was still playing poker. The musicians played another sprightly tune for the lissome young woman to dance to.

The hard-faced pair led him to a door in the far corner. One of them opened it and revealed a short hallway with another door at the end of it. There was an apartment at the back of the building, Braddock realized. It probably served as Hernandez's private quarters.

One of the men knocked on the far door, opened it, and ushered Braddock into a sitting room every bit as luxurious as Shadrach Palmer's on the other side of the river. They really were two sides of the same coin, Braddock thought...except Hernandez didn't look like a dumpy little storekeeper, at first glance.

Hernandez was taller and more powerfully built than Palmer with a full head of dark brown hair lightly touched with silver here and there. He was clean-shaven except for long sideburns. Braddock had a hunch women considered him very handsome.

Hernandez appeared to have been riding recently. A fine film of trail dust clung to his boots and whipcord trousers and short, dark brown jacket. He wore no visible gun but a slight bulge under the jacket might be a pistol in a shoulder holster, Braddock noted.

"The gringo, Señor Hernandez," one of the men who had brought him in murmured.

Hernandez's eyes regarded Braddock from under prominent brows. He said, "You are the one who killed Calvin Larkin?"

"I didn't know his name," Braddock said, maintaining the fiction that Larkin hadn't been his target all along, "but yeah, I reckon I'm him. My handle is George."

"From what I am told of the incident, you are a very dangerous man, Señor George. You killed not only Larkin but the two men who work with him. All three of them had considerable blood on their hands, I suspect, and would not have been easy to kill."

"I wouldn't know about that," Braddock said with a faint shake of his head. "I haven't been in El Paso for long."

"You are not in El Paso *now*. You are in Juarez. And in Juarez, *I* am the law."

"So I've heard. I was protecting one of your employees when I stepped in, though. That ought to be worth something."

Hernandez blew out his breath and said, "A prostitute. Less than nothing. Larkin was a potential...business associate."

"I'd apologize for ruining your plans but I still say the son of a bitch had it coming to him."

"No doubt. Calvin Larkin was a very unpleasant man. And if I were to ever do business with him, it would have been in the future, not now. Now, I already have arrangements in place. So in a way, Señor George, I suppose I owe you my thanks. You have...simplified my life, let us say."

"Always glad to be of help," Braddock said dryly.

Hernandez looked at him for a second, then laughed.

"I think I like you," he said. "You have a certain boldness about you. You remind me of me. I'm told you came in tonight with Dex Wilcox."

It wasn't really a question but Braddock said, "That's right," anyway.

"So you work for Señor Palmer as well."

"Just started."

"And while waiting for me, you spent time with Carmen?"

"Yep."

"You enjoyed your time with her?"

"Very much so."

"Good. You can become accustomed to such pleasures. I'm sure that we will be seeing each other again."

Hernandez turned away in obvious dismissal. The other two men moved up closer to Braddock, who said, "Buenas noches, Señor Hernandez."

Hernandez just grunted and didn't say good night.

The men escorted Braddock out. Once they reached the balcony, he said, "I reckon since your boss gave his seal of approval to what happened, I'm free to go."

"Certainly. And you are welcome back here."

"Obliged for the hospitality," Braddock said. He started down the stairs.

The picture in his mind was even clearer than before and just as ugly as ever.

16

Braddock spotted Wilcox as he went down the stairs. The gunman slouched at one of the tables, playing poker with four other men. Wilcox must have seen him, too. He looked at the cards in his hand, shrugged, and threw them in, folding so he could leave the game. He stood up, nodded to the other players, and then headed for the stairs to meet Braddock at the bottom of them.

"Well, I see Hernandez didn't have you taken out into the desert and left in a shallow grave," Wilcox said with a grin.

"I got the feeling he wasn't too happy about me killing Larkin," Braddock said. "He hadn't decided yet about double-crossing Palmer and throwing in with Larkin."

"Then you came along and made up his mind for him."

"He said pretty much the same thing."

"That's what the boss wanted," Wilcox said. "Hernandez probably suspects Palmer might have sent you here to get rid of Larkin but, the way it all played out, he can't be sure about that. For the sake of keepin' the peace, he'll give Palmer the benefit of the doubt. You wound up doin' a mighty fine job, George. The boss is gonna be pleased."

"I'm glad to hear it," Braddock said. "I could use a nice steady job for a while."

"Until the heat dies down enough in Arizona for you to go back, eh?"

"Who knows?" Braddock said. "I might decide I like it in Texas."

Wilcox's grin slipped a little but he didn't say anything except, "Come on. Let's get back across the river."

They left the place and walked toward the bridge a few blocks away. In the warren of alleys and shacks spreading out on both sides of the main street, a dog barked and a woman cried. Typical nighttime sounds, Braddock thought. He wished there had been some way for him to take Carmen out of Hernandez's but he hadn't been able to think of any that wouldn't threaten his plans.

He decided to probe a little more and said, "You know, I got to thinking about it and I believe I've heard of you, Dex. You used to ride with Black Jack Ketchum, didn't you?"

"What if I did?" Wilcox asked, his voice sharp with sudden suspicion.

"I don't mean any offense," Braddock went on. "In fact, I've always admired fellas who could pull off stopping a train and holding it up. Seems like that would take an awful lot of both guts and brains."

Wilcox grunted and sounded somewhat mollified as he said, "You're damn right about that. "The Reno brothers and then Jesse and his boys showed us all how it's done, 'way back when, but since then the railroads have gotten better about protectin' their trains...and fellas like me have gotten even better at holdin' 'em up."

"Must be sort of tiresome for you, hanging around town like this and running errands for Palmer when you're used to bigger and better things."

Wilcox's voice had a knife edge to it again as he said, "Don't ever mistake me for an errand boy. Palmer's got a damned big deal in the works and he never could've pulled it off without me. He knows it, too."

"I'm sure he does," Braddock said. He'd had a hunch Wilcox had been in charge of the train robbery that had netted Palmer the shipment of rifles. Now Wilcox's boasting made him certain of it. "What's this big deal you're talking about?"

"You'll find out soon enough if the boss hires you. After tonight, I don't reckon there's much doubt about that. In fact, once he hears about the slick way you handled that whole Larkin business, he'll be really happy. You'll be his fair-haired boy, I'd say."

Braddock shook his head as they reached the bridge over the Rio Grande and started out onto it.

"I wouldn't go that—"

Before he could continue, Wilcox yanked out his gun, lunged at Braddock, and chopped at his head with the revolver.

17

FROM THE CORNER OF HIS EYE, BRADDOCK SAW WILCOX make his move. It wasn't a complete surprise. Wilcox had seen what the newcomer could do and feared that, given time, Braddock would worm his way into Wilcox's position in Palmer's hierarchy of hired guns.

Things probably never would have gotten that far but Wilcox had no way of knowing that.

Braddock twisted aside, getting out of the way of the blow so it hammered down on his right shoulder instead of crushing his hat and maybe busting his skull.

It was bad enough getting hit the way he did because it made his arm and hand go numb—and that was his gun hand.

He jerked back and swung his left arm at Wilcox's gun, knocking the revolver aside for a second. That gave Braddock enough time to kick Wilcox in the belly. Wilcox groaned and staggered back a couple of steps but he didn't drop the gun.

The two of them were alone on the bridge. A half moon floated overhead, giving them enough light to see each other. Wilcox straightened up from the kick, bared his teeth in a grimace, and said, "I didn't want to shoot you, George—"

"No, you just figured you'd stove in my skull and drop me in the river to drown," Braddock said. "Then you could tell Palmer I went off on my own somewhere after we left Hernandez's together and you didn't know what happened to me after that. If anybody found my corpse, they'd just think some thief jumped and robbed me before dumping me in the river."

"It could'a happened that way."

"Then I'd never have a chance to take over your spot, would I?"

Wilcox laughed, but it sounded hollow. "You think I'm scared of you, George? You're just a two-bit hard-case. You got lucky against Larkin and his boys!"

"You saw me shoot it out with those two," Braddock said. "That look like luck to you?"

Wilcox snarled an obscenity and jerked his gun up, obviously not caring any more about drawing attention with a shot.

Braddock dived to the side as Colt flame bloomed in the night. He felt the bullet rush past his ear. He tried to slap at the Colt on his hip but his right arm still hung limp and unresponsive. Under different circumstances, he might have worried that Wilcox had broken his arm.

Now, he just worried about staying alive.

Wilcox was already tracking the gun to the side for another shot. Braddock dove at his knees and took his legs out from under him. Wilcox fell on top of him. Braddock rolled desperately to throw Wilcox off of him and grabbed for Wilcox's gun with his left hand.

Braddock missed the revolver but got hold of Wilcox's wrist. He slammed it down hard on the bridge planks. Wilcox cried out in pain. Braddock drove his gun hand down again and, this time, the weapon slipped out of Wilcox's fingers and skidded away.

Braddock scrambled after it. He was a decent shot with his left hand and it was faster and easier to scoop up Wilcox's gun than it would have been to reach across his body and draw his own Colt.

His fingertips had just brushed the gun butt when Wilcox tackled him from behind. Braddock went down. The heel of his hand struck the gun and caused it to skid even farther away.

Wilcox smashed a fist into Braddock's right kidney. Braddock gritted his teeth against the pain, writhed over, and brought his left elbow up into Wilcox's face. That knocked Wilcox over onto his back. Braddock went after him and dug a knee into his groin. Wilcox gasped curses and curled up around the agony.

Braddock climbed wearily to his feet. His right arm began to tingle as feeling inched back into it. Maybe it wasn't hurt too bad after all, he thought.

He looked around, spotted the dark shape of the gun lying on the bridge a few yards away, and stumbled over to it. He bent down to pick it up with his left hand, turned and steadied himself to cover Wilcox.

The question now was what he should do with the gunman and train robber. After this attempt on his life, he couldn't ever trust Wilcox again.

But he couldn't just waltz into the El Paso police station, turn Wilcox over to the lawmen, and tell them how Wilcox had had a hand in holding up that train, killing those soldiers, and stealing all those army rifles. The whole story was too complicated and he was wanted, too, after all. The police would hold him while they tried to sort everything out and word might get to the Rangers that he was locked up.

The simplest thing would be to do to Wilcox what Wilcox had figured on doing to him. Bust his head open and dump him in the river, then go back to Palmer and plead ignorance as to Wilcox's fate. Palmer might suspect he'd had something to do with the disappearance but nobody would be able to prove anything.

It was too bad he didn't have a place he could stash Wilcox for a while...

Braddock considered all those options as he took a couple of steps toward Wilcox and he was still trying to figure out what to do when Wilcox suddenly stopped groaning and rolled over toward him. Wilcox's arm came up and flame spouted from the muzzle of the derringer he'd had hidden somewhere in his clothes.

The derringer made a loud pop like somebody had clapped two boards together. Braddock felt the bullet rip into him. He dropped Wilcox's gun, reeled back against the bridge railing, and toppled over it.

The fall lasted only a couple of heartbeats before Braddock struck the surface of the Rio Grande and went under but it seemed longer than that.

18

IT WOULD HAVE BEEN EASY TO SURRENDER TO THE embrace of the warm, gently flowing water. Braddock could just let himself float away downriver...

The Rio Grande was only about eight feet deep here. Braddock's left hand touched the sandy bottom. He righted himself and kicked with his legs. He heard a couple of muffled booms and knew Wilcox was shooting at him...or at least shooting where Wilcox thought he was.

Braddock was already twenty feet downstream. He kept going that way, swimming underwater and trying to disturb the surface as little as possible. While he was falling from the bridge, he had sucked in as deep a breath as he could so he didn't want to come up where Wilcox could still see him.

His right arm had started working well enough again he could stroke clumsily with it. That kept him from swimming in circles, anyway. The pain in his side where the bullet from Wilcox's derringer had struck him wasn't too bad. He managed to put it aside and not pay any attention to it.

He never had figured out what to do with Wilcox after the gunman tried to kill him but that dilemma had vanished in the pop of the derringer. The boot was back on the other foot. Wilcox would have to go back to Shad Palmer and claim ignorance of the new man's where-abouts. Palmer might be annoyed by "George's" disap-pearance but Larkin was dead and that was the main thing he had wanted out of this night.

Even as he was falling into the Rio Grande, Braddock had realized it might be to his advantage to stay dead for a while.

That required not actually dying by drowning, of course.

He didn't hear any more shots. Wilcox might have left the bridge and started running along one of the river banks, looking for him. Braddock had to risk that because his lungs burned from lack of air.

He stopped kicking and let his legs drop, not a problem because his boots pulled them down. He stroked with his arms and lifted himself enough that his mouth and nose came out of the water. Trying not to be too noisy about it, he gulped down a breath.

He couldn't float very well, not fully dressed and with his boots on, but he managed to tread water and let the river's sluggish current carry him slowly downstream. Braddock looked from side to side, searching the banks for movement. He didn't see any, but that didn't mean he was in the clear yet.

His side began to ache. He put that out of his mind, let himself sink beneath the water, and began swimming again. He stayed under as long as he could, then came up for air again.

No bullets came screaming out of the night.

Wilcox had to believe he was dead. More than likely, he had left some blood on the bridge, and if Wilcox saw that, he would know his shot had struck Braddock. The way Braddock had gone right into the river and not come up again sure made it look like he was dead.

Braddock wanted Wilcox to keep on thinking that. To help ensure the assumption, he stayed in the river and let it carry him downstream until he was just too weak and exhausted to manage anymore. Sensing that he might pass out and drown for real, he struggled to the southern bank and crawled out onto the sand.

The scattered lights of El Paso and Juarez lay to his right, at least a mile away. Where he had left the river was nothing but sand and scrub brush, maybe a rattlesnake or two hunting in the darkness. Braddock hoped he wouldn't run into any of them. He pulled himself farther from the water.

Muffled hoofbeats sounded in the distance. Braddock listened and could tell they were coming closer. Muttering curses under his breath, he came up on hands and knees and moved as fast as he could toward a cluster of mesquite trees barely larger than bushes. The shadows were thick among them, though, and that was all Braddock cared about at the moment.

He thought about those rattlesnakes again as he crawled among the mesquites. He didn't hear any warning buzzes, though, just the faint clicking as night breezes blew mesquite beans against each other. In the thickest shadows, he bellied down in the sand to wait.

The approaching rider might be Dex Wilcox, looking for him, but logically Braddock knew it was probably someone else, someone who had nothing to do with him. He waited, barely breathing. His gun still rested in its holster but he wouldn't trust it to fire properly after having been immersed in the river for so long.

The soft, thudding hoofbeats moved past him, thirty or forty yards from the mesquite thicket where he sprawled. In the light from the moon and stars, he saw the rider's silhouette topped with a broad-brimmed, steeple-crowned sombrero, nothing like the Stetson Wilcox wore. Braddock heaved a sigh of relief as the man rode on.

He was safe but only for the moment. Not only that, but he still didn't know how badly wounded he was or how much blood he had lost. He had been forcing his battered body to go on but that couldn't continue much longer.

He sat up and reached down to his right side where the bullet had struck him. The river had soaked his shirt, of course, so he couldn't tell from feeling it how much blood had leaked from the hole he found. A grimace pulled his lips away from his teeth as he probed the wound and the area around it.

A few inches back from the bullet hole, he found a hard lump under his skin. That was it, he thought. The bullet hadn't penetrated very far, skimming along his side until it came to a stop. He was surprised it hadn't come on out. The derringer must have been a small-caliber weapon not packing much punch.

Braddock reached into his pocket and found the clasp knife he carried. As he opened it, he thought about how awkward this impromptu surgery was going to be. He didn't want to haul that slug around inside him, though. That was a good way to get blood poisoning. He gritted his teeth and started digging at the bullet in his side, trying to get the tip of the blade underneath it.

Suddenly, a vision of his father appeared before him.

"It's just a damn splinter," Pa said, brandishing a giant Bowie knife. "Now hold still and lemme take it outta there. Can't leave it in. It'll rot your whole hand off. Don't want that, do ya?"

George swallowed hard and said, "No, sir." But he saw the way his father's hands trembled and knew Pa had been drinking, and he couldn't stop a tear from trickling down his cheek.

"You know how many bullets I've taken outta men? Hell, I've carved bullets outta my own hide! What're you gonna do, one of these days when you're a Ranger and you're out in the middle o' nowhere by yourself and some damn greaser shoots you? You gonna just lay down and die, or are you gonna take that bullet out and live?" Pa let out a contemptuous snort. "Hell, what am I talkin' about? They'll never take a scared little piss-ant like you in the Rangers. Now hold still—"

George screamed as the tip of the Bowie lanced into his palm, gouging for the splinter...

The bullet popped out of his side and thudded to the sand. Braddock followed it an instant later, collapsing as he passed out.

19

THE MESQUITE BRANCHES THREW A LATTICEWORK OF shadows over his face when he woke up, but the sun still shone brightly enough through them to make him wince and turn his head away from the stabbing glare.

The movement made his stomach roil and his head throb for a moment but the feeling passed. He sat up slowly, stiff, sore muscles complaining as he did so. His injured side caught and twinged sharply. He sucked in his breath.

The mesquite beans rattled to his left. He looked in that direction and saw a small brown face peering at him through the branches. A boy, eight or ten years old, jumped back when he saw Braddock looking at him.

"Don't be afraid," Braddock told him in Spanish. "I won't hurt you."

"You are not dead," the boy said.

"No. Halfway there, maybe, but no further."

The boy started to back off.

"Wait," Braddock said. "Don't run away. Do you live near here?"

"My father's farm is that way." The boy pointed southeast along the Rio Grande.

"Your father...does he drink tequila or mescal or pulque?"

A look of understanding appeared on the boy's face. "I thought you were hurt," he said. "Now I see you have had too much to drink."

He looked and sounded a mite too world-weary for his years, Braddock thought.

"I *am* hurt." Braddock turned a little and pulled up his shirt so the boy could see both the bullet hole and the wound where Braddock had cut out the slug. "I need the tequila for medicine, not for drinking."

The youngster frowned and said, "My apologies, señor—"

"That's all right," Braddock assured him. "Do you have a horse?"

"A burro."

"Can you get him and bring him back here?"

The boy nodded and started to turn away, then paused and said, "My name is Alphonso."

"I'm George."

"Wait there."

"Thank you," Braddock said. In truth, he couldn't do anything *except* wait. He was too weak to get up and wander off by himself.

Alphonso didn't come back for a long time and Braddock had just about decided he wasn't coming back when the youngster walked up to the thicket leading a short-legged burro. Braddock had been saving what little strength he had. He used it now to crawl over to the burro and reach up to grasp the animal's harness.

Alphonso took hold of Braddock's other arm to help him. With all three of them working at it—although in truth, the burro didn't do anything but stand there—Braddock got to his feet.

"Have you told your mother or father about me?" he asked.

Alphonso shook his head. "My father and my brothers are working in the fields. My mother is home with my little sisters."

For a moment, Braddock wondered why the boy wasn't working in the fields, too, but then he saw the unnatural twist to Alphonso's left leg. It didn't seem to keep him from getting around but he would have a difficult time putting in a full day's work.

"What's your mother going to do when you show up with me? She won't shoot me, will she?"

Alphonso looked horrified at the idea. "No, señor! She is a good woman who prays every day to the Blessed Virgin. You are injured. She will care for you."

"I can use it," Braddock muttered. "Let's go."

He leaned on the burro and forced his legs to work. They walked slowly along the river with Alphonso leading the burro. Braddock hoped Dex Wilcox or one of his other enemies didn't happen to come along. He wouldn't be able to put up much of a fight and Alphonso would be in the line of fire.

No one seemed to be around, though, and, after a little while, the adobe jacal where Alphonso and his family lived came in sight. Braddock saw some younger children playing outside but no sign of the boy's mother.

"Are you a bad man?" Alphonso asked.

"What?"

"You have been shot." As if that explained the question.

"A lot of people who aren't bad get shot. It's the bad people who shoot them."

"So a bad man shot you?"

Braddock thought about Dex Wilcox and said, "A very bad man."

"That's all right, then. Mama will help you."

Braddock hoped so because even this short walk had him just about at the end of his rope again.

Because of that, he couldn't do anything except stop and stand there when a woman stepped around a corner of the jacal holding a pitchfork and looking like she wanted to ram it right through his guts.

BRADDOCK WONDERED IDLY IF SHE WAS PART YAQUI. HER face was fierce enough for that to be the case.

Or maybe she just looked like that because she thought she was defending her home and family.

"Alphonso, what have you done?" she demanded.

"It's all right, Mama. This man was lying in the mesquites, hurt. I thought he was dead at first but he isn't. He's been shot and needs some of Papa's tequila as medicine."

The woman looked at Braddock. "You have been shot?"

"Yes, ma'am," he said. Bracing himself on the burro, he half-turned and pulled up his shirt again to reveal the wounds.

"Where are the men who shot you?"

"It was just one man and he's back in El Paso, I reckon. I'm pretty sure he thinks I'm dead."

The woman frowned and said, "I will not have you bringing trouble into my house."

"Well, then," Braddock said, feeling himself growing

weaker, "I'll just sit out here, then..."

His head spun and he would have fallen if Alphonso hadn't caught hold of his arm. The woman looked indecisive for a second, then she leaned the pitchfork against the jacal's adobe wall and hurried forward. She took Braddock's other arm and they helped him to a three-legged stool near the doorway.

"Sit here," she told him after they had lowered him carefully onto the stool.

"Yes, ma'am. I don't really feel like getting up and doing a jig."

The thought of that made him laugh. The sound of the laughter made him realize he was lightheaded and not himself at all. The sun was hot as it beat down on him or else a fever had hold of him. Maybe both.

The three little girls, all younger than Alphonso, gathered a few yards away and stared at Braddock. He was just loco enough, at the moment, that he was tempted to say "Boo!" at them but he knew if he did that, they would scream and run off and their mama might be mad at him. He didn't want that.

She came back with a basin of water and a rag in one hand, a clay cup in the other.

"Can you hold this to drink?" she asked as she held out the cup.

"I don't know but I'll try."

"Alphonso, help him."

With the boy's hand on the cup, too, to steady it, Braddock lifted it and sipped the clear liquid inside. The fiery bite of it told him it was tequila.

"Don't drink it all," the woman said. "I'll use it to clean the wounds after I have washed them."

"Yes, ma'am, that's just what I had in mind."

She lifted his shirt and used the wet rag to swab away

the blood that had flowed from the holes and dried after Braddock emerged from the river. Then she squeezed out the rag, took the cup, soaked the cup in the tequila, and pressed it deep into the bullet hole.

Braddock said, "Ahhhh," and leaned his head back, baring his teeth.

The woman repeated the process with the hole Braddock had made to get the slug out. It hurt just as bad but he expected it this time and didn't react quite as strongly.

"Come inside," the woman said. "You must lie down."

"I *am* mighty tired."

"You must lie on your side so I can pour tequila into the wounds."

"Oh. Well, that's gonna hurt."

Alphonso said, "And Papa will say it is a waste of good tequila."

"Never mind what your papa will say," the woman snapped. "Help the gringo."

With their assistance, Braddock hobbled inside and lay down on a bunk with a straw mattress. It felt good and Braddock might have dozed off right away, except the woman made good on her word and carefully tilted the cup to let raw tequila run into the holes in Braddock's hide. He didn't yell out loud but he didn't miss it by much.

The burning pain still filled him enough he was barely aware of it when the woman slid the Colt from its holster. Braddock wanted to object. His instincts rebelled at the idea of anybody taking his gun.

But he didn't figure she planned to use it against him. If she'd wanted him dead, she could have let him fall down in front of her house and lie there until the sun and the fever killed him. She could get that pitchfork and stab him full of holes. She didn't need to shoot him.

Through slitted eyes, he saw her place the revolver on a table.

"Stay away from the gun," she told Alphonso in a stern voice. "Do not touch it. Do not even get near it."

"Yes, Mama," the boy said.

She turned to Braddock with her mouth open to say something else to him.

He didn't know what it was because, just then, he passed out again.

21

"GRACIAS, SEÑORA SANCHEZ," BRADDOCK SAID AROUND A mouthful of tortilla and frijoles. When he'd regained consciousness that morning, he wouldn't have given odds on him still being alive by now, let alone eating ravenously. He could feel strength flowing back into him from the food and the strong coffee he sipped between bites.

She still didn't look too happy about him being here and neither did her husband, Enrique. Alphonso and the other six children seemed to find the *Tejano* endlessly fascinating, though. No doubt the Sanchezes had used stories of the Texas devils to frighten their children into behaving and now here was one of them sitting right in their own jacal. So far, he hadn't eaten the head off of any of them.

Sanchez said, "You are certain, señor, that the man who tried to kill you will not come here and harm my family?"

"I don't see how that could ever happen," Braddock said. "I told you, he's convinced I'm dead."

"You cannot *know* this, señor. You cannot be certain of what is in a man's head."

"No, I suppose not, but I'm convinced it's true in this case. You see, this fella...he wouldn't want me on his trail. We didn't know each other for very long but I reckon he understood that about me. If he didn't believe he'd killed me, he would have kept on looking for me."

Sanchez sighed and said, "It seems all I can do is trust you. I cannot blame my wife for helping you. She has a good heart."

"You have a good family," Braddock said. "If I can ever pay you back for all you've done, I will."

Sanchez glanced at the open door, where the last light of day faded, and said, "Just go, señor, as soon as it is dark and do not come back here again."

Braddock had slept about half the day, then woken up long enough for Señora Sanchez to clean his wounds again and change the dressings she had put on them after he passed out. While he was awake, Alphonso had fed him some hot stew. Then Braddock had gone back to sleep and when he woke up in the late afternoon, his fever had broken and he was extremely hungry and thirsty.

Since then, he'd had more of the thick stew with chunks of goat meat swimming in it, along with tortillas and beans and a couple of cups of coffee. Señora Sanchez had changed his bandages again, binding them tightly in place with strips of cloth.

"Be careful," she had told him. "Do not move around too much."

That would be difficult, because he had things to do, but he didn't tell her that.

Wouldn't want her to think all her hard work keeping him alive might go to waste before the night was over.

When he'd finished eating, Braddock reclaimed his gun and cleaned and dried it as best he could. It seemed to be in good working order but he wished he had his gear so he could give it a good cleaning. Everything he owned was back in the boarding house in El Paso, though.

Only about thirty-six hours had passed since his meeting with E.J. Caldwell in the Camino Real. With everything that had happened, it seemed more like weeks to Braddock.

Señora Sanchez shooed the youngsters away from the table while Braddock worked on his gun. Her husband sat on the other side of the table and regarded Braddock gloomily. He had some tequila in one of the clay cups and sipped it now and then.

"What are you going to do?" he asked.

"Well, since you don't have a horse I can buy or rent and I figure I'd look sort of foolish riding that burro with my feet scraping the ground, I reckon I'll walk back to Juarez. It's not much more than a mile, you said."

"You are shot last night, nearly bleed to death, and now you would walk a mile back into the face of danger. Most people would say you are loco."

Braddock smiled faintly and said, "I've been called that before and worse." He shook his head. "But what else am I going to do? You don't want me staying here."

"It is true, I do not. This farm provides a living of sorts for us. It cannot support a Texan with your appetite, too."

Braddock laughed and Sanchez smiled a little, then grew more serious as he went on, "You are the sort of man who cannot turn his back on trouble."

"One of these days I might. But not just yet."

"You will keep on saying that until someday it is too late."

"You could well be right about that."

Braddock had resigned himself to such a fate when he put that bullet-holed Ranger badge in his pocket and started riding the dangerous trails alone. But he would do as much good in the world as he could before fate caught up to him.

Tonight, as he told Sanchez, he planned to head back to Juarez. He wasn't sure yet what he would do once he got there but Wilcox believed he was dead, Palmer wouldn't know what happened to him and, by now, Hernandez might have found out that apparently he'd dropped off the face of the earth. None of them would be looking for him.

He had figure out some way to turn that to his advantage.

Satisfied he'd done the best he could with the Colt, he stood up and slid it back into leather. His movements were a little stiff, partially because he was sore and partially because Señora Sanchez had tied the bandages so tight.

He reached into his pocket and found a couple of silver dollars. One he gave to Señora Sanchez, the other to Alphonso.

"Gracias to both of you," he said. "You saved my life and I'll never forget it."

"You are leaving now?" Alphonso asked.

"I have to."

"But you will come back to see us someday?"

Braddock glanced at the boy's father, who scowled.

"None of us knows the future, Alphonso, but this I do know, wherever the two of us are from now on, we will be amigos."

The boy's face lit up in a smile.

Sanchez followed Braddock outside, where the last of the daylight was gone and the stars were beginning to come out overhead.

"I would tell you to go with God," the farmer said, "but I think you already have a companion."

"El Diablo?" Braddock said with a grim smile.

"Es verdad," Sanchez said.

22

IT DIDN'T TAKE LONG FOR BRADDOCK TO DISCOVER HE wasn't as well-rested as he'd thought he was. Putting one foot in front of the other required a lot of effort and determination but he kept doing it anyway.

He followed the river toward the bordertowns on each side of the Rio Grande. After a while, he could see their lights ahead of him.

Señora Sanchez had removed his boots and allowed them to dry outside in the sun during the day but, even so, they still weren't made for walking. Braddock paused, leaned against a mesquite, and pulled them off so he could walk in his stocking feet. He had spent a lot of his life on horseback, so being a-foot rubbed him the wrong way.

Maybe he should have considering borrowing that burro from the Sanchezes after all...

He didn't know how long it took him to cover the mile or so to Juarez. An hour, maybe, although it seemed longer. When he reached the outskirts of town, he stopped and put his boots on again. Then he headed for

Hernandez's place without any clear plan in mind, thinking only that whatever he did next, Hernandez's was a place to start.

The long walk had given him time to think about everything he had learned the night before. The women and girls who had been kidnapped from Santa Rosalia were the key to the whole affair, he decided. Shadrach Palmer had whores upstairs at Casa de Palmer and, if the rumors about his extensive criminal connections were true, he probably had a piece of every brothel in El Paso. He would need a steady supply of women.

Maybe Hernandez, in partnership with the bandit Martin Larrizo, had an arrangement with Palmer to supply those women, in exchange for the shipment of army rifles. Those Krags were worth more than the prisoners Carmen had told Braddock about. That was a callous thing to think, Braddock knew, but it was true. However, those unfortunates might be just the first installment on the payment.

There were plenty of other villages Larrizo, Gonsalvo, and the other bandits could raid.

Braddock wasn't sure why they wanted the rifles, other than the fact outlaws always wanted more and better weapons. Maybe Larrizo harbored some crackpot notion of staging a revolution and setting himself up as dictator of this part of Mexico. Loco schemes like that were common south of the border. Every common bandido fancied himself an emperor, it seemed.

That idea had begun to form in his mind after Carmen had told him about the captives and after turning the theory over and over in his head during the walk to Juarez, it seemed even more reasonable and likely.

If Braddock had made the correct assumption,

hundreds of women, maybe more, eventually would face an ugly fate. And untold numbers of innocent men, women, and children might die if Larrizo managed to rally an army, even a small one, and launch a revolution. The effort might be doomed to failure but it would be a bloody slaughter while it lasted.

Braddock had no proof of the plotters' intentions but his instincts told him he was right.

Even if he wasn't, those women were still being held captive somewhere not far from Juarez. He had to find them and help them somehow.

All those thoughts led him to Hernandez's place, where he circled around to the rear of the big, brightly lit building.

He had in mind seeing if there was a back door so he could slip inside and maybe reach the second floor without being seen. He wanted to talk to Carmen again and try to find out more from her about where the prisoners were being held.

A stable stood behind the building and, as soon as Braddock saw it, he thought about saddling a horse and tying it somewhere nearby, in case he had to make a quick getaway. Before he could even attempt that, however, the question of whether Hernandez's place had a back door was answered. Light slanted out toward the stable from the door as it swung open.

Braddock pulled back in the shadows beside the stable.

Four men walked out of the building and came toward the stable. Braddock eased an eye around the corner to take a look at them.

Hernandez strode along a few feet in front of the other three. Tonight, he wore black trousers, a short black charro jacket, and a flat-crowned black hat.

The other three were dressed like vaqueros in rough clothing and sombreros but the guns they wore told Braddock they were pistoleros, not cowboys. Hernandez's bodyguards, more than likely.

Clearly, Hernandez intended on going somewhere, as he had the previous evening. Braddock wondered where.

One possible answer suggested itself to him immediately.

Braddock heard Hernandez say something about "the mission" as the men went into the stable. He didn't know if Hernandez meant the errand that brought them out tonight or a specific place, a Catholic mission. Plenty of those could be found all over the region.

Braddock could tell from the noises within the stable that the men were saddling horses. A harsh voice, instantly recognizable as not being Hernandez's smooth tones, said, "Something is wrong with my cinch. The buckle is coming loose."

"Fix it and catch up to us," Hernandez snapped. A moment later, he rode out with the other two men. They turned south.

Braddock stood tensely in the shadows. With Hernandez and some of his men gone, he stood a better chance of being able to sneak into the main building without being discovered.

But another opportunity had presented itself and Braddock didn't want to waste it. The chance might not amount to anything but there was only one way to find out.

Hernandez and the other two men had ridden out of sight by the time the third man emerged from the stable.

Braddock was waiting for him, gun in hand.

The pistolero wasn't expecting any trouble, right here behind his boss's headquarters. He rode loosely in the saddle. The horse had taken only a few steps when Braddock dashed out of his hiding place. He grabbed the man's arm and jerked him out of the saddle violently enough that the man's sombrero flew off. Braddock struck swiftly with the Colt which he had reversed in his hand.

The gun butt thudded hard against the pistolero's skull. The man grunted and tried feebly to struggle. Braddock hit him again.

This time the pistolero went limp.

Braddock holstered the Colt and reached down to take hold of the unconscious gunman under the arms. He dragged the man into the stable, which was dimly lit by a lantern hanging on a nail in one of the posts holding up the roof. Braddock spied a pile of straw and dumped the pistolero on it.

The man's breathing was shallow. He might wake up, after a while, or he might not. Knowing the pistolero worked for Hernandez and probably had plenty of blood on his hands, Braddock didn't really care either way. He found a pitchfork and heaped straw over the man until it completely covered the senseless form.

Using the pitchfork made Braddock think of Señora Sanchez. He checked the bandages she had placed on his injuries. Neither of them felt wet, so maybe his exertions hadn't started the wounds bleeding again.

What he hoped he would discover when he followed Hernandez and the other two men made him not mind running the risk of re-opening the wounds.

The horse had danced off a few yards when Braddock grabbed its rider, but it still stood in front of the stable. Braddock approached slowly and carefully, talking in a low voice. Horses had always responded well to him and this one was no exception. The animal let him get hold of the reins.

A thought occurred to Braddock. Before swinging up into the saddle, he looked around and found the pistolero's sombrero lying on the ground nearby. He picked it up and put it on. That would make him look less suspicious to anyone who saw him.

Then, with a grim smile on his face, he mounted up and rode after his quarry.

23

BRADDOCK KNEW ONLY ONE MAIN ROAD LED OUT OF Juarez heading south but he didn't know whether or not Hernandez and the others planned to take it. So he pushed the pistolero's horse at a fairly rapid pace starting out. The men had about a ten minute lead on him, but he thought he could make that up.

He had to be careful, though, because he didn't want to ride right up behind them and have them spot him. Even though he rode the third man's horse and wore his hat, he knew he couldn't maintain the masquerade more than a few seconds. It was a fine line, getting close enough to spot them without being spotted himself.

No doubt Hernandez would wonder what had happened to his third bodyguard but Braddock didn't believe the man would turn back from his errand because of that.

He hadn't seen any sign of the men he was after by the time he reached the edge of town. Braddock reined in for a moment and let out an exasperated sigh. All he could do was keep going on the main road, he decided.

A few minutes later, he came up behind an old, white-bearded peon slowly pulling a handcart. The man must have taken produce or maybe some chickens into Juarez to the market and was late getting started back to his farm. Braddock pulled up beside him and said with the sort of harsh arrogance he figured the pistolero would have used, "Hey, viejo, did three men ride this way a little while ago?"

The old-timer nodded and said, "Sí, señor. They rode very fast. I had to pull my cart aside, else they would have trampled me."

"That's what you get for being in the way." Braddock started to ride on, then paused and added, "But gracias for your help."

"De nada, señor."

Braddock didn't have any more silver dollars but he had a fifty-cent piece, he recalled. He found it and tossed to the old man, who displayed good reflexes despite his age by catching it in the dim moonlight.

Braddock rode on. Hernandez and his men had been in a hurry, according to the old-timer, but whether or not that actually meant anything was open to question. Hernandez might easily be the sort of man who always charged ahead aggressively, no matter what, and to hell with anybody who got in his way. Braddock could believe that even though he had met the man only briefly.

He stopped occasionally to listen, and finally, he heard the swift rataplan of hoofbeats ahead of him. Several horses, judging by the sound. Braddock had a strong hunch he had found the men he was looking for.

But then the next time he stopped, he didn't hear anything. Either Hernandez and his men had increased their speed and gotten out of earshot again...

Or else they had reached their destination and halted. Braddock reined his mount to a slower speed. His keen eyes scanned the shadowed landscape ahead of him.

There wasn't much out here in this semi-desert region. An occasional jacal, dark because the peons who lived there were asleep after a hard day of trying to scratch a living out of the land they worked. Clumps of scrubby mesquite trees and stretches of chaparral. Low but rugged mountains looming darkly in the distance like a great, slumbering beast.

And something else squatted a couple of hundred yards off to the left of the road, an irregular pattern of light and shadow against the gray, sandy terrain.

It was a structure of some sort, Braddock realized, but it wasn't all still standing. The roof was gone and the walls had partially collapsed. The ruins of some old building.

An abandoned mission, maybe, with an intact cellar suitable for holding captives?

A minute later, Braddock came to a trail that branched off from the main road and led toward the ruins. He rode on past it without slowing. Hernandez might have a man watching the trail.

It wasn't likely he would have a man watching the back of the place, though. Not this far from town in such an isolated area.

Braddock rode another half-mile before leaving the road. He struck out across the country, looping wide around the ruins and finally reined in. He swung down from the saddle and tied the horse's reins to a mesquite.

From there, he went ahead on foot and, after a few minutes, he spotted the ruins again. As he worked his way closer, he saw he was right about how the roof and portions of the walls had fallen in. Looming higher at one end of the old building stood the remains of a bell tower. They looked sturdy enough to support a man, and if Hernandez was smart, he'd have a rifleman up there watching the trail from the road.

Braddock crouched in the chaparral and kept an eye on the place for long minutes. Finally, he saw the flare of a match in the tower's remnants. Somebody was up there, all right, and had just lit a cigarette.

Braddock could only hope they weren't looking in his direction as he began to creep closer. As much as possible, he stuck to the shadows cast by clumps of mesquite.

Off to one side of the old mission stood a hitch rack with three saddled horses tied to it. On the other side of the mission, a corral held several more horses. Braddock would have been willing to bet Hernandez's men had had to repair the corral before they could use it, maybe even just about rebuild it.

Everything he saw told him he had come to the right place. Hernandez and the two pistoleros had ridden out here from Juarez and several more men had been here to start with. Maybe the guards were changing shifts. Maybe Hernandez liked to come and check on the prisoners every night. After all, they meant a great deal to him.

If Braddock was right, they represented partial payment for that shipment of Krags.

He hunkered there, ignoring the dull ache in his wounded side, for long minutes. At last three men emerged from the ruins and went to the horses tied at the hitch rack. One of them was Hernandez; Braddock could tell that from his hat. He didn't know if the others were the men who had accompanied Hernandez from Juarez or two of the men who had already been here at the mission and it didn't really matter. All three mounted up and rode off into the night.

That left approximately four men at the old mission —and an outlaw Ranger lurking outside, wondering if those kidnapped women were really here.

He didn't intend to leave until he had the answer.

24

Braddock focused his attention on the bell tower. If anyone was going to discover him as he approached, likely it would be the guard posted there.

Braddock's eyes had adjusted to the darkness, so after a while he was able to tell the guard had a routine of sorts. He spent most of his time watching the trail from the main road but, every few minutes, he turned in a complete circle, pausing at each compass point to study the surrounding countryside in that direction.

Braddock waited until the guard had just finished that survey before he left the thick shadow where he crouched and quickly catfooted forward. He knew he ought to have several minutes before the guard swung around in his direction again.

He covered half the distance to the ruined mission before he went to ground again in the gloom of another mesquite thicket. He might have had time to reach the nearest wall but he didn't want to risk it.

Patiently, he waited for the guard to make another turn. That gave him a chance to spot a small, flickering orange glow somewhere inside the mission. Not surprisingly, Hernandez's other men had built a campfire in there. Enough of the half-fallen walls still stood upright to keep it from being noticed from the road and the flames would provide warmth. It got chilly out here on the desert at night even in the middle of summer.

So Braddock knew where to look for the other men as he slipped up to the crumbling wall a few minutes later. When he listened closely, he could hear the voices of two of them talking quietly to each other.

Like most men, they were complaining about their boss.

"—never know the difference. Hernandez has one of them. Why should we be deprived of the pleasures due us as men?"

"Because he pays our wages and because, if he feels like it, he can have us strung up and lashed within an inch of our lives and there is not one damned thing we can do about it. Besides, he didn't have Gonsalvo bring him that girl for his own use. Gonsalvo said Hernandez wanted to put her to work in his place, to see what kind of whores we had brought him."

Braddock knew they were talking about Carmen. The comments jibed with what she had told him about her experiences.

"It's still not fair," the first man said. "Larrizo had her all the way here, now Hernandez—or his customers—have her, and you and I, we have nothing, amigo."

"Nothing but the promise of an easy life when Martin is the president, you mean."

The first man snorted. "A promise is like the call of a night bird. Here and then gone, nothing but a pleasant memory that actually accomplishes nothing."

A third voice spoke up, saying, "Will you two bastards shut up so I can sleep?"

"Bernardo, you cannot think it is fair for us to be around all those women, yet never are we allowed to touch them."

"When you get to be my age, you dung beetle, women matter very little except for what they can cook."

Both the other men laughed and one said, "I hope I never get to be as old as you, Bernardo."

"It is doubtful you will."

Crouched in the darkness on the other side of the wall, Braddock smiled.

He intended to see to it that none of these men got any older than they already were tonight.

With maybe one exception, he corrected himself as an idea sparked in his mind.

He moved carefully along the wall until he reached a spot where nearly all of it had collapsed. Taking off the sombrero, he eased his head around the ragged edge so he could look toward the fire.

The two men who had been talking sat beside the fire, warming themselves. The third man, Bernardo, stretched out a few yards away in a bedroll. He represented the least threat because it would take him longer to get out of those entangling blankets.

Braddock eyed the Winchesters leaning against a large chunk of adobe that had toppled into the mission at some point. He carried only his Colt and the spare cartridges in his shell belt. While he believed the revolver would work after he had cleaned it at the Sanchez farm, he would feel better about things if he could get his hands on one of those repeaters and maybe the bandolier of ammunition worn by one of the guards.

Braddock pulled back a little and felt around on the

ground until he found a chunk of broken adobe slightly bigger than his hand. He drew back his arm and heaved the chunk in a high arc that carried it across what had been the sanctuary to the other side of the mission. It thudded, bounced, thudded again.

Almost instantly, the two men leaped to their feet with their guns drawn. They wheeled around to face the source of the sound.

"Bernardo!" one of them said in an urgent whisper. "We heard something."

"Well, go see what it was," Bernardo said without getting up. Evidently, he was in charge of this guard detail. "Probably just a coyote."

The men left the rifles leaning against the chunk of fallen wall and stalked toward the far side of the mission. They thrust their revolvers out in front of them in a stiff, tense manner, obviously ready to start firing at the least excuse.

Braddock swung his leg over the collapsed wall and stepped into the old mission. Bernardo had his head tucked down with the brim of his sombrero shielding him from the glare of the fire. When Braddock got close enough, the man would be able to see him but, with any luck, it would be too late to make a difference.

Only a few feet separated Braddock from the rifles when Bernardo suddenly shifted, muttered, lifted his head, and then ripped out a curse.

"Over here!" the older guard cried as he started trying to throw the blankets aside so he could claw for his gun. "Over here!"

25

BRADDOCK'S COLT ROARED AS HE SHOT ONE OF THE guards on the other side of the mission. The bullet caught the man in the side as he tried to turn around. He staggered and fell as bloody froth from his punctured lungs spewed from his lips.

"Felipe!" Bernardo shouted. "Felipe, down here!"

So Felipe was the one in the tower. Braddock would get to him in due time—if Felipe didn't get to him first.

But in the meantime, Braddock fired a round over the head of the second guard across the mission, then turned and shouted toward the front of the ruins, "Wilcox! Get the man in the tower!"

The second guard had ducked away from Braddock's shot and now scrambled for cover behind the collapsed wall on the other side. Braddock's next bullet kicked up dirt at his feet an instant before he flung himself over the wall.

As Braddock pivoted, he saw he had almost neglected Bernardo for too long. The man had gotten untangled from his bedroll and started to raise his gun. Firelight glinted off the weapon's barrel and threw a red glare across the man's angular, gray-bearded face.

Braddock's gun roared a fraction of a second before Bernardo's but that served to throw off the guard's aim as Braddock's slug tore into his chest. Braddock felt the heat of Bernardo's bullet as it skimmed beside his cheek without touching it.

Bernardo gasped and fell back but he didn't drop his gun until Braddock shot him again.

The sombrero flew off Braddock's head as a rifle cracked from the bell tower. Braddock dived over to the big chunk of adobe where the rifles leaned and snagged the barrel of one of the Winchesters. He rolled onto his belly and saw a muzzle flash from the other side of the mission where the second guard had taken cover.

Braddock returned that fire, cranking off three rounds as fast as he could work the rifle's lever. The bullets struck the top of the ruined wall and sprayed chips of adobe in the second guard's face. He cried out as he fell back.

The rifle in the tower continued to crack but the piece of fallen wall protected Braddock. He crawled along on his belly until he reached a spot where he could thrust the Winchester's barrel around the stone and line up a shot.

He and Felipe must have spotted each other, at the same instant, because the man in the tower swung his rifle and fired just as Braddock squeezed the Winchester's trigger. The sharp reports blended together and sounded like one instead of two.

Felipe's bullet whined off the adobe a few inches from Braddock while the outlaw Ranger's shot made Felipe lurch upright on the part of the tower's wooden platform that remained intact. Hunched over against the pain, he stumbled forward a step and dropped the rifle.

A second later, he pitched off the platform, turned over once in the air, and smashed down on his back on the ground just inside the mission.

"You got him, Dex!" Braddock yelled. "There's just one of them left. He can't stop all of us from getting those women."

Braddock sprayed four more rounds toward the guard who had taken cover on the far side of the mission. No shots came in return this time.

Instead, as Braddock lowered the rifle and listened, he heard hoofbeats pounding on the desert floor, heading away from the mission. A bleak grin curved his lips.

He waited five minutes after the sound of the hoofbeats faded out before moving from cover, just to make sure the guard wasn't trying anything tricky. When he was convinced the man had fled, he stood up and moved quickly away from the fire, back into the shadows along the ruined wall. His dangerous life had ingrained such caution in him.

Braddock let a few more minutes go by, then went in search of the entrance to the mission's cellar.

The elements had taken their toll on the adobe walls of the mission. It might have been a hundred years or more since the priests had abandoned it. But the stone and mortar and thick wooden beams that formed the cellar could still be intact.

After a few minutes, set against what had been one of the mission's rear walls, Braddock found a heavy wooden door set into the ground at a slant. It looked fairly new and was barred from the outside. Somebody —Hernandez or one of his men, more than likely—had found this old mission, discovered the cellar was still usable, and decided it would make a good place to store contraband.

There was no better way to describe the women and girls who had been kidnapped from Santa Rosalia, at least where Hernandez, Larrizo, and Shadrach Palmer were concerned. Those captives were a commodity to be traded, nothing more.

That thought made anger smolder inside Braddock. He set the rifle aside, removed the bar from the door, and then grasped its handle. With a grunt of effort, he swung it up and to the side. Its hinges creaked from the sand that had gotten into them.

Then he picked up the rifle, stepped back, and called in Spanish, "You can all come out now. You're safe."

26

IT TOOK A COUPLE OF MINUTES BEFORE ONE OF THE
captives gathered enough courage to stick her head up
into the silvery light from the moon and stars. That glow
shone on her long, sleek dark hair.

"Señor...?" she said.

Without the sombrero, it was more easily discernible
that Braddock was a gringo, not one of the guards who
worked for Hernandez and Larrizo. He said again,
"You're safe now. Nobody's going to hurt you. Those
other men are either dead or gone. You must have heard
the shooting, even down there."

The young woman swallowed and nodded. "Sí, señor.
We did not know what was happening. We were frightened that someone had come to kill us."

"No. I'm getting you out of here. You're free to go."

"Go, señor?" she repeated. "Go where?"

Well, now, that was a problem, Braddock realized. He
had been concerned with rescuing the prisoners and, at
the same time, making it seem as if Shadrach Palmer
were double-crossing Hernandez and Larrizo and had

sent his men to steal the captives away. That was why Braddock had been happy to let the other guard flee.

Probably the man had almost reached Juarez by now, carrying the news of Palmer's betrayal to Hernandez.

Braddock needed to move quickly himself but he couldn't just ride off and leave the women to fend for themselves.

"We'll find a place for you," he said. "Right now you need to go back down into the cellar, talk to the others, and tell them we have to get out of here right away."

"They will be frightened..."

Braddock didn't have time for this but he didn't really have a choice, either.

"You have to convince them. Otherwise it may be too late."

The woman nodded again and disappeared back down the stone steps visible inside the cellar entrance.

The delay chafed at Braddock as he waited for her to reappear with the other prisoners. He could hear a vague murmur of voices from the darkened cellar. After everything that had happened to the women, he wouldn't be surprised if some of them believed this was a trick or trap of some sort.

Finally, though, the young woman he had spoken to reappeared. She came up the steps and out into the ruined mission, leading a long line of women and girls, all of them still wearing the nightclothes they'd had on when the raiders took them from their village.

Braddock had been looking around while he waited. Some low hills lay a couple of miles away, splotched with dark stretches that had to be trees and other vegetation.

He pointed to them and told the women, "You can go to those hills and find some place to hide until I come back for you."

"That is far to walk and some of us are weak," the one who spoke for them said. "Larrizo's men did not feed us well."

"There are three horses in the corral." Braddock pointed. "Take them. The weakest among you can ride, two on each horse if necessary." He nodded toward the sprawled bodies of the three men he had killed. "There are weapons and ammunition. Take them, too, so if anyone tries to hurt you, you can fight."

"And what if you never come back for us, señor? What if you are dead?"

Braddock considered that for a moment. He certainly couldn't rule out the possibility of his luck finally running out.

"The Rio Grande is north of here," he said, pointing again. "There are farms on both sides of it where good people will take you in and help you return to your home. I would take you there myself but there are other things I have to do tonight."

"More killing?" the young woman said.

"More than likely."

One of the older women stepped forward and asked, "Why are you doing these things and risking your life for us, señor? You are a gringo, are you not?"

"That doesn't matter," Braddock said. "There are bad men on both sides of the river and it's my job to deal with them."

He reached into the hidden pocket on his gunbelt and brought out the silver star in a silver circle, the emblem of the Texas Rangers. In this poor light, the women might not be able to see the bullet hole in the center of the badge, but they could make out enough detail to recognize what it was. Braddock heard several of them murmuring about Texas devils.

Let them think whatever they wanted about him. It didn't change what he had to do.

"Señor," the young woman said as Braddock put away the badge. "There was one other kept here for a time...a friend of mine...Her name is Carmen."

"I know her," Braddock said with a nod.

"Then you know where she is? They took her and we all believed we would never see her again."

"I know where she is," Braddock said, "and I plan to set her free before the night's over."

27

THOUGHTS TUMBLED CRAZILY THROUGH BRADDOCK'S HEAD during the swift ride back to the border.

Probably the first thing Hernandez would do when the guard reached him with the news of the attack on the mission was to send men galloping back down there to make sure the prisoners actually were gone.

When they returned to Juarez and confirmed that, Hernandez would be livid. He would believe Palmer had discovered where the women and girls were being held, then decided to double-cross him and grab the prisoners without trading the stolen rifles for them. That way Palmer could sell the rifles to someone else and get a new supply of whores, too.

If Braddock's theory about the arrangement between Palmer and Hernandez being an ongoing one was correct, the double-cross idea wouldn't stand up to prolonged scrutiny.

Braddock had a hunch Hernandez might be too furious for any such scrutiny, though. In the heat of the moment, he would want to strike back at the man he believed had betrayed him.

He would go after Palmer.

It had to be tonight, too, if Braddock's plan was going to work. If Hernandez waited until the morning and investigated further around the old mission, he or his men would see the prints Braddock had left and realize there had been only one attacker. Braddock could only hope Hernandez was more impulsive than that.

Instead of riding directly through the middle of Juarez, Braddock circled around the bordertown and swam the horse across the Rio Grande a short distance downstream. He stuck to the back streets as he made his way toward Casa de Palmer.

When he reached the place, he left the horse in the alley behind the building. He wondered briefly what had happened to the pistolero he had "borrowed" the horse from. He might never know, Braddock thought, so he put the question out of his mind.

A set of rear stairs beckoned him. If he strode openly into the saloon, he might encounter Wilcox, who would surely try to gun him down before he could reach Palmer. Braddock wasn't afraid to match his speed against that of Wilcox but putting the rest of his plan in motion mattered more than settling any personal grudges.

Palmer probably had guards on the second floor to protect him, although Braddock hadn't seen any on his previous visit. As he started up the stairs, he knew he needed to be careful anyway.

When he reached the landing, he tried the door and found it unlocked. A place like Casa de Palmer just about had to have a discreet way in and out because some of the patrons wouldn't want to be seen coming and going, especially if they were conducting "upstairs" business. Braddock's right hand hovered over the butt of the Colt while he used his left to open the door. He stepped inside quickly.

A couple of gas lamps in holders on the wall cast a dim light in the rear hallway. The doors along both sides of the corridor were closed but Braddock couldn't count on them staying that way. Palmer's soiled doves entertained their customers in those rooms.

Some of the women Braddock had freed from the cellar at the old mission would have wound up here, he thought. And those were the lucky ones, the more attractive ones. The less fortunate would have been forced to toil in even worse places.

At the far end, the hall made a ninety-degree turn to the left. Palmer's suite was located in the front part of the building in that far corner, Braddock recalled, somewhat isolated from the whores' section.

Braddock walked quickly along the corridor, his steps muffled by the carpet runner. If any of the doors opened, he would just keep his head down and move on, as if he'd concluded any business he had up here and was on his way back downstairs for a drink or a hand or two of poker before calling it a night.

No one emerged from any of the rooms during the thirty seconds or so it took him to walk to the other end of the hall. He heard noises coming from behind some of those doors but nothing out of the ordinary.

When he reached the corner, he paused to take a look around it. There was the door to Palmer's suite he remembered, no more than forty feet away from him.

But between Braddock and the suite, a tough-looking hombre sat in a ladderback chair with his right ankle cocked on his left knee as he smoked a quirley. The only reason for him to be there was to guard the entrance to the suite.

He looked fully capable of doing that, too, with broad shoulders, a slab of a beard-stubbled jaw, a long-barreled, .44-caliber Remington holstered on his hip, and a double-barreled shotgun leaning against the wall beside him.

Braddock didn't recall seeing the man during his visit to Casa de Palmer the previous night, so there was a good chance the man hadn't seen him either, and wouldn't recognize him. Braddock could approach him, pretending to be a customer returning from one of the whores' rooms. The question was whether the guard would realize he hadn't seen Braddock come upstairs and go around the corner with any of the soiled doves. Braddock had no way of knowing how long the man had been sitting there at his post or how good his memory was but it was a definite potential risk.

A risk, Braddock knew, that had to be run because he had to reach Shadrach Palmer before all hell broke loose.

He put the sort of leering grin on his face that a man would wear after a successful visit to the second floor of Casa de Palmer and ambled around the corner, turning toward the guard. The man sat up straighter and moved a hand toward the Greener as he regarded Braddock with a narrow-eyed gaze.

Braddock just grinned even bigger and stupider at him.

The guard grunted and seemed to relax. He didn't pick up the shotgun. Braddock kept moving and gave the man a friendly nod.

"Howdy," he said.

The guard started to say something, probably a

return greeting, but then his eyes abruptly narrowed again. Braddock saw suspicion spring to life in them.

Too late. Braddock had come within reach and his fist shot out in a powerful blow that landed on the guard's jaw.

It felt about like punching a slab of rock but it jerked the guard's head to the side and knocked him off the chair. As he went down, Braddock leaped closer, pulled out his Colt, and slammed it against the guard's head to finish the job of knocking him out.

The brief scuffle had made a little noise but maybe not enough to be heard in Palmer's suite. Braddock couldn't leave the man lying there to be discovered and cause a commotion, so he pouched his iron, stooped, got hold of the senseless guard under the arms, and hauled him upright.

Pain jabbed into Braddock's side where the bullet from Wilcox's derringer had ripped through him twenty-four hours earlier. The wounds were probably bleeding again but there was nothing Braddock could do about that now.

One way or another, this would be over tonight, he thought, and he could get some proper medical attention then—if he was still alive to need it.

He propped the guard up and held him with one arm while he used his other hand to twist the doorknob. It turned, and he shoved open the door to Palmer's suite. Braddock lurched through the entrance, taking the guard with him, and then dumped the man on the thick rug on the sitting room floor as he heeled the door shut behind him. His right hand dropped to the gun and slid it from the holster in case Wilcox was in here.

The room had only one occupant, though, and she gasped as she shrank back against the divan cushions.

The silk dressing gown she wore hung open almost to the waist, revealing a lot of smooth, curving, swelling flesh.

"George?" Palmer's mistress Elise said as she stared at him. "What in the world are you doing here?"

Then her rich brown eyes widened even more as she stared down the barrel of Braddock's Colt.

2 8

"Where's Palmer?" Braddock asked, his voice sharp.

"George, I...I don't understand. Dex Wilcox said you disappeared, that something must have happened to you—"

"Is Palmer here?"

"No, he...he's downstairs, I think..."

Two glasses, each with a little bit of wine in it, sat on a small table next to the divan. Braddock glanced at them, then asked, "Is Wilcox in the bedroom?"

"What?" Elise's eyes widened even more. "You think Wilcox and I...how dare you! I would never betray Shad like that. What makes you think I would?"

"There are two glasses."

"Left from when Shad and I had drinks earlier."

He couldn't tell if she lied. He never had been able to read women as well as he could men. He motioned with the revolver's barrel and said, "Go over there and open that door."

She glared at him for a second, then pouted. "I won't. You've insulted me."

"I can knock you out like him—" Braddock nodded toward the unconscious man on the floor. "—and then go see for myself if that's what you want."

"You wouldn't," she said, her voice as frigid as a blue norther.

He probably wouldn't, Braddock realized, but he didn't say anything and kept his face hard as stone.

After a few more seconds, Elise blew out an exasperated breath and said, "All right. If I have to show you before you'll believe me..."

She stood up, not being too careful about it so the dressing gown gaped even more, and went over to the bedroom door. She threw it open and stepped back, waving a hand to indicate Braddock should take a look.

"You first," he told her.

Elise walked into the room, turned around to face him, and spread her arms. Braddock ignored all the charms on display and stepped through the door, checking to right and left.

The two of them were the bedroom's only occupants. Braddock stepped over to a large wardrobe and opened it, saw only clothes.

"Are you going to look under the bed like the cuckolded husband in some melodrama?" Elise asked.

"Should I?"

She made that exasperated sound again and pulled the duvet up around the bed. Braddock could see under it without having to bend over.

"Are you satisfied now?"

"I reckon. When do you expect Palmer back up here?"

"I have no idea. He owns this place. He comes and goes as he pleases."

"And he owns you, too, I suppose."

Braddock wasn't sure why he said that. Maybe he just

wanted to put a burr under her saddle because of her attitude.

"No one owns me," Elise said in a low, menacing voice. "Least of all Shadrach Palmer. I'm here for my own benefit, not his."

"All right," Braddock said. "I suppose since we're clear about everything, we can talk civilly now. Did you hear the conversation when Palmer talked to Wilcox last night, after Wilcox got back from Juarez?"

"Why should I tell you anything?"

Braddock figured he would get farther by appealing to her mercenary instincts, rather than any other approach, so he said, "Because Palmer's in trouble, he just doesn't know it yet."

"Shad is in danger?"

"He could well be." Braddock told the truth as far as it went although Braddock himself represented the biggest danger to Palmer right now.

Elise studied him for a moment longer, then pulled the gown closed and tightened the belt around her waist.

"Wilcox came up here to talk to Shad. He told Shad how you killed Larkin and he killed Larkin's two men."

"Wilcox said he killed Larkin's men."

"That's right."

Braddock let that pass. Wilcox had figured he could get away with claiming credit for those two shootings because he wasn't expecting Braddock to show up again. But it didn't really matter.

"What else?"

"He said you wanted to stop at another cantina and told him to come on back and tell Shad what happened. He claimed you said you'd be along later. So Wilcox did what you asked. Only you never showed up today. Shad sent Wilcox back to the other cantina and the people there claimed they had never seen you. Shad was upset when Wilcox told him but Wilcox said you must have been jumped and robbed. He said you might be lying dead in an alley or floating in the Rio Grande." Elise shrugged. "It happens all the time in Juarez."

"So he thinks he got away with it," Braddock murmured.

"Got away with what?" Elise asked.

Braddock stiffened as he heard the sound of a gun being cocked behind him and then Shadrach Palmer said, "That's what I'd like to know. What are *you* trying to get away with, George?"

29

BRADDOCK CURSED HIMSELF SILENTLY FOR NOT HEARING Palmer come into the room. He had been concentrating on what Elise told him and Palmer must have been quiet about it. If he had come along and seen the guard missing from the hall outside the suite, that would have made him suspicious.

The situation was even worse than that, Braddock saw as he looked over his shoulder.

Dex Wilcox stood a little behind and to one side of Palmer, a scowl on his face and his hand on the butt of his gun. Both men had stopped just inside the door of the sitting room.

Palmer gestured with the little pistol in his hand. He no longer looked like a shopkeeper. His eyes reminded Braddock more than ever of a rattlesnake and so did the attitude of his body, poised and ready to strike and kill.

"Back out of there," Palmer went on. "Don't try anything or I'll put a bullet in you."

Braddock backed out of the bedroom. Elise folded

her arms and sauntered after him, a smirk on her face now.

And yet concern still lurked in her eyes. Braddock had said something threatened Palmer and he represented her livelihood right now. She wanted to know more, Braddock thought, so she could protect herself.

"Elise, take his gun," Palmer ordered.

She hesitated, clearly not wanting to get that close to Braddock. A faint smile touched his lips as he told her, "Don't worry. I won't hurt you."

"Damn right you won't hurt her," Palmer said. "If you did, I'd make sure you took a long, painful time to die."

She stepped up to Braddock, licked her lips slightly, and reached out with a slender, long-fingered hand to slide the Colt from its holster. Then she stepped back quickly.

"All right, George, turn around."

"Something's bad wrong here, boss," Wilcox said. "He must figure on tryin' some sort of double-cross. Why else would he drop out of sight like that, then sneak in here, knock out Carson, and force Miss Elise into your bedroom?"

Wilcox talked fast. He wanted to solidify Palmer's suspicions and make sure he considered Braddock guilty of something. Braddock knew that. He just kept a cool, confident smile on his face. It might madden Wilcox into saying too much.

When Palmer didn't respond, Wilcox went on, "Let me take him outta here and deal with him. No need for you to worry yourself about this, Mr. Palmer."

"Wait just a minute," Palmer said as he lifted his free hand. The gun in his other hand remained steady as a rock as he pointed it at Braddock. "I asked George for an explanation and I'm going to give him a chance to answer me."

"Wilcox is right about a double-cross," Braddock said, "only he's the one trying to pull it."

Wilcox's scowl darkened. He had moved aside so he had a clear shot at Braddock. He started to draw his gun as he snarled, "You damn liar—"

"Dex!" Palmer's sharp tone made Wilcox pause with the gun halfway out of its holster. "I have this under control."

"Sure, boss." With obvious reluctance, Wilcox let his revolver slide back down into leather but he didn't move his hand far from it.

"Keep talking, George. And remember...this is the only chance to tell the truth you're going to get."

"I don't blame you for being leery of me, Mr. Palmer," Braddock said. "After all, you barely know me. But I did what you said last night. I went to Hernandez's place and killed that fella' Larkin."

"And then dropped out of sight," Palmer said, nodded. "I know about Larkin. I want to know what else you were doing."

"Trying not to die after Wilcox shot me. That kept me pretty busy."

Wilcox said, "That's a damn dirty lie!"

"If you'll let me pull up my shirt, I can prove it," Braddock said.

Wilcox started to say something else. Palmer motioned him to silence, thought for a moment about what Braddock had said, then told him, "All right, go ahead, but slow and easy. No tricks."

"No tricks," Braddock agreed. He lifted his shirt to reveal the bandages on his side. "Wilcox wounded me with a little derringer he carries. He'd already tried to smash my head in and drop me in the river to drown."

"Why the hell would I do that?" Wilcox demanded.

"So I wouldn't tell Mr. Palmer how you and Hernandez are planning to steal those army rifles for yourselves, so Hernandez won't have to turn over the women from Santa Rosalia."

Palmer's eyes widened and so did Wilcox's. Braddock could feel Elise staring at him as well. But after a moment, the canny look came back into Palmer's gaze, replacing the surprise, and he said, "Just because someone shot you doesn't mean Dex did it."

"No, but how would I know those things I just told you if I hadn't heard him and Hernandez plotting together? Hell, I just rode into El Paso a couple of days ago!"

"He's loco, boss," Wilcox insisted. "Either that, or he's lyin' to save his own hide since you caught him in here with Elise."

"Wait just a minute," she said coldly. "You had better not be accusing me of anything."

"No, no," Palmer said, waving the idea off as ridiculous. "We all know you'd never do anything to risk your comfortable life, my dear." He turned his attention back to Braddock. "Just what else do you claim to have overheard?"

"Boss, you're not gonna listen to this lyin' son of a bitch, are you?" Wilcox protested.

Palmer ignored him and looked steadily at Braddock, waiting for an answer.

"Wilcox told Hernandez where you've got the rifles stashed and Hernandez told Wilcox about the old mission south of Juarez where the women are being kept. Hernandez is sending two groups of men across the river tonight. One group will go after the rifles. The other will come here and kill you so Wilcox can take over your operation. That's the other part of their deal."

"By God, that's all I'm gonna take!" Wilcox yelled. He started again to claw at his gun but Palmer swung around sharply and leveled the pistol at him.

"Stop it, Dex!"

Wilcox stared at him. "Boss—"

"I don't see how George could know everything that's going on unless he's telling the truth," Palmer said. "He knows about the rifles in the warehouse, he knows about the deal with Hernandez...Hell, he even knows where the prisoners are and that's something Hernandez never told me! He must have told you, though."

Wilcox shook his head. "It's all a pack of lies."

"There's one way to sort it out. Gather up all the men you can and we'll go to the warehouse and make sure those Krags are safe. If they are—"

Before Palmer could go on, gunfire suddenly roared downstairs. Pistols cracked and a shotgun boomed and women began to scream. It sounded like a war had broken out with no warning.

And so it had.

30

BRADDOCK HAD HOPED TO STALL LONG ENOUGH FOR Hernandez to make a move. The violent chaos downstairs told him he'd been successful.

Wilcox yanked out his gun. Whether he intended to shoot Braddock or Palmer, Braddock never knew because Palmer fired before Wilcox could pull the trigger.

Wilcox staggered back, blood welling from the hole in his chest. His revolver had swung wide but he jerked the trigger in his death spasms and the gun roared.

The slug whipped through the space Elise had occupied a split-second earlier before Braddock tackled her and knocked her to the floor. Even though Wilcox's knees had buckled, Palmer shot him again, this time in the face. Wilcox went over backward, a red-rimmed hole in the center of his forehead.

Palmer swung around from the dead gunman and said, "Elise! Are you all right?"

Braddock sprawled on top of her, a position that

would have been mighty pleasant under other circumstances. He rolled off her so she could sit up, gasping and wide-eyed.

"My God!" she said. "He...he almost *shot* me!"

She had dropped Braddock's gun when he pulled her down. Braddock started to reach for it, then paused and looked back at Palmer.

Palmer jerked his head in a nod and said, "Pick it up. I think Dex showed just whose side he was on when he tried to shoot me."

If Palmer wanted to believe that, Braddock didn't mind at all. He scooped his Colt from the rug and stood up. He could have killed Palmer then but he needed the man alive.

"Get down there and see what's going on," Palmer said. "We have to deal with this attack and then stop Hernandez from stealing those rifles."

Braddock gave him an equally curt nod and hurried out of the suite.

So far, so good, he thought as he ran along the balcony toward the stairs. He paused at the landing to survey the scene below.

Gunsmoke hung in the air in thick clouds. Hernandez's men must have come in shooting. Palmer's bartenders and bouncers had returned the fire as the customers scattered, scrambling for cover. Braddock didn't see the bodies of any innocents lying around but one of the bartenders lay face-down on the hardwood with a pool of blood around his head. The crimson had spread out enough to start dripping off the front of the bar.

Braddock barely had time to take that in before a bullet sizzled past his ear. The pistolero who had fired it crouched behind an overturned table but he had lifted himself too high when he triggered the shot, giving Braddock a target. Braddock drilled the man through the throat. He flopped backward with blood spurting from the wound.

Some of Hernandez's men knelt on the boardwalk in front of the saloon and fired through busted-out windows. Braddock sent a couple of rounds whistling through one of those windows and saw another shape fall.

Hernandez's men outnumbered Palmer's, though, and Braddock realized they couldn't win this fight. He snapped a shot at another pistolero he caught a glimpse of, then turned and raced back to the suite without waiting to see if his bullet had scored.

"There are too many of them," he reported to Palmer after hurrying into the sitting room. "You need to get out of here while you still can, boss."

The guard Braddock had knocked out earlier had regained consciousness. He sat up, shaking his head groggily but, at the sight of Braddock, he growled and started to get up.

Palmer closed a hand on his shoulder to stop him. "Forget it, Carson," he said. "Get downstairs and help hold off Hernandez's men. George, you come with me and Elise. We have to warn the men who are guarding those rifles. Maybe Hernandez hasn't gotten to them yet."

Braddock nodded. He would have suggested the same thing if Palmer hadn't beaten him to it. He knew now the rifles were hidden in a warehouse somewhere in El Paso but he didn't know its exact location.

"If I'm coming with you, I have to get dressed—" Elise began.

"No time." Palmer grabbed her hand. He still held the pistol in his other hand. "Come on."

Braddock had been thumbing fresh cartridges into his Colt while Palmer talked. He held it ready as he led the way through the rear corridor toward the stairs. Frightened faces belonging to soiled doves and customers peeked out from doors open a few inches. Braddock figured as soon as he and Palmer and Elise were gone, a stampede would follow them down the rear stairs.

When he threw the door open and stepped out onto the landing, he caught a glimpse of two men wearing sombreros on their way up. Each man carried a shotgun, so Braddock couldn't give them time to bring the Greeners into play. He fired three times, flame geysering from the Colt's barrel.

The first two slugs hammered into the chest of the man leading the way up the stairs and knocked him back into his companion. Braddock's third bullet blew that man's jaw off. The pistoleros' legs tangled together, and they both tumbled back down the stairs, leaving splashes of dark blood behind. They landed at the bottom in a welter of dead and dying flesh without firing the shotguns.

Elise screamed, then muffled the sound by clapping both hands over her mouth in horror.

"Get hold of yourself," Palmer snapped. "You knew I'm in a violent business."

"I don't see any more of them," Braddock said. "We'd better move while we can. There are bound to be more of Hernandez's men on the way around here."

He went down the stairs as fast as he could and stepped over the corpses at the bottom. Palmer and Elise followed close behind him. Palmer had his left hand clamped around Elise's arm to help her negotiate the grisly obstacle at the bottom of the stairs. She still wore only the dressing gown and slippers, but that couldn't be helped.

A moment later, the three of them had disappeared into the welcoming darkness of the alley.

31

THE SOUND OF GUNFIRE CONTINUED BEHIND THEM BUT IT
faded as Palmer took the lead and they wound through
the back alleys and side streets of El Paso.

The route actually didn't cover all that much
distance, Braddock realized as they came to a large,
darkened building beside the Rio Grande.

"This is it?" Braddock said. "The place where the
rifles are hidden?"

"That's right." Palmer looked around. "And we've
beaten Hernandez here."

Of course they had, Braddock thought, since
Hernandez didn't know where Palmer had hidden the
rifles. Braddock had just wanted Palmer to think that so
he'd lead the way here.

Palmer took a ring of keys from his pocket. Braddock
said, "You don't have guards posted here?"

"Of course I do, inside and outside both."

As if to prove that, a couple of dark shapes loomed
out of the shadows and turned into a pair of men toting
rifles.

"What's going on, boss?" one of them asked.

"Hernandez is trying to double-cross us," Palmer said. "He and some of his men may show up here at any minute. Some of them attacked the saloon a little while ago."

"Son of a bitch!" The guard added hastily, "Sorry, Miss Elise. We thought we heard shots in that direction, boss but we didn't figure they came from Casa de Palmer. If we had, we would've gone to see what the trouble was."

"No, you did the right thing by staying here," Palmer told the men. "Those rifles will set me up for life before I'm through." He started unlocking the regular-sized door beside the big double entrance. "Stay out here and keep your eyes open. If you see any sign of trouble, come on inside. We'll fort up in there." Palmer laughed. "We have enough rifles and ammunition to hold off an army, after all!"

That was true, Braddock supposed. But rifles still needed people to fire them and he didn't figure Palmer had more than half a dozen men here.

Even if he was right about that number, he still faced steep odds. He couldn't do anything except forge ahead with his hastily formed plan, though.

Braddock followed Palmer and Elise into the warehouse. They stopped in a small office next to the big, open storage space. Palmer lit a lamp on the desk and went out into the warehouse's main room.

Bales of cotton, large tow sacks full of other goods, and stacks of boxes and crates filled about half the space. As a smuggler, Palmer had to have plenty of contraband on hand and in motion across the border.

Braddock had no trouble spotting the particular crates that interested him, however, fifty of them, all long and rectangular and holding twenty Krag-Jorgensen Springfield rifles apiece. Square ammunition boxes rose in stacks next to the crated rifles.

Three men carrying Winchesters emerged from the shadowy recesses of the warehouse's far corners. They nodded politely to Elise, then one of them asked, "Is there some sort of trouble, Mr. Palmer?"

"Damn right there is. Hernandez is on his way here to steal those Krags from me."

"Well, that dirty, double-crossin' greaser! I always figured you couldn't trust a Mex."

"Dex Wilcox was in on it with him."

That shocked the three guards even more. One of them said, "Dex could be a pretty sorry varmint sometimes but I never thought he'd sell you out."

"He tried to kill me not long ago, as soon as George here told me about his deal with Hernandez."

The three men looked suspiciously at Braddock. One of them asked, "Who in blazes is this?"

"His name's George. He just went to work for me last night and already he's saved our bacon by exposing Wilcox's treachery."

The guard's eyes narrowed even more as he stared at Braddock. Then he said, "You're the hombre who killed Larkin and his boys."

Palmer looked at him sharply. "How did you know that?"

"Because I was there, boss. I wasn't on guard duty last night, so I went across the river to Hernandez's place to see a little chiquita there I like. I watched her dance all evenin' but I saw Dex and this hombre come in, and then they left a little while later, after the trouble with Larkin." The man nodded toward Braddock. "George—if

138

that's his name—went upstairs for a while, but Dex was downstairs drinkin' and joshin' with the whores."

"He didn't talk to Hernandez?"

"He couldn't have. I never laid eyes on Hernandez but Dex was where I could see him the whole time." The man bared his teeth in a grimace at Braddock. "If you been sayin' Dex was a traitor, it's a damn lie!"

Any plan, no matter how meticulously laid out, could be ruined by something unexpected. As haphazard as Braddock's plan had been, he was a little surprised nothing had gone wrong with it before now.

But now he had reached the end of the trail, so there was only one thing he could do.

He smacked the gun in his hand against the side of Palmer's head, driving the man to his knees, then darted toward the crates holding the rifles as he triggered the Colt at Palmer's guards.

ONE OF THE MEN DOUBLED OVER AS A SLUG FROM Braddock's Colt punched into his guts. The bullet bored on through and smashed his spine, dropping him to the floor like a discarded rag doll.

Another guard dropped his rifle and staggered back as he clutched at a bullet-shattered shoulder.

The third man got his rifle working, though, and hammered shots at Braddock as the outlaw Ranger rolled over the stacked-up crates. The bullets narrowly missed Braddock but chewed splinters from the wood. He felt them sting his hands and face.

As he dropped behind the crates, he heard Palmer yell, "Circle around! Get the bastard!"

Boot soles slapped the floor as the guard still on his feet ran through the shadows in an attempt to flank Braddock. Knowing the man couldn't draw a bead on him at the same time, Braddock came up on one knee and leveled the Colt at Palmer. He pulled the trigger but Palmer had already dived aside so the bullet missed him.

Elise was just standing there, too stunned by everything that had happened to move. Palmer ducked behind her and looped his left arm around her neck to yank her against him as a human shield. With his other hand, he shoved the pistol under her arm and triggered a couple of rounds toward Braddock.

The hurried shots missed but Braddock had to hold his fire because Palmer had Elise in front of him.

That situation didn't last very long. Elise realized the danger she was in and tried to writhe free from Palmer's grip. Failing that, she grabbed his arm, forced her head down, and sank her teeth into his flesh.

That loosened his hold on her. Elise slammed an elbow against his chest and knocked him back a step. She dived away from him, out of the line of fire.

Palmer tried a desperate shot but Braddock's Colt roared a hair ahead of Palmer's little revolver. The impact of the slug smashing into him knocked Palmer all the way around so he faced away from Braddock. He fell to his knees, looked back over his shoulder, and opened his mouth.

Blood poured out of it and then he slumped forward to land on his face.

The third guard's rifle cracked. Braddock felt the wind-rip of a bullet as it went past his ear. He dived, rolled, and came up just as the guard fired another round. The muzzle flash gave Braddock something to aim at in the gloomy warehouse. The Colt roared and bucked in his hand.

The guard dropped his rifle and stumbled back, gurgling and wheezing. He went to one knee and fought to stay upright and alive as he clawed out the gun on his hip.

Braddock sent the final round in the Colt through the man's brain.

He jammed the empty gun back in its holster, vaulted over the crates, and ran over to the man whose shoulder he had broken with his second shot. The guard had collapsed and started writhing in pain. Braddock snatched up the rifle the man had dropped and put him out of his misery temporarily by knocking him out with a stroke of the Winchester's butt.

Hurried footsteps came toward him again. Braddock swung around and leveled the repeater at the two guards who had rushed in from outside.

The men stopped short, not knowing what was going on. Before they could figure it out, Braddock yelled, "Get out of here! The Rangers are on their way! We've been double-crossed!"

The men stared, clearly uncertain what to do, especially now that they had spotted Palmer's body.

Elise stepped up beside Braddock and said in a voice slightly hoarse from Palmer choking her, "Shad's dead. George is right. It's all gone to hell. Save yourselves."

They knew her as their boss's mistress and didn't see any reason why she would lie to them. Braddock could tell when they made up their minds to light a shuck while they still had the chance.

"Son of a bitch," one man muttered but that was all either of them said before they got out of there as quickly as they could.

"Thank you," Braddock told Elise when they were alone.

"Is that what you really are?" she said. "A Texas Ranger?"

"Something like that."

If the answer confused her, she didn't bother to show it. Instead, she glanced at Palmer's body and her lip curled.

"He didn't give a damn about me."

"Did you really think he did?"

"I didn't think he'd try to get me killed, just to save himself!"

"And that's why you helped me?"

She sighed. "I don't know. Just like I don't know what I'm going to do now. But I'm going to be gone from here before the Rangers show up, I can tell you that."

"Good luck to you, then. And thanks again for your help."

"Maybe I'll see you again sometime, Mr. Something Like a Ranger."

"Maybe," Braddock said but he didn't really believe it.

33

HALF AN HOUR LATER, BRADDOCK KNOCKED SOFTLY ON the door of Elizabeth Jane Caldwell's room in the Camino Real.

With a bloodstain showing on his side where the bandages had soaked through to his shirt, and his face and hands grimy from powdersmoke, he didn't look like the usual denizen of the fancy hotel. Because of that, he had snuck in through a service entrance and hoped he wouldn't encounter anyone on his way up to the room.

He hadn't. Now he hoped the reporter would answer the door pretty soon since someone could still come along. He knocked again and said, "Miss Caldwell?"

She opened the door and peered out at him in shock. Her tousled blond hair and the blue robe she had wrapped around her told him she had been in bed.

Well, why wouldn't she be? It was well after midnight, after all. Most self-respecting people were asleep by now, even journalists.

"Mr. Braddock," she said. He could tell she tried not to sound shocked.

144

"I'm going to make an improper suggestion and ask you to invite me in."

"Wait...you mean...Yes, of course." She stepped back. "Come in." She caught sight of the blood on his shirt. "You're injured!"

"Shot, actually," he said as he stepped inside and she closed the door behind him. "But it happened more than twenty-four hours ago and it hasn't killed me yet, so maybe it won't for a while."

"I...I didn't expect you to get hurt."

"You sent me after people who hold up trains, steal rifles, and wipe out army escorts, not to mention other things just as bad you don't even know about. What the hell did you expect to happen?" Braddock laughed humorlessly. "Never mind. I get cranky when people try to kill me all the time." He held out a key he took from his pocket. "This opens the door of a warehouse down by the river." He told her exactly where to find the place.

She took the key and asked, "What's in there?"

"A thousand Krag-Jorgensen Springfields, and the body of one of the men responsible for stealing them, along with a few of the varmints who worked for him. I dragged one of them who was still alive outside into the alley before I locked the place up but he may well have bled to death by now."

"Good Lord, you're...you're cold-blooded."

"Just trying to get the job done," Braddock said. "It's possible you and I are the only ones still alive who know the rifles are there...Well, one other person," he added, thinking of Elise, "but I don't reckon you have to worry about that. You've got contacts at Fort Bliss, you said. I know it's the middle of the night, but you'd better get dressed, hire a buggy, and get out there as quick as you can so you can tell them where to find the guns."

"Of course. You can stay here. I'll summon a doctor for your wounds—"

"Not hardly," Braddock said. "Once this is all over, I'll write you a letter and explain everything but, for now, just get those Krags back where they belong."

He turned toward the door but she caught his sleeve and stopped him.

"I still owe you—"

"Send whatever you think is fair to the mission in Esperanza, where you sent that letter to me. The padre there will put it to good use if I don't get back to claim it. Hell, even if I do, I'll probably give most of it to him anyway."

"Because you don't really work for money, do you?" she asked, her blue eyes peering up at him. "You do what you do—"

"Because it's my job," Braddock said harshly, "and it's not over yet."

34

Braddock didn't know how the battle at Casa de Palmer had turned out but he didn't give in to his curiosity and steered clear of the saloon instead. After a small-scale war like that, the El Paso police had probably swarmed the place and he was still a wanted man, after all.

Instead, he reclaimed his dun from the livery stable, annoying a sleepy hostler. Some of his gear remained at the boarding house where he had barely stayed but nothing he couldn't live without. This time, he rode across the Rio Grande on the bridge he had fallen from a night and a day and most of another night earlier, then headed for Hernandez's place.

Dawn wasn't far off by the time he got there. Establishments like this never really closed but, usually by this time of the morning, they had settled down to a pretty drowsy state. Braddock counted on that to help him get what he had come here for.

He left the dun by the stable behind the building and walked toward the rear door. Steel whispered against leather as he drew his gun. The Colt had a full cylinder and Braddock would use every one of the bullets if he had to.

He was lightheaded again and felt somehow outside of himself. Exhaustion, strain, and loss of blood would do that to a fella', he supposed. But, as he had told Elizabeth Jane Caldwell, he hadn't finished the job.

By now, the young woman might have notified the army about the location of the stolen rifles. Braddock knew the warehouse's thick walls had muffled the shots inside it. Anyway, nobody paid much attention to gunshots in that part of town. Those Krags would sit there undisturbed until the proper authorities came for them.

Nobody was going to help Carmen, though, and he had promised the women at the mission he would get her out of here.

Not only that but Hernandez was still alive and he was partially responsible for the deadly raid on Santa Rosalia. He had to pay for that.

He would settle up with Martin Larrizo some other time, Braddock told himself. Hell, one man couldn't take on the whole world at the same time, now could he?

The back door of Hernandez's place was locked.

Braddock muttered a curse and fished out his knife. After a few minutes of working the blade at the lock and the jamb, he put his shoulder against the door and pushed. It popped open. He stepped inside and found himself inside a pitch-black room.

After pushing the door up behind him, he fished a lucifer from his pocket and snapped it to life with his thumbnail, squinting against the sudden glare. He was in some sort of storeroom, with crates of empty bottles sitting around. A door on the other side of the room let out into a short hall that ran toward the front of the building.

Close by at Braddock's right hand, stairs rose to the second floor. They would lead just about to where Hernandez's living quarters were located, Braddock recalled.

He went up, staying close to the wall so the steps wouldn't creak as much. When he got to the top, he saw a door he remembered and knew it led into Hernandez's rooms. Braddock closed his hand around the knob and twisted it silently.

He stepped inside quickly, gun up and ready. A lamp on a side table was turned down low, but it cast enough light for him to see Hernandez sprawled in an armchair, legs outstretched, a glass of what was probably tequila in his right hand. He was bare from the waist up and his left arm was wrapped in bandages.

Hernandez stared stupidly at the intruder. Braddock realized the man was drunk. He could have put a bullet in Hernandez right then and there and ended his evil but that would rouse the rest of the place and wouldn't help Carmen.

"You!" Hernandez said. "Palmer's man! Have you come to betray me, too?"

"Palmer's dead," Braddock said flatly. "I'm nobody's man and never have been. As for why I'm here, I'm taking Carmen."

Hernandez frowned and looked confused for a moment before his expression cleared.

"The little whore from Santa Rosalia?" he said. "She's why you risked your life coming here?"

"That's one reason."

Hernandez must have figured out what Braddock meant. His face clouded. Then, even though he didn't appear to have any weapons, he suddenly flung the glass of tequila at Braddock and launched himself after it in a desperate dive.

The fiery liquor hit Braddock in the face and stung his eyes. He chopped at Hernandez's head with the gun but couldn't stop the man from ramming into him. They both went down with a crash that shook the floor underneath them and jolted the gun out of Braddock's hand.

He swung a fist at Hernandez's head and connected with a glancing blow. Hernandez seemed to have sobered up in a hurry, though, because he shook it off and slammed punches of his own at Braddock. Braddock tried to fend them off but his head jerked from side to side under the impacts. He knew if Hernandez hit him many more times, he would pass out.

His hands shot up and grabbed Hernandez by the throat. Braddock mustered all the strength he could and rolled over, putting Hernandez underneath him. He hung on for dear life as he dug his thumbs into the man's neck.

Hernandez bucked and thrashed and flailed at him but Braddock ignored it. He knew if he let go, he was a dead man, so he bore down harder. Hernandez's eyes grew wide and began to bulge out until it seemed they were about to burst from their sockets. His handsome face was ugly now as it turned a deep shade of purple.

Hernandez bucked a couple more times, then a sharp stink reached Braddock's nose. Hernandez's bowels had emptied as death claimed him. The wide, staring eyes began to turn glassy.

Braddock let go. His chest heaved as he tried to catch his breath.

Something crashed into his injured side, filling him with agony until it seemed he would explode. He rolled over, looked up, and through pain-blurred eyes saw a tall, burly man with a heavy black mustache looming over him, ready to kick him again. The man wore only the bottom half of a pair of long underwear but he looked powerful enough to tear Braddock apart with his bare hands, especially considering the shape the outlaw Ranger was in at the moment.

"You've killed Paco," the man rumbled. Braddock realized he meant Hernandez. "No matter. The revolution will go on as soon as I find those damned rifle—"

The man stopped short and gasped. He stumbled a step forward, twisted and tried to reach behind him. He couldn't reach whatever he tried to grab. Slowly, he kept twisting around until Braddock saw the handle of what must have been a long, heavy knife protruding from his back.

Then, with a gurgling moan, the man collapsed and died. With him out of the way, Braddock saw Carmen standing there, nude, hair disheveled, bruises and scratches on her face.

"They both took out their anger on me," she said in a voice that trembled slightly. "First Hernandez, then Larrizo. But now they are dead and I live."

Braddock pushed himself up on an elbow and looked at the man Carmen had stabbed. "That's...Martin Larrizo?"

"Sí. The revolution...is over."

Until some other would-be dictator tried to seize power for himself, Braddock thought, even if it meant the deaths of thousands of innocent people.

He wanted to lie back and rest, but he knew he couldn't. Instead, he struggled to climb to his feet and told Carmen, "Get dressed. I've come to take you out of here. To take you home."

"But you are hurt!"

"I'll make it," he told her. "I'll see that you're safe."

"After all that has happened...how can I ever be safe again?"

Braddock didn't have an answer for that. Time would heal Carmen or it wouldn't. He had done all he could.

At least, he would have once he had delivered her and the other women back to Santa Rosalia.

"We've got to go," he said. "I don't know if anybody else heard that commotion but we can't risk it."

She swallowed and nodded. "You are sure you can make it?"

Braddock wasn't sure of anything but he put a smile on his face and said, "Let's go home."

35

Braddock moved one of the knights on the chessboard and said, "Check."

The padre moved his king out of danger for the moment. Braddock slid a rook across the board to close in on his royal prey and his opponent angled a bishop into position and said, "I believe that is checkmate, my friend."

Braddock looked at the board for a couple of seconds, then said, "Huh. You suckered me. I didn't see that coming."

"You are off your game. But don't worry. You're still recovering. You will be your old self again in no time."

Braddock wasn't sure about that. Two weeks had passed since that hellacious couple of days in El Paso and Juarez. He had lost weight, making him more whip-like lean than ever, and he hadn't regained his full strength yet. Luckily, things had been peaceful in Esperanza.

He wondered how things were in Santa Rosalia as the people there tried to recover from the damage wreaked on their lives by Palmer, Hernandez, and Larrizo. At least he had seen all the women safely home as he had promised, including Carmen, before heading back to Esperanza and practically collapsing on the padre's doorstep.

"Another game?" the priest asked.

Braddock shook his head and said, "Not now. I reckon I've had all the beating I can take for one day."

The padre laughed and started to put away the board and the pieces. Braddock stood up and went to the door of his little house, which stood open to let in the breeze.

He frowned as he looked across the arid landscape and saw a rooster tail of dust rising from it. As he watched, the dust moved closer to the village.

"Somebody coming," he said.

"A harmless traveler, no doubt," the padre said but a worried frown creased his forehead despite the words.

"We don't get many of those around here." Braddock took a Winchester down from a couple of pegs set into the adobe wall. He wasn't wearing a Colt but he figured the rifle would do in case of trouble.

The padre sighed and said, "If it is someone else who wants you to go off tilting at windmills again, I wish you would tell them no, G.W. You are in no shape to be risking your life again so soon." He stood. "Let me go out and meet them, see what they want."

"No. You go on back home while you can, Padre."

The priest still looked worried but he tucked the chessboard and the bag with the pieces under his arm and hurried out. Braddock stood in the jacal's doorway, leaning against the jamb, and watched the rooster tail come closer.

The dark speck at the bottom of it resolved itself into a buggy being pulled by a couple of horses. At least it wasn't an army of gunmen come to kill him and wipe out the village, he thought.

In fact, there seemed to be only one person in the buggy and, as the vehicle rolled closer, Braddock thought he caught a glint of sunlight shining on fair hair.

A few minutes later, Elizabeth Jane Caldwell pulled the buggy team to a stop in front of the jacal and waved a gloved hand in front of her face to swipe some of the dust away.

"You already sent the money you owed me," Braddock said, "and I sent you that letter telling you everything that happened, like I promised. What are you doing here, Miss Caldwell? How'd you even find the place?"

"I'm a journalist," she told him. "I have ways of finding things out. And that's not a very friendly greeting, Mr. Braddock."

"Most of the time, I'm not a very friendly man."

She climbed down from the buggy, brushed her hands off against each other, and said, "Well, despite that, I began to feel guilty and decided to come and check on you. I'm the one who got you into that dreadful mess. In a way, it's my fault you were injured so badly."

Braddock shook his head. "Not really. I think the fellas who actually tried to kill me deserve more of the blame."

She came closer and looked up at him. "How are you doing?"

"I'm all right. Some days are better than others. Still got a ways to go, I reckon—"

"Amigo, is there a problem?"

The question made Braddock look over to where the padre stood with several of the men of the village beside him. A couple of them carried machetes and one had an old blunderbuss in his hands.

Elizabeth glanced nervously at them. "You have friends here," she said.

"They look out for me," Braddock said. He chuckled and told the priest, "It's fine, Padre. Señorita Caldwell didn't come here to kill me." He looked at her again. "Although I'm still not sure why you *are* here."

"I've come to take care of you while you recuperate. I told you, I'm a good journalist but, in a pinch, I'm a damned fine nurse, too."

"You know," Braddock said as he smiled and moved aside to let her come in, "I'll bet you are."

BLACK GOLD

BLACK GOLD

CONTENTS

In memory of Texas Ranger Captain Francis Augustus
"Frank" Hamer (1884-1955)

PROLOGUE

JEFFERSON COUNTY, TEXAS

THE RAIDERS CAME AT MIDNIGHT, NO MOON TO REVEAL them in case anyone was still awake and stirring in the farmhouse they had targeted. Eight men, armed to the teeth—each with a rifle or a shotgun and at least one holstered pistol—all with orders to fulfill.

They hadn't asked about the choice of targets in advance, knew any questions wouldn't meet with favor from the man in charge. Their orders were to raise a ruckus, put a dose of fear into the Boss Man's enemies, and let it go at that. Unless, of course, the homesteaders were dumb enough to fight and put their own lives on the line.

In that case, most especially if there were witnesses who could identify the raiders . . . well, whatever happened after that, the stubborn holdouts would have brought it down upon themselves.

Cletus Crowther, leading the approach, knew how far they could push it, what excuses his employer would

JAMES REASONER

accept. Clete's standing orders were to clear the land and make sure no one carried tales into the county seat at Beaumont, or beyond it to the Texas capital at Austin, where Governor Joseph Draper Sayers abhorred any disturbance in his normal workaday routine.

A subtle operation, then . . . and if the homesteaders decided not to play along, a swift, clean sweep. Whoever cleaned up afterward could sift the ashes for a month of Sundays if they pleased and come away with nothing to support a charge in court.

When they were half a mile out from the farmhouse, barn and all, Clete called a halt and waited for his hand-picked men to circle up around him, hard eyes staring from above the plain bandana masks they'd tied around their faces from the nose on down. None of them spoke as they sat on their restless horses while they waited for some final word to send them on their way.

Clete Crowther didn't stretch it out. Just said, "You all know why we're here. Boss wants the sodbusters to move along and they're too dumb to even haggle over price. I call that stupid pride, but any way you slice it they've run out of time. Tonight, they pull up stakes and git."

A question then, one of the shooters asking him, "What if they won't?"

"No more debating," Crowther said. "There's only one man on the place. If he don't care about his family and wants to start a shivaree, we finish it tonight. The place goes up in smoke and that's an end to it."

Another rider chimed in, making sure. "The boss don't care which way it goes?"

"He's paying us to get it done. Worse comes to worst, nobody squeals. We good now?"

Nods around the circle facing Cletus as he spat

164

tobacco juice into the dust, then pulled his own bandana into place.

"All right," he said. "I'll do the talking if there's any to be done. From there on in, it's each man for himself. Now light 'em up."

Upon his order, each man lit a torch that had been carried braced across their saddle horns, flames leaping in the night, before they swept down toward the ranch they had been ordered to eradicate.

JARED WITHERS SAT bolt upright in his bed, jarred from a dream of plowing endless furrows into unforgiving land. His sudden movement woke Arlene beside him, by which time he was already reaching for his boots.

"Jared?" she whispered. "What is it?"

"Riders. Coming fast."

"Oh, Lord!"

Shod now and on his feet, grabbing the double-barreled Greener shotgun from its place between the bed and homemade nightstand, Jared told his wife, "See to the boys. No lamps."

He thought Arlene was praying as she scrambled out of bed but had no time to think about it as he left their sleeping room, crossed through the combination dining room and parlor, peering through a gun slit in rough shutters facing onto the front porch.

He saw a line of riders bearing torches, passing the barn Withers had built himself, their first year on the land. They fanned out across the farmyard, stopping well back from the house in a half circle. Firelight glinted on the barrels of their long guns and showed Withers that the late arrivals all wore masks.

He had a choice to make, whether to call out from the house, behind a closed and bolted door, or step outside and face them on the porch. It felt wrong, leaving Arlene and their sons alone inside, but Withers had a fair idea of who the riders were and why they'd come. Instead of seeming weak and cowardly, he thought a man would meet them in the open, not stay cringing under cover like a coward.

Pride can get you killed, he thought.

And he stepped onto the front porch anyway.

Before the riders had a chance to speak, he challenged them. "What brings you out so late?"

One of them hollered back, "You want to play dumb, Mr. Withers, that's your privilege. Won't help you none."

In fact, thought Withers, nothing much could help him now. He had the option to surrender, giving up the spread he'd worked with Arlene for the past eleven years, both of their children born inside the house he was defending now. That course of action might put money in his pocket—or it might have, rather, if he'd acted expeditiously six months ago, the first time he was offered cash—and there was still a chance that he could save his family from harm tonight.

All Jared had to do was nod, lay down his gun, and start to pack their things for leaving first thing in the morning.

Going where?

He didn't have a clue, but when he thought of backing down now, turning tail at gunpoint, Withers had to ask himself what would become of him—of Arlene and the boys—if he turned tail and proved himself a yellow coward in their eyes.

How could they start again, when he had lost that

final vestige of respect from anyone who mattered to him in the world?

So maybe he was stupid, like the spokesmen for the nightriders suggested, but a man could only let his adversaries push him so far. Beyond that, he had to stand up for himself.

Cursing under his breath, Withers lifted the Greener to his shoulder, sighting down its double barrels, wondering how many of the riders he could kill or maim before they took him down.

CLETUS CROWTHER SAW the shotgun rising, looking shaky in its owner's hands, and fired his Winchester before Withers could squeeze off his first shot. The hasty slug caught Withers high in his left shoulder, but the farmer still managed to fire one barrel of his scattergun, his aim thrown off enough that half his buckshot pellets hissed through empty air.

A couple of them scored, however, drawing curses from a raider down the line to Crowther's right. Clete hoped that whoever it was, he could survive the wound and stay up in his saddle while others in his party raked the farmhouse with rifle and shotgun fire, some of their horses shying from the thunderclap of noise.

Above the din, Clete shouted, "Torch it! Bring it down!"

Those words had barely left his lips before he fired another rifle shot, his second round drilling through Jared's cheek, erupting from the backside of his skull. The others kept on firing as their lifeless target fell, riddling his corpse, then they rushed in, hurling their torches at the porch and onto the roof of the farmhouse.

Dry wood caught quickly, flames fanned by a prairie breeze that served the raiders as a natural accomplice. Within minutes, fire had started to consume the house, its crackle not quite drowning out shrill cries of panic from inside.

Clete grimaced through his mask. It ran against his grain, frying a widow and her kids, but her husband had decided that for all of them without consulting any of his brood about their thoughts on being cooked alive.

This way, Crowther could tell his boss that there would be no witnesses, unless . . .

"A couple of you ride around in back!" Clete shouted to be heard above the whooping of his men. "Make sure nobody's got another way of sneaking outta there!"

Three men rode off around the backside of the burning house, two on the right, one on the left, and vanished into darkness as the firelight blinded their compatriots. It wouldn't take much longer, Clete decided, for the blazing roof to tumble down on anyone still living in the house, after its oxygen had been consumed by flames.

All Crowther had to do was sit and wait.

ARLENE WITHERS HUDDLED her two sons, Chad and Jacob, one arm around each and hugging them against her. After the first barrage of gunfire from outside, she had known that her husband was dead, and now, smoke seeping through the farmhouse rafters, vicious heat increasing in the boys' shared bedroom, she knew it was time to make her peace with God.

Small comfort there, knowing that in a few more

moments she would have to watch her boys die screaming, wreathed by fire.

As heat intensified within the second bedroom,
Arlene turned her eyes skyward and saw smoke leaking
through the ceiling planks above her. Moments later,
rivulets of flame broke through and lit the boards from
wall to wall. A curtain flared around the room's sole
window as the boys concealed their faces, sobbing,
pressed against their mother's dress.

"Don't fear, boys," Arlene urged them. "This will only
take a second." Knowing even as she spoke those words
of reassurance that she lied.

It crossed her mind to flee the house then, let the
raiders cut them down with gunfire that seemed merci-
ful, considering the bleak alternative, but Arlene could
not bring herself to give their murderers the satisfaction.

Sobbing even as she spoke the words, she prayed,
"Our Father, who art in Heaven . . ."

Before she could forgive her killers, Arlene heard a
creaking sound from overhead and hunched her shoulders as the roof collapsed.

1

LIBERTY COUNTY, TEXAS

IT HAD BEEN A LONG RIDE—TWO HUNDRED AND FIFTY miles, eight days of trekking over desert and grassland, stopping for water when it was available and skirting towns too small to offer anything but headaches. Perched atop a low rise overlooking Liberty, his destination and the county seat, George Washington Braddock felt every yard of that journey and knew that he wasn't done yet.

Not until he met the man who'd summoned him and found out why his presence was desired.

It would be gun work, more than likely, and while Braddock reckoned he was up to any challenge, he still needed to assess the job and find out whether it was right for him, a former Texas Ranger still a tad uneasy without pinning on his star.

In fact, Braddock was born to be a Ranger, son of G. W. Braddock Sr., a sergeant with the Rangers' Frontier Battalion under Major John B. Jones. Christened

"Junior" by his parents, he had never liked the suffix tacked onto his name, and least of all when older Rangers used it in a denigrating style, comparing rookie Braddock Jr. to his father's legend as a manhunter. "Junior" had proved himself while serving with Company D under Captain John R. Hughes, but then Texas state legislators, in their wisdom, had reduced the force to a virtual skeleton crew and cut him loose without any vestige of authority.

Since then, he'd drifted, taking jobs that suited him without a rule book or a legal jurisdiction to constrain him, using what he'd picked up from his father and the Rangers overall to strike a blow for justice when the opportunity arose, skirting the law with no intent of breaking it but stretching it from time to time.

Officially, the Rangers wanted him because he had a habit of pinning on his old badge from time to time and letting folks assume whatever they pleased. Most never noticed that the silver star-in-a-circle had a neat bullet hole punched through it. Enough of the Rangers agreed with his efforts to deliver justice that they weren't too diligent about hunting for him, but one of these days they might have to bring him in. Braddock would deal with that when it came. Until then, he would continue doing what he saw as right.

He wasn't a gun for hire, per se, but he accepted payment when his efforts eased a client's worldly burdens and allowed said client to get on with something close to normal life.

Whatever that meant these days, on the tough Texas frontier.

Observing Liberty from half a mile away, Braddock considered what he knew about the county and its seat of government. Liberty County was created seven decades earlier, in 1831, as a municipality of Mexico, the same year that its county seat was founded on the banks of the Trinity River. Organized as a county in the new Republic of Texas, in 1837, it was named for the American ideal of liberty eight years before the Lone Star State became part of the larger Union. Today it sprawled over 1,158 square miles of land, with a growing population of 8,102 logged by last year's 1900 census. The county ranked as the state's third oldest.

All that history, and yet, in many ways, Liberty County still remained a part of the Wild West as a new century began.

Somewhere below him, Braddock needed to acquire precise directions to his client's—make that *maybe* client's—home, a spread vaguely described to him in a short telegram as lying somewhere north and west of Liberty.

And where better to ask than a saloon?

Braddock carried no mirror with him, but he knew that he must look a sight after his journey. He thought about stopping in Liberty to have a bath but then decided he would rather just get on with it.

His client's telegram sought help, not someone fit to pose for photographs.

That telegram had been sent to an address in Del Rio and then delivered by rider to the village of Esperanza in Mexico where Braddock made his home these days. He had arranged the system so people who needed his help could get in touch with him. Word got around that he was a man who could handle problems the regular law maybe couldn't. He figured people who really needed him could find him, and in the meantime, he kept his own eyes open for situations where his help might be needed.

Braddock entered Liberty along North Main Street, took his time riding past all the normal fixtures anyone might look for in a county seat: the courthouse, with adjacent sheriff's office and the a clutch of local lawyers' hangouts within easy walking distance; sundry stores—dry goods, hardware, a greengrocer's and butcher's shop; a blacksmith's forge and livery; a barbershop that tempted him by renting bathtubs by the quarter-hour; restaurants and two saloons with tinny music wafting from around their batwing doors. Farther along, Braddock glimpsed a hotel he didn't plan to patronize and spires of two competing churches stationed catty-cornered from each other, Catholic and Baptist squaring off.

Braddock supposed he could have asked directions from the county clerk but didn't crave official notice of his mission yet. The same held true for the barbershop, where long experience had taught him that hair-trimmers loved to talk, impartially dispensing facts and rumors to their customers.

With that in mind, he steered his dun horse toward the first saloon along his course of travel, standing to his right. A slightly faded sign painted between its street windows and balcony anointed it the Lucky Strike.

There was a hitch rail out front, with access to a water trough, and Braddock tied his horse there, scanning North Main's pedestrians before he left his rifle in its saddle boot and went inside.

Business was slow at that time of the mid-morning, three men standing at the bar and sipping beers, three others playing poker at a table to the left as Braddock entered. There were no soiled doves in evidence, which told him they were likely sleeping in their cribs upstairs after a hectic night. He liked it better that way—no one to offend right off, when he declined to spring for watered drinks—and the barkeep was busy wiping glasses, trying not to be caught watching Braddock from the corner of his eye.

Braddock moved past the cardplayers, who scarcely seemed to notice him, and headed for the twenty-something bartender, standing apart from his three drinkers off to Braddock's left-hand side.

"Help you?" the barkeep asked, facing Braddock directly for the first time since he'd pushed in through the batwing doors.

"I'll take a beer," Braddock replied. "And some directions to a spread outside of town if you can help with that."

"Do what I can," the bartender allowed. "Who are you looking for?"

"A Mr. Lucius Haverstock, runs someplace called the Circle H," said Braddock, hoping that he was imagining a subtle change that swept across the barkeep's face at the mention of the name.

HALFWAY THROUGH HIS second term as sheriff, Noah Ransom liked things nice and quiet in his county, though he rarely got his wish in that regard. Liberty County was not situated on the border with Mexico—a blessing in itself—but saw its share of rowdy drifters passing through, some of them on the dodge from Houston or Beaumont, and riffraff off the ships that docked around Trinity Bay, facing the Gulf a few miles to the south.

A day seldom elapsed—and never on a weekend—without Ransom locking up a few rough customers and either holding them for trial or else collecting fines imposed by Justice of the Peace Tom Daley. Some of those resisted and he had to rough them up a bit, but Ransom was relieved that he had only shot two men so far—clumsy bank robbers, in his first year on the job—and only one of them had died.

The remedy for trouble, Ransom had concluded long ago, when still a sheriff's deputy, was watching out for potential problems early on and dealing with them then.

With that in mind, he had been exiting his office, next door to the courthouse, when he saw a rangy horseman stop outside the Lucky Strike saloon, tie up his mount, and make his way inside the barroom. Ransom never claimed that he could name all of the county seat's eight hundred some odd residents on sight, much less the other seven thousand plus who toiled throughout his jurisdiction, but experience had taught him how to sniff out new arrivals with a certain look and feel about them that suggested trouble coming down the road.

The dun's rider looked like one of those.

Delaying plans to grab an early lunch at Dale O'Grady's steakhouse, Ransom stepped down off the wooden sidewalk, crossing North Main toward the Lucky Strike. He recognized the music coming from the barroom as a product of its wind-up Pianola, a relatively new contraption and costly at two hundred fifty dollars, that could crank out tunes from rolls of perforated paper and avoid the need of hiring live musicians other than on Friday nights and Saturdays. That meant the joint wouldn't be doing any major business yet, so there'd be fewer eyeballs on the sheriff if he had to call the stranger out, resulting in a public scene.

Maybe the dusty-looking rider was just passing through to somewhere else, in which case, Ransom would be pleased to help him move along and see the last of him. Conversely, if he planned to stick around a while, the sheriff yearned to know what brought him into Liberty and how long he might plan to hang around.

Call it insurance, preferably without any major premium to pay up in advance.

Halfway across the street, Ransom considered on his six-gun's load but let it go. He always kept an empty chamber underneath the Colt's hammer unless he knew the extra round was likely to be needed in a hurry, and the sheriff reckoned that he wouldn't need six .45 slugs to put the stranger down if simple talk degenerated into mayhem. If Ransom couldn't do the job with five shots at close range, he knew a sixth wouldn't do him a damn bit of good.

And if he wound up on the losing end of that exchange, at least no one in Liberty could say he'd died from lack of shooting back.

Small consolation, granted, but from what he knew of life and sudden death in Texas, Noah Ransom was not worried about what awaited him beyond the mortal pale. A cold hole in the ground would always be a careless lawman's due.

Reaching the boardwalk on the east side of North Main, Ransom peered through one of the Lucky Strike's windows facing the street. He picked out the stranger at once, his back turned toward the saloon's entrance, a beer in front of him, talking to barkeep Bobby Travis. Bobby could be talkative enough with folks he knew, but Ransom sensed that he was being cagey with the stranger, finally replying briefly with a leftward-tilting head that might mean anything.

Ransom considered entering the Lucky Strike, taking a place beside the new arrival at the bar and striking up a conversation in the guise of simple curiosity, but then decided to hang back and wait it out. If simple talking turned to shooting, he would rather it was in the open air, without six customers and Bobby Travis catching any random lead.

Of course, that would put passersby along North Main at risk, as well as merchants in their shops, but Ransom figured that a bit of mental preparation in advance could see him through in that eventuality.

He kept it on the safe side, reaching casually down to free the hammer thong that kept his Colt Peacemaker firmly settled in the holster tied down on his right leg.

The stranger, whoever he was, looked to be finishing his beer and saying *adios* to Bobby Travis at the bar. The other early drinkers lined up there ignored him, same thing with the trio playing cards as he passed by their table, headed for the exit onto North Main Street.

Ransom backed off, clearing the window he'd been peering through and briefly checking out foot traffic on the thoroughfare. He didn't want the stranger spotting him first thing. Better to take him by surprise, see how he handled that, and if he became shifty once he glimpsed the badge pinned onto Ransom's vest.

Most men were just a trifle nervous when confronted by a lawman, even if they had done nothing wrong that anybody knew about. What was it that the Good Book said? *For all have sinned*, or words to that effect, but thankfully, most sins weren't elevated by state legislators to the level of a crime—and some that were, in Ransom's reckoning, were hardly worth tossing a fellow into jail.

He'd always tried to get along with others if they made that possible, negotiate a settlement when trouble reared its head at first, and only clamped down hard when nothing else would serve to keep the peace.

With strangers, though, you never knew. He might be

looking at a man in need of work or staring down a killer with a stack of warrants filed against him and no end to notches on his gun.

Whatever happened in the next few minutes, Noah Ransom meant to be prepared.

BRADDOCK HAD GOTTEN what he could out of the barkeep. Travel six miles north and west of Liberty, approximately, and watch out for riders posted on his client's spread, the Circle H. So far, the information had only cost him twenty cents for the beer, and it would take another ninety minutes on the trail or so, unless he pushed the dun to a gallop underneath the Texas sun.

No rush, he thought. Arriving close to lunchtime might have its advantages, in terms of getting fed in case he turned the client's offer down.

One thing about a telegram, when someone reaching out for help was chintzy about paying by the word, the message rarely spelled out any details about what the sender's problem was or how he hoped to see it all resolved. Gun work was not the sort of thing newspapers advertised, so Braddock always counted on a twist or two when he came face to face with somebody seeking urgent aid.

But maybe, even if he turned down this latest offer, he might still get a free meal for his time.

That wasn't much for eight days on the trail, and seven nights of sleeping rough, but Braddock had a list of things he wouldn't do for money. The jobs he took on were ones that he might have handled as a Ranger . . . if he still wore the star.

He cleared the Lucky Strike's exit, was moving

179

toward the hitch rail in front of him, when a male voice reached out to stop him, saying, "You'd be new in Liberty."

Braddock stopped short, turned slowly, taking in the man who'd spoken to him. First, he noted gray eyes with determination in them, and a cautious frown below a beaklike nose, then Braddock saw the round badge of the speaker's vest with SHERIFF stamped into its brass. Not DEPUTY, but the county's top man himself, it seemed.

"That's true," he granted, giving nothing else away.

"Just passing through, I'd guess," the lawman said.

"And you'd be right again, Sheriff," Braddock replied.

"Not stopping off in Liberty?"

"Not to my knowledge, yet."

"Is there some doubt about it, then?"

The riddle in this kind of situation was how much to give away without exciting further curiosity or making matters escalate.

Braddock replied, "I'm visiting a fellow who lives a few miles out of town."

"Old friend of yours?"

"Never laid eyes on him before."

The sheriff's frown deepened a bit. "That makes me wonder why you've come to see him, Mister . . ."

"Braddock."

"Sounds familiar," said the lawman. "I believe there used to be a Texas Ranger by that name."

"Two, if you want to get it straight," said Braddock. "You're most likely thinking of my father, used to be a captain."

"And yourself?" the sheriff asked.

"Cutbacks on manpower," Braddock replied. "Political showboating. You probably heard about it."

The sheriff nodded. "I didn't think it was the best idea they ever had in Austin."

Braddock shrugged. "I didn't get a vote, just walking papers." This lawman obviously knew what had happened, so there was no point in trying to make the man believe he still had any official standing.

"That's often the way of it. What brings you to my county, Mr. Braddock?"

"Like I said, going to meet a fellow."

"And this fellow has a name?"

"He does." Braddock allowed himself a narrow smile that stopped short of provoking anything.

"I'm not a dentist, son. Never cared much for pulling teeth."

"Well, as I said, I've never met the man. Name on his telegram was Lucius Haverstock."

That raised one of the lawman's eyebrows, telling Braddock that his client was a local man of influence. He'd done some basic research and learned that Haverstock was big in cattle, but he wasn't reaching out through Western Union to recruit new ranch hands.

"You're familiar with him, then," Braddock surmised.

A slow nod from the sheriff, who still hadn't offered up his name. "I'd hate to see a solid citizen disturbed in any way," he said.

"Well, as I mentioned, Sheriff . . . what's your name, again?" A gentle nudge to show he hadn't been intimidated.

"Ransom. Noah Ransom," the reply came back.

"Well, as I mentioned, Sheriff Ransom, Mr. Haverstock got in touch with me."

"Requesting that you come down here and visit him?"

"Some kind of business that he wants to talk about."

"And what might that be?"

181

"Sorry. I won't know until I've spoken to him personally. If you'd like to come along . . ."

"Nope," Ransom said. "I don't go out and pester folks unless they have some kind of trouble."

"That sounds like a solid policy," Braddock replied.

"I've found it so."

"But you make an exception when it comes to strangers passing through."

"I've learned the best way to prevent a fire is not to let one start," said Ransom.

"Well, I haven't planned on lighting any, Sheriff."

"That could happen when you least expect it, Mr. Braddock. All depends on who you're working for and what the job might be."

"I've given you the name of the man I've come to see," Braddock replied. "I won't know what he has in mind before we've talked about it privately."

"You ought to know that Mr. Haverstock's been having trouble recently," said Ransom.

"What kind of trouble, Sheriff?"

"Not for me to say, except that he's been under pressure and it has to do with oil along the Gulf Coast."

"That's tied in with Spindletop somehow?" asked Braddock. He got the San Antonio papers sent to him and had read about that oil strike over by Beaumont.

"Not directly," Ransom answered, "since that happened east of us, across the county line in Jefferson. Let's say it lit a fuse that's burning faster by the minute, and I'll let it go at that."

"And now you're worried that he's hiring guns?"

"It's crossed my mind."

A nod from Braddock, as he said, "I don't know how to put your mind at ease on that, except to say that I don't work as an assassin, Sheriff."

"But you *do* take gun work, right?"

"When I'm on a job I will defend my client and myself within the law."

"And that's the part that worries me. Your Mr. Haverstock has competition breathing down his neck to buy up land that may have oil beneath it. Those competitors have private armies on their payroll who claim they also work within the law, for whatever that's worth."

"I'll keep all that in mind," Braddock replied, "and I appreciate the warning. If there's nothing else . . .?"

"Nothing that I can hold you on," Ransom replied, half-smiling now. "At least, not yet."

"Then I'll be on my way, Sheriff."

"*Vaya con Dios,*" Ransom said. "With any luck, we may not meet again."

LEAVING LIBERTY, Braddock followed a rutted trail of wagon tracks that ran northwestward at an angle from the broader road he'd followed into town. He met no one along the way, and while he started clocking off the miles, his thoughts focused on oil.

Braddock was no geologist, much less an expert on the subterranean deposits that newspapers had begun to call "black gold." He knew that Native tribes had found it oozing from the Texas soil before the first Spaniards arrived, telling invaders that the thick black substance had healing properties. In 1543, survivors of Hernando de Soto's expedition caulked their leaky boats with the tarry stuff a few miles from the site of present-day Port Arthur, Jefferson County, near the border with Louisiana, and it saw them safely home.

The first intended drilling in Texas by a white man,

one Lyne Barret, had occurred a year after the Civil War in Melrose, Nacogdoches County, but it generated no rush by competitors. More crude wells were completed during 1889 and 1893, in Bexar and Hardin Counties, but the first real strike of any notable significance occurred at Corsicana, in Navarro County, during June of 1894. That operation ran with more sophisticated gear, prompting construction of the state's first oil refinery in 1898, shipping its first loads of refined oil in 1899.

And then came Spindletop.

On January 10, 1901, a Croatian immigrant named Anthony Lucas struck what experts called "salt dome oil" at the Spindletop site near Beaumont, so surprised by his find that nearly one hundred thousand gallons spilled on bare soil before Lucas got the well properly capped. Within a year Texas produced more than eight hundred thousand barrels of oil, fully expected to quintuple in the next year of a new century.

That discovery caused a global sensation and made Anthony Lucas an instant millionaire, as factories from the United States to Europe and beyond retooled, converting from coal to oil as the fuel that drove their endlessly roaring machines. Aside from heavy industry, a whole new market opened up: private use in lamps and heating homes, leading to impending disaster for the whaling industry at sea.

Meanwhile, as the United States became the world's top oil producer and prospectors ranged afield from the Arabian Peninsula to India and China, the fortune reaped by Lucas brought competitors flocking to Jefferson County, Texas. Some names that came to Braddock's mind straight off were David Beatty, the Heywood brothers, Colonel J. M. Guffey, Pattillo

Higgins, and the Hogg-Swayne syndicate, led by former Texas governor James "Big Jim" Hogg and Tarrant County judge James Swayne.

From that, Braddock figured that competition for a prime role in the Texas oil boom would be turning would be turning rough-and-tumble any day now, and for all he knew, might already have spilled its share of blood. Unlike the quest for gold, silver, and copper, which inspired claim-jumping in some cases or sent prospectors off to the frozen reaches of Alaska seeking an isolated "mother lode," oil spread beneath the Earth's surface in massive pools, produced as Braddock understood by rotting prehistoric plants and animals. One pool might spread across multiple counties or bridge state lines, allowing anyone who sank a well to siphon crude away from furious competitors nearby.

In short, you could not simply buy a thousand acres, claim all rights to minerals beneath the surface, and proceed to mine in peace. Not while some other upstart drained your black gold via wells erected on his property nearby. Lawsuits concerning who owned what and where might drag on over years or even decades, but in isolated regions of the Great Southwest there was a simpler, more straightforward way to settle things.

And that could pose a problem.

Braddock had a short, inviolable list of rules where his work was concerned. He wouldn't serve as an assassin or participate in driving any lawful settlers from their land to serve the interest of a would-be oil baron. He *would* defend a paying client and his property from harm by interlopers, and while that might lead to killing, he was not a gunfighter per se. He didn't roam from town to town, inviting challenges and building up a reputation for himself that would require lethal defending farther down the line.

While no longer a lawman, with no legal jurisdiction, he was still a Texas Ranger in his heart. For good or ill that mattered to him and would likely never change.

But Lucius Haverstock deserved a hearing before Braddock either took the latest job or turned him down.

With any luck, the question would be settled by that afternoon. He would assess the situation, judge if it was right for him or not, and either sign on or bid the owner of the Circle H farewell.

Whichever way it went, whatever he had done since separating from the Rangers, Braddock wouldn't compromise his basic principles.

If he ever did, that bullet-punctured star, safely hidden away in a compartment on the back of his gun belt, more than likely would burn a hole right through his soul . . .

2

Five miles out from Liberty, holding his dun to an easy canter, Braddock felt a sense of being watched. Instead of reining in to look around, he only slowed down to a trot and lifted the canteen slung from his saddle horn, miming the gesture he would use to take a sip of water, while his sharp eyes scanned to left and right.

He saw the lookouts on his first pass, three of them on horseback, half concealed in shadows cast by camphor trees and red cedars. A glint of sunlight from a round glass lens told him that one of them was staring at him through some kind of telescope, likely a pocket model easily concealed when not in active use.

Instead of veering to approach them, Braddock kept on riding down the trail to the Circle H. Without knowing the spread's extent, he could not guess if the observers were employed by Lucius Haverstock or simply passing by. For all he knew, in fact, they might be trespassers, but it wasn't his place to challenge them before he'd spoken to the man in charge and listened to his story.

The watchers, likewise, made no move to intercept Braddock or to obscure themselves from view beyond remaining still while he passed by. If they had sought to stop him, he assumed that they had rifles and could have picked him off easily by now.

A warning, then? Or were they simply keeping track of who came visiting the Circle H and its proprietor?

Playing it cautious, Braddock offered them no threat, no reason to start shooting from a distance. Riding on as if he hadn't noticed them, he watched the trio from a corner of his eye until his progress took them out of sight behind the screen of trees they'd used for half-hearted concealment. Even then, he knew the rider with the spyglass might be tracking him, and while Braddock had faced odds worse than three to one before, this seemed neither the time nor the place to gamble on the motives of three strangers.

He'd take it up with Lucius Haverstock in due time, when he made it to the would-be oilman's ranch, and try to find out if the three posed a threat. If so—and if he decided to help Haverstock—then he would think about what should be done with any lurking spies around the rancher's property.

The last half mile or so seemed to take longer, Braddock watching out for other riders, trying not to let a lurker catch him at it. Finally, he saw a looming wooden gate ahead of him, surmounted by an "H" ringed all around with barbed wire strands. A fence of logs stretched off to either side and vanished into trees that formed a second barrier around the property.

That made him think again about the watchers who had spied him earlier. If they belonged to Haverstock, it meant their news of his arrival would be too late for the rancher to prepare himself for company, unless they had some other access to the fenced-off ranch that Braddock couldn't see.

No matter.

He had reached his goal and would see what happened next.

That turned out to be more horsemen, closing in on the gate from its far side. Only a pair of them this time, advancing with the confidence of men who felt at home around the Circle H, not taking any pains to hide. One had a rifle resting crossways on his thighs. The other man, a southpaw, had his left hand resting lightly on the curved butt of a holstered six-shooter.

As Braddock reached the gate, the rifleman spoke up, asking, "Would you be Braddock?"

"In the flesh."

"You should be carrying an invitation from the boss man."

"Right again," Braddock replied. "I'll have to reach inside my vest."

The spokesman nodded. "Just keep it nice and slow. No sudden moves."

Braddock obeyed. He saw no point in traveling so far, only to turn around and ride off in a fit of pique because two total strangers didn't recognize his face on sight.

He figured they were concerned about a shoulder holster or some kind of belly gun, so he used his left hand to draw back his vest, revealing that he had no secondary weapons tucked away. Two fingers of his right hand plucked a folded piece of paper from his shirt's breast pocket and held it waiting for one of the guards to sidle closer, sharp eyes ready as the Western Union telegram changed hands.

The rifleman examined it, lips moving as he read it silently. At last he nodded, kept the telegram, and said, "Okay, then. Follow us. I'll show this to the boss, and if it's straight, you're clear."

Braddock could have protested that he didn't know yet why Haverstock wanted to talk with him, but there was no point raising that topic with underlings. Instead, he'd wait and hash it over with the man who'd summoned him, find out what was expected of him at the Circle H, how much it paid . . . and whether he could live with it.

IT TOOK twenty minutes longer just to reach the ranch house and its outbuildings. Before leaving the gate, the leader of the two watchmen ordered his pal to stay in place, then slipped his rifle down into a hand-tooled saddle boot and turned away from Braddock, saying simply, "Follow me."

They rode along a narrow track through pastureland with longhorns grazing off to either side, more trees beyond them, and a lone oil derrick creaking as it labored, trying to extract oil from the ground below. Two men on foot were tending the machinery, their horses tied well back, both pausing to observe Braddock and his escort as they passed by.

The derrick looked like something prehistoric, or perhaps a giant animal from Africa, bobbing its massive head over a waterhole. In this case, though, there was no pond or lake, only a pipe descending from what would have been the creature's nose—a sucker rod, as Braddock understood the basic oilfield terminology—while horizontal pipes off to one side led to a vat resembling a silo, where crude oil would be accumulated prior to shipping out for a refinery.

As such, it didn't seem to be a thriving operation, but there could be other derricks spotted all around the Circle H, depending on the acreage it covered. Braddock didn't know how much a single vat of crude was worth—how much it even held, in fact—but with the Gulf Coast boom in progress, any oil at all was money in the bank.

And any property of value tempted thieves to take it for themselves.

Braddock added more questions to his ever-growing mental list but kept them to himself for now. He would get nowhere trying to milk information from subordinates, especially when they were already on edge.

He *did* ask, just to break the ice, "Have you got men on watch outside the fence?"

He escort case a wary eye toward Braddock, frowning. Answered with a question of his own. "What makes you think so?"

Braddock shrugged, trying to keep it casual. "I thought I saw some riders, back three-quarters of a mile or so before I reached the gate. Could have been wrong, I guess."

"How many of 'em?" asked the man riding beside him.

Time to hedge again. "A couple," Braddock said. "Could have been more. I thought one of them had a spyglass on me, but it could have been a trick of the light."

"Don't count on it," his escort said, and let it drop at that, as the headquarters of the Circle H came into view at last.

The ranch house was a two-story affair, with wings that stretched away on either side, a broad front porch, and balconies upstairs. Braddock saw a corral out front and two large barns, one standing off to each side of the house, to east and west. There was a water well in the front yard, built up with fieldstone, and outbuildings farther back. Three bunkhouses had room enough to house at least a dozen hands apiece.

As Braddock and his escort neared the covered porch, a front door opened and a tall man dressed in white shirt over denim jeans, a string tie at his throat, face shaded by a tan wide-brimmed hat, emerged, standing with arms folded across his barrel chest as he watched them approach.

The boss man wore no pistol, but he had no need of one just now. Three ranch hands dropped whatever they'd been doing, moving toward the porch to flank their lord and master, all of them with guns riding on their hips. They must have recognized the rider who delivered Braddock to their midst, but every face betrayed suspicion backed by edginess that could explode with one false move on Braddock's part.

Instead of tensing up, Braddock relaxed, keeping his left hand on the dun's reins, his right well clear of any movement toward his Colt or the Winchester hanging in its saddle scabbard.

Eight days on the dusty trail, and he had no wish to be killed before a formal introduction to his host.

LUCIUS HAVERSTOCK WAS forty-eight years old and looked it, in a way most women found ruggedly handsome. Widowed nine years earlier, with no children to carry on his line, he lived for *things*, success measured by acquisitions, be they animal or mineral. He'd carved a minor empire from the wilderness, prospered in beef, and now was branching out.

It irked him that he had to ask for outside help at this stage in his life, but there it was. If life had taught him anything so far, it was that stubborn pride could kill a man.

A shouted summons from the yard had tipped him off that horsemen were approaching. One of them was Blake Drury, a watchman posted on gate duty, while the other, Haverstock assumed, was the import he'd been expecting from down on the border.

Discreet inquiries among contacts in Austin had gotten him this man's name. A former Ranger let go for political reasons, G.W. Braddock still had friends among the force and in the State Capital, despite the fact that some of his activities had branded him an outlaw. Some folks believed that he still did a lot of good, though, and were willing to steer people with trouble in his direction.

The stranger was a decade younger than his host, roughly equivalent in height and weight to Haverstock, and sat his dun like a man accustomed to long hours in the saddle. Whether he lived up to any other aspect of his reputation still remained to be discovered.

"You're G. W. Braddock," Haverstock declared by way of greeting, not a question.

"That's right," said the former Texas Ranger.

"Sometimes known as Junior Braddock?"

"Never to my friends."

"Point taken," Haverstock allowed. "I hope we can be friends, or at the very least, associates."

"That would depend on the problem you need help with," Braddock replied.

"Of course. Let Blake, there, see about your horse while we go on inside. Maybe a drink to cut the dust before we talk some business over lunch. Unless you've had your midday meal, that is?"

"Not yet."

"Care for a steak?"

"I never turned one down," said Braddock, as he climbed down from his saddle and passed the dun's reins to Drury. "He could use some oats and water."

"We'll take care of that," said Haverstock, before his watchdog took offense at Braddock's tone.

The big house at the Circle H was built for comfort, staying reasonably cool in summer, holding warmth in from its four fireplaces through the harshest winters Texas had provided yet. It helped that temperatures near the Gulf of Mexico were fairly moderate year-round, unless a hurricane blew in from time to time and brought flash floods along with raging winds.

"The dining room's this way," said Haverstock, trusting his guest to follow through the parlor, down a long hallway, past a well-stocked library and a room containing mounted trophies from his hunting days, which now seemed long ago. Strangely, the master of the Circle H no longer missed the tracking, culminating in a kill.

He reckoned that was because of the forces breathing down his neck that would love to hang his own head on a wall.

The dining room was paneled in loblolly pine with carpet underfoot. Its central table was surrounded by a dozen matching chairs, but Haverstock couldn't remember the last time he'd welcomed guests into the house and found he hardly missed them. Since his wife had passed from cholera, the days were work and more work, always trying to expand, bring in more cash to keep the Circle H afloat.

And nights, of late, were spent sleeping with one eye open, primed and ready to respond if trouble came calling.

There was a bar to one side of the dining room, and Haverstock veered toward it, asking Braddock, "What's your poison?"

"Bourbon, if you've got it," said his guest.

"I do, indeed. Old Forester, Knob Creek, Woodford Reserve, or Jefferson's?"

"Knob Creek's the only one I know by name, offhand."

"One double, coming up."

Haverstock poured himself the same and brought the glasses back to where Braddock was standing at the table's head.

"Sit anywhere you like," he told Braddock. "We seldom stand on ceremony here." As if to prove it, Haverstock crossed to a nearby doorway, stuck his head into the kitchen, and advised the chef, "Two rib-eyes, Clancy, with potatoes and whatever greens you've got on hand."

The "Yessir" from his cook sounded perfunctory but was delivered with all due respect.

When he turned back to face the dining table, Haverstock saw Braddock lounging in the chair located just left of his normal seat, the one a stranger might have figured was reserved for the proprietor.

Before he had a chance to speak, the former Ranger said, "I met your county sheriff earlier today. He shared a little of the problem that you mentioned in your telegram. Why don't we lay that on the table right up front?"

Instead, the rancher turned oilman led off by asking Braddock, "What did you think of Sheriff Ransom?"

"Seemed concerned about his town and strangers raising Cain, like any other local lawman I've run into in my time," Braddock replied.

"He told you about the problems I've been having, then?"

"No details," Braddock answered. "Just that you were after oil, which I've seen for myself, and that you might be getting pressure from outside."

"To put it mildly," Haverstock said, nodding, as their meals arrived on sizzling platters, piping hot. While Braddock tried a bite of steak and smiled in pleasure, Haverstock pressed on. "Whoever strikes crude anywhere along the coast is up against two major players in a game where no one's bothered writing any rules so far. One calls itself Gulf Oil and claims to be home-grown."

"I've heard of it," Braddock allowed.

"Who hasn't? Starting with the well at Spindletop, it's spread like wildfire on the prairie, roping in investors like the Mellon family from Pittsburgh, up in Pennsylvania. Gulf's front man, based in Beaumont, southeast of here in Jefferson County, is Hal Baker. Short for 'Harold,' that is, and no conscience to speak of. As we speak, he's branching out and sinking wells across Louisiana, up in Oklahoma, anywhere he catches the scent of crude."

"And who's the other player?" Braddock asked his host.

"That would be Standard Oil, a company launched by the John D. Rockefeller family in Ohio, back around the time of Gettysburg."

"That long ago?" Braddock shook his head. "I didn't know anybody started drilling that early."

"Oh, yes. No flies on Johnny D., his brother William, or their brother-in-law Ollie Jennings. They formally incorporated in 1870, with headquarters in Cleveland, made a sweetheart deal with New York's railroad kings, and shifted to New Jersey for a hefty tax advantage in 1885. The Sherman Anti-Trust Act's had them ducking various investigations for the past eleven years, but they're still going strong. Their man in Texas, covering the Gulf, is Roger Jamison, a shady character if ever there was one."

"And both sides put the squeeze on independent operators like yourself," Braddock surmised.

"Along with anybody else, if they imagine oil lies underneath a homestead or a ranch, regardless of its size. They start with monetary offers, pennies on the dollar for a strike's potential, and if landowners don't play along right off, they raise the stakes from there."

"You've contacted the government in Austin?" Braddock asked.

"Time and time again," said Haverstock. "You can forget about Joe Sayers. He's so busy banking payoffs that he can't be bothered with what's happening to his constituents. Same thing with Charlie Bell," he added, naming the state's current attorney general.

"And what about the Rangers?" Braddock countered.

Haverstock restrained a laugh at that. "I know you still feel a connection there, but there aren't many of them left. Four companies, with eighty men in all policing two hundred fifty-four counties spread out over two hundred sixty-nine thousand square miles. Allowing for the trouble caused by red hostiles and border-hopping outlaw gangs, on top of natural disasters like the hurricane that tore up Galveston last year and killed at least eight thousand folks, besides the yellow fever epidemic on its heels."

Braddock nodded, knowing only too well how the

Rangers had declined in recent years, himself a casualty of the Lone Star legislature, but he had to say, "You've still got county sheriffs and their deputies."

Haverstock laughed aloud at that, shaking his head. "You know the story there as well as I do. Every sheriff has his little kingdom, run his way. Some play it straight, but others have their hands out and they'll run with anyone who tops their basic salary. I grant you Noah Ransom is a fairly decent man, but I have doubts about some others. Isaac Prentiss out of Jefferson County, for instance. As for Cody Lawson, he runs Chambers County like his private red-light district. Anything you want—and I mean *any*thing—he can arrange it for a price."

"What about the U.S. Marshal?" Braddock asked.

"That would be a deputy along the Gulf," said Haverstock. "One Jonas Henshaw. He's a decent man, unless I've read him wrong, but he's spread thinner than the Rangers are these days, patrolling some six hundred miles of coastline, mostly chasing smugglers."

"Who are Standard Oil and Gulf using for muscle?"

"It sounds ridiculous, I know, but both of them are signed up with the Pinkertons out of Chicago."

"Pinkerstons fighting one another?"

"If it comes to that," said Haverstock.

"Sounds like a clear conflict of interest to me," Braddock replied with a shake of his head.

"You'd think so. Turns out headquarters doesn't care, as long as cash keeps rolling in from both sides. The Pinks can always hire more guns, same way they do with strikebreakers."

"With that in mind," Braddock said, "which side do you suppose has lookouts posted on the south edge of your property?"

Haverstock paused, lowered his fork, and cocked an eyebrow at his guest. "How many did you see?" he asked.

"I counted three," Braddock replied. "Could have been more back in the trees. One of them tracked me with a spyglass until I was out of sight."

"Well, damn," the oilman said at last. "I won't pretend to be surprised, but I've had no reports from any of my hands of spotting them on trips to Liberty."

"Could be that they're getting bored and careless," Braddock said.

"Or turning up the heat to see how I'll respond," said Haverstock. "If you saw three, smart money says they'll have more stationed all around the Circle H. I'll have to double up my guards at night to stop them sneaking in and doing God knows what."

"How many men do you have on your payroll?" Braddock asked him.

"With the normal hands plus oil rig workers, close to ninety," Haverstock replied.

"I saw one derrick, riding in," Braddock observed.

"That's one of four that pumps around the clock so far. Each has a driller and assistant driller, plus a chain-hand and a derrickman, with roustabouts and rough-necks on eight-hour shifts. I wouldn't reckon them as fighters though unless you count some scuffles in saloons."

"So call it fifty you can count on?"

"Right around there," Haverstock said, then added meaningfully, "if I don't count you."

Braddock countered with, "I still haven't heard what you expect from me."

"Let's settle the money first," said Haverstock. "How does two hundred bucks a month sound to you?"

When he'd started on this campaign of his, Braddock

had never even thought about taking money for what he did. But without the resources of the State of Texas behind him, eventually he had realized that he had to support his efforts somehow. As long as he kept it to jobs that he deemed worth doing, his conscience didn't botehr him.

"Better than the salary the Rangers ever paid me," Braddock said honestly. "And what do you expect in return for that?"

"Help me defend my property."

"Be more specific. You could hire ten normal hands for what you're offering. I don't bust broncs or clean out barns."

"It might involve some travel," Haverstock replied. "Delivering some messages."

Braddock began to see the light. "And would those messages be written down?" he asked.

"Or word-of-mouth, depending. Does that make a difference?"

"It would depend upon the message, Mr. Haverstock. I won't involve myself in threats or blackmail, anything like that."

"Nor would I ask you to. A time may come when pressure placed upon me will require an answer face to face. Some circumstance where I don't feel secure in going by myself."

"I won't square off against another lawman," Braddock cautioned.

"Even if he tries his best to murder you?"

"I'd judge that situation if and when it happens."

"Fair enough. And what about the spies you noted shadowing my property this afternoon?"

Braddock considered that. "If they're still hanging around when I pass back that way, no reason why I couldn't have a word with them. Bearing in mind there's nothing legal I can do if they're not trespassing."

"Or if they pull on you."

"It would become a matter for the sheriff then."

Haverstock smiled. "Of course. And there might be a witness hanging back to tell the story your way, if Ransom has any problem with it. Say, Blake Drury for instance?"

"Never heard of him."

"He brought you in to see me from the gate."

"Oh, him."

"Could come in handy," Haverstock advised.

"And do you plan on having him trail me around wherever I wind up?"

"Let's take it one step at a time."

Braddock considered that. Asked Haverstock, "You've been negotiating with your opposition personally, from Gulf Oil and Standard?"

"That would be a stretch," his host replied. "They've offered cash to clear me off my land. I've turned them down."

"Is there a price you would accept?"

"No, sir. My wife is buried here. I plan on joining her someday."

"But not just yet," said Braddock.

Haverstock allowed himself a smile at that. "I'd rather put it off a while, that's true."

"So you expect a war of sorts."

"If that's the way they choose to play it," Haverstock agreed. "You up for that?"

"How many Pinkertons between them?" Braddock asked.

"Twenty or thirty each, I'd guess."

"Long odds."

"Figure you're up to it?"

"Don't let the Rangers' motto fool you," Braddock said.

He had in mind the slogan coined by Captain Bill McDonald five years earlier, when he was sent to halt an illegal prize fight between contenders Bob Fitzsimmons and Pete Maher. On arrival, someone had inquired whether McDonald needed reinforcements to disperse the angry crowd of bettors, whereupon he had allegedly replied, "One riot, one Ranger."

Braddock couldn't say if that story was true or not, but he had always liked the sound of it and felt it captured something of the Ranger spirit, call it boast or warning, as you might prefer.

"Three on one or maybe more," said Haverstock. "I'd hate to see you killed before you draw your first paycheck."

"Maybe you ought to pay me for this month up front," Braddock replied.

"Sounds like a good idea," his host agreed.

"But first," Braddock said as a smile creased his lean face, "I'd like to finish off this steak."

3

"So LET ME GET THIS STRAIGHT," BLAKE DRURY SAID, HIS bay mare keeping pace with Braddock's dun. "You're expecting three men, maybe more, to jump us—"

"To jump me," Braddock corrected him. "If they're still keeping watch over the Circle H."

"And I'm supposed to let you take them all by yourself. Right?"

"Hang back and see what happens," Braddock answered. "You're my witness if I need one. If push comes to shove and I wind up delivering dead men to Sheriff Ransom back in Liberty."

"Uh-huh." His escort didn't sound convinced. "And what it you're the dead one? Did you think about that?"

"Then," Braddock replied, "you turn around and ride straight back to Mr. Haverstock. Tell him he saved two hundred dollars."

"I don't follow that," said Drury.

"You don't have to. Just remember it."

"Okay. You don't want any help against three guns or more, then count me out."

"Exactly."

A silent moment passed, then Drury asked him, "Have you done this kind of thing before?"

"Not quite," Braddock replied. "Never with Pinkertons."

"Which gang of them you figure this might be? Hal Baker's or Roger Jamison's."

"No telling if both men are breathing down your boss's neck. Maybe we'll get a chance to ask."

"Not if they're dead. And I don't plan on chasing 'em across the county line to ask them for their bona fides."

"No," Braddock agreed. "I wouldn't ask you to."

"Just watch and see what happens, right? No matter who comes out on top."

"That's it, in a nutshell."

"If you don't mind me saying so . . . or even if you do . . . that must make you the nut."

"I've been called worse," said Braddock, with a smile.

Drury muttered something underneath his breath at that and Braddock let it go. His mind was on which weapon he should choose if lookouts on the trail accosted him.

His pistol was a Colt Single Action Army revolver, widely known as the "Peacemaker," chambered in .44-40 Winchester to match the lever-action rifle in his saddle boot. Both guns had been produced for the first time in 1873, and matching ammunition for them saved Braddock from carrying around two different calibers.

His Colt measured eleven inches with a 5.5-inch barrel, while the rifle's twenty-four-inch barrel hurled two hundred-grain bullets down range at 1,245 feet per second, killing reliably out to one hundred yards. The Colt's range, naturally shorter, was still more than adequate for any distance he was likely to encounter in a standup fight. Between the two of them, Braddock could get off twenty shots without reloading unless someone dropped him first. Twenty-two if he kept one in the rifle's chamber and a full wheel in the Colt.

Which one to choose this afternoon?

Braddock favored the Colt, eleven inches long next to the rifle's forty-nine inches and nearly eight pounds lighter, but he'd have to let the final situation dictate which he used if called upon to fight.

And, then again, he knew a wily sniper hidden in the tree line as he passed could pick him off before Braddock had time to draw and fire.

Speaking of trees, he saw the stand of camphor and red cypress coming up, reversed from when he'd passed it earlier. Without turning, he told Blake Drury, "This is where you need to fade back. Watch those trees off to the right. If anybody shows, they'll come from over there."

"All right, then," Drury answered, letting Braddock pull ahead.

When he had cleared another hundred yards, Braddock saw two men, rather than the three he'd seen originally, sitting easy on their horses in the tree line's shadow.

Any time now, if they're coming, he decided.

If they didn't . . . well, Braddock supposed he'd have to start the ball himself.

That was the only way to find out who wanted to dance.

"He's coming back," Doc Webber said.

"Somebody tell you I was blind?" asked Arnie Folger without turning toward his fellow Pinkerton detective.

"Huh? No, Arnie. I just meant—"

"Take a look for Zeke but don't be obvious about it. Is he hidden back there, from the road?"

"Can't see him," Webber said a moment later. "You know Zeke. He's good at hiding."

Folger knew Zeke Bodine's talent for lying low and understood that Zeke was equally proficient with his rifle if it came to that, although his orders should prevent him using it if anything went wrong. Their temporary boss in Beaumont wanted someone on the scene reporting back to him pronto if surveillance on the Circle H went south on them, and Folger was in charge, meaning he could not lie back in the weeds and play it safe.

His orders were explicit: check out any strangers he saw visiting the ranch—those without badges, anyhow—and warn them off from helping Lucius Haverstock. In fact, the cattleman and would-be oil tycoon had few callers these days, which suited Folger fine. This solitary rider was the first one in a week of covering the Circle H, and while he had a kind of lawman's air about him, Folger knew from telescoping him when he arrived that there was no badge on his chest.

"What now?" asked Webber, even though they'd been over the plan a dozen times.

"Same as I said before," Folger replied. "We head him off and ask his business. Make the point that it ain't smart palling around with Haverstock, then send him on his way."

"And what if he gets feisty?" Doc inquired.

"We've been all over that. We put him down."

Nothing they hadn't done before in service to their

masters in Chicago, managing the famous "Eye That Never Sleeps." In Folger's time with Pinkerton's Detective Agency he'd infiltrated labor unions, sent some of their men to prison or the gallows, and had planted others in forgotten shallow graves, depending on the task at hand. Railroads and banks fielded private detectives in pursuit of bandits dating back to the James Gang, and Pinkerton's provided muscle for whoever paid the going rate—in strikes, range wars, around the nation's lawless mining towns, wherever.

Arnie Folger never lost a moment's sleep over his job as long as he went home alive when all was said and done.

"All set, then?" he asked Webber.

"Ready as I'll ever be," Doc answered back.

"Come on then. I don't wanna chase him all the way from here to Liberty."

Webber said something Folger didn't catch and didn't care about, trailing Arnie as he left the tree line, trotting down to intercept the stranger who'd been visiting the Circle H.

BRADDOCK DIDN'T BOTHER PRETENDING that he hadn't seen the two riders in tweed suits and bowler hats approaching him. In those outfits, with their burly shapes and full mustaches, they couldn't have looked more like Pinks if they'd been playing the parts in some melodrama.

He reined in, waiting for them, while he wondered where the third man was and whether any more were hiding back among the trees.

Easily, half turning his dun to conceal the subtle

move, he freed the leather thong around his Colt's hammer and brought his right hand back onto his saddle horn.

When the two horsemen were twenty yards away, he called out to them, "Finally decided to stop skulking in the trees?"

The leader of the pair, smiling a bit, hands well clear of his twin six-guns, replied as he approached, "We got a job to do is all."

"And how do I fit into that?" Braddock asked.

"We're paid to keep an eye on whoever comes visiting the Circle H."

Braddock switched gears and said, "It appears you lost a man since I saw you the first time."

Looking startled, their spokesman tried to cover it, replied, "Shift change." Sprouting a smile, he added, "We're plenty as it is."

Braddock kept his face expressionless. "Depends on what you've got in mind, I guess."

"A couple questions," said their spokesman. "Friendly like."

"You've got a funny definition of it," Braddock said.

"No reason to get touchy, mister. We get paid to keep an eye on who goes in and out."

"Since neither of you wears a badge, I'd have to ask how that's your business."

The point man frowned and came up with obviously the first thing he could think of. "Mr. Haverstock—I guess you've met him—owes our boss some money and he's late on paying. Simple, see?"

"I don't see anything," Braddock replied, "except you ought to take that up with him if it's the truth."

"You calling me a liar, son?"

"I'm not your son," said Braddock, "and I'm not the

Circle H's bookkeeper. You want to see the man about a bill, why not try knocking on his door?"

"He gets his back up, prickly like. We shy away from trouble."

"There's a sheriff back in Liberty. Seems like an amiable sort. Tell him your story."

"Listen, friend—"

"I'm not your friend any more than I am your son. Fact is, I've never met you before in my life and don't know you from Adam."

"All I'm asking you—"

"Is details of my private business. I don't share that kind of thing with strangers, much less highwaymen."

"Hey, now!" Color rising in his bristly cheeks, the mouthpiece for the pair said, "I don't stand for any insults."

"Then you need to move aside and let me pass," Braddock replied.

"Nobody's stopping you, mister."

In fact, the riders hadn't blocked his way, but Braddock felt their confrontation at the tipping point, no turning back.

"Thing is," he said, "I look at the pair of you, and I have to wonder if you'd shoot a fella in the back."

The lookouts shared a glance, both of them tense, their spokesman on the verge of fuming. "Damn you! I don't take that kinda talk from any saddle bum."

"Your call," Braddock replied.

And smiled.

ARNIE FOLGER COULD NOT GRASP how things had gotten out of hand so quickly. That had been a fault of Folger's since he was a kid, temper running away from him and getting him in trouble, sometimes into fights he couldn't win and once or twice locked up in jail.

He'd tried to overcome that since he signed on with the Pinkertons. His job allowed an outlet for the violence he kept penned up inside, as long as he controlled and channeled it down avenues that his employers found acceptable. That ran to clubbing union strikers on the picket line, jumping a claim from time to time when mining companies wanted relief from two-bit prospectors or sodbusters, that kind of thing. He'd killed a few men in his time—and sure, he'd shot a couple of them when their backs were turned, just like this cowpoke said—but Folger couldn't bear to take an insult from some saddle bum.

Particularly if it hit him with the sting of truth.

"Arnie?"

The sound of Doc's voice grated on his nerves, the very last thing that he needed now, when he was working overtime to get his thoughts in order and decide what he should do within the next few vital seconds.

"Hush!" he snapped at Webber without turning back to face him. To the stranger, then, name still unknown, he said through gritted teeth, "You owe me an apology."

"Agree to disagree on that," the saddle bum replied without dropping his smile.

Only he looked less like a saddle bum to Folger now than like a gunman, someone comfortable with the big Colt on his hip.

Stalling for time, Arnie replied, "Say what?"

"Which part of that confused you?" asked the stranger.

Still that smile.

"He's mocking you, Arnie," his sidekick muttered.

"Shut your pie hole, Doc!" Folger hissed back at Webber. Then, to the stranger, "What's your game, mister?"

"No game," the dun's rider answered back. "You boys stopped *me*, remember?"

Folger felt as if his brain were spinning on the inside of his skull, the same rage that swept over him before he ran amok and had to clean up afterwards. His right hand trembled, inches from the pistol on his belt, and that was bad. He needed clear eyes and a steady hand to make the first shot count.

And where was Zeke Bodine? Still hiding in the trees as he'd been ordered, maybe smart enough to have his rifle out and cocked by now, or maybe not. Doc Webber was a fair hand with a six-gun at close range, but Folger knew he could not count on anyone except himself right now.

Drawing a deep breath, Arnie Folger held it as his hand dipped toward his holstered gun.

BACK IN THE trees and out of sight, Ezekiel Bodine—Zeke to his friends—watched Doc and Arnie while he wondered what the deuce was going on. He couldn't hear what Folger or the man he'd stopped were saying, but it didn't take a genius to read their attitudes and realize that both were on the verge of slapping leather.

In that case, Bodine's orders were explicit: see which way the action went, but not to intervene if it went sour on his fellow Pinkertons. Arnie, in charge, clearly didn't believe that such a thing could happen, not with Doc supporting him against the rider they had reckoned was some kind of drifter seeking work, but if by some outlandish chance it *did*, Zeke has been tasked with carrying the bad news back to Mr. Jamison in Beaumont. He was absolutely *not* supposed to pull his Winchester and join the fight, no matter how much it ran against his grain to cut and run.

Although, the truth be told, Zeke wouldn't mind that part at all.

He followed orders to the letter when he could remember what they were, and failing that, tired his damnedest to stay alive when other bodies started dropping. His real worry, if it came to scuttling back to Beaumont, was the possible reaction of the man who had employed them to enforce his will during the escalating Lone Star war for oil.

He'd seen enough of Roger Jamison so far to know the man fronting for Standard Oil was unpredictable, likely to go off like a half-cocked pistol if you didn't handle him exactly right. Zeke wondered if the man was crazy on some level, but that didn't matter once he'd signed a contract with Chicago and the word came down that Bodine and his fellow Pinkertons do whatever was required of them to keep a wealthy patron satisfied.

Zeke knew what *that* meant and he knew that questioning the man who paid his salary and made the rules was not a healthy proposition.

So he'd watch and wait, see who came out on top, and if the saddle tramp turned out to be a gunfighter, he'd ride like hell to break the news before it came to Mr. Jamison some other way. No stopping off in Beaumont first to fortify himself with pop skull at the first saloon he spotted, prior to checking in.

Better to keep his fingers crossed, praying to long forgotten gods that Folger and Webber could pull it off

212

before Zeke had to be the bearer of bad news who took the heat for it.

BRADDOCK WAS ready when the mouthpiece of the two men facing him went for his gun. No trick to that, seeing intention in the rider's eyes, the way his shoulder dipped, his right hand clutching at his holstered shooting iron.

Braddock was there ahead of him, Colt Peacemaker in hand, already cocked, its hammer poised above the firing pin. It only needed two pounds of pressure on the trigger to dispatch a .44 round from a range of twenty feet or less, drilling his adversary's chest and cancelling whatever hope he'd had of beating Braddock to the draw.

The impact punched his human target over backward, worn boots flailing as he vaulted off his piebald gelding's rump and hit the ground like three weeks' worth of dirty laundry. By the time the dead man's horse veered off and galloped toward the tree line, Braddock had his pistol's hammer cocked again, its front and rear sights lined up on the second rider's chest.

The second shooter hadn't tried to pull yet, but his mind was obviously clicking over, calculating his odds of success now that he'd seen his partner die in front of him. His narrowed eyes were focused on the smoking muzzle of the Colt confronting him, like staring down a railroad tunnel with a freight train barreling toward him.

"You don't have to do this," Braddock told him, watching for the tells that usually marked a fighting man's decision to proceed even without a hope of coming out on top.

"You kilt Arnie," the other said, sounding half-witted as he spoke.

"Was that his name?"

A head bob, followed by a question. "How am I supposed to tell the boss about this?"

"Maybe I can help you out with that," Braddock replied. "Tell me his name and where to find him, for a start."

As if he hadn't heard, the trembling rider said, "He'll have my hide for sure. Won't wanna hear about it if I don't do something."

"Think about that long and hard," said Braddock. "I don't like your chances."

"You don't know the boss."

"If you're resigned to this—"

"I got no choice, mister."

"All right. What was your name?"

"They call me Doc," he answered back and made his move.

The second round from Braddock's Peacemaker sent Doc to join his friend. A splash of crimson and a puff of dust on impact with the soil.

ZEKE BODINE DIDN'T WAIT AROUND to see Doc Webber drop. He wheeled his palomino mare around and dug in with his spurs, hunched down over his saddle horn as branches whipped across his chest and shoulders, nearly ripping off his hat before he raised a hand to clamp it down.

Scared spitless, for a moment he imagined that the gunfighter was coming after him, then realized the thrashing sounds he heard were generated by his own retreat from watching his companions die.

There was no doubt in Bodine's mind that both of them were dead. Nobody hit the ground like that if he was ever getting up again without somebody lifting him, and Zeke's next thought was, *Good. At least they can't spill anything on Mr. Jamison or what he'd have in mind for tenants of the Circle H when Bodine broke the news to him.*

Not that he hoped for one split-second that their silence at the end would spare Bodine himself from Jamison's explosive wrath.

He still hoped to survive that, though, combining fast talk with the Beaumont oilman's fear of losing Pinkerton support by killing off the agency's so-called detectives he'd been renting by the week to stake his claims along the Gulf of Mexico. The Pinkertons' top man serving with Roger Jamison was a hard-nosed veteran, Emery Grimm, who tried to keep the client happy while he looked out for Chicago's interest at the same time.

And there were two things that headquarters didn't need right now: a scandal in the press, or agents getting picked off due to orders their impulsive client handed down. Bodine hoped that a fear of either possibility might save his life—though there was still no guarantee of that—and if he wound up being reassigned . . . well, he could live with that.

In truth, he had no love for Texas, the wide open spaces so unlike his Brooklyn birthplace or the Windy City, where he felt much more at home. He didn't like the way things had been shaping up of late, particularly with the mounting risk that he'd be going up against more Pinkertons retained to back another side in the accelerating range war.

No, Zeke thought, he wouldn't mind a change of

scene, even a pay cut if it came to that. Demotion struck him as an option preferable to a cold hole in the ground, likely without a marker, fifteen hundred miles from home.

The fear that nagged Bodine was that he might not have a chance to pick between the two.

BRADDOCK WHISTLED BETWEEN HIS TEETH, a rising note, and had his Colt's spent rounds replaced as he saw Blake Drury approaching on his dapple gray gelding, eyeing the dead men on the ground.

"You saw all that?" he asked the Circle H drover.

"Enough to testify if it comes down to that," Drury replied.

"That's all I need," Braddock confirmed. "Now help me fetch their mounts and get them settled for the ride to Liberty."

That took a bit of time, the horses acting skittish after losing both their riders, then they had to be secured while Braddock and his helper from the nearby ranch hoisted each corpse in turn, draped them facedown over the saddles of the animals they'd ridden to their deaths, and used the dead men's lariats to link their wrists and ankles underneath each horse's abdomen. The five- or six-mile journey back to Liberty was short enough that Braddock didn't bother draping anything over them to keep the flies off as they rode.

Drury was breathing heavily as they finished that task, but he still found the breath to say, "These two weren't all that I expected."

"Oh?" Braddock replied. "How's that."

"We hear a lot about the Pinkertons, you know, how

tough they are and all, but you took these two down like it was nothing. I begin to wonder what we've all been so afraid of since they started showing up down here."

"Don't underestimate them," Braddock cautioned. "These two weren't expecting trouble, but the first one let his temper get the better of him. That's always a hazard in a fight."

"You know a third one got away, right?" Drury asked him.

Braddock nodded. "I was afraid he might start sniping from the trees. That could have turned the whole thing upside down, but he got spooked or maybe had his orders in advance."

"Orders?" Drury was frowning now.

"To run back home with a report if anything went wrong."

"Wherever home is," Drury said.

"I was about to ask you that."

"No telling, since the Pinkertons are split between two companies and both of those are after Mr. Haverstock to sell his land. I've never seen these two before, so I can't help you out with that."

"It makes a difference for the one who got away," Braddock replied. "How long it takes for him to pass the word along."

In fact, he knew that Anahuac, the seat of Chambers County and headquarters of the Gulf Oil outfit, was located twenty-four miles south of Liberty, while Beaumont and the team from Standard Oil were situated forty-six miles to the east. If the escapee traveled eastward at a steady gallop—and his horse could make it that far before giving out—he might reach Beaumont within three or four hours. Say half that time for Anahuac.

Allow whoever sent the spies out in the first place to

assess their options and decide on how they should respond, then put a larger force of gunmen on the road, it would most likely be tomorrow at the earliest before the Circle H felt any repercussions from the double killing.

But he didn't like the sound of *likely* echoing inside his head.

Whichever company his killing of the lookouts might arouse, Braddock knew either or both of them could have more agents in the area, awaiting orders to respond in case of any trouble.

"Right," he said after he'd hauled himself into the dun's saddle. "Let's get these two into town and try to satisfy the sheriff."

"Then what?" Drury asked him.

"Then," Braddock replied, "we wait and see who turns up next."

LIBERTY, TEXAS

SHERIFF NOAH RANSOM LIT A THIN CHEROOT AND PEERED across his desk through rising smoke to eye his unexpected visitor. "What brings you by today?" he asked Deputy U.S. Marshal Jonas Henshaw, trying not to sound suspicious as he spoke.

Henshaw patrolled the coastal counties between Jefferson, along Louisiana's border, down to Cameron, beside the Rio Grande where it spilled into the Gulf of Mexico. That covered some sixteen thousand square miles, plus seven good-sized barrier islands and various small spits of land beloved by smugglers as hideouts and layover points for illicit cargo. That kept him on the move, explaining why he'd never married and had killed more than a dozen fugitives during as many years.

"Ear to the ground as usual, you know," Henshaw replied. "Your oil war's heating up."

"Was bound to happen," Ransom granted. "Little fish attract the sharks, including some from out of state."

"Like Standard Oil, you mean." The marshal didn't phrase his statement as a question.

"Not to mention Gulf Oil, which has roots in Pennsylvania despite its name that makes it sound homegrown."

"Squeezing the independent operators," Henshaw noted.

"While they last."

"I hear you've got one in your own backyard, Noah. Fella named Lucius Haverstock who runs the Circle H."

Ransom nodded. "He's got a few wells pumping. Gulf and Standard both would love to buy him out, but he's rejected them. Says that he runs cattle for a living, even though he's banking more from oil than beef these days."

"That has to raise some hackles with the money men from up north."

"Two of them, anyway," Ransom agreed.

"Baker and Jamison." Again, it didn't come out sounding like a question.

"You've been studying up on this, Jonas."

Henshaw shrugged. "Enough to know they've both been hiring Pinkertons. I guess Chicago has less scruples than the big oil boys."

"They'll chase the money. Pinch a penny till it screams," said Ransom.

"I've been looking at them for some raids in Jefferson. Homesteaders run off when they wouldn't sell their land. Four dead in one raid just last month."

"I heard about it," Ransom allowed.

"Nothing like that here in Liberty so far?"

"I try to keep a tight lid on."

Henshaw nodded. "I know you do, and I appreciate it. But the pressure's building up, Noah. Smart money says it's bound to blow."

"If something happens, I'll reach out to you, Jonas."

Another nod. "Assuming that you get the chance."

"And if I don't, Pete Withers will be burning up the Western Union line to Austin," Ransom said, referring to the aged mayor of Liberty.

"Except that could be where he hits a snag."

"Payoffs, you mean," said Ransom.

"Did you ever know a politician to refuse one, Noah?"

"Don't believe I have." As Ransom answered, for the first time since he'd known Henshaw, it struck him that they both had given names selected from the Bible, and he had to wonder if that was some kind of cosmic joke, since both of them had jobs that placed them in the company of sinners constantly.

"Keep this under your hat," Henshaw advised. "Word is the governor and the attorney general, along with half the legislature, likely more, are taking campaign contributions from the oilmen left and right. Standard or Gulf, their money's all the same."

"You think they'd leave us hanging?" Ransom asked, frowning.

"Who knows? They've got a ready-made excuse, what with the Rangers cut back to a handful spread across the state."

"Speaking of Rangers . . ."

But before Ransom could finish, a young boy he recognized as Tommy Clanton burst in through the office door, hollering, "Sheriff! Sheriff!"

"Take it easy, Tommy," Ransom urged him. "What's the hubbub?"

"Two horsemen coming down the street, Sheriff."

"That's not exactly news," said Ransom, putting on a smile.

"No, sir. Except they've got two other horses with 'em, both with dead men tied across their saddles."

Ransom bolted from behind his desk and brushed past Tommy, making for the sidewalk. Jonas Henshaw beat him to it and the lawmen stood together, watching death approach.

BRADDOCK AND DRURY took their time once they had crossed the city limits, neither locking eyes with any of the spectators who watched them riding slowly toward the sheriff's office. On the wooden sidewalk he saw Noah Ransom standing with a second lawman whom he didn't recognize, although his badge—a circlet with a bright five-pointed star inside—identified him as a U.S. Marshal.

"More trouble," Drury muttered as they closed the gap.

"Relax," Braddock advised. "Just tell them what you saw, like we agreed."

As they drew near, Ransom spoke up. "We talked about this, Braddock."

"I remember, Sheriff. But unfortunately, no one passed the word on to these boys."

"And who are they?"

"I haven't checked their pockets," Braddock answered, "but my guess would be they're Pinkertons. As far as who they're working for, I leave that up to you and Marshal Henshaw here."

The marshal looked surprised. He asked Braddock, "Have we met?"

"Never had the pleasure," Braddock told him, "but I

heard your name from Lucius Haverstock this afternoon."

Now, sizing up the deputy, he saw a solid man, mid-thirties, with a pale scar on the right side of his jawline, sideburns showing just a touch of early gray amid the sandy hair. His eyes were gray and steady, attitude at ease, although his right hand rested on the curved butt of his Colt.

Braddock saw something click behind the marshal's eyes before he said, "I'm guessing you're George Braddock's son."

"And you'd be right," Braddock agreed.

"That kind of reputation takes some living up to."

"Used to," Braddock said, "until the Rangers started cutting back on men."

The sheriff, frowning, interrupted. "Can we get back to these carcasses now if you all don't mind?" he asked.

"They're all yours, Sheriff," Braddock said. "Or we can drop them at the undertaker's if you'll point us there."

"Hold up on that," Ransom replied. "What makes you think they're Pinkertons?"

"Three of them watched me ride up to the Circle H after I talked to you, and Mr. Haverstock suspected that his place was being watched. These two stopped me while I was heading back to town."

"And what about the third one?" Ransom asked.

"He hung back out of sight and then skedaddled when the shooting started. I could hear him riding off but didn't get another look at him."

"Reporting back to somebody," Henshaw suggested.

"That would be my guess, Marshal," Braddock agreed.

"And I suppose they pulled on you," said Ransom.

"Starting with the fellow in the blue shirt," Braddock

said. "He took offense at me not answering his questions."

"And the other one?"

"Had due time to consider it. Pride got the better of him in the end."

Ransom's eyes shifted toward Blake Drury. "I've seen you in town before."

"Yes, sir," Drury replied. "Come in sometimes with others from the Circle H on Friday nights or Saturdays."

"And you're a witness to these shootings?"

"That I am, Sheriff."

"They happened just like Braddock tells it?"

"Down the line," Drury agreed.

"So, nothing I can take before a court, then." Ransom sounded disappointed.

"Not unless you're prone to prosecuting men for self-defense," Braddock advised.

"Can't say I like the smell of this," said Ransom. "Your first day in Liberty and all."

"You want to check with Mr. Haverstock, he'll tell you that I'm on his payroll," Braddock said.

"As what?" Henshaw inquired.

"Extra security around the spread," Braddock replied. "The sheriff's seen his telegram inviting me. Seems like I got the job."

Ransom made an exasperated sound, then said to Drury, "You know where the undertaker's parlor is?"

"I've seen it," Drury granted.

"Drop them off with Eulon Wells down there and tell him I'll be stopping by to look them over, see if anything helps to identify the two of them."

"Yes, sir," Drury agreed, and set off with the two death-laden horses, leaving Braddock to catch up with him.

In parting, Braddock tipped his Stetson to both lawmen, saying, "I suppose we'll meet again sometime."

"Can't hardly wait," Ransom replied, then started back inside his office, Marshal Henshaw on his heels.

JEFFERSON COUNTY, TEXAS

Zeke Bodine was roughly halfway back to Beaumont when he had to stop and rest his palomino mare, knowing that it would be no benefit for him to kill his horse and wind up hiking back on foot to face the music for his fellow agents getting killed.

Those fatalities weren't Zeke's fault, granted. He had followed Arnie Folger's orders to the letter—hide and watch, then high-tail it back with a report to Mr. Jamison if anything went wrong—but he was well acquainted with the boss's temper and knew someone had to pay for such a hitch in the established plan.

He chose a spot due south of Sour Lake and north of China Grove, a watering stop for the Texas and New Orleans Railroad with no population in residence. The mare drank its fill from a creek, cropped some grass while Zeke dismounted, rolled himself a quirley, smoked it to a stub, and ground that out beneath his bootheel.

Relieved, if only for the moment, he rode on to eastward, working on his story, making sure he had the details ironed out in his mind. It might not fly, could even get him slapped around some, when he broke the news, but Zeke supposed that sticking to the truth as much as possible might save his life.

Mr. Jamison was known for flying off the handle, but he was a businessman as well. He'd know that losing two

Pinkerton agents on a half-baked spying mission had to cost him money for replacements. If he went berserk and killed a third himself . . . well, that could terminate his contract with the company and maybe even leave him open to some legal repercussions that the men above him in the ranks of Standard Oil might not appreciate.

Running a few shiftless homesteaders off their land was one thing, when it served the greater good, but murdering his own employees . . . well, the cost of white-washing a thing like that could boomerang and hit the boss where it hurt.

"Just tell it straight," Zeke muttered to himself. "Stick to your guns."

The mare beneath him offered no opinion of her own.

Zeke's only other option was to turn tail and vamoose, vacate the county and the state of Texas altogether before someone tried to track him down. That meant abandoning his steady paycheck from Chicago, living on the dodge if other Pinkertons were sent to find him and erase that stain upon the company's good name.

Bodine snorted a laugh at that, considering the things he'd done in service to the Eye That Never Slept, but none of that would be revealed if they caught up with him and silenced him for good. He'd simply be another casualty of the endless labor wars—and might well disappear from formal records altogether if headquarters deemed it wise.

No. Lighting out would only make Zeke's troubles worse. If he could talk to Mr. Jamison and get a word in edgeways, he could likely save himself, get off with just a dressing-down, and maybe even be left out of future missions for a while.

Which might not be a bad thing, Zeke decided, just as long as Mr. Jamison didn't suggest Chicago firing him as useless in the field. And if worse came to worst, he could survive that too, maybe move on to find a new job riding shotgun for Wells Fargo, chief competitor of Pinkerton's and growing all the time with banking and express shipments across the country.

Feeling somewhat better, Bodine whistled at his mare for greater speed and started eating up the miles ahead, prepared to meet his fate.

LIBERTY, TEXAS

After delivering the bodies to the undertaker's parlor, telling Eulon Wells to see the sheriff about funeral arrangements, Braddock rode with Drury to the Lucky Strike saloon, where Braddock stood the Circle H hand to a shot of whiskey and a beer chaser.

When he had wet his whistle, Drury asked, "You see that kind of action very often?"

Braddock didn't bother keeping score, like certain Rangers he could name. "I don't go looking for it," he replied, without taking offense. "When trouble finds me, I like to be ready for it."

"Well, you were ready for them two today, all right," Drury allowed.

"It could have gone the other way," said Braddock, "if they hadn't put somebody jumpy in charge. Once he was down, his sidekick must have figured it would go hard for him, taking back the news."

"Damn fools," said Drury.

"I suppose they had to like their odds at two-to-one."

227

"We saw how that worked out for them."

"Too bad you didn't recognize them," Braddock said. "It would be helpful, knowing which side sent them out prepared for killing."

"Wish I knew 'em," Drury answered. "Truth is, Mr. Haverstock's hemmed in by people hoping they can buy or spook him off his land. They know he's pumping oil and want it for themselves."

"Standard or Gulf," Braddock acknowledged.

"Them two at the very least," Drury replied. "I wouldn't be surprised if more came crawling out from under rocks before too long. This 'boom' the papers write about has put a squeeze on anyone who doesn't take the first offer they get from one bunch or another. I hear tell of people being run off homesteads granted to 'em by the government when they just try to raise a decent crop and make ends meet. Some stranger *thinks* there may be oil under their fields and little houses, that's enough to bring the pressure on."

"Who makes that call?" asked Braddock.

"College boys who study rocks and such," Drury replied.

"You mean geologists?"

"Or so they call themselves. We've got one on the Circle H, working for Mr. Haverstock. His name's Tom Forman. Calls himself an oil prospector, and I guess he's worth the money the boss is paying him. Four wells so far, and there could still be more."

"Brings in a lot of cash from drilling in the dirt," said Braddock.

"I suppose. Ask me, we weren't bad off just running beef."

Drury was halfway through his beer when he glanced

over at the saloon's batwing doors and muttered, "Damn! Here comes the law again."

Braddock followed his gaze and saw that it was Marshal Henshaw on his own, without the sheriff this time, eyeballing the room until he spotted Braddock and his drinking partner at the bar.

"Maybe he's just relaxing," Braddock said, while not believing it.

"Don't bet on that. I'm lighting a shuck," said Drury. "You coming along?"

"Thought I might try for a hotel room overnight," Braddock replied. "Clean up a bit and see what happens next."

"You've got a choice of three or four," groused Drury. "Any parting words for Mr. Haverstock?"

"Tell him I'm on the job. I'll be in touch as soon as I have any news."

Drury finished off his beer and left, passing by Marshal Henshaw on his way back toward the street. He stopped briefly, exchanged some words with Henshaw, then moved on and through the swinging doors to reach the sidewalk and his tethered dapple gray gelding.

Braddock saw Henshaw approaching, flagged the bartender, and said, "I'd better get a refill on that beer."

JONAS HENSHAW STEPPED up to the bar beside Braddock, maintaining a respectful distance so their elbows didn't touch. "Mind if I join you?" he inquired.

"Free country, last I checked," Braddock replied.

Spotting the empty whisky glass beside Braddock's fresh beer, he told the barkeep, "May as well give me one of those boilermakers, Bob."

"You stop in here from time to time I guess," Braddock observed.

"Recalling names and faces is a big part of my job. Of course, you know that from the Rangers. Saves you carrying a stack of WANTED fliers everywhere you go."

"And helps with spotting enemies," Braddock added.

"You have a lot of those in Liberty? Ones still alive, I mean?"

"I never saw those boys before today," said Braddock. "If they hadn't called me out, they'd be having their supper anytime now."

"Hey, don't get me wrong," said Henshaw. "I believe your explanation. So does Sheriff Ransom, though he's not happy about it."

"Maybe he should take that up with whoever employed them."

"As to that," the marshal said, "your thought was right about them being Pinkertons. That doesn't narrow down the field much, sad to say, the way oil companies are hiring so-called detectives to promote their interests."

"Meaning you can't say who paid those two to hang around the Circle H, messing with lawful traffic in and out."

"Not yet. I'm working on it though," Henshaw replied.

"From what I hear," said Braddock, "you've got two main suspects."

Henshaw nodded, tossed his whiskey down, and grimaced. "I know who you mean," he said a moment later. "Neither one of them is based in Ransom's county."

"Bad for him," Braddock allowed. "But you've got jurisdiction all along the Gulf, and anywhere in Texas if you want to press the point."

"On paper, sure. But I answer to a superior in Austin,

and *he* answers up the line to Washington. Between those capitals a lot of men with influence and interests of their own butt in whenever possible to keep their own wheels turning smoothly."

"Nothing you can do about that?" Braddock asked him.

"Such as?"

"Dusting off the Sherman Anti-Trust Act, for a start."

"The president is no great fan of intervening in states' rights," Henshaw replied.

Meaning William McKinley, starting off his second term in the White House, who had burned his fingers badly on a tariff bill while he was still in Congress.

"But he doesn't mind starting a war with Spain that let him capture Cuba and the Philippines," said Braddock.

"Well, officially the war was *their* fault," Henshaw countered. "Remember the *Maine* and all that."

"I remember," said Braddock. "Just not sure I buy it."

"Either way," Henshaw replied. "Looks like your buddy left without you."

"Not my buddy," Braddock said. "He works for Mr. Haverstock."

"Like you."

"And I just met him for the first time earlier this afternoon."

"He backed your story on the shooting, though," Henshaw observed.

"You mean to say he told the truth."

The marshal shrugged. "It makes no difference to me. Less Pinkertons around can only make life easier on my end."

Braddock smiled at that but dodged the snare. "First time I ever met them, too," he said.

231

"You've had a busy day, then, Mr. Braddock." Switching tacks, he said bluntly, "To the best of my knowledge, there are no federal charges against you."

A thin smile curved Braddock's lips. "To the best of *my* knowledge, that's true."

"The Rangers may have your name in their book, but they don't seem to be looking very hard for you."

"Some of them seem to think the things I do aren't necessarily bad."

"Well, far be it from me to do the Rangers' job if they don't want to do it themselves. Are you sleeping at the Circle H tonight?"

"Reckoned I might stay over here in Liberty if they've got any rooms to rent."

"You shouldn't have a problem there," Henshaw advised. "I'm booked into the Palace, two blocks east of here."

"Sounds pricey on a lawman's salary," Braddock observed.

"Just average," Henshaw corrected him. "They went all out on naming it, but there's no bedbugs, anyway."

"I'll have a look at it," said Braddock, finishing his beer. "After the trip from the border sleeping in a bed sounds like a luxury."

"You want me to, I'll show you where to find it," Henshaw offered.

"Why not?" Braddock said. "But just to have a look. No promises."

"I don't get a commission from the management," Henshaw replied, smiling. "Are you about done here?"

"Lead on. I'll check it out and grab a bite of supper afterward."

Henshaw paid off his tab. "By coincidence, they've

got a fairly decent restaurant across the street, O'Grady's. Serves three squares a day."

"You sound more like a civic booster all the time," Braddock remarked.

"What can I say? The food's good and the price is right," Henshaw replied.

"Meaning they let you eat for free."

"My theory is they like to have a badge around the place from time to time. Makes them feel safer," Henshaw said.

"You never know," said Braddock. "I'm a newcomer in town, but I suspect there's trouble on the way."

IT WAS DUMB LUCK, Frank Mandelbaum supposed, that let him spot two gunmen bringing in the corpses of his fellow Pinkertons, Folger and Webber, just as Mandelbaum was stepping from a barbershop a block north of the sheriff's office.

Seeing them head-down across their saddles had surprised him, knowing as he did that they'd been sent to watch the Circle H, but there was no sign of their team's third member, Zeke Bodine, so Mandelbaum supposed that he had managed to survive somehow. That wasn't Frank's concern, however. His job, once he saw the bodies, was to find out what had happened and report back to his boss in Beaumont with the news.

As to the "what" of it, that much was fairly plain. Instead of simply spying on the Circle H one of the now-dead men—likely Folger, considering his temper and propensity for going off half-cocked sometimes—had likely chosen to accost the riders who had brought them into Liberty to drop them off.

Mandelbaum made a show of dawdling past the windows of a hardware store, watching reflections in the glass as the two new arrivals stopped outside the county sheriff's office and palavered with a pair of lawmen standing there. He recognized the sheriff, Noah Ransom, and had seen the U.S. Marshal standing at his side roughly a month ago, on a prior visit to the local law. The marshal, name of Henshaw, didn't visit frequently, and Frank hoped it was mere coincidence that he was present when Mandelbaum's unlucky colleagues made their last visit to town.

Frank kept an eye on Liberty for Roger Jamison—or, rather, by the order of his boss working for Jamison, Emery Grimm, one of the agency's top men in Texas, known for solving problems that had stymied other detectives before Grimm stepped up to sort things out. In that capacity, keeping a low profile, Frank had collected scraps of information on the Circle H, its owner, and his quest for oil, passing the tidbits on to Beaumont as they came his way.

But two dead Pinkertons . . . well, that was on a whole new level of bad news.

Mandelbaum kept his distance as the escorts for his late compatriots jawed for a while with Sheriff Ransom and the marshal, then he'd casually trailed them to the undertaker's place, where they deposited the stiffs, then moved on to the Lucky Strike saloon. He hadn't followed them inside, too obvious, instead dawdling half a block away while they went in to wet their whistles at the bar. A short time later, Marshal Henshaw turned up on his own and entered the saloon, shortly before one of the Circle H riders—Frank knew his face, but not his name —came out alone.

More time had slipped away, before Henshaw

emerged in company with the gunman whom Frank had never seen before. That one had trouble written on his face, provoking Mandelbaum to guess that he had done the killing earlier, while the other one hung back, stayed out of it. Frank couldn't prove it, but this fellow had that look about him, like he'd buried other men before and didn't let it eat away at him.

Mandelbaum trailed the two men at a distance, saw them go inside the Paradise Hotel after the shooter tied his dun to the hitch rail outside. The best part of a quarter hour passed before the stranger came back out again, this time without the marshal at his side. Frank gave the man a decent lead, then came along behind him on a three-block walk to reach the livery. He came back out after a while, no horse, and started back in the direction of the Paradise, ignoring Frank in his position on the far side of the thoroughfare.

Staying the night, apparently, and that meant Mandelbaum had time for his next task. He moved off toward the Western Union office, knowing he could pick the stranger up again at his hotel if all else failed. The clerk who greeted him inside was in his twenties, with a rash of acne hanging over from his teens.

He perked up at the prospect of a customer and said, "Yes, sir. May I help you?"

"Hopefully," Frank said. "I need to wire someone in Beaumont right away."

5

BEAUMONT, TEXAS

The offices of Standard Oil were located downtown on Pearl Street, one block west of Main. Emery Grimm's office was down the hall from Roger Jamison's, filling the second story's northwest corner, overlooking Bowie Street, named for a hero of the Alamo.

Grimm was a supervisor of the Pinkerton Detective Agency for Jefferson County, assigned to Jamison and Standard Oil for riding herd on three dozen detectives in the field. Each of his men was armed and had a badge that carried no legal authority beyond what Jamison had purchased from the county sheriff's office with hard cash that most observers would have labeled bribes.

Still, that was all a private army needed on the coast where crude oil gushers rivaled the proceeds from any record-setting cattle drives before the latest Texas boom began.

How long that lasted would be anybody's guess, but

Grimm had no more interest in black gold than he possessed for beef, pork, wool, or any other product of the Lone Star landscape. He was in the law enforcement business with a twist, protecting clients of the Eye That Never Slept no matter how they trampled on the laws of man.

It was the same with mining, banking, railroads, pick your poison. Every corporation that he'd ever served while working for the Pinkertons was hip-deep in corruption of some kind, slipping bribes to any politician who could help them, throwing their weight behind contenders if the current officeholders wouldn't fall in line. Today he served one of the nation's rapidly expanding oil producers. Next month or next year he might be hunting members of the Wild Bunch farther west or breaking up some labor union that was threatening the power of an eastern robber baron.

It was all the same to Grimm, as long as it put money in his pocket.

Right now his mind was focused on the Circle H, next door in Liberty County. Roger Jamison was chafing at the lack of progress when it came to getting rid of Lucius Haverstock and Emery was running out of fresh excuses for the failure of his efforts up to now. On top of that, Chicago had been breathing down his neck, wanting results before they lost the Standard Oil account, and Grimm was bound to get the blame for that as well.

He didn't fancy looking for another comparable job at forty-two, if he was cut loose by the Pinkertons, and anyway—

A rapping on his office door distracted Emery. He swung his chair around to face the door and growled, "Who is it?"

"Zeke Bodine, sir."

One of three men who should be watching the Circle H right now.

"Come in!"

Another second and Bodine was standing slump-shouldered before Grimm's desk, his dusty hat in hand.

"Well, spit it out," Grimm snapped. "Why aren't you at your post?"

"Um, Mr. Grimm, sir . . ."

"Spit it out, man!"

"I'm afraid I've got some bad news for you."

"Well? Am I supposed to guess it?"

"No, sir. There's been some trouble at the Circle H."

"What kind of trouble?"

Leaning forward, Grimm felt color rising in his cheeks. An angry pulse was throbbing in his ears.

"Folger and Webber, sir. I'm pretty sure they're dead."

"What do you mean by *pretty sure*?"

"Well, um, I heard some shooting."

"*Heard*? Not *saw*?"

"Arnie told me to hang back in the trees and—"

"Stop right there!" Grimm was already on his feet and striding toward the office doorway. "Come with me," he ordered. "You can tell it to the man himself."

Emery glanced back as he reached the outer hallway and found Boding trailing him, pallid, dragging his feet, as Grimm had seen condemned men trudging toward the gallows.

And in fact, he thought, that image might not be far wrong.

THERE WERE DAYS, since signing on with Standard Oil, when Roger Jamison felt on a par with modern royalty, if such a thing existed in the USA. He represented men of power, wealth, and social stature that he hoped might someday fall within his grasp, exalting him above the lowly status of a lowly oil prospector with a second-rate geology degree from Howard Payne College at Brownwood, up in central Texas.

He had been in the right place, at the right time, when Spindletop erupted and the lords of Standard Oil turned their greedy eyes upon the Lone Star State. Today, seated behind his spacious desk, most people would have viewed him enviously, as a rising star.

But every silver lining had a thunder cloud behind it and today, right now, Jamison thought it a deluge was about to wash his hopes away.

The Western Union telegram had reached him moments earlier, sent by Frank Mandelbaum in Liberty County. One of the Pinkertons Emery Grimm had brought to Beaumont with him, Frank stood out as brighter than the rest and Jamison had chosen him to play a covert role in Liberty, assuming the part of a vacationer with time to kill, money to spend, collecting any gossip that he could about the Circle H and feeding it directly back to Jamison, bypassing Grimm and Pinkerton's chain of command. That was not strictly kosher, but Grimm knew better than to complain.

Now this, the telegram laid out on Jamison's wide desk in front of him.

It read—

Two agents down, Folger and Webber. No sign of the third man on their team.

An unidentified stranger apparently responsible, presumed hired by the Circle H.

Sheriff involved, along with U.S. Marshal for the district. Suspect staying locally.

Advise soonest. F.M.

Two Pinkertons scratched off the payroll and the law was looking into it, of course. Not only Sheriff Ransom, but the federal marshal who had come sniffing around not long ago, asking about suspicious fires and such driving homesteaders off their land in Jefferson County. He'd gone away dissatisfied, getting no useful information out of Jamison, but obviously hadn't given up.

Presumably he had an eye on Gulf Oil's people too, harassing Hal Baker, but that was no great consolation and wouldn't assuage the men from Standard who had chosen Jamison to run their operation out of Beaumont. If their trust in him evaporated . . .

Tapping on his office door drew Roger's thoughts away from Liberty, back to the here and now.

"Enter!" he said.

Emery Grimm was first across the threshold, trailed by someone Jamison suspected he should recognize but couldn't call by name. One of the Pinkertons, no doubt. Grimm prodded his companion with an elbow and said, "Go on and tell your story."

Jamison spoke up before the worried-looking man could start, asking, "Would this be about two dead men of ours in Liberty?"

Both new arrivals in his office gaped at Jamison. The one who'd been about to speak seemed on the verge of passing out before he stammered, "Y-yes, sir."

"I'm not a mind-reader," the boss informed his visitors, lifting the telegram to wave it at them without giving either a chance to read it. "And you weren't the only eyes I have in Liberty."

Grimm blinked at him. Began to say, "You mean—"

"No names!" said Jamison, cutting him off. "Just spill the details of what happened."

Grimm gave his subordinate another poke and fairly spat at him, "That's you."

"Yes, sir," the second Pinkerton began. "The three of us were sent to watch over the Circle H, see who was going in and coming out."

"I know that," Jamison replied. "Get on with it, will you?"

A quick head-bob, then, "Well, we seen a rider going in, a stranger to us, gone about an hour and a half before he came back out again. So Arnie—Folger, that is—rides down to have words with him, taking Doc Webber, and he tells me hang back in the trees—"

"In case something went wrong," said Jamison. "And so it did."

"Yes, sir."

"Which one of them drew first?" he asked the Pinkerton.

"I'd have to say that Arnie did—or tried to, anyhow."

"Then Webber?"

"Yes, sir."

"Which turned out to be the dumbest thing they ever did." Instead of waiting for an answer, since he hadn't asked a question, Jamison pressed on. "All right. Get out of here, the two of you. I'll try to clean this up before it ruins everything for all of us."

When they were slow departing, Jamison pounded a

fist against his desktop. Raised his voice to ask, "Well? What in blazes are you waiting for? Out! Now!"

Another mess for him to rectify, and he would have to clean it up before reporting back to his superiors before they got the notion it was his fault and he ought to be the next dead wood under the axe. There was a way to pull it off, thought Jamison, but it was risky.

Still, what wasn't, nowadays?

ANAHUAC, CHAMBERS COUNTY

Telephones had been in use for eight years now in Texas, and while Harold Baker had one of the county's first receivers in his Gulf Oil office on Hamilton Street, he still wasn't accustomed to the jangling device's shrill demands for his attention during any given working day. It set his teeth on edge, but that was progress, and since no one had his office number but the men who pulled his strings, there was no option to ignore incoming calls.

Baker, known to his doting wife and various wealthy associates as "Hal," had no idea who might be calling him this afternoon, but there was only one way to find out. Frowning, he lifted the bell-shaped receiver from its cradle, leaned in closer to the instrument's mouthpiece, and said, "Hello?"

A faraway voice answered back, "Um, Mr. Baker?"

"Speaking. Who is this?"

"Lemuel Givens, sir, calling from Liberty."

Of course. The Pinkerton his top enforcer, Cletus Crowther, had dispatched on Baker's order to watch over things across the county line.

"Go on," Baker commanded.

"Thought you ought to know, sir, that a couple men from the Circle H brought in two bodies here a while ago. I didn't know 'em personally, but they worked for Standard out of Beaumont."

"And the men who took them down?"

"One of them was a Circle H hand that I've seen in town before," Givens replied. "The other, I can't say. Hard-looking fella, though. I'd guess these aren't the first two men he's bedded down."

"So things are heating up between our friends at Standard Oil and Mr. Haverstock."

"I don't see any other way to figure it, sir. Should I try to stir the pot a bit?"

"Not yet, Lemuel. Watch and wait for now but call me back or get in touch with Clete first thing if there's more trouble."

"Yes, sir. I'll do that. One other thing you ought to know."

"Which is?"

"That U.S. Marshal's back in town. Henshaw, I think his name is."

"Good to know," Baker replied. "You keep your head down now, your eyes wide open. Right?"

"Yes, sir."

The line went dead, a distant humming that indicated Baker's telephone was ready to receive more messages as soon as he hung up.

So, two dead Pinkertons in Liberty, but they were on the Standard Oil payroll, hence no concern of Baker's. It was troublesome, a U.S. Marshal butting in, but Henshaw made a point of roaming up and down the Gulf, sticking his nose in musty corners where it was not welcome. For the moment, he'd be focusing on Roger Jamison in Beaumont, and whatever cramped the competition's style pleased Baker in the long run.

Watch and wait would be his bywords for now, going after other likely properties near Anahuac while he observed events in Liberty from a safe distance. When it came to blows between his Standard Oil competitors and Lucius Haverstock, Baker would see who got the worst of it and find an opening, perhaps to offer reinforcements for the Circle H, or make a deal with whoever Haverstock's heirs turned out to be.

Relaxing in his high-backed swivel chair, Baker remembered that sometimes, in a quandary, the best thing he could do was nothing.

And if action was required he would have time to act decisively, perhaps emerging as the savior of the day.

LIBERTY

G. W. Braddock dined alone, relieved when Marshal Henshaw didn't trail him to O'Grady's restaurant, an easy walk north from the Palace Hotel where he'd booked a second-story room facing the street. A pert red-haired waitress, all smiles and freckles, showed him to a window seat, table for two, and went to fill a mug with coffee while he scanned a menu posted on the wall.

Considering the owner's name, he ordered Irish stew that came with lamb, potatoes, carrots, onions, and fresh parsley in a creamy broth. The bowl was huge, its contents steaming and delicious, with a side order of soda bread to let him savor the last dregs. While eating slowly, savoring his meal, Braddock studied the street traffic outside and picked up nothing that would put him on alert.

Killing two Pinkertons, whether they'd worked for Gulf or Standard Oil, was bound to have its repercussions. Blake Drury's eyewitness account had let him off the hook with Sheriff Ransom, but he wasn't quite so sure of Marshal Henshaw, judging him the kind of lawman who could watch and wait indefinitely for a case to break. If that meant staking Braddock out as bait for anybody craving vengeance, Henshaw seemed the sort who'd make his peace with that and take things as they came, from any side, to deal with strife in his bailiwick.

Braddock had no desire to buck the law, but in his present situation, trying to accommodate Henshaw, much less befriend him, might not be a viable option. As an ex-Ranger, stripped of all legal authority, he naturally raised suspicion—or at least concern—with anyone who still carried a badge.

In fact, by hiring out his services, Braddock knew he walked a fine line between upholding public peace and vigilantism, between protecting persons under siege and serving as a gunfighter for hire. He hadn't drawn a paycheck from the Circle H yet, but had slain two men already, and his ingrained lawman's instinct told him there was more trouble ahead.

The good news: no one on the streets of Liberty appeared to notice Braddock as he left O'Grady's, having paid his tab, and pleased his waitress with a decent tip, yet Braddock still felt—or imagined—that someone was watching him as he returned to his hotel through early evening shadows. He didn't use any of the techniques he'd learned for smoking out surveillance—using storefront windows as a mirror to detect a follower, or doubling back as if he had forgotten something, to surprise a tail—but Braddock knew he would feel better once he'd locked himself inside his second-story bedroom, with a spare Colt and his Winchester ready to hand.

If someone came at him, Braddock was going to be ready, waiting. Neither Sheriff Ransom nor his U.S. Marshal friend—a fellow tenant at the Palace—would find any charge to hang him for that.

"I WIRED my Austin office for information on Braddock," Marshal Henshaw said, lounging across from Sheriff Ransom in a straight-backed chair facing the sheriff's desk. "He's clean, straight as an arrow down the line. His father's still revered among the Rangers, and George Junior would be on the force today if not for legislators angling for political advantage during an election year. The only law he's really broken is letting folks believe he's still a Ranger when it suits his purpose."

Ransom fired up a fresh cheroot. Nodded as he replied, "I know all that. His old man's pretty much a legend anywhere you go in Texas. Best be careful you don't call him 'Junior,' though. It tends to get his back up."

"But he worries you," said Henshaw.

"Sure he does. Only a few hours in my county and he's killed two men already, after I warned him to keep his nose clean."

"Sounds like clear-cut self-defense to me," Henshaw replied. "He's got a witness."

"From the Circle H."

"That's no cause to believe he's lying, in and of itself."

"Proves nothing either way," Ransom countered.

"And that's my point," said Henshaw. "I was with your undertaker when he looked over the two bodies. Clean shots from the front, like you'd expect in any showdown, and the two of them were packing these."

Henshaw leaned forward, tossing four small objects onto Ransom's desk. The sheriff squinted at them, recognized two matching badges from the Pinkerton Detective Agency. The marshal's other offerings were business cards, bearing the signature of William Pinkerton below a plea asking all law enforcement officers to show Pinkerton men "the proper courtesy," whatever that might mean.

Ransom knew that founder Alan Pinkerton, a Scotsman, had succumbed in 1894, though no one seemed to know exactly how or why. There were at least three stories—apoplexy, virulent malaria, or gangrene from an accident where Pinkerton had stumbled on pavement, bit his tongue, and failed to see a doctor afterward. Whatever, sons William and Robert had inherited the agency and were not shy about expanding it, fighting a string of bloody labor battles in the Midwest, chasing Bill Doolin's Oklahoma Long Riders, and following Butch Cassidy around the West in vain. The agency's excesses in the Homestead Strike of 1892 drove Congress to pass an Anti-Pinkerton Act the following year, banning any federal bureau from employing agency "detectives," but that hadn't stopped proliferation of their services to railroads, banks, and such.

"I know their reputation," Ransom granted. "And it worries me as much as Braddock does. I hear about Standard and Gulf putting the squeeze on homesteaders in other counties, if they won't sell out for pennies on the dollar, but it hasn't happened here as far as I can tell, unless you count this afternoon."

"You've spoken to the men in charge?" asked Henshaw.

"Can't do it legally," Ransom replied. "Both live outside my jurisdiction, Jamison over in Beaumont, Baker down in Anahuac. They're friendly with the sheriffs where they live and don't stray far from home."

"I know the sheriffs from my normal rounds," said Henshaw. "Isaac Prentiss covers Jefferson—"

"And Cody Lawson runs the show in Chambers County," Ransom finished for him. "They put on a show of law and order, but neither one's been known to shy away from feathering his nest with what our *federale* friends south of the border call *soborno*."

"Bribery," Henshaw translated Ransom's Spanish into English.

"Nothing I could ever prove in court, of course," Ransom replied. "Not that their county judges would agree to hear the case regardless."

"I might swing by and have a word with them before this thing gets out of hand," Henshaw proposed.

"Your call but leave me out of it. I don't need anybody claiming I've been talking out of school."

"With people dying in my territory, I've got a perfect right to nose around."

Ransom waved toward the objects on his desk. "Nothing here connects those men with either company so far. Word is they've both hired Pinkertons for muscle. The Chicago office doesn't seem to mind as long as Jamison and Baker pay their bills on time."

"That tells me something stinks."

"You'll get no argument from me," Ransom replied. "Now just try proving it."

"Sounds like a challenge," Henshaw answered, smiling. "Care to place a wager?"

248

"On my pay," Ransom scoffed, shaking his head, "I couldn't buy into a penny-ante game."

FRANK MANDELBAUM OPENED the Western Union envelope, removed the telegram inside, and read it silently.

> *Message received. Require that you tie up loose ends before we may proceed.*
>
> *Discretion paramount. Report outcome of cleanup operation soonest. Fail not.*
>
> *R.B.J.*

The signature, such as it was, denoted Roger Bentley Jamison, responding to the wire that Mandelbaum had sent to him in Beaumont earlier that day. Frank didn't need to question Jamison's intent, which seemed as clear to him as daybreak on the Gulf of Mexico.

Jamison wanted whoever had killed the Pinkertons watching the Circle H repaid in kind, eliminated from the scene for good. And in that world, where Jamison served as the face and voice of Standard Oil, his edict had the force of a commandment handed down from God on high.

Or maybe not.

In all his twenty-seven years on Earth, Frank Mandelbaum had never seen Jehovah take a hand in the affairs of men. Conversely, Jamison gave orders that affected many lives—and ended some if they displeased him—seven days a week.

From a sheriff's deputy who always needed extra

cash, Mandelbaum knew the killer's name already. He was one G.W. Braddock, while the man who'd helped him bring the bodies to Liberty was just an onlooker and flunky at the Circle H, a cowpoke by the name of Drury who apparently had seen the killings without playing any part in them himself.

Braddock had a room at Liberty's Palace Hotel, tonight at least, and Frank had spotted Braddock walking from a restaurant back to the Palace through the first long shades of dusk. He had waited in an alley opposite until he saw a lamp lit in a second-story window facing on the street. One last glimpse of his quarry, just as Braddock pulled his curtains shut, confirmed it was the man's room.

From there, all that remained was to complete the deed and vacate Liberty, ride back to Beaumont while some other Pinkerton employed by Standard Oil was sent to take his place as Jamison's sharp eyes and ears around the county seat.

Bearing in mind that Braddock had already killed two of Frank's fellow agents in a stand-up fight—or rather on horseback from what the deputy had spilled— there was no question of a shootout face to face. Mandelbaum reckoned he was fast with a six-gun but only bet money or his life on a sure thing.

In his upstairs room at Martha Jessup's rooming house, after informing his landlady that he would be having supper out, Mandelbaum rummaged in his closet and withdrew a bulky blanket-wrapped parcel. Inside, when he opened it upon the comforter of his small bed, he found a Magazine Lee–Enfield rifle, introduced in 1895, now standard issue for the British army and associated military services. It measured just a fraction under fifty inches, tipped the scale at 9.24 pounds, with ten rounds packed into its integral box magazine.

The Lee-Enfield fired .303 Mk VII ammunition with a maximum range of three thousand yards, and in skilled hands could manage twenty to thirty aimed shots in one minute, though that meant reloading it with five-round stripper clips through the bolt action. For tonight's work, Mandelbaum supposed one or two shots would get it done, the range a trifle under forty yards across the thoroughfare.

Simple.

And when he'd finished, slipping out of Liberty should be no problem with the law tied up examining his handiwork.

He might even receive a bonus from the hand of R. B. J. himself, and some time off in which to spend the extra cash.

6

DESPITE HIS LONG DAY ON HORSEBACK AND UNEXPECTED battle with the Pinkertons, Braddock felt restless as he lay down on his hotel bed and counted knotholes in the ceiling while he tried in vain to fall asleep.

Killing the gunmen who'd been spoiling for a fight didn't disturb him, though he took no pleasure in it. Riding with the Rangers he'd gotten used to fighting for his life. He still carried his former badge but kept it either in his saddlebag or in the pocket on the back of his gunbelt, out of sight, since it didn't give him any legitimate authority.

That hadn't stopped him tracking fugitives and renegades, however, and Braddock had left more than his share in dusty graves without any problems from his conscience.

No, it wasn't any qualms about a double killing in self-defense that made left him sleepless now. Rather, he wondered whether he had wandered inadvertently into a brewing war that was beyond his powers to contain—a clash of titans, as it were, wherein the state and U.S.

governments appeared to have no interest in tactics or the final winners as long as crude oil kept pouring from its subterranean reserves into refineries and from there to fuel both industry and an expanding navy that was bidding to become the strongest military force on Earth.

In bygone days, Great Britain's Royal Navy was a tool of conquest, standing ready to police a global empire over which the sun quite literally never set. During its war with Spain, America had overtaken Britain's battleship construction and surpassed it, with no end in sight, and while the war as recognized in headlines lasted barely sixteen weeks, it still dragged on interminably in the Philippines, where natives fought against replacing Spanish rule with domination by America. Aside from that ongoing battleground, the U.S. had acquired outposts from the Caribbean to the vast Western Pacific Ocean, including Cuba, Puerto Rico, and Guam.

The only way to reach those far-flung islands was by travel over water, and the U.S. Navy had begun converting rapidly from coal to oil for powering its mighty engines, with reliance on domestic oilfields rapidly increasing. Newly inaugurated Vice President Theodore Roosevelt had served for thirteen months as Secretary of the Navy before war propelled him to the forefront as a hero of the "Rough Riders" and put him on the Republican ticket as William McKinley's running mate in 1900. They had triumphed with 52 percent of the popular vote in November, and while Roosevelt was better known for hunting wildlife, storming Spanish forts in Cuba, and struggling to reform New York City's police department, he retained strong interest in the navy almost as an absent father watches over adult children from afar.

So oil was in and coal, while far from fading out of

use, was also taking a back seat in powering domestic energy. Oil seemed to be the future of America and nothing would forestall discovery of more unless the major companies became embroiled in war amongst themselves and forced Congress to intervene somehow.

Meanwhile, Texas had turned into a new frontier where pioneers played by a set of ancient rules, where might made right and money had the final say, backed up by guns.

Who was it that declared, "The more things change, the more they stay the same?"

Some foreigner, Braddock suspected, though he neither knew nor cared just now. It was the sentiment—and its inherent accuracy—that had placed him on another firing line with only two ways out. He could quit the contest and depart without drawing his first paycheck from the Circle H, or he could forge ahead and see what happened next.

And to the one-time Texas Ranger, that was no real choice at all.

Still sleepless, he decided that a shot of red-eye might help tip the balance toward slumber. Rising from bed, his room's sole lamp still burning, Braddock crossed to the free-standing wardrobe where his saddlebags hung suspended from a wooden peg. Rummaging inside one, he retrieved a pint bottle of Old Overholt rye whisky, took a hefty sip that lit a fire inside him, then replaced the bottle and retraced his steps toward bed.

He'd traveled half that distance when the window to his left shattered, spraying him with broken glass.

THE LEGAL FIRM of Chase and Houser occupied a plain two-story building directly across from the Palace Hotel. The structure's second floor was storage, and while it was shorter than the Palace its flat roof was on a level with the hotel's second-story rooms facing the thoroughfare.

Frank Mandelbaum had scouted the location after trailing Braddock to his lodgings, noting that a ladder bolted to the law firm's eastward-facing wall served double duty as roof access and a fire escape of sorts for anybody stranded on the second floor if flames broke out.

Tonight he thought the roof would serve him just fine as a sniper's roost.

Moving through town along back streets and alleyways, bearing the Magazine Lee-Enfield rifle in its wrapping underneath one arm, Mandelbaum took advantage of the dinner hour and full darkness settling over Liberty. He'd reached the legal offices and scaled their ladder without being seen by anyone except a slat-ribbed street dog gnawing scraps in back of Weissman's butcher shop along the way. Frank got along with dogs all right and this one hadn't given him a second look after it realized he didn't plan to filch its meal.

Now, kneeling of the roof with gritty tar paper beneath him, he removed his long-range weapon from its covering and peered along its barrel toward the second-story hotel window he had marked as Braddock's room. The place was dark so far, but it was early evening and Frank had time to spare.

The Lee-Enfield had sliding ramp rear sights, a fixed-post at the business end, the combination known to shooters as a "buckhorn" setup. To adjust the rear sight for a long shot would require a screwdriver, but Mandelbaum had judged his distance in advance and satisfied himself with the arrangement prior to leaving Martha Jessup's rooming house. All he required now was a target and a light inside the hotel room to help him find his mark.

A long half hour passed and he was getting antsy when the lamp came on behind thin linen drapes. Frank guessed that Braddock must be restless on his first night in a new town, having killed two men already and assuming that there would be more to come.

On that score, anyway, the former Texas Ranger was mistaken.

This was meant to be his final night on Earth.

Frank raised the British rifle to his shoulder, pressed his cheek against its polished walnut stock, peered down its thirty-inch barrel, and willed himself into a state of relaxation, focused on his respiration rate as much as on the window opposite.

If Braddock only showed himself . . .

There!

But the man was quicker than Frank had expected, moving from the sniper's left to right and out of range. Mandelbaum mouthed a silent curse and waited, trying not to think of what Braddock was doing in the room behind those drapes, waiting for him to cross back toward his waiting bed.

And there he was again.

Frank sighted on the moving shadow, tried to lead it by a fraction, tightening his index finger on the trigger, taking up the slack. The MLE—dubbed "Emily" by British troops—kicked back against his shoulder and he racked the bolt-action instinctively, prepared to fire a second shot if it should be required.

Or had he dropped Braddock the first time out?

The answer to that question, when it came, was in the form of an orange muzzle-flash from Braddock's window, angled more or less toward Mandelbaum's point of concealment. Frank felt the wind-rip of the heavy slug as it breezed past his face and knew in that moment that he wouldn't get a second chance.

Cursing aloud this time, he scurried backward toward the ladder, rifle clutched in one hand and its blanket thrown over his shoulder, running for his life.

MARSHAL JONAS HENSHAW was a light sleeper, roused from an instantly-forgotten dream by gunfire close at hand. Instinctively he rolled from bed in his third-story hotel room and landed on the floor, his pistol already in his fist.

It took another moment for him to confirm that neither shot had been directed his way. Edging toward the window, he nudged back a curtain with his gun's barrel and peered down toward the street. He was in time to see G.W. Braddock burst from the hotel's front doorway, wearing jeans over long underwear and carrying a rifle in his hands.

"Damn it!"

Henshaw scrambled to snatch his own trousers, felt precious time escaping from him as he slipped his head and right arm through his buckled gun belt, draping it across his torso like an awkward shoulder holster. Bursting from his room as other tenants stirred around him, he didn't bother to lock his door, sprinted to reach the stairs, and hammered down them, gasping air and thinking he was in no shape for a prolonged footrace.

Not that he had a choice.

Night clerk Jack Tatum, watching Henshaw pass him in a sprint, the hotel's door still yawning open from George Braddock's exit, shouted at him, "Marshal, what the—?" but Henshaw was outside before he heard the rest Tatum's question and had no spare time to answer it.

Braddock had disappeared already, likely down an alleyway that ran between a law firm opposite and a dress shop for women who were disinclined to sew their own at home. Taking a gamble, Henshaw crossed the street and ducked into the alley, slowing his pace there as he moved through brooding shadows, almost tripping over an ill-tempered cat he had interrupted in its nightly search for mice.

The feline snarled and hissed at him as Henshaw edged along the alleyway and exited into another street with homes ranked boxlike, side by side. Off to his right, a scuttling movement caught his eye as Braddock ran around another corner, elbows pumping in his haste.

Who was he chasing? Who had fired the first shot of this skirmish in the dark?

Henshaw knew it would likely be connected to the Pinkertons Braddock had slain that afternoon, but guessing games were futile until he could clap eyes on the other shooter in this running gunfight.

As he labored toward the corner where he'd last seen Braddock, another gunshot split the night, then again after a four- or five-second delay. Dead silence followed that, and Henshaw knew that he was probably too late to interrupt another killing as he picked up speed.

He only hoped that he was not about to find G.W. Braddock lying dead.

BRADDOCK GLIMPSED his moving target as the gunman ran around a corner without looking back. He might have winged the sniper at that distance with his Winchester but couldn't take the risk of missing him and injuring or killing some innocent citizen of Liberty.

As he approached the corner, Braddock wondered if the hotel shooting had alerted Marshal Henshaw, or if Jonas had been elsewhere when it happened, maybe stopping off at one of the saloons in town or huddling with Sheriff Ransom at the latter's office. Either way, if any more shots were discharged, it was a safe bet someone would be sounding an alarm before much longer.

At the corner, Braddock hesitated, half expecting to be ambushed if he showed himself, but knowing that he could waste the whole night waiting where he was and let his would-be killer slip away. Rejecting that alternative, he cocked his rifle, sank into a crouch, and swung around the corner, dropping to one knee, prepared to fire at the first sign of opposition from an enemy.

Nothing.

No, he corrected that impression as he glimpsed a shadow-shape hurdling a picket fence down range, nearly two blocks ahead of him, and barging into someone's yard. Furious barking from at least one watchdog drove the runner back, kicking his way straight through the wooden fence this time and into Braddock's line of fire.

The Winchester bucked once and Braddock pumped its lever-action, chambering a fresh round as his target staggered, reeling, clutching at his left side as if wounded. Still, the man refused to drop and kept on going, though the pace was slowed considerably and his left leg dragged behind him as if each step sent pain jolting through him.

Braddock knew he could drop the sniper then but held his fire. He wanted answers, knowing that Ransom and Henshaw would demand the same. Attempted murder in the county seat was sheriff's business first and foremost. Marshal Henshaw would be left to follow any leads that led to other jurisdictions. Tracking down that evidence might be facilitated by a living witness, while a dead one could be written off as any one of countless enemies who bore a grudge against Braddock from bygone days.

But failing that . . .

Braddock was following the wounded shooter from a half-block back, ready for anything, when suddenly the stranger spun around and raised his own long gun as if to fire. Ready and waiting, Braddock beat him to it, trying for a shoulder wound that would prevent his adversary from succeeding in his murder mission, but between his tension and the night's dark shadows, the ex-Ranger couldn't call the hit precisely.

As it was, his target vaulted backwards, lost his rifle as it spun from nerveless fingers, and collapsed onto the unpaved residential street. He shivered once, a final tremor of departing life that Braddock clearly recognized, and then lay still.

Braddock closed in, still wary just in case it was a bluff, some kind of last-ditch ruse, but as he stood over the gunman it was clear his enemy wouldn't be sharing any information with the local law or anybody else, this side of Judgment Day.

The shot intended for his shoulder had been off just an inch or two, and from the quantity of blood in evidence had likely snipped one of the arteries located in his throat or upper chest, turning his face into a dripping crimson mask.

Movement behind Braddock brought him around, Winchester leveled from the hip, relaxing when he recognized Deputy U.S. Marshal Henshaw. Glancing back and forth between Braddock and the corpse at his feet, Henshaw inquired, "You know this fellow?"

Braddock shook his head, replied, "I've never seen him in my life before tonight."

"DID YOU HEAR THAT?" asked Noah Ransom.

Deputy Joe Pilcher, reading something in a magazine sent out bimonthly by the state Sheriff's Association, raised his doughy face and answered with a question of his own. "Hear what?"

"A gunshot, maybe," Ransom offered.

"Close or far?"

"I couldn't tell you, but—"

There was no doubt about the second shot, its echo battered back and forth between various buildings before reaching Ransom's ears.

Pilcher closed up his magazine. "Could be one of the saloons."

Ransom frowned at that, thinking the first shot seemed more like a rifle's *crack*, the second like a pistol's bark, and who carried a long gun into any barroom unless he was loco in the first place.

Rising, settling his Colt more comfortably on his hip, the sheriff said, "We'd better check it out."

"Wanna split up?"

"Not this time," Ransom said. "I'm thinking we should check the Palace Hotel first."

"Why there?" asked Pilcher.

"That's where Braddock's staying."

"Guy who shot them Pinkertons?" Pilcher was on his feet now, flicking nervous glances toward the office door.

"One and the same," Ransom replied.

"Why him, Sheriff?"

"Said it yourself. Because he shot two Pinkertons this afternoon. The others won't take kindly to a thing like that."

"You think they'd try something in Liberty?"

"Won't know until we check it out. Come on."

Ransom sensed a peculiar reticence from Pilcher that he'd never seen before whether it came to breaking up a brawl in one of Liberty's saloons or backing Ransom's play against a fugitive wanted for rape and murder. Shrugging off the feeling, Ransom grabbed a rifle from the gun rack on the wall behind his desk and started for the street while Pilcher took a double-barreled twelve gauge.

Whatever they found, and wherever they found it, Ransom thought they ought to have it covered now.

Jack Tatum met them on the wooden sidewalk running past the Palace Hotel, fidgeting, wringing his hands, as if he were an anxious would-be father waiting on the birth of twins. He rushed to meet them, jabbering so fast that Ransom had to raise a hand and urge him to slow down.

Tatum told the two lawmen what he knew, although it wasn't much. At least two gunshots fired, one into the hotel, the other from an upstairs room that he assumed was occupied by Mr. Braddock, since the man ran out moments later, through the lobby and across the street. He hadn't seen where Braddock went from there or who he was pursuing, but the clerk directed Ransom and his deputy as far as he was able, toward a corner where the chase had turned off to the left.

"Come on!" the sheriff snapped at Pilcher. "Pray that we catch up to them before somebody else gets killed."

"Pray, right." The deputy's echo was glum and held out little promise of an answer from Above.

THE SOUND of footsteps coming toward him on the run made Braddock turn, his rifle cocked and braced against his hip. Beside him, Marshal Henshaw held his Colt steady, prepared to deal with any hostile new arrivals on the scene.

Instead, Braddock saw Sheriff Ransom jogging toward them, followed closely by a deputy he didn't recognize. The local lawmen pulled up short, Ransom raising an open hand, asking Braddock and his companion from a distance, "Someone want to tell me what the shooting's all about?"

"It's your story," said Henshaw, leaving Braddock to explain.

"Someone took a potshot at me through my hotel window," Braddock said, keeping it brief. "He missed and so did I, returning fire. I hit the street in time to see him run this way and winged him, slowed him down enough to make him turn around. He clearly didn't plan on giving up. I tried to shoot the rifle from his hand but you know how it is, Sheriff. That hardly ever works."

"So now it's three dead," Ransom answered.

Henshaw interrupted, said, "You'll note his rifle, Noah. It's some kind of foreign military piece and it still smells of being fired."

263

"Okay, I get it," Ransom answered grudgingly. "Another case of self-defense. I don't suppose this was the third man from your set-to earlier this afternoon?"

"Can't answer that," Braddock replied. "It's like I said before, I never saw the one who got away."

"Well, can you think of any other reason he might try to kill you?"

"I might have one," Henshaw interjected, holding up a badge stamped with the Pinkerton identifying name. "I found this in his vest pocket."

"Well, damn!" The sheriff's shoulders sagged as if a sudden weight had settled on them from above.

Behind Ransom, his deputy coughed nervously, clearing his throat, and said in a small voice, "It might be that I recognize him, Noah."

Ransom turned on his subordinate. "Might be? You wanna clear that up for me, Joe?"

"Well . . . I've seen him around Liberty." Another nervous hesitation, then, "Fact is, I talked to him a couple times, I guess."

"You *guess*?" Ransom's voice was a whiplash now.

"Okay, boss," Pilcher said, staring down at his boots as if he wished the ground would open up and swallow him. "I ran into him one night, making my rounds of the saloons. Told me his name's Frank Mandelbaum—or *was*, I guess. Said we were both in the same line of business, him being a Pinkerton and all."

"Just passing time, shooting the breeze." Ransom's obvious disbelief was withering.

"Until this afternoon, that it," his deputy replied.

"You want to spit it out, or do you need a jailhouse cot to sleep on while you think about it, Joe?"

"After the shooting at the Circle H today, I saw him on the street. He asked some questions about *him*"—

nodding toward Braddock — "asking who he was, if he was staying overnight in Liberty, that kinda thing."

"And I suppose you helped him out with that?"

"I didn't see no harm in it."

"You being fellow lawmen, right?"

"I guess."

"How much?" Ransom demanded.

"Huh?"

"Don't clam up on me now," the sheriff said. "I'm guessing that he must have paid you something, or you're just so dumb you pass out information to whoever stops you on the street. And that makes *me* the fool for ever hiring you."

"Cost of a beer or two, is all," Pilcher replied. He sounded like a broken man.

Ransom relieved the deputy of his tin star and pistol. Told him, "Go back to the office now and wait for me, while I fetch Eulon Wells. You even *think* about absconding, Joe. You try it and I'll hunt you down and drop you where you stand."

"No, sir. I got no place to go." Pilcher seemed on the verge of weeping now.

"That's where you're wrong, boy. You go straight to jail."

Braddock could almost sympathize with Pilcher as he turned away, dragging his feet back toward the office where he was no longer an employee, but a prisoner.

Almost.

But thinking how he'd nearly died tonight, over the price of watered beer, his sympathy evaporated in an instant, turning into bitter gall.

7

Before depositing the late Frank Mandelbaum with Eulon Wells to seek out next of kin and plan his burial, Sheriff Ransom and Marshal Henshaw had gone through the dead man's pockets and retrieved a telegram dispatched to Mandelbaum from Western Union's office in Beaumont.

Braddock and Henshaw now sat facing Ransom in a mismatched pair of chairs while ex-Deputy Pilcher watched and listened from a nearby cell, while the sheriff read that telegram aloud for all to hear.

"It says, 'Message received. Require that you tie up loose ends before we may proceed. Discretion paramount. Report outcome of cleanup operation soonest. Fail not.' The sender signs off, 'R. B. J.'"

"Well, that's no mystery at least," said Henshaw. "Roger Jamison runs things for Standard Oil along the Gulf from offices in Beaumont."

Ransom swung his swivel chair around to face Pilcher. "Joe, looks like you stepped in something smelly this time. Bribery and dereliction of your duty was enough to get you sixty days, but now we've got conspiracy to murder."

"Hold on, now!" said Pilcher, lunging to his feet from where he had been sitting on a cot. "Frank never told me what he had in mind, and that's God's honest truth."

"You want to blaspheme," Ransom chided, "go ahead. Lucky for you, state law won't tack on any extra prison time for that, but I can't speak for the Almighty."

"Come on, Sheriff! Noah, this is *me*!"

"And I'm fed up with hearing you," Ransom shot back. "You'd best shut up and hope I don't forget to fetch you breakfast in the morning."

Braddock watched the sheriff turn from Pilcher, facing Henshaw and himself. "Jonas," Ransom went on, "let's say you're right about this wire coming from Jamison. I won't dispute it, but we all know I can't lay a finger on him over there in Jefferson County."

Braddock chimed in, saying, "There's bound to be a judge in Beaumont."

Ransom snorted. "Sure there is. Old Truman Beck. He's crooked as a sidewinder and halfway senile, but the boys with money like him. It's a toss-up whether he or Sheriff Prentiss pocket more in bribes. He'll laugh you out of court on a good day."

"And on a bad one?" Braddock asked.

"He likely won't remember why he's there, himself."

Jonas Henshaw leaned forward. "Before we all throw up our hands and say there's nothing to be done, I'll take a run at Jamison."

Ransom lit one of his acrid cheroots and answered, "Well, at least you've got due jurisdiction, if he's plotting crimes across the county line."

"And maybe something more than that," Henshaw replied.

"Such as?" the sheriff asked.

"Maybe the Sherman Antitrust Act. Congress passed it back in 1890, banning what they call restraint of trade, price fixing and the like."

That put a frown on Braddock's face. "I may be wrong," he said. "The Rangers took no part in that while I was with them, but as I recall that only covers trade between two states or countries."

"Lawyer talk," said Henshaw, "and it might not stick in court, but maybe I can make this R. B. J. think twice before he orders killings in another county where he's not protected by a paid-off sheriff."

"And suppose he doesn't scare?" Ransom inquired. "Suppose he laughs it off? What, then?"

"I take a run at Austin," Henshaw answered. "Show my boss the evidence and let him pass the case along to Washington if he's afraid of acting on his own. Another way, maybe convince the Rangers that it's worth a closer look."

"They're spread thin as it is," Braddock advised. "And if you're trusting Charlie Bell to sic them onto Standard Oil, don't bet on it. He gets more headlines when they're chasing Indians or Mexican outlaws."

"Don't sell me short before I give it a try," Henshaw advised.

"No, sir," Braddock replied. "I wouldn't dream of it."

"And while we're on the subject," Ransom interjected, "we might have an unexpected ace laid by."

"What's that?" asked Braddock.

Ransom cocked his head toward Pilcher behind bars. "A witness under lock and key," he said.

"Witness!" The cashiered deputy was on his feet again, clutching the bars in front of him. "Witness to *what*, I'd like to know? I told you everything already, Noah. That's God's honest truth!"

"Maybe it is," Ransom allowed. "Or maybe you'll remember something else after you've had some time to sleep on it."

"Like what?" Pilcher demanded.

"How should I know?" Ransom made no effort to disguise his tone of mockery. "Conspiracy to murder buys you ten to fifteen years behind the walls at Huntsville Prison, Joe. Convicts don't get a lot of former deputies to play with. You should make a lot of friends up there."

"Noah—"

"It's 'Sheriff Ransom' when you speak to me from now on, Joe."

"Sheriff, I swear to you, I don't know any more than what I've said." Pilcher sounded as if he might be on the verge of tears.

Ransom allowed himself a shrug. "That may be true. I might even believe you, Joe, but how can Roger Jamison be sure of that, sitting behind his desk over in Beaumont? He'll be getting worried soon. And when *he* worries, you can bet his Pinkertons will hear about it."

"Sheriff, what are you doing to me?" Pilcher whined.

"Not a thing, Joe," Ransom answered. "Not one thing at all. I figure other folks will take care of that . . . depending on how this business plays out."

BEAUMONT, JEFFERSON COUNTY

"You know, you didn't have to tag along," said Marshal Henshaw as they crossed the city limits.

"Let's say I got tired of sitting around Liberty," Braddock replied.

"We could be riding straight into a hornet's nest."

"I've managed to survive a sting or two," said Braddock. "What's your plan for bracing Jamison?"

"My badge should get me in the door. Beyond that I'll just question him and see how he responds."

"And if he won't?"

"There's only three ways he can go: admit, deny, or call a lawyer in and try to stonewall me."

"I doubt that he'll admit to anything," Braddock advised.

"Same here. If he denies a link to Mandelbaum, I've got the telegram to wave under his nose. If he falls back on a lawyer, I may have to pester old Judge Beck and let him know storm clouds are gathering."

"I'd love to be a fly on that wall," Braddock said.

"Can't help you there," Henshaw replied. "At best you're an intended victim with no standing in the case unless you plan on suing Jamison."

"Now there's a thought," said Braddock, smiling.

"Just remember who'd likely be ruling on that matter."

"Truman Beck. Who else?"

"I think it's best if you lie low while we're in Beaumont," Henshaw offered. "Chances are that no one on the Standard payroll has researched your background yet, much less fixing your face in mind."

"Guess I'll grab dinner, then, or plant myself in some saloon."

"Back to the wall," Henshaw suggested. "Just in case."

"I never sit in public any other way," Braddock replied.

"I'd say that's wise, all things considered."

Beaumont was a significantly larger town than Liberty, double the former's area, its population roughly ten times greater, although Liberty was four years older counting back to its founding date. It was no surprise to Braddock that the man in charge of Standard Oil's prospecting on the Gulf would choose it for his headquarters. A major bonus would be its proximity to Spindletop, barely five miles to the southwest, and to Louisiana on the east, where avid drillers were expecting gushers any time now.

When they reached the Standard Oil building on Pearl Street, Braddock left Henshaw and rode another block to reach The Gusher, a saloon and gambling house whose upstairs balcony, he guessed, might grant a long view of the winding Neches River, the dividing line between Jefferson County and Louisiana's steaming bayous.

Reining his dun in to hitch it at a rail with easy access to a water trough, Braddock dismounted, stepped onto the raised boardwalk, and cast a backward glance at Marshal Henshaw as he disappeared through double doors beneath a sign that simply gave a street number, without naming the company with offices inside.

Before he pushed in through The Gusher's batwing doors, he wished his traveling companion well and wondered when—or if—they'd meet again.

Would Roger Jamison try anything inside his own headquarters, during normal business hours, much less with a lawman? Braddock doubted it, but still could not be positive. Before they'd parted, Henshaw had agreed to come and find him at The Gusher but had no clear idea how long his unscheduled meeting with the oilman might go on. On the off chance that Jamison was out somewhere and unavailable, they planned to overnight at some hotel or rooming house nearby and try again tomorrow morning, after breakfast.

Braddock had been through Beaumont on several occasions, in his Ranger days, and knew the city's layout fairly well, though it had obviously grown by leaps and bounds since his last visit. As a rule, he felt more comfortable in a smaller settlement, or even camped out on the prairie, than in crowded towns where bustling people vied for sidewalk space.

Dallas and Houston, with their tens of thousands, always made him feel hemmed-in and short of breathing room. Even the Texas capital at Austin, half the size of Houston or "Big D," seemed cloying on the rare occasions when he'd visited on Ranger business, back before the state had cut him loose. Now that he'd spent most of his time the past few years in the Mexican village of Esperanza, big cities really did give him the fantods.

Suddenly anxious for a drink or three, he navigated through The Gusher's smoky atmosphere to find a place against the bar.

DEPUTY MARSHAL HENSHAW made his way upstairs, following small signs that directed him to the third floor. A husky bouncer type had tried to intercept him in the lobby but thought better of it when he spotted Henshaw's badge and tied-down Colt, together with the grim look of determination on his face. While Henshaw climbed the stairs, the other scuttled off somewhere, presumably to warn his masters through some kind of speaking tube or telephone connection.

Let the games begin, thought Henshaw as he reached

the building's top floor, following signs that pointed him toward MANAGEMENT.

When he was halfway down a walnut-paneled hallway, counting off the numbered doors, one opened in front of him. A well-dressed man of thirty-some-odd years emerged, wearing a strained smile on his pink clean-shaven face. The left side of his tailored jacket bulged slightly from what Henshaw supposed must be a compact shoulder holster.

"Marshal, can I help you?" he inquired, confirming Henshaw's guess about communication from the ground floor.

"Not unless you're Roger Jamison," Henshaw replied, moving to step around the human obstacle.

The younger man shifted a bit, again blocking the corridor. "No, sir, but I believe he's occupied just now."

"I'll wait," said Henshaw, stepping forward more aggressively.

"If I may introduce myself, Marshal . . ."

"Suits me, if you can do it walking."

That wiped off the phony smile at last. "I represent the Pinkerton Detective Agency and speak for Mr. Jamison."

"Is he a mute?"

"What? No, sir. As his legal representative."

"You've been to law school, then?" asked Henshaw. "If I step into your office, will I find a sheepskin hanging on the wall?"

"No, sir. I've just explained—"

"That you're some kind of private snoop, or maybe muscle. Either way, it cuts no ice with me."

That brought a tinge of color to the other's cheeks. Catching himself before he answered back too angrily, the Pinkerton stuck out a hand and introduced himself. "Emery Grimm. And you are . . . ?"

"Marshal Jonas Henshaw, going in to see your boss now."

They had reached the final third-floor office. Henshaw barged in without knocking, Jamison's hired interceptor on his heels, and found himself inside a spacious waiting room. A pretty secretary glanced up from her paperwork, appearing flustered by the sudden presence of a stranger in her bailiwick.

"Excuse me, gentlemen," she said, then recognized Grimm bringing up the rear. "Is there a problem, Mr. Grimm?" she asked, bypassing Henshaw.

"I'd say so," the marshal answered, moving past her desk to open one last door, invading what he took to be the inner sanctum of the man who he'd come looking for.

Roger Jamison was rising from behind his desk as Marshal Henshaw entered, trailed by Grimm. The Pinkerton seemed on the verge of offering an explanation when Henshaw raised a warning hand to silence him.

Half turning, Henshaw told his shadow, "You can take a walk now, sonny."

Glaring past him, Grimm addressed his boss. "Sir, if you need assistance—"

"I know where to find you, Emery. Leave us."

The door closed softly at his back and Henshaw moved to take a seat before the oilman's desk, not waiting for an invitation to sit down.

Jamison settled in his swivel chair before saying, "I'll need to see your warrant, Marshal . . . ?"

"Henshaw. And we both know I don't need court paperwork for simply asking questions."

"I believe—"

"Feel free to call your lawyer if you like," said Henshaw, talking over Jamison. "I'm not here to arrest you, search your office, or make off with any files."

One eyebrow raised, Jamison said, "In that case, may I ask what brings you here?"

"You may indeed," Henshaw replied. "I've come from Liberty, across the county line, where three men met their maker yesterday."

"Three men, you say?" The number seemed to take him by surprise.

"Three Pinkerton detectives, like your watchdog out there in the waiting room."

"I'm sure I don't know—"

Good at interrupting when it helped him, Henshaw butted in once more. "The first two, as I understand it, may have worked for you, watching the Circle H and stopping visitors."

"*May have?*" Jamison fairly sneered the words. "If you have any proof of that—"

"They're on the undertaker's books in Liberty as Arnie Folger and Doc Webber, actual first name unknown as yet. Ring any bells?"

"I can't say that they do," the oilman answered back.

"And how about Frank Mandelbaum?"

That caused a moment's hesitation, then a frown. "Again, I'd have to say—"

"Save it," Henshaw suggested. "I already know he took his orders from you."

"Oh? It's news to me."

Smiling, Henshaw withdrew the Western Union telegram that last night's ambusher had been carrying. "Turns out he wasn't smart enough to burn this message that you sent him yesterday."

"*I* sent? Marshal . . ."

Henshaw held up a hand for silence and began to read the telegram aloud. "You wrote, 'Message received. Require that you tie up loose ends before we may proceed. Discretion paramount. Report outcome of cleanup operation soonest. Fail not.'"

"And you say that came from me, allegedly?"

"Unless you know somebody else with the initials R. B. J."

Jamison's voice was stiff as he replied, "May I see that?"

"Maybe in court," said Henshaw.

"Court, is it?"

Henshaw took his time folding the telegram and putting it away. "I'm not sure what to charge you with just yet, which is the reason that I haven't bothered with a warrant."

"Charge me?" Jamison could do a decent imitation of a parrot when he tried.

"Your Mr. Mandelbaum ran out of luck last night, after he tried to kill a fellow who works for Lucius Haverstock, the owner of the Circle H."

"And you contend that I put him up to it?"

"Unless you've got another handy explanation for 'Require that you tie up loose ends,' after the man he tried to ambush killed your other Pinkertons."

"This is preposterous! No judge in Texas would believe that accusation."

"Maybe not, particularly if you've paid them off. My other angle would be charging you under the Sherman Act."

"And what have I monopolized, exactly, Marshal?"

"Glad to see you don't play dumb on what the law's about. That means you *also* know it doesn't say you have to have an actual monopoly in place, just that you're making various illegal moves in that direction."

Rising, Jamison said stiffly, "I believe we're finished here."

"For now, maybe," Henshaw replied. "But if you're half as smart as I suspect, you'll lay off Haverstock and any other land grabs that you might be working on. Or maybe hire a better class of bushwhackers who can get the job done without making such a mess. I'll find my own way out for now, but I suspect we'll meet again."

JAMISON GAVE the lawman time to clear the premises, then punched the button underneath his desk to buzz for his enforcer. Grimm arrived a moment later, still red-faced and trying to apologize for letting Henshaw past him until his employer raised a manicured hand to shut him up.

"We'll talk about that later," he assured the agitated Pinkerton detective. "Did you follow him from here?"

"Yes, sir. He took his horse and went across the street, into The Gusher. Met another man inside there, at the bar."

"Another marshal?"

Grimm responded with a head-shake. "No, sir. Or at least, if so, he didn't bother putting on a badge today."

"Describe him," Jamison commanded, frowning as his underling did so. When Grimm was done, he asked, "That sound like anyone you know?"

A moment of consideration, then another negative shake of the agent's head. "No, sir."

Jamison had a flash of inspiration then. "But maybe

someone poor Frank Mandelbaum could name for us, if he was still alive."

"Frank's dead, sir?" Emmett truly sounded shocked now.

"As a doornail," Jamison replied. "Got himself killed in Liberty last night, which brought the marshal to my door."

"How's that, sir?"

"He was stupid, Mr. Grimm. A blockhead if you must know."

Blinking, Emery replied, "Sir, I don't follow you."

"Consider this. I ordered him to deal with whoever it was that put away our watchdogs on the Circle H. Do you remember that?"

"Yes, sir. Of course." Looking embarrassed now.

"Well, he botched that, for starters. Got his orders turned around somehow and wound up dead himself. Worse yet, the marshal found my telegram still in his pocket, telling him to tie up the loose ends in Liberty."

"That doesn't mean—"

Jamison cut him off. "It's clear enough to anyone with half a brain. So now I've got a U.S. Marshal sniffing up my backside, threatening to file some charge or other, maybe tie us up in court for months on end. Do you think our investors will appreciate that, Emery?"

"No, sir!"

"You got that right. We have to put a stop to this before it gathers steam and leaves us staring down an empty track."

"Just tell me what you need, sir, and I'll get it done."

"First thing, I want a tail on Marshal Henshaw and his drinking partner. Find out where they go from here, whether it's back to Liberty, the Circle H, or all the way to Austin."

"Yes, sir. And . . .?"

"And put an end to this damned foolishness. I never want to hear of them again unless I'm reading their obituaries."

"Yes, sir! If there's something else . . ."

"There is, but I'll take care of that myself," said Jamison.

"If I can be of any help, sir . . ."

"Not this time. I'm going to explain this situation to Hal Baker down in Anahuac."

Grimm's eyes narrowed at hearing that. "Baker. But sir, he's—"

"Standard's opposition," Jamison cut in. "I know that, Emery. But you know that old line about how misery loves company?"

"I've heard it said, sir."

"I surmise that Baker doesn't want the U.S. Marshals Service butting in on what we're doing down here anymore than I do."

"I guess not, sir."

"And if he should lend a hand in dealing with the problem, strictly in his own best interest, let us say, perhaps he'll draw attention from our operation, back onto himself."

Jamison saw the essence of his plan sink in with Grimm, bringing a cautious smile onto the Pinkerton detective's face. "Yes, sir. It might, at that."

"I'm thrilled that you approve," Jamison said dryly. "Now kindly get your people mounted up before we lose Henshaw and whoever his partner is."

"Yes, sir! Right now!"

"But under no conditions make a move against them until we know where they're headed and who else they're dealing with, if anyone."

"No, sir. I'll make that crystal-clear."

"And Emery? For God's sake don't write any of this down."

"No, sir."

Once Grimm was gone, Jamison reached for his telephone. He had Hal Baker's number memorized, although they'd only spoken once before, and then in abstract terms regarding oil that Lucius Haverstock was pumping from the Circle H.

With any luck, Jamison thought, he might just turn the marshal's visit to his own advantage, killing two birds—make that *four*—with but a single stone.

ANAHUAC, CHAMBERS COUNTY

Hal Baker glowered at the telephone as it began to jangle on his desk. He was no enemy of progress, wouldn't have been toiling long and hard for Gulf Oil otherwise, but there were moments—such as this one—when he wished the future could be postponed.

Drawing the instrument closer across his polished desktop, Baker lifted the receiver to his ear and spoke into the mouthpiece. "Yes?"

Give nothing up for free had been his rule in life since he was old enough to turn a dollar on his own. Baker saw no reason to ditch it just because some new-fangled device tried to control his life.

"Harold?" a male voice answered down the line.

He recognized it instantly. First thing, incoming calls were few and far between, most of them emanating from Gulf's founding headquarters in Pittsburgh and the rest from Baker's local agents in the field. Second, because it was the very first time he'd received a phone call from his competition, what he naturally thought of as an enemy.

"Well, glory be!" Hal answered back. "What have I done to rate an interruption from the high and mighty Roger Jamison? Trouble in paradise, R. B.?"

He pictured Jamison behind his own desk, a couple dozen miles to the northeast, a pinched frown on his face. "You've heard, then?" Jamison inquired, sounding a tad surprised.

Baker leaned back into his leather-covered chair, affecting nonchalance. Give nothing up until you knew what it would cost you, versus what you stood to gain.

"Heard what?" he asked.

"Oh, so you *don't* know, then?"

"Roger, I've got a desk piled high and deep with paperwork," Baker lied, scanning the barren plateau of mahogany in front of him. "I don't have any time to spare for guessing games."

"Sorry to bother you, old friend," said Jamison. "If you already know about the U.S. Marshal sniffing around oil prospecting on the coast . . ."

"What U.S. Marshal?" Baker asked, then nearly cursed himself for sounding overeager.

"Jonas Henshaw."

Baker felt himself relax a bit. "I've heard of him," he granted. "Works the Gulf counties, the last I heard."

"That's him, all right."

"So, what about him?"

"I just had him in my office, making noise about indictments, some damned thing."

That put a narrow smile on Baker's face. "Indicting you? On what charge, Roger? Won't that be embarrassing?"

"Plenty of that to go around," said Jamison. "He's making noise about big companies trying to squeeze sodbusters off their land. Gunplay in Liberty, with Pinkertons caught in the middle of it."

"Are you missing some detectives, Roger?" Prodding Jamison a little. "Mine are all accounted for."

"He rambled some," Roger replied. "Mentioned something about the Sherman Act as he was headed out the door."

"Monopolies?" Baker knew all about the Sherman Antitrust Act, its provisions, and the fact that it had only been used twice since it was passed eleven years ago. The first time, in the so-called Sugar Trust Case, eight of nine Supreme Court justices had barred Congress from regulating manufacturing and left that power to state governments. Three years later, though, the court reversed itself and split five votes to four, allowing Washington to regulate the railroad industry because it carried goods across state lines.

In short, next time around, it could go either way, with national concerns like Gulf and Standard on the chopping block.

"It's likely nothing," Jamison assured him, with a gloating tenor to his voice. "Just thought you ought to know in case it blows up in our faces somewhere down the road."

"Well . . ."

"Anyway, he's gone now. Back to Liberty, I understand, nosing around those killings that I mentioned."

"Ah. Nothing to do with me, then."

"That's the same thing I told him," Jamison said. "No point thinking about it anymore."

"Well, thanks for calling, anyhow," Baker replied. "If

you've got shooting up your way, best keep your head down."

"First thing that I ever learned in business," Jamison responded, chuckling as he cut the link between them.

Baker cradled the receiver, glared at it for half a minute, then rang through for Clete Crowther. The Pinkerton enforcer stood before him moments later, saying, "Sir?"

Baker peered up at him and asked, "How soon can you have men in Liberty?"

8

LIBERTY, TEXAS

Braddock and Henshaw made it back to Liberty by dinner time and separated after dropping off their horses at the livery, where owner Liam Campbell took the animals in hand and pocketed their coins for food and lodging overnight. Outside, they separated, Henshaw voicing his intent to speak with Sheriff Ransom, Braddock moving on in search of sustenance.

And hoping that there'd be no repetition of last night's festivities ending in death.

As far as Braddock knew, no one from Standard or the Pinkerton Detective Agency had spotted him in Beaumont, but it preyed upon his mind that whoever had tried to have him murdered previously might be in the mood for a reprise of that endeavor while he was within their easy reach.

Aside from that, he owed his latest client at the Circle H a briefing on his progress since he had agreed to work for Lucius Haverstock, regarding last night's showdown and the U.S. Marshal's putting Roger Jamison on notice that his movements would be under scrutiny, with legal repercussions for the oilman if Standard Oil continued on its present course.

And where did that leave Gulf?

During their ride from Beaumont back to Liberty, Henshaw had mentioned plans to visit Hal Baker in turn, put him on notice that the days of forcing people off their land were done, but Braddock knew from personal experience that wealthy bullies seldom paid attention to such warnings unless they were hammered home by force.

That was a subject for another day, however, and his growling stomach urged Braddock along the street in search of hospitality.

He had enjoyed O'Grady's fare, but when he found himself in a town of any size, he tried for variety in meals, if nothing else. To that end, he stopped at a homey-looking eatery called Valenzuela's, checking out a menu posted on the outer wall before he entered and was instantly surrounded by enticing smells.

The restaurant was doing lively business. Diners were roughly split between Mexicans and whites, ignoring Texas's Jim Crow laws enacted during recent years, requiring segregated cars for railroad travelers and dining establishments. That said, there seemed to be no mingling between patrons of respective races and no blacks at all were present in the restaurant.

Braddock opposed discrimination and had always tried for even-handed law enforcement as a Ranger, unlike some he could have named, but at the moment hunger took priority over his social sensibilities.

The café had no windows, so he took a corner table set for two that provided him with a sight line toward the street entrance and swinging kitchen door. A harried-looking waitress in her early twenties took his order for a combination plate including enchiladas, a tamale, rice, and beans, with freshly baked tortillas and a mug of steaming coffee on the side.

After his round trip with Henshaw, out and back from Beaumont, Braddock had no fear of coffee keeping him awake that night, but he could always chase it with a shot of red-eye to make sure.

His meal arrived in good time, piping hot, and Braddock dug into it avidly, careful to keep an eye on both potential entrances while checking out his fellow diners on the sly. None of them looked like Pinkertons, based on his personal experience in dealing with the agency, but he also knew headquarters in Chicago had a knack for fielding agents in disguise—including women on occasion.

Still, the Pinkertons he'd met and buried so far around Liberty had all been rough-hewn men cast from the mold of gunfighters. None would have passed inspection as a swell from high society if such a thing existed locally, nor would they fit the role of horny-handed farmers seeking momentary respite from their plots of soil.

When he was pleasantly full, Braddock paid his tab and tipped the waitress, offered her a smile that was returned without enthusiasm, and began the stroll through purple dusk to his hotel. He had a sense of being watched but shrugged it off, impossible to verify with broad shop windows and the smaller glinting eyes of private homes along the thoroughfare.

In search of relaxation from a nightcap, without letting down his guard, Braddock stopped at the Lucky Strike saloon, surveyed its patrons briefly from outside, then pushed in through the swinging doors and made his way up to the bar.

EDDIE GEYER STOPPED his men a mile outside of Liberty to take them through their strategy once more before they put it into action. He could tell his fellow Pinkertons were tired of going over it, but Geyer didn't care. If anything went wrong, *his* neck was on the chopping block with Mr. Jamison and being sent back to Chicago with his tail between his legs might be the least of it.

"Stop belly-aching," he commanded, talking over their muttered complaints, and waiting until all of them were still.

"We know all this," said Charlie Hampton, loudmouth of the bunch who doubled as a joker when the mood came over him.

"Terrific," Geyer answered back. "Then you won't mind explaining it to us."

Hampton allowed himself a weary sigh, then launched into the spiel they had rehearsed in Beaumont and again, repeatedly, since heading west.

"We're looking for a county deputy named Phillips—"

"Pilcher," Geyer angrily corrected him.

"Okay," Hampton agreed. "If he ain't on patrol we check the sheriff's office."

"And?" A prod from Geyer.

"*And* he tells us where to find this U.S. Marshal and his pal who came to Beaumont, giving Emery the fits."

"That's Mr. Grimm, to you," Geyer reminded him.

"Right. Anyhow, he tells us where the marshal's staying and we take care of him. Likewise for his friend if Pilcher knows him."

"What about the sheriff?" Dallas Inman chimed in.

"If he tries to bother us, we drop him with the rest," Geyer replied. "He's not our first consideration, though. If we can make it in and out while he's at home asleep, so much the better."

"And he's got no right to chase us past the county line, regardless," Brett Chandler chimed in.

"Best not to test that theory if we can avoid it," Geyer said. "He comes at us, then take him down, along with any witnesses."

That sobered his companions, but they each nodded in turn, confirming that they understood their orders. None of them were keen to disappoint Emery Grimm in Beaumont, much less run afoul of Mr. Jamison and Standard Oil. Worse yet, failure might get them all in Dutch with their Chicago headquarters, cost Pinkerton's a major contract, and result in those responsible getting the gate—or worse. It was not past the agency's ability to hunt down and eliminate failures who cost the Eye That Never Sleeps that kind of payday from a major company.

Nods all around told Geyer that his men were clear on what awaited them in case they botched the job. Their choices: either die in Liberty tonight or else wake up tomorrow unemployed if they were lucky.

Geyer, for his part, had already decided how he'd handle failure in the worst scenario.

He'd leave no one alive who could identify him, then he'd light out for some territory far from Texas, praying that his ex-employers in Chicago could not track him down.

On second thought, Geyer decided that was likely hopeless.

Tonight's raid on Liberty could be a case of do or die.

INSIDE THE LUCKY STRIKE, Braddock noted a few more drinkers casting cautious glances toward him, whispering among themselves and trying not to make it obvious. That was a natural reaction to a stranger who had shown up out of nowhere, trailing corpse-draped horses, and then killed a third man right in town after the Palace Hotel ambush.

Fortunately, none of them approached him as he crossed the busy room, and Bob the barkeep didn't turn a hair at the sight of his returning customer. If others at the bar edged back a bit away from him, the former Ranger didn't mind. It simply granted him more elbow room.

He ordered whisky with a beer back, quaffed the liquor down in two swallows, then slowed down with the chaser, letting cool amber dilute a measure of the fire inside him. When a painted lady sidled up to him and asked him for a drink, Braddock ordered another shot, then courteously told her that he didn't crave a jaunt upstairs. She shrugged it off, gave him a smile that could have been mistaken for a grimace, and moved on in search of other prey.

Some other time, Braddock might have accompanied the soiled dove if they could agree on price, but after yesterday and Marshal Henshaw tossing down a gauntlet to the local head of Standard Oil, the time didn't seem opportune for letting down his guard. That same reasoning stopped Braddock from ordering another glass of red-eye, though he risked a second pint of peer after the first, feeling no ill effects to slow his eye or gun hand in a pinch.

A live pianist had replaced the wind-up Pianola for a

more discerning crowd, although in truth, most of the drinkers and the men bent over poker hands didn't impress Braddock as music lovers for its own sake. When the clamor started grating on him, he paid up and made his way outside once more, into the night.

It was a relatively short walk back to his hotel, but Braddock took his time, eyeing the alleyways and any other source of brooding shadows as he neared them, ready for a quick draw with his Colt if so required. No one stepped out to challenge him before he crossed the street and made his way into the hotel's lobby, where Jack Tatum stopped just short of flinching at the sight of him.

"Good evening, sir," the clerk offered.

"And quieter tonight, I'm hoping," Braddock answered.

"That would be most welcome, sir," Tatum agreed.

"To both of us, I'm sure. You put that broken window on my tab?"

"The management prefers to take that up with Mr. Mandelbaum, sir."

That would be a neat trick, Braddock thought, unless the Pinkerton had died with money in his pocket and enough left over for hotel repairs after his funeral expenses. Braddock couldn't see Standard Oil admitting any link to the attack, nor did he reckon that the Pinkerton Detective Agency would bother to involve itself in after-hour follies by a member of its team.

Upstairs, with no one else to see him in the corridor, Braddock drew his Peacemaker as he neared the door to his bedroom. A listen at the panel picked up no sound of intruders on the other side, but he still kept the six-gun handy as he plied his key and pushed the door wide to reveal an empty chamber on the other side.

So much for what the alienists in New York and other major cities had begun to label paranoia, meaning delusions that a patient was beset by phantom enemies created by an addled mind.

No paranoia here, Braddock decided, as he started to undress for bed.

He had no end of real-life enemies who would be pleased to see him lying in a box, and that meant keeping up his guard around the clock until his work for Lucius Haverstock was done.

THE RIDE from Anahuac to Liberty was roughly half the distance between Liberty and Beaumont, but a late start had slowed down Harold Baker's team from getting on the road with Angus Fletcher leading five subordinates: Ben Greene, Floyd Meachum, Mel Norton, Tommy Shattuck, and Hosea Flynn.

All had a reputation as fair gun hands and Clete Crowther trusted them to deal with Baker's enemies— some U.S. Marshal and his unknown traveling companion—before either of them caused any headaches for Gulf Oil.

Beyond that, they could deal as they saw fit with anybody else in Liberty who tried to give them any grief.

One major problem: Fletcher and his men had no idea if Standard Oil was also sending men to Liberty, but if its Beaumont leader *did*, that raised the unwelcome prospect of Pinkerton agents from separate camps crossing paths, perhaps even fighting in the streets. Chicago wouldn't like that, but it wasn't Fletcher's place to question Cletus Crowther, much less Harold Baker in his luxurious office atop Gulf Oil headquarters.

Fletcher was employed to follow orders and make sure the agents working under him did likewise. Beyond that, full responsibility rested upon the shoulders of the men who styled themselves as his superiors, whether or not they lived up to that role in his opinion.

Taking out a lawman—and a U.S. Marshal, yet— might well come back to haunt him later, but Fletcher would do as he'd been told . . . up to a point, at least.

Beyond that point, he would be looking out for number one, whatever was required to save himself.

"Who did you say we're meeting up with?" Tommy Shattuck asked when they were a couple miles due south of Liberty.

"Lem Givens," Fletcher said. "He's been watching the town for Clete the past three weeks or so, down from Chicago special, putting word around that he's a prospector for Gladys City Oil and Gas. They're playing catch-up since the strike at Spindletop, which gives the law someplace to look aside from Gulf if anything goes wrong tonight."

"Goes wrong?" chimed in Hosea Flynn. "Like what, for instance."

"Never mind that," Fletcher answered back. "Just follow orders, do your jobs, and we'll be back across the county line before you know it."

Or they wouldn't, Fletcher thought.

In which case he supposed the agents riding with him might not be in a position to protest.

"SHERIFF, ain't there some way we can work this out?"

Ransom was sick and tired of Pilcher whining from his cell. He glowered at the pudgy man who had disgraced himself and Ransom's office. Said, "You should have thought about that in advance, before you started taking bribes."

"Beer money didn't seem like any kinda bribe to me, Noah."

"And did you drink that beer on duty?"

"Well..."

"So that's a second strike against you, Joe."

"Come on! I've seen you take a drink when you were on duty yourself."

"It's not the beer, Joe. If you can't see that, there's nothing I can do for you."

"What *is* it, then?"

"It's selling information to the Pinkertons, you horse's ass! You nearly got a fella killed by talking out of turn. The one who paid you off *was* killed, the only thing that stopped him from committing murder in my town. If anybody else had been caught up in the cross-fire, their blood would be on you and I'd be charging you as an accomplice, meaning five to ten years behind bars."

There was a snivel to Joe Pilcher's voice as he replied, "I swear to God, Noah, I'm sorry!"

"Tell it to Judge Martin," Ransom said. "And count your lucky stars I didn't wake him up to deal with you last night. You know how he gets after playing poker with the mayor."

Another snuffle from the cell before Joe Pilcher asked, "What do you think he's gonna do with me?"

"I'm not a mind-reader," Ransom replied. "My best guess, you'll get off with thirty days or so on the road gang."

More snuffling. Then, "What am I gonna tell my folks, Noah?"

"What folks? You claimed to be an orphan when I hired you."

"My friends, then. What about Amanda?"

"At the Lucky Strike?" Ransom suppressed a smile at that. "Don't worry about that one missing you. She keeps her dance card full the way I hear it."

"Supposing I'm in love with her?"

"You need to ponder that a while. Now go to sleep. It's time for me to make your rounds."

Joe was still yapping from his cell when Ransom left the office and closed the door behind him. Another turn around downtown, shaking the doorknobs on selected shops, should see him homeward bound and ready for another night of fitful dreams.

Starting off on his final patrol, Ransom heard laughter and piano music emanating from the Lucky Strike saloon, where he would stop and peer in through the smoky windows as per usual, alert to any sign of discord among drunks or losing players at the joint's card tables. Winding up his tour of the darkened streets, their gloom barely dispersed by widely-paced street-lamps fueled by piped coal gas, lit up an hour after dusk, extinguished with the first pale flush of dawn.

Besides the Lucky Strike, he had two more saloons to reconnoiter before heading home at last, the Gold Rush, smaller than the Lucky Strike and somewhat shabbier, and La Taberna on the east side, catering primarily to Liberty's Mexican residents. With any luck, he wouldn't have to stop at either one or haul another prisoner back to the office, although that would give his former deputy someone to gripe at as the night wore on.

Mostly, he thought about the oil companies feuding over rights to poach crude from the Circle H and cursed the day when Patillo Higgins first decided he should pump natural gas into his brickyard and struck oil instead at Spindletop.

In Ransom's view, progress was overrated and if that made him a fuddy-duddy, he could live with it.

The problem now, with hostile private armies on the prod in two adjacent counties, came down to the question as to whether he could stay alive at all.

DEPUTY U.S. MARSHAL JONAS HENSHAW left the Gold Rush feeling slightly flushed, thinking that his third double bourbon might have gone a step too far. He was not *drunk*, mind you, but with the challenge he had issued to the local head of Standard Oil that very day, a clear head should have been his top priority.

"Too late," the lawman muttered to himself, smiling. "At least this way I'm bound to get some sleep."

Once he was well away from the saloon, the streets were quiet, no pedestrians in evidence, no shops still open for nocturnal business. Before signing with the U.S. Marshals Service Henshaw had put time in as a deputy in Dallas County, riding heard on sixty-seven thousand citizens within an area of nine hundred square miles. During his time there, he had handled every kind of crime from petty theft to rape and murder, been forced to kill three men within a four-year span when they decided it was smart to draw down on a lawman.

Each time, they'd been wrong.

His present job was easier in some respects, although working his territory along the Gulf meant long days in the saddle and as many nights sleeping beside a campfire as in hotel rooms. The government covered his basic tab with a per diem, but his salary and constant traveling precluded purchasing a home. The benefits, if you could call them that, included six cents paid per mile in search of suspects, and a dime per mile while transporting arrestees to the nearest court for trial, plus fifty cents for each subpoena served. On balance, Henshaw would be lucky to earn five hundred dollars in a given year, and there were penalties attached as well. If he were forced to kill a suspect and could find no relatives to foot the bill for funeral expenses, those came out of Henshaw's pocket.

Deputies received no part of any federal reward offer but might get paid if they bagged a fugitive with money on his head from private individuals, a state or local government, or from railroad and express firms. On the downside, 25 percent of any fees a deputy collected went directly to the top Marshal in charge of a respective state for lounging at his desk.

Henshaw rounded a corner, glimpsed a pair of riders as they crossed the thoroughfare a few blocks down, toward his hotel. The hour made him feel that they were somehow out of place, and Henshaw ducked back into shadow as he watched them pass by, moving out of sight.

None of my business, he decided, even if they were up to no good. Liberty had a sheriff on the job, with deputies to back him up, even if one of them was sitting out the night behind bars.

It crossed his mind that he should double back to look for Noah Ransom, warn him that there might be something going on in town, but that seemed foolish when he thought it through. Two riders moving after hours through the county seat? So what?

"Just let it go," Henshaw advised himself aloud, but knew that wouldn't fly. He'd always had a nose for trouble, whether getting into it when he was younger or attempting to resolve it once he'd donned a badge. And yet . . .

It was not far to his hotel, the fairly comfortable bed awaiting him. Why should he deviate from the agenda he had set himself, unless—

The next two riders settled it, both clearly following the horsemen who'd preceded them. There were no saloons in the general direction they were headed, rendering their appearance on the street at this hour more strikingly peculiar.

Hansen thought about G.W. Braddock and the botched attempt to kill him only one night earlier.

Heaving a weary sigh, his right hand loosening the six-gun holstered on his hip, he picked up speed moving along the wooden boardwalk to find out where they were going and discover what they had in mind.

UPSTAIRS in his room at the Paradise Hotel, Braddock had removed his vest and shirt, his boots and gun belt, standing in his union suit, barefooted, as he tidied up for bed. The Paradise provided each room with a basin and pitcher of water, two small towels, and a mirror—cracked at one corner in Braddock's case—for guests who chose to make themselves presentable or merely to relax after a weary day at one job or another.

After last night, Braddock finished his ablution with the lamp's wick turned town to its lowest setting and his curtains tightly drawn. Precautions wouldn't stop another sniper firing through the window, with its glass lately replaced, but he could minimize the target visible to anyone lurking outside and keep his fingers crossed, for all the good that it might do.

With any luck, he hoped the Pinkertons had learned their lesson, even if it didn't stick long-term. He knew the agency by reputation for tenacity in hounding lawbreakers—or, on the other hand, pursuing a vindictive course against people whom Chicago or its agents in the field perceived as enemies.

Braddock had made that list without fully intending to, but he wasn't alone. Thinking of Marshal Henshaw, he wondered again how long the man in charge of Standard Oil in Beaumont might preserve his reputation if he let a threat of prosecution go unanswered.

If the course pursued by Roger Jamison was normal business, honest and above board, Braddock would expect his adversary to consult attorneys, maybe file some kind of writ in court where he could pay a judge under the table, but last night's events had proved that there was more at stake. Jamison, whether approved by his superiors or not, was plainly willing to exert illegal force in moving obstacles out of his way.

And what about Standard's competitors from Gulf Oil, based in Anahuac? How long would Henshaw's interest in predatory efforts be concealed from them? Would they react as Jamison had done already, fielding gunmen to eradicate a threat before it turned on them?

Deciding that should be a problem for another day, Braddock blew out his lamp and lay down on the hotel bed beside his Winchester, gun belt coiled beside it, without slipping off his jeans. It was a compromise he chose in case of trouble, more comfortable than a night on stony ground beside a campfire, fully dressed, yet still prepared for an emergency.

Sleep was about to overtake him when a distant shout roused Braddock from the brink of slumber, followed a split-second later by the sound of gunfire from a distance, echoing between Liberty's clapboard buildings.

He was face down on the floor in nothing flat, dragging his rifle and his pistol belt along with him. It came as a surprise when no glass showered down on him from the window, until Braddock realized the gunshots weren't aimed his way.

Who was the target this time?

Jonas Henshaw came to mind, and in another moment Braddock had his boots on, rising in a crouch as he prepared to face more mayhem in the street.

And this time, from the sound of it, more than two gunmen were involved.

9

ANGUS FLETCHER FELT UNEASY AS HE LED HIS FOUR MEN closer to the Palace Hotel. They'd received directions and a hand-drawn map from Lemuel Givens before he took off and left them to it, saying he had other work to do and there was no way they could miss it.

He had been right about that, anyway, although the hostelry wouldn't have sprung to mind if someone had asked Fletcher to describe a palace. Baker had his Pinkertons lodged at a nicer place in Anahuac, but if he had to answer honestly, Fletcher had yet to see a hotel anywhere below the Mason-Dixon Line that held a candle to the stately buildings on Chicago's Loop.

Fletcher had been only a child when fire had swept the Windy City thirty years ago, cremating some three hundred people in its path and leaving at least one hundred thousand homeless in its wake. His parents had regaled him with the horror stories, but honestly, Fletcher couldn't recall any part of the disaster, even though he'd come to think that it had hardened him somehow and helped to make him what he was today.

As for a town like Liberty, he calculated that a lit match and a prairie wind would wipe it off the Lone Star map, scatter its residents for miles around, and once initial shock wore off no one would think about it twice.

Pushing that useless thought away, he focused on the vaguely seedy Palace one long block in front of him. Givens had told him that the U.S. Marshal, Jonas Henshaw, had a room there, while his pal—someone named Braddock, totally unknown to Fletcher—also lodged somewhere beneath its roof, but Lemuel had been unable to provide specific room numbers. Eyeing the hotel now, Fletcher guessed that it must have something like three dozen rooms for rent, some of them empty based on the darkened windows he could see.

No problem, then.

His team's first job would be to rouse the night clerk, shake him down for the room numbers, then head upstairs and get their jobs done. They would have to shut the clerk up too, once he had seen their faces, but a silent knife thrust could accomplish that without arousing anybody else within the hotel's walls.

Gun work would be required for that, which meant some racket, but the guests with any sense would stay behind locked doors and keep their heads down, so the killing should be minimized. Beyond that, if the local sheriff heard something and tried to intervene, that was his tough luck.

What was one lawman added to the list of corpses, more or less?

"Let's get 'er done," Fletcher commanded, agilely dismounting, tying up his horse directly opposite the Palace.

Half of his team had already descended from their

saddles when a voice called out behind them, asking, "You boys hoping to find someone in particular?"

Turning, Fletcher made out a stocky man wearing a badge, and then his thoughts became a blur as he went for his holstered gun.

BRADDOCK REACHED the hotel's lobby as Jack Tatum was emerging from his backroom office, blinking at him, exclaiming, "Not again!"

"They're not shooting at me this time," Braddock remarked in passing, and the clerk ducked out of sight once more before he reached the exit.

Opposite the Palace he saw five men either mounted or standing beside horses, all drawing weapons as they faced a sixth man farther down the boardwalk on the east side of the street. Braddock was unfamiliar with the new arrivals on the scene but recognized Deputy Marshal Henshaw at first glance, crouching with Colt in hand, his eyes sweeping the group arrayed before him.

Someone from the raiding party must have fired the shots that rousted Braddock from his room. A haze of gun smoke hung before them now, already dissipating as Henshaw triggered his six-gun and one of the riders who'd dismounted clutched his stomach, dropped to his knees, then toppled forward on his face.

Braddock figured the shooters must be Pinkertons, dispatched after Henshaw confronted Roger Jamison in Beaumont, but in the present circumstances any question of their motivation was irrelevant. He had befriended Henshaw, and Braddock couldn't simply watch the lawman killed before his eyes.

No time for niceties.

Raising his Winchester, Braddock lined up one of the mounted gunmen in the rifle's sights and plugged him in the back, between the shoulder blades. Explosive impact punched the raider forward, falling to his left and sliding past the horse's neck before it bucked and lashed out with its rear hooves at the other men and animals surrounding it.

The rifle shot and its chaotic aftermath put two of the remaining gunmen in a spin to face the unexpected threat on the Palace Hotel's porch. Both leveled pistols but they weren't fast enough to stop Braddock before he vaulted to his right and dropped from view behind a sturdy water trough. Their bullets drilled through wooden planks, producing spouts of water jetting toward the thoroughfare, but neither slug reached Braddock in his makeshift hiding place.

Beyond his line of sight, gunfire continued, punctuating the background noise of men cursing, their horses nickering and neighing in reaction to the close-range gun-thunder. Braddock couldn't tell the reports apart from where he huddled out of sight but hoped that Henshaw was alive and holding up his end of the engagement.

Probably, the former Ranger thought. *If he were dead, they'd all be angling their shots in my direction.*

Braddock knew he had to break that stalemate and he had to do it now, while time remained for cracking the unequal odds.

"WHAT'S THAT SHOOTING?" Dallas Inman asked, rotating in his saddle as if he could spot the shooters from the spot where they had paused outside the darkened sheriff's office.

"How should I know?" Eddie Geyer snapped back in reply.

"Did Emery send anyone besides us?" Brett Chandler asked, addressing Geyer as their team's leader.

"He didn't say anything to me about it," Geyer answered, forced to wonder now if Roger Jamison's top Pinkerton had hedged his bets by calling out a second team to cover Geyer and his men in Liberty.

He couldn't rule it out, knowing the way Emery Grimm's devious mind worked, but it made no sense to Geyer that the second squad would be off wreaking havoc somewhere else while Eddie and his riders carried out the task they had been given.

That was simple, as Grimm laid it out for him: locate the sheriff's deputy who had been dealing with Frank Mandelbaum and silence him before the lawman had a chance to spill his guts in court.

That kind of testimony was enough to prove conspiracy if laid before a jury under oath, and Roger Jamison was not about to sacrifice himself if he could put someone else up on the cross.

"Sounds like somebody's catching hell," Charlie Hampton observed, a hint of tremor to his voice.

"None of our business," Geyer answered back. "We've only got one target, and the sheriff's office is our starting point for finding him."

"Let's get it done, then," Inman offered, "before anything goes wrong."

"You read my mind," Geyer replied, dismounting from his horse, looping its reins around a nearby hitching rail, and moving toward the door with "SHERIFF" stenciled on its window glass in silver paint.

The door hadn't been locked, but Geyer saw no one inside until he'd entered. Only then did he spot a heavyset man peering at him from behind jail bars. The prisoner examined him, then scanned the others crowding in behind Geyer, before he said, "You fellas here to help me out?"

Geyer put on a smile, no mirth behind it, and replied, "That all depends on who you are."

DEPUTY MARSHAL HENSHAW saw a figure sprint across the street but only recognized his unexpected would-be savior when Braddock joined him on the opposite boardwalk.

"You made it," Henshaw cracked, not joking quite so much as offering a prayer of thanks.

"Wouldn't have missed it for the world."

"I bet," Henshaw replied.

At least four of the nameless raiders still remained in fighting trim, all now afoot, ducking and dodging around horses as they used their frightened mounts for cover, pegging shots at Henshaw and Braddock, thus far with no effect. That was a fluke that couldn't last, as Henshaw realized full well.

"We need some cover in a hurry," he advised Braddock.

The former Ranger glanced back at the millinery shop behind them, saying, "How about in there?"

"Seems locked up tight to me," Henshaw replied.

"I'd say it was a case of pressing need," Braddock advised.

"Okay. You first."

Those words were barely spoken before Braddock

rushed the shop's front door and kicked it open with a bootheel. As he ducked inside, dropping behind a rack of hats and bonnets on display in the window, Henshaw scrabbled across the sidewalk, firing once more with his Peacemaker, an unaimed shot, before he crossed the threshold and ducked low.

The whole place smelled of women and their various colognes. For sixty years or more the millinery trade had been regarded as a female venue, both in terms of manufacturing and sales, while men's headgear was mostly found in dry goods shops or stores where guns were sold.

Henshaw imagined dying there, among the frilly women's things, and nearly laughed out loud but caught himself in time to keep Braddock from wondering if he had lost his mind.

While reloading his six-gun, Henshaw felt Braddock rise from hiding, squeezing off a rifle shot that made his ears ring in the crowded confines of the shop. "There goes another one," said the ex-Ranger, sounding neither satisfied nor out of sorts at having dropped another man.

"Leaving how many?" Henshaw asked, since he'd lost count.

"I make it three, but with them ducking all around out there I can't be positive."

"That's half the number that I saw first thing," Henshaw allowed.

"But still determined from the look of them," Braddock replied.

"Let's try to change their minds on that score, shall we?" Henshaw answered, rising from a crouch to pick a target from the moving shapes outside.

JOE PILCHER WAS NOT sure he'd understood the question properly, which gave him pause and sparked what felt like worry in the space around his heart, facing four men with guns he didn't recognize.

"Who am I?" He considered that and asked the one who'd spoken to him, "Didn't someone send you over here from Beaumont?"

The cashiered deputy's sense of uneasiness increased as the four men standing before him in the office traded glances, then their spokesman answered, "Nope. We're not from Beaumont. So let's try that name of yours again."

"Joe Pilcher."

"What's the charge against you, Joe?"

"I was a deputy, but then . . ."

"Then, what?"

Pilcher decided he would try to put a favorable twist on what was otherwise a drab, depressing tale. "Sheriff found out that I was talking to a Pinkerton agent in town from time to time, keeping him caught up on troubles we've been having hereabouts."

"A Pinkerton," the spokesman said. "Now that's a wonderment. *We're* Pinkertons, ourselves."

Hope dawned in Pilcher's mind, then did a rapid fade. "You are? But not from Beaumont? See, the one I talked to worked for Mr. Jamison."

"I've heard of him," their spokesman said. "He calls the shots for Standard Oil, from what I understand."

"That's right! But you . . .?"

"We deal with someone else entirely." Turning to the gunman on his left, he asked, "Think I should tell him?"

"Can't hurt anything," the other said.

"That's true enough. We work for Gulf Oil out of Anahuac."

Pilcher tried to wrap his frazzled mind around that. "So you're like, competitors of Mr. Jamison's or something?"

"Something like that, right."

"I reckon you're not here to help me out, then," Pilcher said, his shoulders slumping with the weight of disappointment.

"More to help ourselves, you might say," the anonymous leader replied. "Which doesn't mean that we can't make your burden lighter while we're at it."

"Oh? How's that?"

The leader of the four men let that pass and asked, "Which Pinkerton were you having those conversations with before your boss caught on?"

"Frank Mandelbaum," Pilcher replied. "You *must* know him."

"I might have heard the name, Joe. Seems to me he came to grief a little while ago."

"That wasn't my fault. I mean, sure, I told him where the guy who shot a couple of his friends out by the Circle H was staying, but I didn't know what Frank was planning, much less that he'd go and get himself shot dead."

"So you're the only one who can connect all this with anybody from the agency?"

Joe wasn't sure he liked the sound of that but answered anyway, saying, "I guess so."

"Well, that just might make things easier."

"Not sure I follow that exactly, but if you just wanna let me go, the keys are hanging over there behind the sheriff's desk."

"I think we can improve on that," the speaker said, drawing his six-gun.

Off to either side of him, the other three did likewise, aiming down the barrels of their smoke wagons toward Pilcher in his cell.

"Hey, now! Hang on a second! All you gotta do is—"

He was staring down four muzzles as they all went off at once and filled the intervening space with smoke.

Pilcher was dead before he hit the floor and never saw the leader of his firing squad step forward, reach in through the jailhouse bars, and pump one final slug into his face.

BRADDOCK COULDN'T FEEL the moment when the tide of battle turned, but he could feel it shifting all the same. It was a skill he had acquired from countless other situations where his life was riding on the line and there were only two ways out: elimination of his adversaries or a cold hole in the ground.

Outside the millinery shop, survivors of the raid on Liberty were scattering, trying to disengage from their initial aim of ending Jonas Henshaw's life. Confusion, gun smoke, and the dust raised by their milling horses' hooves still made a head count difficult, but Braddock wasn't worried about that.

He'd know when all of them were down and out, no further danger to himself or his companion.

For a split second he wondered what was keeping Sheriff Ransom from arriving on the scene, perhaps accompanied by any deputies he hadn't jailed for bribery. The shooting must have wakened half of Liberty by now and it would only take the local law's arrival to prevent the remnant of the raiders from escaping into darkness.

That is, unless Braddock and Henshaw disposed of them in the meantime.

Which meant more questions and more paperwork before he even had a chance to check in with his new employer at the Circle H.

Was Lucius Haverstock concerned about him? Maybe wondering if Braddock had skipped town after the first attempt on his life? If so, he would owe Braddock nothing for the favor of eliminating three Pinkerton agents hired by Standard Oil to run him off his land.

Not quite a win, but under the circumstances . . .

"Watch out on the left!" Henshaw alerted him, but Braddock had already seen one of the gunmen vault into the saddle of a palomino, clinging for dear life as it tried hard to buck him off.

Braddock lined up a rifle shot, squeezed it off, and knew that it was wasted when his target ducked low in the saddle, nearly toppling from his seat. Braddock's slug flew across the street and smashed a window over there while he was pumping the Winchester's lever, then his fleeing enemy turned down a narrow alley, vanishing into the night.

That still left two and both were fanning pistol shots into the ruined millinery store, trying to run in opposite directions in their effort to escape. Beside Braddock, Henshaw lunged to his feet, shot one of them just as his target was returning fire, then made a grunting sound and toppled to the floor.

Braddock lined up the last remaining shooter as he tried to grab a horse at random, but the animal eluded him and left the raider standing in the street, exposed. Without a second thought, Braddock dropped him where he stood, then swept the street with one last look before he turned toward Henshaw.

"Are you hit?" he asked the marshal.

It turned out to be a futile question. Henshaw sprawled on the floor, clutching his chest with one hand while a crimson stream spilled from his gasping mouth, joining an ever-growing pool of blood spreading across the shop's glass-littered floor.

———————

WHEN SHERIFF RANSOM reached the scene, panting and vowing to cut back on the cheroots, he found a slaughterhouse waiting for him. Five bodies lay like heaps of castoff laundry in the dusty street, as many horses trotting off in various directions, riderless, clearly relieved that the shooting had ceased.

The fallen men were fanned out like a worthless hand at poker, two lying faceup, the others nuzzling dirt. It made no sense to Ransom, but it seemed they'd been cut down while storming Sadie Gilmore's millinery shop, the very last place on God's earth he would have thought a gang might try to rob by night in Liberty.

And even as that wayward thought took shape, Ransom saw furtive movement in the store, cocking his Peacemaker and dropping to a crouch as he called out, "You there! Inside the shop! Come out and show me empty hands!"

He recognized Braddock's voice responding, "Sheriff? We need help in here, and fast."

Cursing under his breath, Ransom had one more look along the street, filling up with sleepy-looking citizens now that the storm had passed, and answered Braddock. "Who's in there with you?"

"Henshaw," the call came back. "He was the target this time and he's hit. Looks bad to me."

Ransom shoved through the shop's door with its shattered window, saw Braddock hunkered down beside the U.S. Marshal's body, leaving boot prints in the lawman's blood. It didn't take a sawbones to make out that Henshaw had stopped breathing sometime earlier, his face a crimson mask from choking as he died.

"Bad doesn't cover it," Ransom observed, shoulders slumping. "He's gone."

"Those men outside—"

"How many were there?" Ransom interrupted Braddock.

"Six to start with."

"Then one of them got away. You've only got five bodies and five horses on the street."

"I don't know if they came for Henshaw or he took them by surprise," said Braddock, coming to his feet beside the murdered lawman. "Maybe on his way back to the hotel from supper or whatever."

"Can you keep the townsfolk off those others while I go for Eulon Wells?"

"No problem," Braddock said. "I'll give you even money that they're Pinkertons."

"I try to stay away from sucker bets," Ransom replied, fairly certain that a thorough search of the bodies would link them to the Eye That Never Slept, even if he should come up short on names.

And that meant he would have to make a hard choice in the morning, either palming off the case on Austin, looking like a fool to his constituents in Liberty, or else stray from his lawful jurisdiction to invite more trouble home.

ANGUS FLETCHER PULLED up short a mile outside of Liberty, to clear his head and think. The palomino stallion he was riding had belonged to Floyd Meachum, who had no need of transport now unless it was a boat to carry him across the River Styx.

Five agents killed, trying to do what should have been a simple job, and Fletcher was amazed to find that he'd come through the massacre without a scratch on him. He might have counted that as lucky, but he knew he wasn't in the clear.

Not yet.

The way he saw it, two choices lay before him. On the one hand, he could ride straight back to Anahuac, report his team's failure to Cletus Crowther at the Gulf Oil offices, and wait while Hal Baker decided what to do with him. It never entered Fletcher's mind that he would walk away from that unscathed, and when he lingered on that thought, he had to wonder whether he would walk away at all.

From Baker's point of view—and maybe from the agency's as well—it might be preferable if he simply disappeared without a trace. Someone came asking later, they could all shrug, feign confusion, and pretend they'd never heard of him.

Angus *Who*? No sir, that doesn't ring a bell.

Fletcher supposed it wouldn't be the first time that Chicago purged its personnel files to erase embarrassing employees. Commerce was the top priority, and no man —maybe not even the brothers who were running things since burying their father seven years ago—could be permitted to derail the money train.

As for Hal Baker, lining up an oil bonanza if he could beat Standard to the finish line, he cared no more for any given individual than for a housefly battering itself to death against his windowpane. Given the opportunity he would swat Fletcher without thinking twice and by day's end might well believe that Angus never worked for him at all.

A fantasy that Cletus Crowther would be happy to facilitate, as long as he was paid.

What was the difference with five men lying dead in Liberty? Maybe the fact that only Fletcher could connect the dots and make them stick in court.

That tipped him toward considering a change of scene. Fletcher had never cared much for the Lone Star State to start with, just another job that called for someone unafraid to get his hands dirty, but he was well and truly soured on it now. Trying to kill a U.S. Marshal, even failing at it, meant that he would likely die while breaking rocks at Leavenworth, which rated near the very bottom of his long-term plans.

But what would happen to him if he simply picked a compass point at random, rode hell-bent for leather toward that far horizon, never looking back? When lawmen finished counting heads in Liberty, maybe tomorrow morning, would they be aware that someone from the raiding party had escaped?

With any luck, Fletcher decided, *I won't be around these parts by then.*

THE CROWD of townsfolk that surrounded Braddock and the five dead men outside the millinery shop regarded him with hostile eyes, which came as no surprise, but none spoke to him or advanced closer than ten to fifteen feet after they noted that he had two guns ready at hand.

Instead of trying to converse with total strangers,

Braddock told them all, "The sheriff should be back with Mr. Wells most any time now."

As he finished speaking, an excited woman showed up on the sidewalk, gaping at the bullet-riddled shop, and wailed, "My store! What's happened to my store?"

The scattered corpses seemed to have less impact on her as she moved in closer to what still remained of the shop's door. Braddock edged back to intercept her, saying, "Ma'am, you need to wait outside for now."

She rounded on him, snapping, "Who are you to tell me that? This is my property!"

"And it's already occupied," he said, voice lowered, with a nod toward Marshal Henshaw sprawled on the floor inside.

That vision stopped her and she turned away from Braddock, one hand at her mouth as she fought back a sudden wave of nausea. She backed off to a nearby alley's mouth, still muttering, "My shop. My lovely shop."

Ten dreary minutes passed before Braddock saw Noah Ransom jogging back. The crowd turned toward their sheriff, several of them asking questions all at once, while Ransom started easing them aside, clearly frustrated by their sluggishness.

"Back off," the sheriff said at last. "We've got a wagon coming through to take these boys away."

Braddock saw Eulon Wells driving the wagon that pulled up a moment later, flanked by two much younger men atop the broad bench seat. Wells reined the two black geldings to a halt, then waited for his aides to clamber down before he followed suit, clucking in evident distress as he surveyed the carnage before him.

"Lord Almighty!" said the undertaker. "Ben, Edward, start loading up this bunch and have a care. We'll need to check their pockets when we get back to the parlor."

While his helpers set to work, Wells faced Ransom. "There's one more in the shop, you said, Sheriff?"

Ransom nodded, leading the way. Over his shoulder, he advised the undertaker, "Brace yourself, Eulon. It's Marshal Henshaw."

"God have mercy!" Wells blurted before he crossed the shop's threshold, then paused, as if he might be thinking better of it. "No, I suppose it's too late for that now."

Braddock and Ransom waited while the six corpses were stacked in the mortician's wagon bed. The sheriff parried questions from the growing crowd with vague non-answers, saying they would have to wait upon a finding from the undertaker and from Justice of the Peace Tom Daley, hopefully sometime tomorrow.

As the wagon pulled away at last, Ransom and Braddock left the townies muttering among themselves, drifting off to homes nearby. Five minutes later they were at the sheriff's office, when they found the door standing ajar and both went in behind drawn pistols.

"If somebody came along and let Joe out of here—" Ransom began, then caught himself and rushed to stand before the cell where his late prisoner lay stretched out on the blood-slick floor. As Braddock followed, his nose readily identified a heavy scent of gun smoke in the air.

Ransom stood before him, staring through the bars at what was left of Joe Pilcher. From Braddock's vantage point he guessed the former deputy had stopped at least six bullets, likely more.

"I never heard a thing," Ransom observed, sounding surprised.

"You were distracted, Sheriff."

Leaning closer, forehead pressed against the bars, he

said, "Sweet Jesus, will you look at that? What happened to his *face*?"

Braddock replied, "Looks like somebody wanted to make sure he didn't talk."

"Well, they did that, all right. Just let me lock up here and go tell Eulon that he's got another customer. Then we can check the pockets on those other boys."

"You're thinking they were Pinkertons?" asked Braddock.

"It's a safe bet," Ransom said. "And if I'm right, that tells me where I'll be most of the day tomorrow."

"Let me know if you want company," Braddock offered.

The sheriff's voice was stone-cold as he said, "I thought you'd never ask."

10

LIBERTY

BRADDOCK AND SHERIFF RANSOM MET FOR BREAKFAST AT
O'Grady's, both men weary after a long night examining
the dead, sorting the raiders' Pinkerton credentials,
winding up with whisky shots at the Gold Rush to help
them catch a little sleep.

"Business is down," Ransom observed, as the familiar
waitress showed them to a table facing on the thoroughfare outside.

Braddock had only patronized the restaurant for
lunch or supper, so he had no way to assess its morning
trade but took the sheriff at his word.

"A massacre puts off some people's appetite," he said,
to fill the silence between them.

"It doesn't help my prospects for employment,
either," Ransom said. "Especially when one of my
own deputies winds up in jail and then gets killed
there."

"One of your *ex*-deputies," Braddock corrected him.

"Not that it matters to my kind constituents," the sheriff said.

Casting an eye around the sparsely-settled dining room, Braddock had to agree that both of them were drawing hostile stares this morning, after all of last night's bloody havoc.

Both ordered steak and eggs, anticipating a long day ahead, Braddock ordered his cackleberries scrambled, while the sheriff liked his over easy so the yolks were runny. Waiting with their mugs of coffee, both men scanned the street while Braddock asked, "You get an answer back from Austin yet?"

"One of the U.S. Marshal's deputies wired back that he'd received my message about Henshaw but their boss is traveling. Fort Smith, he said."

That meant a visit to Judge John Henry Rogers, Braddock easily surmised. Rogers, a U.S. district judge, had jurisdiction over western Arkansas and the vast span of Indian Territory, serving as successor to notorious "hanging judge" Isaac Parker, who'd retired a bit over four years ago, after hearing some 13,500 cases in two decades, sentencing 160 men to the gallows. Rogers had a somewhat gentler reputation but didn't hesitate to place a killer on the gallows when it came to that.

"He could be gone a while," Braddock observed.

"And I'm stuck waiting for him in the meantime," Ransom groused, just as their meals arrived.

A search conducted at the undertaker's parlor overnight had turned up five Pinkerton badges but without identifying any of the dead by name—or indicating whoever sent them on their killing mission into Liberty. In Braddock's mind that left two possibilities, including front men serving either Gulf or Standard Oil

"What's next then?" he asked Ransom.

319

Talking with his mouth full, Ransom answered, "What I *don't* intend to do is sit around here twiddling my thumbs while outside forces use my county as a shooting gallery. I don't have deputies enough to post a guard around the Circle H, but nothing's stopping me from running down the problem to its source—or maybe *sources*, in this case."

Braddock reminded him, "That means going outside your jurisdiction."

"So? What have I got to lose at this point?"

Braddock almost said that Ransom's job was riding on the line. Instead, he offered up, "Maybe your life?"

"I was elected in the first place to keep order," Ransom said. "By anybody's gauge I'd say I've failed at that. It cost Henshaw his life and I refuse to let it spread from there."

"Outnumbered and outgunned, you may not have a choice," Braddock replied.

"What's the alternative?"

The former Ranger shrugged. "Beats me. Who did you plan to visit first?"

"I'm thinking Jamison in Beaumont. Care to ride along?"

Braddock responded with a nod. "I have to stop in for a word with Mr. Haverstock before we leave, though, or he'll start thinking that I've flown the coop on him. When did you plan on leaving?"

"Once we're finished here and fetch our horses from the livery suit you?"

"Down to the ground," Braddock replied.

THE CIRCLE H RANCH

Braddock expected to see more spies watching Lucius Haverstock's domain but spotted none this time around. He noted where the first two Pinkertons had called him out and lost their lives accordingly, but Sheriff Ransom didn't seem concerned.

"That's blood under the bridge," he said. "With any luck, somebody's running low on mercenaries and they'll have to send off to Chicago for replacements. That ought to buy us three, maybe four days, allowing for stopover and switching trains."

Shortly before they reached the spread's main gate, two riders met them on the trail. Braddock immediately recognized Blake Drury on his dapple gray gelding and stopped Ransom from reaching for his Colt, saying, "These boys come with the property."

Ransom nodded. Said from the corner of his mouth, "That one helped bring the first stiffs into town day before yesterday."

"That's him all right," Braddock agreed.

Drury reached up to graze his hat's brim with an index finger as he said, "We were starting to wonder if we'd lost you, Braddock."

"And yet here I am."

"Lucky for you, from what we've heard about the goings-on in Liberty of late."

"We've had some fireworks," Braddock granted. "Is the boss available?"

"Be mighty glad to see you, I expect," Drury replied. "The sheriff too."

"It's nice to be made welcome," Ransom said.

"You both know how to find the house, I guess," said

Drury, as he turned his mount away. "We're on patrol for trespassers these days."

The riders parted company, Braddock and Ransom trotting on until Haverstock's spacious home and outbuildings came into view. Another rider met them there and trailed them to the ranch house, where they found the spread's owner already standing on his broad front porch.

"Sheriff," the rancher greeted Ransom first, befitting his authority, then turned to Braddock. "I'd begun to think you might have left us one way or another."

"I'm still kicking," Braddock said. "No thanks to the best efforts of the Pinkerton Detective Agency."

"How many have they lost now?" Haverstock inquired.

"I make it eight over the past two nights."

"Good news for us, I guess," said Haverstock.

"Against one U.S. Marshal and a sheriff's deputy," Ransom advised.

"Sorry to hear that, Noah. I suppose it could be worse, though."

"And it still might," Ransom said. "That's why I plan on paying calls in Beaumont and Anahuac."

"Beyond your reach under the law," the rancher noted.

"I'm aware of the legalities. But nothing says one man can't warn another that his actions may have consequences down the line."

"Nothing that I know of," Haverstock agreed. "You two have breakfast before riding out?"

"I might have saved room for a shot of bourbon if you have it," Ransom said, smiling.

"I reckon that can be arranged. Climb down and

come inside," said Haverstock. "I'll see what I can do for you."

BEAUMONT

Lunchtime was closing in as Braddock and Ransom entered the Jefferson County seat of government. Nothing seemed out of place, but some pedestrians noted the badge on Ransom's vest and may have recognized that he wasn't a local lawman.

Granted, as Ransom had explained, Beaumont employed more men under his counterpart as sheriff— Isaac Prentiss—than the smaller population next door to the west could justify or fund out of its treasury. Braddock was curious to see what might transpire if they encountered any of the local deputies en route to Standard Oil's office, but as with his prior visit in the company of Jonas Henshaw, none appeared.

"Nice quiet town," said Ransom as they reached their destination. "On the surface, anyhow."

"It's normally the undertow that gets you," Braddock offered in reply.

"I hear that."

They tied up their horses at a hitch rail outside of Standard's coastal headquarters, across from the saloon where Braddock had retired to cool his heels while Marshal Henshaw went in on his own last time. A lithesome secretary rose behind her desk, flicking a glance at Braddock, leveling a frown at Ransom's out-of-county badge.

"He's in a meeting, gentlemen," she said.

Ransom gave her a smile and said, "That's good. You want to tell my fortune while you're at it?"

From behind them a man's voice chimed in, saying, "I'll handle this, Nadine."

"Yes sir," the secretary said and sat back down, without returning to her paperwork at once.

Braddock and Ransom turned to face a well-dressed man, hands clasped behind his back, a telltale bulge under his coat betraying concealed weaponry.

"And who might you be?" Ransom asked.

"Emery Grimm. I represent the Pinkerton Detective Agency on Mr. Jamison's behalf."

"I guess you've got a permit for that hogleg under your arm then?"

"Indeed I do," Grimm said. "Not that you have authority to ask me that in Jefferson County."

"So you can read," said Ransom, reaching up to flick an index finger at his badge. "When we're done with your boss, I'd like to ask about your fellow so-called detectives who keep dropping dead around my town."

"With my attorney present, naturally," Grimm replied.

"And who might he be?"

"Bertram Knowles," said Grimm.

"County solicitor," said Ransom, filling Braddock in. "You all appear to have this district pretty well sewn up."

"It's Standard's policy—and Pinkerton's as well—to make friends where we can."

"Well, if you plan to be my friend, go fetch your boss out of his meeting so that we can have a word."

"About . . .?" Grimm pressed.

"About ten killings in the past two days, most of them Pinkertons like you."

Grimm nodded, putting on a quirky little smile.

Moving to find his boss, he said, "It sounds like Liberty has gone to hell, Sheriff. Maybe you need some help controlling it."

"Don't worry about me," Ransom replied, and fell in step behind the Pinkerton to follow him.

Jamison had no meetings scheduled for today. He had his feet up on a corner of his desk and was enjoying a cigar imported from Havana when the sound of voices in his outer office brought him to his feet.

Emery Grimm was first across the threshold, followed by a lawman dusty from the trail whose badge read "LIBERTY COUNTY SHERIFF." The last fellow in line was yet another stranger but he wore no badge of office. Jamison dismissed him out of hand as a civilian undeserving of his time.

Addressing Grimm, Jamison said, "Emery? Would you care to introduce these gentlemen?"

"Yes sir," the Pinkerton replied. He stopped just short of snapping to attention as he said, cocking a thumb toward the lawman, "This is the sheriff from across the line in Liberty. I didn't catch your name, Sheriff."

"His name is Noah Ransom," Jamison provided. "While we've never met, I know the sheriff from his reputation."

Ransom took over for the final introduction, saying, "And my friend here is G. W. Braddock."

"Possibly a deputy of yours?" asked Jamison.

"Or something," Ransom said.

"I notice that he doesn't wear a badge."

"He speaks, though," Braddock answered on his own behalf. "I used to be a Texas Ranger."

325

"Used to be? Meaning no longer are one?"

Braddock just shrugged.

"So you're without authority of any kind, then," Jamison observed.

"We're not here to discuss his bona fides," Sheriff Ransom said.

"Then pray tell why I have the pleasure of your company?" asked Jamison.

"You had a visit from a U.S. Marshal by the name of Henshaw recently," Ransom replied.

"That's true enough."

"You talked about three Pinkertons who ran afoul of Mr. Braddock here and wound up on the losing end of things."

"There was some mention of—"

Ransom, clearly not used to proper office etiquette, continued talking over Jamison. "Two of those Pinkertons were spying on a ranch across the line, the Circle H. I have good reason to believe that they were on your payroll."

"Your 'good reason' being . . .?"

"Let's just say a little birdie told me."

"Ah. No evidence, in other words," said Jamison.

"And then a third one tried to murder Mr. Braddock that same night."

It was an effort not to laugh as Jamison replied. "Astonishing! And what connects all that to me, in your imagination?"

"It's well known that you hire Pinkertons and some of them are putting pressure on the Circle H's owner to sell off his land—where he's been pumping oil, coincidentally."

"Sheriff, what's 'well known' in Liberty means nothing here. If you had any evidence there'd be a warrant in your hand right now and I'd be wearing manacles."

"Before you jump the gun on that, you ought to hear the rest."

"All right. I'm listening."

"Last night five more Pinkertons showed up in my town. They killed the very U.S. Marshal who came calling on you earlier."

"When you say Pinkertons—"

"I mean they were too dumb to leave their badges in the bunkhouse before heading out."

"From that I take it they're not talking to you," Jamison observed.

"Nobody does much talking from a coffin."

"So they're dead as well."

"Except this time, one got away. We're searching for him now. And when I get my hands on him, smart money says he'll sing until his lungs wither away."

"Perhaps," said Jamison, "but with all due respect, you'd be a fool to think that I'm the only Gulf Coast businessman employing Pinkertons these days."

"I know you're not," Ransom replied. "Just thought I'd warn you first, before we go to see Hal Baker down in Anahuac."

"Warn me, Sheriff?"

"To keep your thugs out of my county and stay well away from Lucius Haverstock."

"I made an offer on his land—most generous if I say so myself—and he declined to sell. Beyond that I have no affiliation with him whatsoever."

"I hope that's true for your sake," Ransom told him. "Otherwise, next time you see me I'll be carrying that warrant and those manacles you mentioned earlier."

"I think we're done here till that happens," Jamison

replied dismissively. "Emery, kindly show out visitors the exit, then come straight back here. We need to have a word about these tiresome interruptions."

ANAHUAC

Braddock was edgy on their ride south into Chambers County, watching out for followers who might be Pinkertons employed by Roger Jamison. When none appeared before they reached the city limits he relaxed a bit, but just enough to let his hand stray from the Colt Peacemaker on his hip.

The Chambers County seat was larger and more populous than Liberty, but smaller than Beaumont, an in-between whose value was enhanced for Gulf Oil by proximity to Lake Anahuac and Trinity Bay. The swampy land around it teemed with alligators who had learned to coexist with pumping oil derricks and stay well out of rifle range by daylight.

Stopping at a tamale stand, they wolfed down two apiece and got direction to Gulf's offices a few blocks farther on. Its building was not quite as large as Standard Oil's but had been freshly painted in a shade of pink that stood out from its neighbors on the street. After they'd let their horses drink and hitched them to a rail outside, Ransom preceded Braddock into the lobby.

A small sign on the left-hand wall directed them upstairs to Gulf's regional headquarters, where neither was surprised to find another fetching secretary at her desk, surprised by their appearance, peering narrowly at Ransom's badge. The sheriff asked to speak with Mr. Baker and she crossed the ante-room to knock upon a door which Braddock guessed might be mahogany, then passed inside.

A moment later she was back, escorting them into the private realm of Harold Baker, number two employer of the Pinkertons at large along the Gulf of Mexico. He rose, dusting his palms together as if he had been engaged in tiresome labor, though his polished desktop boasted no more than a fountain pen, an inkwell, and a leather blotter with no trace of any papers waiting to be signed.

"Gentlemen!" Gulf's front man beamed. "This is an unexpected pleasure."

"You may want to rethink that," Ransom replied.

"Oh?"

The sheriff introduced himself, then Braddock. Baker didn't ask about the latter's lack of any badge and Braddock settled for a silent nod.

"Won't you sit down, please?" Baker urged.

"Thanks," Ransom said. "I'll try not to waste too much of your time."

"Perhaps if you explained the reason for this visit . . .?"

Ransom told the same story he'd shared with Jamison in Beaumont—eight dead Pinkertons in Liberty, plus Marshal Henshaw and a deputy he didn't bother to explain had been locked up in jail when he ran out of time.

"I never met the marshal," Baker said, "but I knew *of* him, certainly. And now he's dead? Gunned down by Pinkertons, you say?"

Ransom ignored the question. Countered with, "You keep some on your payroll if I'm not mistaken."

"Yes, indeed. As do some of your banks along the coast and certain Texas railroads."

"Not to mention Standard Oil," Braddock chimed in, speaking for the first time."

"Indeed. We have that much in common, although very little else."

"Aside from both of you hunting for oil," Ransom corrected.

"Well, yet. There *is* that. But I fail to see how that involves Gulf with the unfortunate events in Liberty."

Again Ransom avoided answering the query aimed his way. Instead he responded with a question of his own. "Are you familiar with a rancher by the name of Lucius Haverstock?"

"I don't believe so," Baker said.

"His spread is called the Circle H."

"Ah, yes. After his surname. How original."

"He got his start in cattle, but he's found oil on the land and has some derricks pumping now. Seems like potential buyers started showing up almost before he got the first well capped."

"That stands to reason. Sadly, I'm not one of them, but maybe I should get in line."

"So long as all you do is make an offer, understanding that he's free to turn it down."

"Of course, Sheriff. It's a free country, after all."

"I've heard that, but some folks might disagree."

"That's more your area of than mine."

"Thing is," Ransom pressed on, "some of the Pinkertons who've turned up dead in Liberty were squeezing Mr. Haverstock to make him sell, like it or not."

"Some of them?" Baker asked, frowning.

"I can't be sure about the bunch who met their sorry end last night. They murdered Marshal Henshaw right around the time somebody killed my deputy inside the county jail."

Not mentioning that Pilcher was a prisoner awaiting trial when he went down.

Baker affected shock as he replied, "If you're suggesting that Gulf Oil had any part in those activities I can assure you—"

"That you know nothing about it," Ransom interrupted. "Sure. I know. What I'm doing now is warning anyone who has a bunch of Pinkerton's on their payroll to keep close watch on where they go and what they're getting up to after hours. Call it a word to the wise before matters get worse."

"I'll take all that under advisement, Sheriff. If there's nothing else . . .?"

"We'll let you get back to your work," Ransom replied, fanning one hand across the oilman's empty desktop.

On their way downstairs, Braddock spotted a shifty-looking character tracking their progress with dark, narrowed eyes. As with Emery Grimm in Beaumont, the man had a gun under his jacket, this one holstered on his hip.

Outside, as they were mounting up, Braddock asked Ransom, "Are we finished kicking hornets' nests today?"

"My work is done," Ransom allowed. "At least for now."

———————

"THEY'RE GONE," Clete Crowther told his boss as he entered Baker's office through a private side door to avoid the oilman's secretary. "Do you want them followed, sir?"

"Don't bother," Baker said. "This late, they should be

headed back to Liberty unless they plan to camp out on the trail."

"It's no great shakes to track them," Crowther said. "All kinds of accidents can happen on the open road."

"Forget that," Baker ordered. "Any word from Angus Fletcher since last night?"

"Nothing. The men who rode with him are lining up for Boot Hill burials unless some of them have kin on file who won't mind coughing up the fare to have their bodies freighted home by rail."

"I don't care where their bones wind up," said Baker. "But I *do* care about Fletcher running wild somewhere and telling tales to God knows who if he goes on a drinking binge."

"I've got good people on the lookout for him," Crowther said.

"I hope they're better than the first team," Baker answered back. "They were sent to plug a leak and put one marshal in the ground, not all get killed themselves."

"Something went wrong."

"Oh, yeah? 'Something went wrong,' you say"? Baker made no attempt to mask his sarcasm. "Like someone stubbed his toe and we can just forget about it?"

"No, sir. What I meant was—"

"Never mind that. Find Fletcher, no matter what it takes. And while you're at it, get some men together for another trip across the county line. No shirkers this time, Cletus. Understand me?"

"Yes, sir. Absolutely."

"Excellent," Baker replied. "Because you're leading them this time."

THE FIRST PART of their ride back into Liberty passed silently, Braddock assessing what he'd seen and heard in Ransom's confrontations with the two oilmen. At last the sheriff said, "If you've got something stuck inside your craw, let's get it out and have a look at it."

Braddock resisted drifting into personal opinion as he answered, "It's none of my business."

"But there's something on your mind. I've watched you gnawing on it for the past five miles."

"All right," Braddock replied. "If it was me—which it was not—I likely wouldn't have invited two armies of Pinkerton detectives to head for Liberty and take me down. I mean, you being short-handed right now and all."

"I can't argue with that," Ransom replied. "It's not the smartest move I ever made, I grant you. But a man just gets fed up sometimes, you know?"

Braddock nodded, thinking about his own activities of the past few years. "I've been there a time or three."

"Besides, I figure that it's even money one way or another."

"Say again?"

"I mean, whether they come for me or make a run at Lucius Haverstock. It's obvious both companies are looking at the Circle H, no matter what their local bosses claim. Lighting another fire in Liberty's no good to them if Haverstock keeps pumping crude or turns arounds and sells off to some other outfit."

Braddock had to smile at that. "So when you rile them up you're really hoping they'll come down on me?"

"Not you alone," Ransom replied. "Although I have to say you've held your own against them pretty well so far. Eight detectives down and not a scratch on you that I can see."

"Henshaw might disagree with that," Braddock replied. "Also your deputy."

"My *former* deputy," Ransom corrected him. "I planned to let him think about the error of his ways while digging ditches on a county chain-gang for a while. I *do* feel bad about the marshal, though."

"You might try to remember that he did exactly what you're doing with the oilmen. Only he was satisfied to threaten Jamison, without roping Hal Baker into it."

Ransom surprised him with a throaty laugh, then said, "I never like to do a job halfway."

"How are you fixed for extra guns tonight, Sheriff?"

"Two deputies that I can count on, although one of them lives up in Cleveland, covering the northwest corner of the county. We have trouble sometimes with drifters and outlaws slipping over from Montgomery County, where they like to hide out in the piney woods up there."

"He's out of action, then?"

"I sent a cable to him on my way to meeting you for breakfast and our little trip. He hadn't answered by the time we left."

"So, maybe one spare gun is all you've got."

"Make that one extra hand," Ransom replied. "I've got more guns than I can handle at the office."

"It gets awkward, carrying a load like that around with you," Braddock observed.

"Maybe I'll borrow some kid's wagon. Drag the whole load on my rounds."

Braddock could almost picture that. It made him smile, but only for a second. "I'm asking you," he said, "because I plan to spend the night out at the Circle H. Maybe the next couple of days, waiting to see if any Pinkertons turn up."

Ransom nodded. "You need to justify that salary."

"And they're as likely to come after Mr. Haverstock as after you," Braddock noted.

"Or Jamison and Baker might just flip a coin," the sheriff speculated. "See which one of 'em goes after me or you."

"Divide and conquer," Braddock answered back.

"I never took you for an optimist," the sheriff said.

"Keeping my fingers crossed. At least until it interferes with shooting," Braddock said.

"I'll hope to see you later then," said Ransom. "This would be your turn-off to the Circle H, coming up just ahead."

"Be safe tonight," said Braddock. "I'll try to make contact with you somehow, in the morning."

"If the morning comes," Ransom replied.

"Smart money says it will," Braddock replied.

While thinking to himself, *The question is whether we'll be around to see it when it happens.*

11

LIBERTY

DEPUTY ASA CARTER — "ACE" TO ALL HIS FRIENDS IN town—awaited Sheriff Ransom when he stepped into his office, weary from a long day on the road. He came around the desk bearing a folded piece of stationery in his outstretched hand, no writing visible on its outside.

"You had me worried, Sheriff. Thought some of those Pinkertons might have waylaid you."

"Well, I'm back," Ransom stated the obvious. "What's this?"

"One of the mayor's flunkies dropped it off around noontime. He's likely chewing on his nails by now."

"The flunky or the mayor?" Ransom asked.

Carter snorted a laugh but didn't answer. Ransom unfolded the sheet of vellum to reveal a printed letterhead reading "PETER WITHERS, MAYOR OF LIBERTY, TEXAS." The hand-scrawled message was succinct: "Come see me now."

"Guess I don't have to ask what's got him up in arms," Ransom observed.

"And not just him," Carter advised. "The runner said he wants to see you with our justice of the peace."

"It just gets better. Well, I'd better get on over there," said Ransom.

"Yes, sir. I'll get started on my rounds."

"No sign of any strangers loitering around so far?" Ransom inquired.

"Not yet," his deputy replied. "O' course, they seem to favor sneaking in by night." Ransom had turned to leave when Carter added, "Sorry about Pilcher, Sheriff."

Ransom shrugged it off. "He made his bed and now he's lying in it. Let it be a lesson to us all."

Five minutes later he was on the steps of City Hall, a block north of his office on Sam Houston Street. The edifice, in need of paint, housed both the mayor's quarters and the small courtroom where Justice of the Peace Tom Daley meted out his brand of justice, married folks, and dealt with civic legal business as the need arose. Upstairs, a larger courtroom was reserved for monthly visits by a circuit-riding judge who handled felonies that carried sentences beyond the misdemeanor limit of twelve months in custody. Today the building echoed with the sound of Ransom's steps on pricey marble brought from somewhere overseas that he was fairly sure taxpayers had been called upon to subsidize without fair warning of its price.

He didn't bother knocking on the mayor's office door, just opened it and stepped into the claustrophobic anteroom. Pete Withers came out of his private office, ruddy-faced as usual, but with a darker tinge of color in his cheeks that indicated his annoyance.

"Sheriff Ransom, finally," he groused.

"I came directly when I got your note."

"Which was delivered to your office hours ago," Withers observed. "Where have you been all day, if I may ask?"

"Around." Ransom was in no mood for explanations that would only further excavate the hole in which he found himself.

"Around," Withers repeated, not quite sneering. "I appreciate your candor, Sheriff. Now, if you would deign to join us . . ."

The "us," as Carter had warned him, meant Withers and old Tom Daley, both men glaring at him now with eyes like gun barrels, though Daley's were bloodshot as usual, matching the color of his drinker's nose. The JP cleared his rheumy throat and growled, "At last, the man himself."

Ransom ignored that, sat down in the office's remaining empty chair without awaiting invitation, doffed his hat and placed it on a corner of the mayor's desk as Withers went back to his swivel chair. The cushions wheezed under his weight.

"We need an explanation for last night's atrocity," said Withers, leaning forward with his elbows on the desktop.

"And the night before," Daley amended, not to be left out where giving orders was concerned.

"You know as much as I do at the moment," Ransom answered. "Pinkertons from outside Liberty came into town gunning for targets, but they couldn't pull it off. First night, they tried to nail a patron at the Palace. Last night, more of them came back and killed Deputy U.S. Marshal Jonas Henshaw, but most of them never made it out of town."

"*Most* of them?" Withers prodded.

338

"One of 'em got clear, it looks like. And before you ask, I don't know who that was."

"But you're investigating?" Daley interjected.

"Which explains my absence when the mayor's boy came by my office with his summons."

"*Where* were you investigating?" Withers asked him.

"Where the Pinkertons hang out these days," Ransom replied. "In Anahuac and Beaumont."

"Both outside your lawful jurisdiction," Daley challenged.

"Yes, Tom. I can read a map."

"By what authority?" the mayor asked.

"My oath of office to pursue and apprehend felons who do their crimes in Liberty."

"Did you consult with Sheriffs Lawson or Prentiss while you were traipsing through their counties?" Daley pressed him.

"Couldn't find them," Ransom lied without compunction. "But I had words with the Pinkertons' employers."

"Would those be the men in charge of Gulf and Standard Oil, by any chance?" asked Withers.

"Locally, at least," Ransom agreed.

At that point Daley shifted gears. "And what about the murder of your deputy, Sheriff."

"Ex-deputy. He was in jail for bribery and dereliction when somebody came around and shot him."

"In your absence, I believe," the mayor said.

"That's right, Pete. I was picking up the pieces of the Henshaw shooting and the Pinkertons who died trying to kill him. Try my hardest, I still can't be everywhere at once."

"You weren't alone though, were you?" Daley challenged.

"No. G.W. Braddock reached the scene ahead of me and helped Henshaw deal with the detectives."

"Braddock," Withers said. "Same man the sniper tried to murder night before last? The same man who brought two corpses in before that all occurred?"

"More Pinkertons who braced him at the Circle H, after he took a job with Lucius Haverstock."

That moneyed name silenced Ransom's interrogators for a moment, then the mayor asked, "Working as what?"

"Security," Ransom replied.

"We'll need to speak with him as well," Daley intoned.

"Then I suppose you'll have to ride out there and ask him nicely, Tom. Of course, the Circle H is well outside your legal jurisdiction. Same for Mayor Withers here."

The pair sat staring at him for a long moment, until Ransom got tired of waiting for more questions, took his hat, and rose to leave. "I'm going back to work now," he advised them. "If you think up something else to ask me you can find me on patrol."

THE CIRCLE H

The ranch was fairly quiet when Braddock returned, except for the steady grinding sound of derricks pumping crude. Blake Drury found him as he walked his dun to the barn and got the stallion settled in, unsaddled, well supplied with oats and water for the night ahead.

"Hell of a thing in town last night," the cowboy said.

"It was that," Braddock readily agreed.

"I heard eight men got killed?"

"Just seven by my count, with Marshal Henshaw and the deputy in jail."

"And those who killed the marshal were more Pinkertons?"

"Unless they stole the badges they were carrying," Braddock replied.

"Any idea who did for Pilcher?"

"Nobody's admitting they saw anything so far," said Braddock.

"But you reckon they were Pinkertons, same as the rest?"

"Can't prove it, but they didn't try to help the first bunch," Braddock answered. "Maybe someone else who didn't want Joe Pilcher dropping any names beyond Frank Mandelbaum's."

"And who was he, again?" Drury inquired.

"The one who tried to snipe me at the Palace night before last."

"So, another Pinkerton."

"He was," Braddock agreed.

"All smells like oil to me. Standard or Gulf, just flip a coin."

"Have there been any more approaches to the boss?" asked Braddock, with a head tilt toward the spacious Haverstock abode.

"Not so far," Drury answered. "He was pretty firm about not selling when the weasels came around last time."

"And since then you've been under siege out here?"

"Until you shot those two the other day. Making my rounds, I've seen no more of them. Of course, that doesn't mean they ain't around, just hiding better than they did before."

"How are your numbers for tonight?" the former Ranger asked.

Drury shrugged. "We're making do. I know you've had a long day in the saddle . . ."

"I could use some shut-eye," Braddock granted. "Slot me in for midnight and I should be good."

"Midnight it is," Drury replied and moseyed on about his rounds.

BEAUMONT

"Consider this your second chance," Emery Grimm declared. "Your *last* chance. Understand me?"

"Yes, sir," Zeke Bodine said, fighting a servile urge to doff his Stetson. "I won't let you down."

Grimm nodded. "You're the last one who came close to scouting out the Circle H, much less spotting the saddle bum who killed your friends."

Bodine nodded. He could have told his Pinkerton superior that Doc Webber and Arnie Folger hadn't qualified as friends, but knew he had to be accommodating in that moment prior to their departure from Beaumont toward Jefferson County.

"This goes sour, and you're absolutely out of chances," Grimm advised. He didn't draw a finger-blade across his throat, but Bodine got the message without any need for graphic illustrations.

"Yes, sir. You can count on me."

"Or count you out," Grimm said, driving it home one final time.

The other members of their party, rounding out an even dozen this time, were Jules Alvord, two-gun Larry Ringo, Cullen Diehl, Frank Colcord, Morgan Eaton, Virgil Ford, Pat Hodges, Mike Musgrove, Jesse McCarty, and George Loving—who was just the opposite in Zeke Bodine's opinion, with his ugly knife-scarred mug. Each one of them, besides the normal complement of six-guns, packed a rifle or a shotgun and at least one knife.

Going for blood this time and no mistake.

The Eye That Never Slept was done messing around with Lucius Haverstock.

"All right, you lead," Grimm ordered, holding back, the others grouped behind him, until Zeke nodded and started off to westward, toward the county line and his final destination at the Circle H.

He didn't like the *final destination* part of that, wished he could think or something better—more encouraging —but Bodine knew this was the price for him surviving last time, when he'd followed orders, watching Doc and Arnie die before he high-tailed back to Beaumont and reported in on the fiasco he had witnessed.

That, in turn, had led Frank Mandelbaum to his spot on Boot Hill, so Zeke supposed he owed the Pinkerton Detective Agency three lives already, one of them perhaps being his own.

But couldn't Grimm and Mr. Jamison have waited for another night or two, for Lucius Haverstock to let his guard down just a little bit, before they went all-in with an attack which, if it failed, would leave their numbers pared down to the bone, requiring more delays and more expense while reinforcements caught the next train south?

To hell with them, he thought now, as they headed out of town. His top priority was personal survival once again, and if he pulled that off a second time, Zeke thought it just might be a miracle.

LIBERTY

Walking the streets as dusk crept in, it seemed to Noah Ransom that he'd just about used up his meager store of luck. Pedestrians and shopkeepers he passed along the way avoided locking eyes with him, their greetings—if they offered one at all—muttered and grudging, telling Ransom that they'd lost all faith in him or were well on their way to doing so.

The sheriff couldn't blame them, which piled fresh embarrassment on top of his self-doubt.

He had considered seeking volunteers to help defend the county seat but gave up on that notion. He had one deputy prepared to back whatever play he called, assuming anything at all should happen overnight, and that was it. He'd left Ace Carter at the office, where Joe Pilcher's blood still stained the floor in one of their two holding cells, to make this circuit of the town alone. From there on, they'd switch off in shifts, perhaps with both of them patrolling as the night wore on and they grew weary from a day without relief.

Ransom supposed the waiting might come down to nothing after all, Baker and Jamison alike delaying their responses to his challenge from this afternoon. In truth, it would be wiser for them to do nothing for a while, lie back and let the strain of waiting grate on Ransom's nerves until it broke him down, and that was why he'd pushed it in his confrontations with both oilmen, hoping he could rile them to the point of no return—or one of them, at least, which would be all he needed for a warrant on the man responsible.

It never crossed his mind that either Jamison or Baker would take part in any action by their Pinkertons that put their own privileged lives in danger. It would

take a criminal indictment, followed by a drawn-out trial
and ultimate conviction, to put either one of them away.

And in the present circumstances, Ransom thought
that was about as likely as a rooster waking up
tomorrow and greeting the sunrise with a rousing
chorus of "I Wish I was in Dixie's Land." Not quite
impossible, but close enough that Ransom wouldn't
want to bet his life on the outcome.

Too late, he thought, knowing that he had overstepped
that boundary already.

As another night came on, he grasped the hard truth
that his life and everything that had propelled him
toward this moment was already riding on the line.

ANAHUAC

Cletus Crowther didn't like his new assignment, not one
bit, but there was nothing he could do to weasel out of it.
He'd worked too long and diligently for the Pinkerton
Detective Agency to throw it all away now, when
Chicago had entrusted him with an assignment that not
only brought a raise in salary but a substantial increase
in his personal authority.

So Crowther would be riding with a dozen of his best
men, north to Liberty, as soon as all their gear was
squared away and he could think of no more good
excuses for delaying their departure.

As to whether he'd be coming back victorious or in a
rough pine box . . . well, that was anybody's guess.

The men he'd chosen from the whittled ranks
remaining to him were all bona fide man-killers, tested
in the heat of battle or at least proved equal to the task of

shooting adversaries in the back without a semblance of remorse. Their ranks included Ben Newcomb, Lucas O'Folliard, Solomon Poole, Nat Rudabaugh, Ab Stephens (given name Albert), Cole Yarberry, Shea Bascom, Warren Hume, Cyrus Tracy, Seth Daniels, Kimball Breckinridge, and Joshua Vaugh.

That brought their total to an unlucky thirteen, as Crowther realized, but he had never been a superstitious man and when the chips were down, he knew an extra gun might just make all the difference between success and lying stone cold dead.

Their task tonight was relatively simple on its surface: find the sheriff who had strayed beyond his jurisdiction to insult and threaten Mr. Baker, then eliminate him. Naturally, someone else would take his place, but Crowther understood that Gulf Oil could exert its influence and spend sufficient money to ensure that the replacement was a man more sympathetic to their cause.

Less likely to make waves, that is. And maybe he would even take Gulf's side against its Standard Oil competitors.

If nothing else, simple neutrality would do.

But first the current sheriff had to go.

No one had ever called Crowther a genius but even he knew that confronting Mr. Baker ranked among the worst mistakes a man could make. Directly challenging his power, threatening his income, was a grievous error no one could survive.

Cletus was on his way to prove that now, despite whatever risks he faced in doing so, and he expected a nice reward for his efforts.

If he could just get back to Anahuac alive.

BEAUMONT

Roger Jamison, as usual, dined alone at Beaumont's finest restaurant, the Occidental Arms, his private corner table commonly reserved and screened from prying eyes by folding screens beyond which only waiters and the French sommelier could trespass with impunity.

A creature of routine, Jamison ordered prime roast beef, medium rare, together with a lobster from the Gulf coast, freshly caught that morning. On occasion he might substitute crayfish or crab, but only on weekends, washing the whole lot down with Cabernet Sauvignon or Riesling, all depending on his mood. He always finished up with cognac — "extra old" preferred—before departing either for the mansion where he dwelt alone or for a pricey brothel run with great discretion by one Madam Chloë on a quiet side street if he felt the urge on Saturdays.

What was the point of being wealthy and pursuing even greater gain without the simple joys of living well?

Tonight Jamison tried to put the long day's aggravation out of mind, beginning with the rude invasion of his office by an out-of-county sheriff who gave no more thought to legal jurisdiction than one might expect from a roadrunner chasing desert reptiles. The audacity of that event—the sheer unmitigated gall—had left Jamison's stomach roiling through midafternoon, until he'd issued orders for a raid against the Circle H.

Jamison blamed its owner, Lucius Haverstock, for stirring up his local sheriff to cross county lines and try throwing his weight around where he had no authority. With any luck the problem would be solved tonight, with Haverstock eliminated and his heirs—whoever those might be—amenable to selling out before they suffered even more misfortune. Should the stubborn rancher manage somehow to survive . . . well, there would still be time try again when things cooled down a bit.

Jamison had considered reaching out to Standard Oil headquarters, operating thinly veiled as the New Jersey Holding Company, but his superiors didn't appreciate reports of fumbling failure. They preferred—in fact, demanded—constant progress in the field, impressing their investors with new acquisitions, greater output, and a bottom line with no tinge of red ink to agitate them in their lavish offices.

Jamison knew enough to keep them pacified, thereby assuring that he would, in turn, survive and prosper in a cutthroat industry that might, before much longer, dominate the field of U.S. commerce and expand from there to rule the world.

A two-bit county rancher with pretensions of grandeur was nothing by comparison.

Soon, he would be a fading memory.

ANAHUAC

While Roger Jamison enjoyed his supper fifty miles away, Hal Baker ate a poor boy sandwich—shrimp and oysters, fried upon a bed of shredded lettuce, all contained within a French roll—at his desk and pondered what he might have done to spare himself and his Gulf Oil employers from the storm that was about to break.

He couldn't think of anything specific but it was a

given that, should this night's mission fail, his headquarters in Pittsburgh would devise some way to blame him for the whole fiasco, in which case dismissal from his post would be the very least of Baker's problems.

Other men had suffered fatal accidents for lesser errors. Some had simply disappeared with no prospect of ever being seen again.

For that reason he hadn't once considered reaching out to his superiors, although the prospect of another call was weighing on his mind. If Cletus Crowther and his riders failed at their appointed task tonight, Baker would need more Pinkertons to fill the thinning ranks and the initial outlay for employing them would have to come from his own pocket, to avoid sounding alarms in Pennsylvania before he had the situation under his control.

His choice had come down to a strike against the Circle H or at the sheriff who had dared disturb him, straying twenty-five miles from his own preserve to challenge Baker with veiled threats. With Chambers County's lawmen in his pocket, not to mention every other politician worth bribing in the neighborhood, Baker had no great fear of being prosecuted but he dreaded bad publicity that would reflect upon his work for Gulf and start headquarters breathing down his neck, reviewing every move he'd made over the past six months or more.

No modern businessman could stand such scrutiny and Baker was not in a mood to try.

Instead, he would eliminate the lawman who had dared defy him and the smug companion who had tagged along in hopes of seeing Baker humbled. Noah Ransom was the main target, the sheriff's sidekick

349

secondary to that master plan but still slated for summary removal from the earthly plane.

Once Baker managed that, he could regroup, move in, and pay off any local leaders who would settle for a reasonable bribe or start planning removal of recalcitrant holdovers at the next election cycle. That would take more time, but Baker had abiding faith in the corruptibility of small-town office holders up and down the Gulf.

With Sheriff Ransom's stark example set before them, he expected most of the survivors to accept whatever they were offered, meekly falling into line.

And when the gun smoke cleared a bit, Baker could turn his mind toward getting rid of Roger Jamison, his nemesis from Standard Oil.

One project at a time, and if he kept his wits about him, Baker had faith in his own ability to triumph in the end.

THE CIRCLE H

Blake Drury rousted Braddock out of bed at midnight, as agreed. Leaving the bunkhouse, Braddock drank a cup of lukewarm coffee—black and strong, regardless—and saw lamps still burning in the ranch house where it seemed that Lucius Haverstock was working late.

Or maybe he was simply worrying about what to expect from his encroaching enemies.

Recovering his Winchester, Braddock embarked on his patrol of Haverstock's spread, stopping at the barn to check his dun first, then circling around the sprawling house where his employer lived alone. There was a photograph inside the home of a brunette woman whom Braddock guessed had been the rancher's wife, but questioning her absence fell outside the ex-Ranger's job as hired help at the Circle H.

It was none of his business anyhow, and he had suffered loss enough in his own life that there was no need to start borrowing from others met by chance. Each person had a story and the course of living dictated that none of those eventually ended well.

Moving around the grounds, he counted half a dozen other hands on watch, making their rounds on foot. Braddock assumed there must be others ranging widely over Haverstock's domain on horseback, shadowing the herd of sleepy cattle, checking up on personnel who kept the rancher's derricks pumping day and night.

Braddock imagined that he was observing the creation of a whole new world, but with the old one's problems amplified by greedy men who had discovered fresh ways to squeeze profits from the soil, pursuing fortunes that would only grow with new petroleum discoveries and applications to the nation's former coal-fired industry. He didn't like to think about the troubles that were bound to follow, spreading out from smoke-filled boardrooms through a vast landscape waiting to be despoiled.

A Texan to his core, Braddock believed in the ethos of enterprise, taking advantage of the nation's natural resources for the benefit of all, but something in him bridled at the thought of fat old men in prideful cliques, making and breaking rules behind closed doors and paying law enforcement officers to look the other way.

Another problem that he couldn't solve alone, except where he encountered it on a small scale during his travels, doing what he could with any tools at hand.

Tonight it was enough to earn his salary from Lucius Haverstock, ensuring that no trespassers moved in to tamper with the life his present boss was building for himself. Braddock didn't regard it as a new career by any means—the Rangers had been that for him, and they were irreplaceable—but once he gave his word to carry out a certain duty he would meet that challenge, never mind the risks involved.

There was a chance, of course, that nothing would happen tonight, but Braddock didn't trust that cautious hope.

Take it one minute at a time, he thought, *and hope to see another sunrise when it rolled around.*

12

LIBERTY

EMERY GRIMM CALLED FOR HIS TEAM TO STOP A QUARTER of a mile outside of town, the edgy Pinkertons huddling around him in the darkness to receive final instructions. Crowther minced no words as he addressed his troops.

"We want the sheriff first and foremost," he reminded them. "If anyone tries helping him, a deputy or whoever, take care of them while you're at it."

"Sparing the town?" Jules Alvord asked him.

"No more damage than is necessary," Crowther answered. "If you're fired on from some building then defend yourselves, but don't go setting fire to anything or shooting up the place to make a point. If possible, we go in, get the job done, and get out."

Pat Hodges groused, "Seems like we ought to get paid extra, bedding down a lawman."

"Take it up with Mr. Jamison next time you see him," Grimm advised. "Or maybe you could send a wire up to

Chicago. Tell the brothers why you want a raise in pay down here."

That brought some chuckles from the others, maybe picturing how Rob and William Pinkerton would take it if an agent in the field complained he wasn't being paid enough to kill duly-elected lawmen on behalf of paying clients. There'd been bad publicity enough a quarter century before, when operators in Missouri bombed the home of outlaws Frank and Jesse James, wanted for robbery and murder. As it happened, neither of the bandits was at home, although the blast had killed a younger brother, Archie, barely nine years old, while also blowing off one of their mother's arms.

Today, after the Homestead Strike and other labor scandals in the 1890s, it could finish off the agency if evidence emerged that its some of its "detectives" were cold-blooded murderers who didn't draw the line at killing law enforcement officers.

"I reckon not," said Hodges, to another round of laughter from the team.

"Okay, then. If there's no more stupid questions," Grimm scolded, "we'll split up here, half of us approaching from the south, the rest circling around to come in on the north side. Bodine, Ringo, Alvord, Colcord, and Diehl, you come along with me. We'll take the south end. Eaton, Ford, Hodges, Musgrove, Loving, and McCarty take the north. I'll give you a ten-minute lead to circle up that way before we come in from the other end. If we don't find the sheriff on patrol, head for his office and we'll box him in there. Got it?"

Nods of affirmation made their way around the ring of shadowed faces while the agents gave a final check to their weapons, confirming all of them were fully loaded and prepared. That done, the northbound group rode off, their horses trailing dust under the wan light of a quarter-moon.

Grimm felt jumpy now that they were on the verge of getting down to it, entering mortal combat with the constituted law in Liberty. He would have trouble counting all the rules he'd broken during service to rich patrons of the Pinkerton Detective Agency, but he was on the verge of stepping over an indelible line now, beyond which no excuse would cover the transgression.

There could be no turning back.

But did he even want to wriggle out from that responsibility when he had come this far?

Deciding it was already too late, Crowther drew a brass watch out of his vest pocket and checked the time.

"Four minutes," he informed his troops. "Line up and follow me."

THE CIRCLE H

Braddock had learned from grim experience that sometimes his surroundings just *felt* wrong, nothing that he could put a finger on precisely, but he trusted his instincts to help him stay above ground in a world peopled by enemies he often didn't recognize until they made a move to take him down.

Tonight that restless feeling nagged at him although he couldn't pin it down, beyond determining what it was not.

First thing that came to Braddock's mind, it wasn't any kind of preternatural silence that unnerved him. Everywhere he turned, guards trudged along on foot patrols, others were mounted with their horses making all of the expected sounds, while grazing cattle lowed and creaking derricks labored round the clock to pump more crude. Snatches of conversation reached him on the night breeze, from the bunkhouse or various points around the house and outbuildings, the constant murmur of a working ranch.

At the same time, he heard no skulking sounds of enemies approaching, saw no shadows that seemed out of place or set his teeth on edge. Nothing to make him cock the Winchester he carried, raising it in preparation for a shot into the night.

The only movement that surprised him came when Lucius Haverstock emerged onto his covered porch, head wreathed with fragrant vapors from a meerschaum pipe. The rancher stood at ease, scanning his property the way a watchful rooster oversees a henhouse, ready to attack—or at the very least raise an alarm—if it beheld a fox or weasel on the prowl.

Braddock drifted toward the porch, rifle braced casually in the crook of his left arm, and Haverstock saw him approaching, raising his pipe in greeting before he returned it to a corner of his mouth.

"All quiet," he declared, not making it a question.

"Seems like," Braddock answered in the same subdued tone, stopping at the foot of wooden steps that granted access to the porch.

"Too much to hope they've given up, I guess," said Haverstock, in a sardonic tone.

"I'd say so," Braddock granted.

"Feeling restless for the road?" the rancher asked him.

"No, sir. When I take a job I like to finish it."

A nod from Haverstock. "And hope it doesn't finish you, instead."

"Always my goal," Braddock agreed.

"It must be tiresome, solving other people's problems for them," said the rancher.

"All depends on how you look at it," Braddock replied. "It's basically the same thing I was doing as a Ranger, trying to stop rustlers messing with the herd."

"Is that how you see people, Braddock? Like some kind of livestock?"

Braddock shrugged. "There's a certain herding instinct. Otherwise there'd be no towns and cities, nothing like the operation you've got going here."

"And those who try to poach what isn't theirs by right would be the rustlers?"

"Rustlers, bandits, whatever you want to call them," Braddock said.

"What if they plant their crimes in fancy offices?" asked Haverstock.

"It makes no difference. When they flout the law, they stand on level ground."

"But money matters, you'd agree," the rancher said. "Some outlaws buy lawmen and judges, politicians all the way from City Hall up to the State House—or the White House, as we've seen from time to time."

"You'll get no argument from me on that score, sir."

"Did it upset you when the Rangers took your badge, Mr. Braddock?"

"I still have it," Braddock said, correcting him. "I just don't wear it nowadays."

"It didn't hurt you, though? Make you feel . . . used, I guess?"

"The legislature didn't ask for my opinion. They prefer to sit behind closed doors and talk about economy, like you can put a price on keeping people safe."

"We put a price on everything," said Haverstock. "A budget's worthless if it doesn't balance."

357

"I can see both sides of it," said Braddock. "I just thought that cutting back so much on manpower was . . . premature, let's say."

Haverstock allowed himself a smile at that. "The wild frontier. Reminds me of when I first settled here. Now, with the oil and all, we're moving into a new age."

"But will it be a better one?" asked Braddock.

With a shrug, the rancher said, "No one can ever answer that until they're on the other side."

Braddock was mulling that one over when a shot rifle rang out, not close at hand, but loud enough to let him know it had been fired within a couple hundred yards. Shifting his Winchester to readiness, he said, "You'd best hole up inside the house, sir."

"Not with raiders on my property," said Haverstock. "They bring a fight to me, I'm going to be in the thick of it."

As Haverstock stepped back inside the house, presumably to arm himself, Braddock decided it wasn't his place to tell the rancher where he could and couldn't go on his own land. A second shot, immediately answered by a ragged volley from the darkness, had the former Ranger moving forward, seeking out an enemy he couldn't see.

CLETUS CROWTHER RESERVED the first shot for himself, not trusting his subordinates to run off on their own and start the ball before all members of his raiding party were in place. Some of them were invisible from where he sat astride his bay roan gelding, but they'd all had time enough to reach their designated places, and he had to trust that none of them had gotten lost.

If they had, so be it. Clete wasn't prepared to sit and wait on them all night.

His target was a ranch hand riding circuit some two hundred yards removed from Lucius Haverstock's ranch house and working structures ranged around it. He lined up the cowboy in the sights of his Lee-Enfield rifle, a bolt-action model holding ten .303 cartridges inside its magazine, loaded with five-round stripper clips. He carried extras in a bandoleer across his chest, enough to drop a hundred men if necessary, though he seriously doubted that would be required.

Nailing one individual—the rancher who aspired to be an oilman—would be adequate, and they could all go home to Anahuac, where they would celebrate a job well done. Hal Baker could negotiate from that point with whoever might inherit title to the Circle H, and that was how you closed a business deal along the Gulf of Mexico these days.

But first, they had to locate Lucius Haverstock and smoke him out, put him on the spot.

Or maybe he would come to them.

Watching the puncher topple from his saddle, dead before he hit the ground, Grimm spurred his mount forward, working the Enfield's bolt, ejecting the spent cartridge, and replacing it inside the rifle's chamber with a live one.

All around him on the property, more guns were blazing now, like fireworks lit in celebration of a holiday. Keeping a likeness of his primary targets in mind, the Pinkerton charged off through darkness speckled by dozens of muzzle flashes, racing toward the front line of a battlefield he'd set aflame.

JAMES REASONER

LIBERTY

Ace Carter roamed the city streets at random, stopping here and there to shake a doorknob and confirm a shop was locked up for the night, wondering where his boss was—and above all how he, as a simple deputy, had stepped into the middle of an all-out war.

It didn't feel that way tonight, of course, the county seat as quiet as it ever was until he came upon one of its various saloons. And even then, the sounds of celebration from within seemed muted, the piano music more off-key than usual. When he peered through the lighted windows of the Lucky Strike he saw only a handful of determined drinkers and there had been no more customers inside its competition two blocks over, dubbed The Inside Straight.

Only a few townsmen—and likely none with families they cared about—had dared to seek amusement in the county seat tonight, barely a full twenty-four hours after seven men were gunned down, one of them inside the sheriff's office, locked up tight inside a cell.

That boded ill for Noah Ransom, Carter knew, from hearing gossip around town. Liberty's mayor and justice of the peace were out to find a scapegoat for the rash of violence their town had suffered, and they naturally blamed the man who drew a meager monthly salary to keep the peace. Neither would challenge Lucius Haverstock, much less the Pinkertons who worked for Gulf and Standard Oil, since they remained in awe of money and the power that it spawned.

It was no secret that Mayor Withers craved a seat in the state legislature. As for Tom Daley, he was looking forward to retirement if he could acquire a better job and Carter wouldn't be surprised if he went shopping his degree from Waco's Baylor Law School to the highest bidder he could find before much longer. Neither of them wanted a blood-red stain on his record when they cast about for new employers, and if sacrificing Sheriff Ransom helped remove that stigma, Carter knew they wouldn't think twice about letting Noah take the fall.

A small voice in his head piped up, asking, *So who'll be sheriff then?*

Embarrassed by the thought, Carter dismissed the thought but knew it would come back to haunt him before long. Promotion meant more pay, but he would also have to win elections to the office and Ace wasn't sure he had the traits required for making a majority of Liberty's inhabitants appreciate him when his job was riding on the line.

"Forget about that now," he muttered, thankful no one else was on the street to overhear him talking to himself.

Ace turned the corner past Sol Weissman's butcher shop and froze, surprised to see six riders moseying along in his direction, moving slowly as if they had no clear destination and weren't in any hurry to arrive there.

Ducking out of sight into a recessed doorway, Carter saw all six of them were armed—no great surprise there —and he didn't recognize a one of them on sight. A tremor of alarm bristled the short hairs on his neck, thinking that after the bloody events in Liberty over the past two nights, this had to be a hunting party on the prowl for human prey.

And that brought Noah Ransom instantly to mind.

Uncertain where the sheriff was right now, Ace knew it was his job to intervene and try to find out what the strangers wanted, maybe even warn them to reverse directions and head out of town, camp somewhere on the plains tonight and make another run at Liberty tomorrow, when the town was wide-awake.

He also knew that move could get him killed, but they were bound to spot him soon, partly concealed as he might be by shadows, with no streetlamp near enough to light him up.

But hiding out, letting them pass, would be the coward's way.

Cocking both hammers on his double-barreled shotgun, Carter stepped from cover, noting as the leader of the hunting party saw him and spoke softly to his followers.

"Deputy Sheriff Carter," Ace announced himself, holding his weapon at what soldiers liked to call port arms. "What brings you into town this late?"

The leader spoke up with a gravel voice to say, "We're looking for your sheriff."

"Guess you'll have to catch him in the morning," Carter said, "and there's no place open at this time of night where you can rent a bed."

"Can't wait that long," their spokesman said. "Where would we find the sheriff now?"

"Like I just said—"

Ace had no time to finish as the riders started pulling guns and aiming them his way. He fired both barrels of his scattergun, loaded with buckshot, then jumped back into the doorway that had sheltered him a moment earlier, a storm of bullets breaking all around him like sudden claps of thunder.

THE CIRCLE H

Emerging from his ranch house with a rifle cocked and ready, Lucius Haverstock beheld a battlefield he scarcely recognized as home.

His chosen weapons were the newest Winchester available, a Model 1895 chambered for .30-06 cartridges, with one round in the chamber and four more in its internal magazine. Haverstock wore a bandoleer of spares across his chest and had a Smith & Wesson Model 10 on his right hip in fast-draw leather, a .38 Special double-action revolver that required no cocking of its hammer for a shooter to discharge six rounds as rapidly as he could pull the trigger. Bright brass for the sidearm ringed the rancher's waist in leather loops that gave him twenty-five more cartridges ready at hand.

Now all he needed was a target and there seemed to be no shortage on that side of things.

Haverstock knew his hired hands at a glance, familiar with their faces and their choice in hats. Mingled among them now were mounted strangers who he didn't recognize and who had never been invited to the Circle H.

One of them spotted Haverstock emerging from his house and swung in that direction, brandishing a pistol as he shouted at his horse for greater speed. Instead of looking for a place to hide, the rancher turned oilman stood tall, his rifle shouldered, peering down its twenty-eight-inch barrel fitted with a sliding ramp sight at the rear, a fixed post at the muzzle.

Aiming only took a fraction of a second but his enemy was fast, determined. Both men fired their weapons almost simultaneously, Haverstock absorbing the Winchester's recoil as he heard a bullet whisper past him, almost close enough to bite a chunk from his left ear.

Almost.

His .30-06 slug sped straight and true, striking dead-center on the hostile rider's chest. The gunman made a *whoof* sound while rolling over backwards from his saddle, boots clearing the stirrups without any conscious signal from his dying brain. He hit the ground, raising a little cloud of dust as he rolled over once and came to rest facedown.

The dead man's horse, a scared gray, veered instantly off course and vanished into darkness, trying to escape the sounds of combat that surrounded it. Haverstock let it go and started searching for another adversary on property that had become a battleground.

And found it quickly, this one running toward the house, dismounted, with a rifle in his hand that looked like a Winchester "Yellow Boy," the classic Model 1866. Haverstock met the runner's eyes over his rifle's sights, pumping the action on his Model 1895, and was about to fire his second shot when a bullet out of nowhere grazed his left forearm and staggered him, immediately drawing blood, spoiling his aim.

He dropped, trying to reacquire the target that immediately threatened him, but someone beat him to it with a shot that made the hostile runner stumble, clutch his side, and sprawl into the dust. The gunman struggled to recover, lurching up on one knee, but it came too late to save him. Haverstock silently cursed the pain in his left arm but held his rifle steady for the length of time required to score his second killing shot.

Just as he pumped the Model 1895's smooth lever action, someone else approached him at a dead run from the general direction of the barn. Haverstock swung around to meet the new threat, then he recognized G.W. Braddock as the former Texas Ranger shouted at him, "Are you hit?"

LIBERTY

Emery Grimm had been expecting trouble scouting through the streets, searching for Sheriff Noah Ransom, but he thought his group had struck it lucky when a lawman with a shiny badge pinned to his vest had hailed them, stepping out of shadow with a sawed-off shotgun in his hands.

That gave him two shots against Grimm and five more Pinkertons itching to cut him down, and even with the prospect of a buckshot charge expanding as it traveled thirty feet enough of them should still remain uninjured, able to return fire and complete their mission for Hal Baker.

What Grimm required now was confirmation of the lawman's name, and he provided that himself, announcing that he was a deputy named Carter, asking them, "What brings you into town this late?"

Grimm saw no point to lying as he answered back, "We're looking for your sheriff."

"Guess you'll have to catch him in the morning," the response came, sounding nervous-like, adding, "There's no place open at this time of night where you can rent a bed."

Instead of dragging out the futile conversation, Grimm went for his Colt and heard his five companions slapping leather off to either side of him. Before he had a chance to fire, though, the obstructive deputy triggered both barrels of his scattergun, trusting to luck instead of aiming, and the whole thing fell apart.

Grimm's palomino shied, tried turning from the hail of leaden pellets, but he gripped its reins fiercely and pegged a shot in the direction of the enemy who was retreating toward a shop's recessed doorway, drawing a sidearm without trying to reload his double-barrel, useless now with both rounds spent.

The Pinkertons poured pistol fire into his hiding place and all around it, bringing down the storefront's picture window with the racket of a frozen waterfall. Deputy Carter was returning fire—a .44 it sounded like —and from a corner of his eye Grimm saw Cullen Diehl sprawl from his saddle, landing in the street head-first with an unnerving *crunch* of vertebrae.

"Somebody kill him, will you?" Grimm yelled at his four surviving Pinkertons and suited words to action with a second aimed round from his Peacemaker.

It missed, splintered the doorjamb that was covering the deputy, and brought another round that sizzled close enough to make a hissing sound in Grimm's right ear. Hunching his shoulders while he cocked his Colt, Grimm could feel his palomino rearing on its hind legs, heedless of him yanking on its reins.

Another second and the Pinkerton team leader found himself airborne, tumbling, trying to brace himself for impact as he landed in the dusty thoroughfare with stunning force.

THE CIRCLE H

Braddock examined Lucius Haverstock's left arm, determined that the wound was just a graze, bloody but nothing that should incapacitate the rancher.

"You should go inside the house," he cautioned Haverstock.

"Forget it!" his employer snapped. "This is my land and I'm defending it."

"Well, then, at least get off the porch where anyone can see you," Braddock urged, descending the short flight of wooden steps, and glancing back to make sure Haverstock was following.

A rifle slug from somewhere in the darkness zipped between Braddock and Haverstock, missed both of them, and smacked into the front door of the ranch house. Haverstock glanced backward, growling, "Damn! I had that wood imported from Brazil."

"Least of our problems," Braddock answered. "We need decent cover and I mean right now."

"If this trash thinks I'll run and hide on my own place they need to think again," said Haverstock.

"No shame in hiding," Braddock told him, "if it helps you live to win a fight."

Another narrow miss that raised a spurt of dust between his boots persuaded Haverstock. "All right," he answered grudgingly. "The bunkhouse, then?"

"Suits me," Braddock replied, sprinting to reach the structure that had emptied out of hired hands when the shooting started moments earlier.

Its door stood open and the two men ducked inside, each moving to a window with a clear view of the nearby property. A horseman Braddock didn't recognize raced past, and Braddock let him go, uncertain whether he was an employee of the Circle H or one of their attackers.

Chaos around the ranch house and its outbuildings made Braddock leery of unloading on potential allies, realizing that he couldn't recognize the hostiles unless they were firing on ranch hands he personally recognized. Frustration made him clench his teeth until he finally made out a face that was familiar from his trip to Anahuac with Noah Ransom.

"That one!" he directed Haverstock's attention to one of the riders. "In the black hat, using the bolt-action rifle."

"Got him!" Haverstock replied, raising his Winchester.

They fired almost together, no more than a half-second between their shots, and Braddock couldn't say whose bullet swept the Pinkerton out of his saddle. It hardly mattered as their target hit the ground, tried struggling to all fours, and then collapsed where he lay.

"You think he was important?" Haverstock inquired.

"Can't answer that," Braddock replied, "but seems to be plenty of them left."

"I dropped two of them near the house."

"Still more to go," said Braddock.

"And we need to find them in a hurry," Haverstock replied.

"All right," Braddock agreed reluctantly, sensing the truth of it. "Your place, you lead the way. Don't let me pick off any of your men."

LIBERTY

Zeke Bodine witnessed Emery Grimm's tumble out of the saddle from a distance, grimacing and wondering which was the quickest path to clearing out of Liberty. He'd been reluctant to accompany the raiding party, cornered into it, but now his mind was focused on escape.

The trick to that was getting out alive, avoiding both sides as he cut and ran.

Zeke wondered if he'd always been a coward, keeping that a secret even from himself. He hoped not, but he'd definitely been relieved to ride off clean when Doc Webber and Arnie Folger made their foolish play against the stranger who had killed them without thinking twice about it. Now, with Grimm apparently dead and their raiding party leaderless, all Zeke could think about was making tracks and getting clear before he wound up dead as well.

This time around, if he could manage to escape, Bodine knew that he wouldn't be returning to Beaumont or to the Pinkerton Detective Agency. He had soured on that, craving a new perspective that would let him start from scratch and not look back at his mistakes.

He only hoped that it wasn't too late.

The key was leaving *now*, before one of the ranch hands picked him off, and being quick enough that none among his fellow Pinkertons caught on and shot him as a traitor turning tail. Once he was free and clear, Zeke planned on riding to the southwest, maybe getting lost a while in Houston with its population climbing rapidly toward fifty thousand souls, then pushing on to cross the Rio Grande at Laredo riding south until he found some tiny town in Mexico where he could change his name and disappear.

But first . . .

He fired a wild shot toward the doorway where the deputy was hiding, then dragged on his horse's reins and spurred the mare back toward the point where his half of the raiding party entered Liberty.

Behind him, Morgan Eaton shouted, "Where you going, Zeke?"

"To fetch the other boys," Bodine replied, not even glancing back.

He'd traveled half a block or so when Sheriff Ransom suddenly appeared in front of him, armed with a rifle, running to assist his cornered deputy. The lawman spotted Zeke approaching, shouldered his long gun, and fired it without breaking stride. The bullet struck Bodine below his breastbone, knocked him sprawling from his saddle, landing with enough force on the ground to drive the breath out of his lungs.

And suddenly, shelter in Mexico seemed very far away.

13

THE CIRCLE H

G.W. Braddock followed Lucius Haverstock on a dash from the bunkhouse to the larger of the spread's two barns, where half a dozen riflemen were firing shots into the darkness farther out. One of the battlers spotted them approaching, recognized the leader, and called out, "Boss coming in with the new guy!"

That suited Braddock well enough, as long as no one from the ranch he was defending tried to pick him off.

Arriving at the barn's southwest corner, he paused to catch his breath and sweep the field in front of him for targets, spotting only muzzle flashes winking back at him. He couldn't count the raiders accurately, knowing some of them would fire and move on to a safer vantage point, but a rough estimate told Braddock there were still at least nine enemies trying to whittle down the defenders' ranks.

And if they couldn't be forced to flee, it would be necessary to eliminate them one by one.

The good news: skulking into their approach, it seemed that none of the attackers had come bearing torches—or, at least, they hadn't thought of starting any fires around the spread so far. Whichever rival company had sent them, Braddock guessed they would have orders not to damage any of the working oil wells, but that still left the barns, Haverstock's home, and several outbuildings that could be set afire, lighting the battle-ground and wreaking destruction.

Worse yet, from Braddock's point of view, his dun was inside the other, larger barn, where it might be consumed by flames if someone got the bright idea of turning the midnight assault onto a scorched earth attack.

Braddock wasn't a sentimentalist, but he had grown accustomed to the horse and it had served him well, with courage, on their travels. Add to that his feeling of revulsion at the Circle H's other horses trapped and panicking, surrounded by gunfire and threats of worse, and it kindled an angry blaze inside him.

Waiting for Haverstock to aim and fire another rifle shot, Braddock leaned in and told the rancher, "Stay under cover if you can. I'm heading for the other barn."

"But why—"

Cutting him off, Braddock said, "I fight better on the move," and took off in a crouching run across the open field of fire.

Ahead of him and somewhere to his right, a voice cried out, "Watch that one!"

Instantly, at least two rifles started firing from the shadows, tracking Braddock as he ran. Their bullets buzzed around him with a sound like angry hornets swarming to defend their nest, Braddock expecting to be struck down any second while he loped ahead, boots raising tiny clouds of dust behind him. It was chilly out but Braddock barely felt it as he concentrated on his next stride, ducking, weaving, as he ran the gauntlet with more hostile weapons chiming in.

Would the next step be his last? No time to think about that now, as his mind focused on the barn ahead of him, the cover he would find there, plus a vantage point from which he would retaliate against his would-be murderers.

A fighting chance as all that Braddock needed.

And he needed it right now.

LIBERTY

Sheriff Noah Ransom saw the horseman he had fired on receive his rifle slug, center of mass, and tumble from his horse without a cry of pain or fear. He took that for a fatal wound and gave it no more thought, working the lever on his Winchester as he advanced along the sidewalk, moving toward the doorway where he'd spotted Ace Carter fighting back from cover, under fire.

Ransom had no doubt that the gunmen must be Pinkertons as two of them spun toward him, horses acting jumpy in the middle of a crossfire on the open street. He had a slight advantage over horsemen grappling with their nervous mounts while trying for a kill shot, but the closer he came to them, the easier their task might prove to be.

To spoil their aim, the sheriff rapid-fired three rounds from his Winchester, one target reacting with a cry of pain but staying in his saddle all the same. Instead of running closer to them, giving them a better shot,

Ransom veered to his left as he approached the recessed doorway to Bert Jackson's feed store, smashing through it, dropping to a crouch behind a stout barrel of oats as pistol bullets whined around him from outside.

Jackson would throw a fit when he observed the damage to his shop, maybe go after compensation through the court, but Ransom had no time to worry about that just now. Nothing would matter if he died within the next few moments and he hated thinking that he'd lose another deputy, this one through no fault of his own.

Ducking more lead and watching for a chance to bring his adversaries under fire, the sheriff wondered which oil company had sent this bunch to kill him. Was another force moving against the Circle H while gunmen dealt with Ransom at the county seat?

He'd issued challenges to both Baker and Jamison, by implication threatening the men behind them who were building unimaginable fortunes from the Gulf's oil boom. From what he knew of the competing rivals, Ransom guessed that neither would stop short of decisive victory, no matter who suffered or died in that pursuit.

They'd proved that much by killing Marshal Henshaw in a challenge to the U.S. government itself, and likely with collusion from a pack of money-hungry politicians stretching from Austin to the District of Columbia.

But if Ransom survived this night, he was determined that their depredations would end here, no matter what grim steps he had to take.

Survival first, and then . . .

He shouted to his enemies, "Come on then, trash! Take your best shot and see what happens next."

Another storm of bullets answered him, making the sheriff wish he still believed wholeheartedly in anything beyond this earthly life, some force that he could ask for help in need.

But this time, Noah Ransom figured, he was on his own with no one but Ace Carter to pitch in against their common enemies.

THE CIRCLE H

Braddock didn't enter the larger barn as he slid into cover there, preferring to defend it as a roving sniper rather than slipping inside to check his dun and the other animals. He couldn't stop the Pinkertons from firing random shots into the barn, but it might only make things worse if he opened the building's double doors and risked admitting enemies.

As if in answer to his silent thought, he heard a bullet strike the wall some six or seven feet behind him, either a stray shot or fired by someone who had trouble with directing rounds toward man-sized targets in the night. A quick visual sweep along that portion of the property revealed no lurking enemies, and Braddock knew the bullet could have come from one of Lucius Haverstock's ranch hands, either a clumsy miss or someone simply making noise to keep the raiders moving and off-balance.

Either way, he needed clear-cut targets before wasting ammunition he couldn't afford to spare.

A rider galloped past without detecting Braddock where he crouched in shadow, but the former Ranger thought he recognized one of the cowboys Haverstock employed and held his fire. A moment later he heard more hoofbeats, maybe pursuing the rider who had just passed him, and this time the faces didn't spark even the faintest memory.

Not roughnecks from the derricks, whom he guessed would either be in hiding now or fighting for the Circle H as grounded infantry rather than makeshift cavalry. Deciding on his course of action in a heartbeat, Braddock raised his Winchester and sighted down its barrel toward the nearer of the two horsemen.

He had fired only one shot so far, which left another fourteen for the Winchester and six in his Peacemaker's cylinder before any reloading was required. Braddock squeezed off his second shot on pure instinct, the .44 slug lifting his selected target from the saddle of his straining mount and dropping him into a boneless heap in the dust the horse's hooves had raised.

Working the rifle's lever, Braddock shifted his position, fired again, and caught the second gunman as he started to react, raising the pistol in his right hand, seeking someone—anyone—he could eliminate for taking down his friend. Braddock's next round caught him beneath his grizzled chin and must have clipped a vertebrae, the way he suddenly went limp and sprawled out of his saddle to the left. One of the gunman's boots got caught in its stirrup and dragged him out of sight, a wail emerging from his ruptured throat.

Two more Pinkertons down, but how many remained in action?

The only way to answer that was moving out to track them down while trying not to stop a bullet on the way.

LIBERTY

Emery Grimm recovered from his stunning fall, spat road dust while he struggled onto hands and knees, finding his horse long gone and another of his men—Jules Alvord—sprawled out lifeless in the street. Larry Ringo was firing at the deputy, crouched in his hidey-hole, while Cullen Diehl and Frank Colcord were dealing with a late arrival on the scene.

A second glance told Grimm the man confronting them was Sheriff Ransom, who he'd been dispatched to kill. Now, having made a hash of that, Emery had a second chance to put things right and possibly escape before a mob of townsfolk gathered, working up the nerve to riddle him with lead or string him up, dispensing with the small formality of a trial.

Shoving that thought aside, Grimm started crawling toward a nearby water trough and hitching post that would provide minimal cover while he tried to nail his man. Frustration gripped him as the sheriff kicked his way inside a feed store labeled JACKSON'S, momentarily concealed from view.

The good news: Grimm knew where he was, well separated from his deputy farther along the block and trapped inside the shop unless he high-tailed it out the backdoor and took off into the night.

Don't let him be a yellowbelly, Grimm thought. *Stand and fight, lawman. Just long enough for me to take you down.*

From there, he'd simply have to find a horse, skedaddle out of town, and hasten back to Beaumont with the news that he'd succeeded where the previous attempts by Mr. Jamison had failed.

That ought to be worth something, Grimm surmised, if he could pull it off and manage to escape from Liberty without some townie getting off a lucky shot and dropping him.

"Just take it one step at a time," Grimm muttered to himself. "And wrap it up as soon as possible."

But he had *two* lawmen to cope with now, and that doubled the odds against success. While he was dealing with the sheriff, what would stop the deputy from sneaking up behind him?

Two-gun Larry Ringo for a start if he could take care of the deputy himself. Plus Diehl and Colcord if they kept their wits about them and assist him. Four-on-two made decent odds for Grimm to work with, but—

As if his thought had drawn down trouble like a lightning rod, Grimm saw a muzzle flash inside the feed store and Frank Colcord toppled from his saddle, landing with a dull *thud* of finality before his mount bolted away.

Which left Alvord and Ringo, both still firing, getting nowhere with their targets under cover, but at least the racket they were making covered Grimm as he began to crawl on all fours toward the boardwalk and the shop where Sheriff Ransom was concealed.

THE CIRCLE H

Braddock moved along the barn's wall, pocked with bullet holes, keeping his head down as he covered ground in the direction of the building's northeast corner, watching out for enemies along the way.

His Winchester was down to ten rounds now— another clean kill and a miss—and the ex-Ranger was averse to wasting them on any shot that wasn't virtually guaranteed to shift the odds between the spread's defenders and the Pinkertons who'd come to kill or wound as many of them as possible. It seemed to him that fewer hostile guns were firing now, but Braddock wasn't taking any chances while a threat of any kind remained.

He guessed the raiders had been sent to murder Lucius Haverstock and that he might rank second on their list of targets, after he and Sheriff Ransom had confronted the prime movers of both Gulf and Standard Oil that afternoon. He'd been prepared for any come-back stemming from those conversations, but whichever oilman was responsible, the move in force had still come as a rude surprise.

Each escalation in the struggle raised its danger level, but the other side of that coin was a whittling down of hostile ranks, whichever company might be involved. Despite each firm's resources in the Lone Star State, Braddock presumed the number of their hired guns on retainer must be limited and each so-called detective lost reduced their strength, at least until fresh reinforce-ments could arrive.

Clearing his mind, Braddock approached the north-west corner of the barn and froze there, at the sound of muffled voices arguing.

"I've had enough of this," one said.

"You gonna tell Hal Baker that?" the other challenged.

"Baker don't care what happens to us, Ab, as long as he keeps wallowing in crude down here."

"So, what about the brothers in Chicago?" asked the one addressed as Ab.

"To hell with 'em," the other answered back. "They wanna dock my salary, so what? I can't spend any of their money if I'm dead."

"Dock you?" the other said. "How 'bout if they decide to shut you up for good?"

"Who's gonna do that?" Ab replied, a sharp edge to his voice. "Would that be you, Warren?"

Before Warren could answer, Braddock edged around the corner, shouldering his rifle. "No," he interrupted their debate. "That would be me."

Both raiders spun to face him, raising weapons, but they weren't near fast enough. Braddock's first shot, directed toward the shooter on his left, drilled through the target's forehead, lifting off his Stetson in a spray of vital fluids, spattering his friend.

Before the other—Ab or Warren, made no difference —recovered from that shock, Braddock had worked his rifle's lever and squeezed off a second shot, punching a clean hole in the raider's chest from ten feet out. The impact pitched his target over backward, bootheels drumming on the sod before his body trembled and lay still.

Two less to think about as Braddock moved on, covering more ground.

Continuing the hunt.

LIBERTY

Sheriff Ransom craned his neck to see outside, beyond the feed store's shattered window, bags and kegs spilling their aromatic contents on the hardwood floor from bullet holes. He thought about Bert Jackson's anger when he saw the mess, wondered again if Bert would file a damage claim against the county, then dismissed that thought as pointless with the battle still in progress.

From the glimpse he'd managed, Ransom calculated that at least two Pinkertons were still alive out front, but there was no call yet for celebration in the shifting tide of combat. Even as that thought took shape, he heard a clatter of hoofbeats approaching, guessing that no townsmen would have mounted up and ridden to assist him in the middle of a raging fight.

So, reinforcements for the other side, then, which increased the odds against himself and Ace Carter. As validation of that guess, a voice the sheriff didn't recognize called out, "What in blue blazes are you chuckleheads up to?"

A shot from Carter's general direction drew a yelp of pain from one of the arriving horsemen, followed by a *thump* as he spilled from his saddle to the ground outside. Ransom fired off a wild round of his own, not aiming properly, and heard a window shatter on the far side of the street.

More damage and another bill, he thought, which meant no more to Ransom at that moment than the price of tea in far-off China. Hearing voices and the sound of riders scrambling from their saddles, Ransom risked another look outside, cocking his rifle in the process, counting half a dozen enemies at least and guessing that was on the low side.

Instead of sighting down on one of them he risked a shout to Carter, hoping that his deputy could hear him over the commotion of gunfire. "Ace!" Ransom shouted. "Are you still with me?"

"So far, Sheriff," his deputy replied, immediately drawing more fire from the Pinkertons.

"Hang on, I'm coming your way," Ransom offered, hoping that would keep his enemies distracted, covering the feed store's entrance while he carried out another plan that had occurred to him.

Most of the shops along the thoroughfare had two doors, front and back. Ducking below an outside shooter's line of sight, Ransom moved through the feed store to its rear exit, unlocked that door from the inside, and slipped out into the moonlit night, pacing along the backside of the shops that stood between Jackson's and where he thought Ace Carter had concealed himself inside the hardware store.

No doubt another mess by now, to salvage later if they managed to survive this evening.

He reached the door he sought, rapped lightly on in, then a little louder when his first knocking brought no response. The second time around, Ace answered from the inside, not far from the doorway, voice low-pitched and asking, "Who in hell is that?"

"It's Noah," Ransom told him, knowing any fool could use his rank and try to bluff it out, but Carter still required convincing.

"Where's the last place we went fishing?" he demanded.

"Sutton's creek," Ransom replied, grateful when Ace unlocked the door. He didn't even mind the double-barreled shotgun pointed at his face.

"You want to point that somewhere else?" he asked his deputy. "Then maybe we can try to wrap this up."

THE CIRCLE H

Cole Yarberry knelt close beside Nat Rudabaugh, hiding behind a privy whose noxious aroma fairly turned Cole's stomach. Normally that wouldn't have disturbed him much, just ducking in and out to do his necessary business, but tonight had come apart on him and what Nat had reported to him seconds earlier gave Yarberry the shakes.

"You're wrong," he challenged Rudabaugh, not daring even now to come right out and tell Nat he was lying.

"You think so? When did you see Crowther last?"

Cole thought about that, couldn't pin it down. "I rode in right behind him," Yarberry replied, "then we got separated when the shooting started. Haven't seen him since."

"Well, *I* have," Rudabaugh hissed back at him, keeping his voice down. "Seen him shot right off his stallion by at least one sniper, maybe more."

A rising surge of panic gripped Cole then. The raid had come unraveled right away, just minutes after Cletus fired the first shot from his fancy European gun to get things started, and each passing moment only seemed to make things worse.

"Well, are you sure he's dead?" Cole challenged his companion.

"Didn't make a peep when he went down," Nat answered back. "Just hit the ground and lay there like a sack of spuds."

That sickened Yarberry and scared him spitless. Finally he found his voice and said, "I seen a couple others hit, myself. Stephens and Hume. They're either dead or on the way there."

"Damn!" said Rudabaugh. "That tears it. Close to one in four of us already down and out. The only thing makes sense to me is clearing out of here, pronto."

Yarberry frowned at that. "And then what?" he demanded. "What do we tell Mr. Baker?"

"Tell 'im nothing," Nat responded. "We go back to Anahuac without the others, who you think he's gonna blame for all of this?"

"How 'bout himself?" Cole asked. "It was a harebrained scheme to start with and he never thought it through."

"When was the last time you told any kinda rich man he was wrong, much less stupid? First thing he's gonna do is plant us in a hole to shut us up."

"So what's your plan then?" Yarberry demanded.

"Get to hell and gone away from here," said Rudabaugh. "Haverstock's men ain't taking inventory, Cole. What's one or two less men when they start counting bodies?"

The thought of getting clear excited Yarberry, until his mind coughed up another problem. "I got no idea what's happened to my horse by now," he said.

"Me neither," Nat replied. "So what? This was a cattle ranch before they started pumping oil, right? Horses ain't exactly scarce."

Cole thought about that for another moment, but he didn't really need persuasion.

"All right, then," he said. "Let's do it!"

He and Rudabaugh were rising cautiously, Yarberry thinking that they could find mounts inside the barn where they'd been sheltering, until a stranger stepped from out of the shadows, brandishing a Winchester.

"Not so fast, boys," he cautioned both of them. "If you've got any brains between you, drop those guns."

LIBERTY

Emery Grimm was still trying to catch his breath as he crawled toward the boardwalk, gasping like a catfish out of water. Shouting orders at his riders who were still alive took more wind than he had to spare, but by the time he reached a hitching rail and hauled himself upright, Grimm reckoned he could manage it.

Six Pinkertons were still alive and fighting, less than he'd expected until he spotted Virgil Ford lying face down, unmoving in the street. Grimm found that he had lost his rifle when he toppled from his horse, long gone now, but found his Colt still snug inside its holster, kept there by its hammer thong. He drew it, looked around, and saw his men were split into two groups of three, only George Loving still on horseback, while the others ducked and dodged, unloading at two shops with three doors in between them, where he guessed the lawmen had concealed themselves.

From sundry places in the dark townsfolk were calling back and forth to one another, excited gibberish that Grimm couldn't make out with any clarity, but he supposed they would be fetching weapons, working up the nerve to rally and defend their town. Unless Grimm got his business done and managed to collect the raiding party's animals for an escape, the scene could quickly turn into a massacre.

And Emery knew that he would be on the losing end.

He raised his voice, a croak at first but swiftly growing stronger, to be heard over the gunfire echoing along the thoroughfare.

"Cease fire!" he shouted. "Dammit, hold up now!"

Finally his riders got the message, some reloading pistols hastily while others crouched or knelt and eyed the storefronts pocked with bullet holes, their window glass cleared out of shot-up frames. They waited, eyes flicking between their leader and the places where they'd last met fire from living enemies.

The sheriff and his deputy, two targets still outnumbered more than three to one.

"Where are they?" Emery demanded. "Come on! Somebody speak up."

The answer came from Larry Ringo, pointing off to left and right with his two pistols. "In the feed store," he told Grimm, "and in this hardware store."

"You're sure about that?" Grimm demanded.

"Sure as can be. Haven't seen 'em poke their heads out."

"Well then, Larry, Cullen, Eaton, take the feed store," Emery instructed. "McCarty, George, and Musgrove, move in on the hardware joint."

It was poor practice, using names aloud during a raid, but Grimm felt confident the two law dogs wouldn't survive to offer any evidence in court. As for the townsmen, they were out of earshot, yammering among themselves, and couldn't hear him anyway.

His agents hesitated long enough for Grimm to feel a surge of irritation. "You all heard me!" he called out to them. "Get moving now. We need to wrap this up."

Reluctantly, the three-man teams moved forward, weapons poised, none of them firing yet. The three off to their leader's left reached their objective first and bulled their way inside, sweeping the shop's interior with wary eyes and gun muzzles. No shooting, though, and an alarm bell started going off inside Grimm's head before one of them stuck his head out, telling Emery, "Hey, boss, there ain't nobody here!"

A curse was forming on Grimm's lips as hellfire

suddenly erupted from the hardware store, *two* guns—a rifle and a twelve-gauge by the sound of it—blasting his three men on the sidewalk. Choking on the epithet, Emery saw Jesse McCarty, George Loving, and Mike Musgrove blown backwards off the sidewalk, tumbling like three tailor's dummies caught up on a twister.

Dropping to his knees, Grimm shouted at the three survivors, "Get back here! One of them slipped around you! Both of 'em are in the hardware store!"

Ringo, Diehl, and Eaton took their time about advancing, gaping at the bodies of their fellow Pinkertons now twitching in their death throes on the street. Clearly, no one among them wanted to lead the charge after their numbers had been whittled down by eight without eliminating either of the lawmen.

Grimm knew how they felt but couldn't let his nerves paralyze him in the face of danger when he'd come this far. Rising, he lurched around the hitching post and stepped onto the boardwalk, understanding what some people meant by saying that their hearts were in their throats.

Somehow Grimm regained his voice, cocking the Colt he hadn't fired so far tonight, and shouted at his men, "Come on, you slowpokes! Now or never!"

And with that, he charged across the threshold of the hardware store.

THE CIRCLE H

In retrospect, Braddock decided that the Pinkertons hiding behind the barn indeed were short on brains. Both must have figured they could shade him, even taken by surprise, one lifting his rifle while the other raised a six-gun, drawing back its hammer with his thumb.

It was a coin toss, from a range of fifteen feet or less, which one was more likely to constitute the greater threat. On impulse, Braddock shot the rifleman, his bullet glancing off the weapon's frame before it tore into the shooter's jaw, his lower face imploding from the impact with a spray of gore that doused the pistolero on his left.

That shocked the other Pinkerton and spoiled his shot, a .45 slug whispering past Braddock's ear and off into the night. Before his adversary had a chance to cock and fire his single-action piece again, Braddock had worked his rifle's lever, swiveled to his right, and fired a shot into the detective's chest at something close to point-blank range. The .44-40's impact toppled his adversary over backward with a rush of breath from emptied lungs and stretched him out at Braddock's feet.

All done.

And how many raiders remaining on the ranch?

Braddock paused long enough to strip the freshly dead of their firearms, unloaded each in turn, and tossed the guns off into darkness for later recovery, whichever way the battle went. That done, he set off toward the house in search of Lucius Haverstock, hoping to find the master of the Circle H alive and in command.

14

THE CIRCLE H

BRADDOCK INDEED FOUND HAVERSTOCK ALIVE, THOUGH he was bleeding from a fresh scalp wound that had occurred since they last parted company.

The rancher-oilman guessed what Braddock must be thinking, smiled and said, "I'm fine. Turns out my head is harder than it looks."

I could have guessed that Braddock thought, but kept it to himself.

Gunfire still popped and crackled in the night, around the fringes of the area where Braddock stood with Haverstock, surveying scattered bodies around the outbuildings.

"Just mopping up," said Haverstock.

"The head count?" Braddock asked, knowing the question might be premature.

"Still waiting on it," Haverstock replied. "If some of them turn tail and run for home, that's fine with me."

"And if whoever sent them wants to try again?"

"We won't run out of ammunition for a while."

"And what about these here?" asked Braddock, with a sweeping gesture toward the ground littered with cadavers.

Haverstock considered that. "I may send to town for Eulon Wells, or maybe haul them off beyond my property and dump them. Coyotes need to eat, the same as worms," he added, with a twisted smile.

Braddock was in no mood to join in repartee just now. Leaving Haverstock to work out the logistics of disposal, hopefully with some nod toward his conscience, Braddock said, "I've got a hunch whoever sent these fellas here might take a run at Liberty tonight, as well."

"Wouldn't surprise me," Haverstock replied, cocking his head to listen as the scattered gunfire petered out and died away. "You feel a debt toward Noah Ransom?"

"Not exactly," Braddock answered, "but we called on Jamison and Baker as a team. I'm thinking that we may have forced somebody's hand instead of warning them away."

A nod from Haverstock signaled agreement. "And you want to check on Noah. Make sure he's all right?"

"I'd feel better about it," Braddock granted.

"Off you go, then. From the sound of it, you won't be needed anymore tonight."

"If you're sure . . ."

"*No hay problema*, as they say south of the border," Haverstock replied. "Your dun likely wants to stretch his legs a bit after this racket, anyhow."

"I'll be back sometime tomorrow," Braddock said.

"Whatever suits you. We can talk about our options then, or if you're tired of fighting Pinkertons we'll settle up and you can move on."

Braddock jogged back toward the bunkhouse for his saddlebags, then moved on to the barn. He found his horse relaxing in its stall now that the killing storm had passed. It seemed happy to see him, standing stock-still as he saddled it and stowed his Winchester, freshly reloaded, in its leather sheath.

The last familiar face that Braddock saw before he left the ranch was Blake Drury's. The cowboy waved to him as he passed by on his way to the main gate. There seemed to be nothing worth saying since the tide of mayhem that had washed over the Circle H, and Braddock left the cowhand to his sentry's duty undisturbed.

Clearing the main gate felt like regaining his freedom, even though he knew that he would be returning to the spread tomorrow, whether to prepare for more attacks or just collect the pay he'd earned so far. Braddock would leave that choice to Lucius Haverstock, as long as his employer didn't plan on waging private war outside the law.

In Braddock's mind there was and always would be a clear line between killing in self-defense and signing on for an assassination.

Once beyond the gate, he let the dun put on speed toward Liberty, hoping his intuition had been wrong and he'd arrive to find the townsfolk safe.

But something told the former Ranger that his long night was not over yet.

LIBERTY

Noah Ransom saw one of the Pinkertons he recognized from Roger Jamison's office, although the man looked

391

nothing like he had before, during the confrontation in Beaumont. Instead of dressing nattily, he wore clothes fit for riding and appeared as if he'd rolled around in dirt before he rushed the hardware store.

Likewise, instead of covering his pistol with a suit jacket, he had the six-gun in his hand and blazing as he cleared the threshold, firing like a madman, shouting curses as he tried to bring down targets he could not have clearly seen.

The sheriff and his deputy were hunkered down behind stout kegs of nails, already bullet-punctured, with their shiny contents dribbling out onto the wooden floor. A bullet snapped by Noah Ransom's head, inches to spare, before he got his rifle sights lined up and slid his index finger through the weapon's trigger guard. Across the narrow aisle from him, Ace Carter had reloaded his shotgun and squeezed one barrel off—a smoky thunderclap—just as the sheriff fired from four or five yards at the charging Pinkerton.

Their one-two punch lifted Emery Grimm completely off his feet and blew him backwards, out the door, rolling across the sidewalk there before his body came to rest against a water trough. Ransom had seen enough corpses to know the raider wouldn't rise again under his own power, unless perhaps on Judgment Day.

In which case, Ransom guessed, he would be in for disappointment at the end result.

Outside the hardware store and out of sight, Ransom heard unfamiliar voices jabbering in mock whispers. He calculated that the Pinkertons still standing were debating how they should proceed—perhaps whether they should turn tail and flee after seeing their leader slain. He couldn't make out any of their words, aside from random curses, but he *did* hear weapons being reloaded and cocked, presumably in preparation for another rush at the bullet-riddled store.

He met Ace Carter's eyes across the aisle that separated them and mouthed the words "Stand ready" to his deputy. Carter responded with a nod, his scattergun already primed with two more buckshot rounds, which Ransom guessed would be about the last Asa had carried with him when he let the sheriff's office earlier.

However many foes remained—approximately six to eight if Ransom had it right from glimpses of them on the street—they could annihilate two lawmen if they played their cards right, willing to forsake more lives in the accomplishment of what they'd come to do in Liberty this night.

At least, now that he'd seen and finished off Emery Grimm, Ransom knew which oilman to blame for the assault. If he survived the night he would be burning up the wires to Austin and to Washington, D.C., demanding that charges be filed against Roger Jamison, whether they stuck in court or not.

But in the meantime . . .

With a scuttling rush of boots on weathered sidewalk boards, the Pinkertons attacked.

APPROACHING LIBERTY, G.W. Braddock heard the *pop* and *crack* of gunfire carried to him on the night breeze, still the best part of a mile ahead, telling him he had run out of time. A nudge was all his horse required to pick up speed, seemingly anxious to rejoin the very sort of action it had recently escaped back at the Circle H.

Arriving late didn't mean he was *too* late, but unbidden images of Noah Ransom and his sole remaining deputy in town filled Braddock's mind, depicting them face down and bullet-riddled by another small army of raiders sent by one foe or another in a bid to wipe the local slate clean and be done with it.

As Braddock reached the city limits he removed his rifle from its saddle boot and held it braced across his thighs with his right hand, his left holding the dun's reins. The street seemed clear at first, but as he neared the sounds of battle he saw townsfolk, mostly men, emerging from their residences, some with weapons, others peering out of upstairs windows in an effort to make sense of what was happening.

At one point Braddock passed three men grouped on a street corner and thought he heard one of them call out toward him, "This is your fault!" Rather than confronting them and wasting further time, he rode on toward the source of rapid gunfire, trying to anticipate what he would find upon arrival.

If a fight was still continuing, it had to mean that either Ransom or his deputy could still defend the town, at least to some extent. Whether he would find one of both alive—or maybe wounded now—remained a mystery, but he would pitch in and provide whatever aid he could supply.

And failing that there was revenge.

THE RISKS of a career in law enforcement were no mystery to Noah Ransom. He had faced death in the past, killed men, and had been shot himself on one occasion, though it didn't come to much. This was the first occasion, though, where he had faced a gang of gunmen, well equipped and seemingly determined, who were motivated by the solid intent of killing him.

He didn't like the feeling and it wasn't over yet.

The Pinkertons had hatched a plan of sorts for storming the hardware store. It was a scheme suited to their declining numbers, dangerous but feasible if they assumed that Ransom and his deputy were running low on ammunition in the shop.

Ransom's best hope, just now, was that they hadn't thought to send a man or two around behind the store to come in through the back, thus catching him and Carter in a crossfire they couldn't survive.

But hoping got the sheriff nowhere in his present situation.

All that he could do was fight to stay alive.

His adversaries had been wise enough to make their final dash in pairs, knowing a larger clutch of men would jam up in the shop's doorway and wind up being cut to pieces there while grappling for a way inside. Once they were in the store and fanning out to form a firing squad, Ransom knew that his final moments would be numbered and his doom assured.

From out of nowhere came a pang of sorrow for Ace Carter, wishing that the deputy hadn't been sucked into this fight he hadn't bargained for.

This situation was on Ransom's shoulders and the weight of it might kill him yet.

Ransom didn't recognize the shadowed faces of his would-be murderers as they entered the hardware store, although he guessed he might have passed some on the streets of Liberty at one time or another without realizing it. Tonight he cared no more for individual identities than for their taste in clothes or breakfast fare.

These men had come to kill him and he meant to stop them by whatever means he could.

Ace Carter beat him to it, triggering a twelve-gauge blast to greet the first pair through the door. His buckshot pellets gutted one of them and clipped the other's right arm, forcing him to drop one of the two revolvers he was firing aimlessly around the shop. Cursing, the wounded raider lurched off to his left, raising his second six-gun, just as Noah Ransom found his mark and put a bullet through the mercenary's face.

The force of that shot pitched his dying adversary backwards, tumbling through the shattered ruins of the front window. Undeterred, the other Pinkertons continued in their mad rush forward, firing over and around each other as they came, trusting dumb luck to let them score a telling hit.

Ace Carter cut loose with the second barrel of his scattergun, toppling another enemy, and then, with no time to reload it, dropped the shoulder gun to draw the Smith & Wesson Model 3 Schofield he carried tied down on his right-hand side. The pistol was a single-action model first adopted by the U.S. Cavalry a quarter of a century before, chambered for man-stopping .44-caliber rounds. Hs draw was fast enough to let him wing the fourth man through the shop's doorway before Ransom lined up his rifle for the killing shot.

So far, so good, if that dismissive phrase could be applied to such a massacre. Looking beyond the doorway jammed with fallen bodies now, Ransom saw four more gunmen lingering outside, considering their options.

In the next split second one of them was leaping through the shattered window of the hardware shop, firing a lever-action rifle as he came.

BRADDOCK SAW the skirmish underway when he was still a long block from arriving on the scene. Rather than risk his dun riding up behind the raiders, he reined in and left it standing in the street, while he advanced on foot, holding his rifle at the ready.

From a half block out, he had no doubt of what was happening. Four shooters had somebody trapped inside a hardware store, firing through its door and window, trying to get past the first line of defense within. As he approached, one of the gunmen took a hit and lurched back through the window frame, fell heavily on the wooden sidewalk, and began struggling to rise.

Braddock took care of that with one clean shot from his Winchester, clearing the attacker's mind of all aggressive thoughts, along with half the normal contents of his skull. The man collapsed into a heap, reminding Braddock of a puppet with its strings cut, folding in upon itself as if it had no skeleton.

That left three raiders still alive and in the fight, one of them turning to face Braddock while his two companions rushed the hardware store again, one through the doorway heaped with bodies and the other leaping through its open window frame facing the thoroughfare.

Braddock put those two out of mind for now and concentrated on the one who'd chosen him. The Pinkerton got off a snap-shot from the hip that came uncomfortably close to Braddock's face, making the former Ranger drop into a kneeling posture while he sighted quickly down his rifle's barrel. When the raider fired again their guns went off in tandem, bullets passing in midair from twenty feet or so apart.

Braddock was slightly faster that time, and more

accurate, drilling his adversary's chest, while the incoming round passed inches overhead. The impact of his .44-40 on flesh and bone lifted the pistolero off his feet and dropped him sprawling on his back, his bootheels drumming on the street until the final vestiges of life ran out.

As Braddock rose to stand erect a final flurry of gunfire erupted from the hardware store. He jogged in that direction, worried about Sheriff Ransom and whoever else was trapped inside, but not reckless enough to risk his life unnecessarily. When he was halfway to the shop one of the Pinkertons who'd made his way inside came lurching through the half-blocked doorway, staggering, his face a mask of blood, then dropped into a heap on the sidewalk.

The other never made it out at all, which didn't prove that he was dead. Slowing as he approached the shop, working the lever on his rifle one last time, Braddock called out, "Hello inside the store! Who's there?"

A now-familiar voice came back at him. "Is that you, Braddock?"

"Running late," he answered, shoulders slumping with relief.

Ransom emerged, not through the doorway, but by stepping through the window frame. Behind him came a younger man whose tin star marked him as a county deputy.

"I thought you'd have your hands full at the Circle H," said Ransom.

"Did," Braddock agreed, "and then we didn't. Thought I'd better see if Gulf or Standard took a run at you to balance out the books."

Ransom glanced down, surveyed the nearest corpse

and forced a smile as he replied, "I'd say their books are in the red tonight."

No time for levity, perhaps, but in the wake of battle men were prone to laugh at things which otherwise might make them weep.

"So what's the next step?" Braddock asked the sheriff.

Ransom looked past him, down the street, where townspeople were gathering, then making way for two figures shoving their way past troubled citizens.

"Next," Ransom said, "we get to hear the city fathers blow off steam."

MAYOR WITHERS AND TOM DALEY, Justice of the Peace, were in high dudgeon as they approached the bullet-riddled hardware store. Ransom faced the two public officials, saying, "We tried to save the shop as best we could. The Pinkertons had something else in mind."

"*Save* it?" Daley raged. "It's *ruined*, Sheriff. Absolutely ruined!"

"Nothing that can't be fixed up," Ransom replied.

"Why, you—"

The mayor's voice interrupted his companion, fairly sneering as he asked, "How many dead this time, Ransom?"

"No one who didn't try to kill me or my deputy," Ransom replied. "I'd say we won this round."

"You call this *winning*?" Withers challenged him. "This is a massacre!"

At that, Ransom's young deputy chimed in. "I guess you're rather have two lawmen dead and let the killers ride away without a scratch?"

"I'm not addressing you," Mayor Withers fumed.

"Then talk to me," said Ransom, interrupting him. "I'm sheriff of this county and you're too damned tight to hire a city marshal, so you've passed enforcement of the local law to me."

Withers looked as if he might suffer a bout of apoplexy where he stood, trembling, his fat face turning crimson. "You may be the sheriff *now*," he answered back, "but when I'm through with you—"

"I'll still be sheriff," Ransom cut him off again. "You have no power to remove me, but feel free to nag the governor about it if you want to. When he hears my side and sends an auditor around to check your bank account, you may not like what he uncovers." Half turning toward Daley, Ransom added, "Either one of you."

The livid mayor seemed to be choking now. "I . . . I . . ."

Ransom let him off the hook, saying, "Or you can find someone else to run against me at the next election. That's the privilege of any citizen. Pick someone you can bully to your heart's content and run that by the voters. Of course, by then, they may have thoughts about replacing you as mayor."

"You're going to regret this, Sheriff," old Tom Daley offered in a weak rejoinder.

"I already do," Ransom replied. "Which doesn't mean my job is finished yet."

The mayor and Daley, both looking deflated, turned, and stalked off toward the crowd of shaken townspeople, who instantly surrounded them.

"I need a drink right now, and supper feels like it was yesterday," Ransom said. "You want to come along?"

"Don't mind if I do," replied Braddock.

BEAUMONT

The telephone woke Roger Jamison from a delightful dream of oil wells gushing crude, the cascade turning into greenbacks in midair, cascading through a skylight set into the roof of a palatial bank where Jamison was the proprietor and sole depositor, wealthy beyond imagining and getting richer by the moment from that deluge of thousand dollar bills.

Scowling at the disturbance of his reverie, he lifted the receiver, leaning toward the telephone's mouthpiece, and said a gruff "Hello?"

He recognized the distant voice that answered him across some sixteen hundred miles of crackling air. "We have one question for you, Roger."

We meaning the board of Standard Oil, his lords and masters.

"Yes, sir?"

"Have you completely lost your mind?" the voice demanded, offering no hint of levity.

"Excuse me, sir?"

"We keep a close eye on our various investments, Roger. We are informed of matters as they happen—and when they go wrong. You've been a busy boy, sending your Pinkertons around the countryside down there, to Liberty and elsewhere. Now they're dead, Chicago's in a snit, demanding recompense and concealment of their own involvement in your schemes."

The phrase *to Liberty and elsewhere* baffled Jamison. Trying to organize his thoughts, he said, "Sir, I sent men to deal with a small problem in the county seat next door. As to the rest of it—"

401

"A *small problem* you say? Is that your notion of a joke, Roger?"

"No, sir. I—"

"Twelve men dead in Liberty tonight. Another thirteen at the Circle H, and all you have to show for it—"

"The Circle H?" Jamison felt as if his head were spinning. "Sir, I can assure you—"

"Shut your mouth and *listen*, Jamison! We want this mess settled with no more bad publicity. Settled to our advantage without any further loss of life. If you can't handle that, just say so, and we'll find someone who can."

"I understand completely, sir," said Jamison.

"I hope so, for your sake."

The sudden humming in his ear told Jamison that the connection had been severed at the caller's end. A sudden surge of fury almost made him fling the telephone across his spacious bedroom, but he stopped himself in time to think twice, then begin to dial another number stored within his memory.

There still might be a way to save himself if he was willing to eat crow.

It seemed a small price if it kept him gainfully employed—and breathing, too.

Yes, there was always that.

LIBERTY

Two stiff whiskies with a beer back at the Lucky Strike helped Braddock unwind sufficiently to think of supper. Still behind the bar—the only place Braddock had ever seen him—Bob Travis made no inquiries about what had happened earlier, though half a dozen other customers cast cautious glances toward where Braddock stood with Noah Ransom, carefully ignoring them.

It felt late when they took their leave from the saloon but Braddock didn't check his pocket watch until they'd reached O'Grady's Restaurant and found it shut up tight, no lights showing inside. The same proved to be true at La Taberna, which served Mexican food with its beer and tequila, driving home the point that Liberty—except for Eulon Well's mortuary—had shut down this night while townsfolk sheltered in their homes behind closed blinds.

"Forget it," Ransom said, as they began the trek back to his house. "I've got a couple beefsteaks in the icebox. And you might as well sleep over while you're at it."

"Just as well," Braddock agreed. "I doubt that I'd be welcome at the Palace anyhow."

"Their loss."

"And what about tomorrow?" Braddock asked his unexpected host.

"We get some breakfast, then I'm heading for the Circle H to see about the damage you described out there. I need to find out if those Pinkertons were taking orders from the same fella who sent the bunch in town."

"You doubt it?" Braddock asked.

"Can't say just yet. We braced the men in charge of both oil companies, each with a gang of mercenaries on his payroll. Maybe it was all one guy's idea, or they were acting separately. Hell, for all I know they tossed a coin and split the difference."

"And neither one's inside your jurisdiction," Braddock said, knowing it must have crossed the sheriff's mind already. "Do you have a way around that?"

"I'll be starting off with telegrams to Austin, asking for some Rangers, trying to contact the U.S. Marshal, wherever he's dallying these days. If need be, I can rattle the attorney general's cage."

"Which one?" Braddock inquired.

"Both of them," Ransom said, cracking a smile. "I'll start with Austin first, then back that up with a request for help from Washington. If I get lucky, someone, somewhere, might take time to read a telegram."

"And if they don't appreciate it?"

Ransom shrugged. "The governor can still remove me, like I told our precious mayor, but aside from that I'll keep on making noise until somebody pays attention. I might even get Ed Farnsworth, owner of our local newspaper, *The Libertarian*, to get some of our citizens riled up in self-defense, demanding answers."

"Which would take some of the heat off you," Braddock observed.

"As long as it stops killing in the streets, I'm satisfied. Whether the men behind all this wind up in court or not, behind a battery of high-priced lawyers, may not make a difference. Big companies, from what I understand, hate bad publicity worse than a dirt farmer hates drought."

"I'll ride out with you in the morning then," Braddock allowed. "If nothing else, I've got some wages to collect."

EPILOGUE

THE CIRCLE H

"YOU'D NEVER KNOW THAT ANYTHING WENT ON OUT HERE last night," said Sheriff Ransom as they neared the spread's main gate. "Except for them, I guess."

Two weary-looking horsemen, one of them Blake Drury, sat astride their animals outside the gate, with Winchesters in hand, relaxing as they recognized the sheriff and Braddock drawing near. Pausing to greet the guards, Braddock asked Drury, "What became of last night's visitors?"

Blake made a sour face. Answered, "The boss decided not to bother Mr. Wells with 'em. Had us haul 'em off and dump 'em half a mile or so beyond the property. I reckon coyotes have been at 'em overnight. Whatever's left, the buzzards will be circling pretty soon."

Ransom frowned at that news. "It would have helped me to identify them," he declared.

"The boss took care of that, Sheriff," Drury advised. "Got all their badges and whatever else they carried in their pockets just in case you wanted it. All Pinkertons, o' course. Their guns are stored up at the house to . . . what was it he called it, Chet?"

Drury's companion spat tobacco juice into the dust before he said, "To supplement the stock on hand, in case more of 'em come sniffin' around."

"I'll need to see those, too," Ransom advised.

"Ain't up to us, Sheriff," Drury replied. "Go on ahead and see the boss man at his place."

Braddock and Ransom took their time approaching Lucius Haverstock's ranch house, aware that some of his men might be jumpy after last night's battle, prone to shooting first and asking questions later. As it was, nobody tried to stop them, probably assuming that if they had cleared the gate they must have passed inspection by the watchmen posted there.

By daylight, hours after the last shots were fired, it would have taken a discerning eye to note the signs of overnight combat. Obvious bullet holes were visible, scarring the walls of Haverstock's mansion, the barns, and other outbuildings, but with the bodies gone and bloodstains raked over, the damage might have dated back a year or more.

Before they reined in at the house, its owner came out the covered porch, holding a mug of steaming coffee in his left hand, while his right hung near his holstered Smith & Wesson Model 10. Smiling, he greeted them.

"Good morning, Sheriff. Mr. Braddock."

"Rough night, from what I hear," Ransom replied.

"Most of us made it through. I've got two customers for Mr. Wells, although I understand he's busy at the moment."

"Got his hands full, true enough."

"More Pinkertons," said Haverstock, not asking.

"Right again," the sheriff said. "My question is who sent them."

"Well, whoever did, they've learned the error of their ways," the rancher said.

"Not sure I follow you on that," Ransom replied.

"Fact is," said Haverstock, "I had two visitors this morning at the crack of dawn. Risked getting shot to see me on an urgent point of business, coming in with just a single guard."

"And who might they have been?" the sheriff asked, his voice wary.

"A most apologetic pair of businessmen," said Haverstock, "explaining how this all got out of hand and they were keen to make amends."

Braddock could feel the sour churning in his stomach now. He held his tongue and let the county sheriff handle it.

"Amends?" Ransom echoed. "The penalty for murder is a short rope and a long drop, Lucius. Anyone involved in it is culpable. They can't just 'make amends' and wish it all away."

"Their explanation satisfied me, Noah. All about two groups of Pinkertons colluding on their own and taking actions that were absolutely not approved."

"Approved by whom?" Ransom inquired. "I need those names."

"You met them yesterday, I understand. Hal Baker and his good friend Roger Jamison."

Good friend? Braddock couldn't believe his ears. The two competitors had spent months at each other's throats while riding roughshod over anyone whose property obstructed prospecting for oil along the Gulf.

"And they convinced you that they didn't sent the Pinkertons to root you out last night? Or murder me in

Liberty? They knew nothing about the death of Marshal Henshaw either, I suppose?"

"News that appalled them and their own employers in the East," said Haverstock.

Ransom considered that, a grim expression on his face, before he asked, "And did they happen to suggest a price to settle all of that?"

Haverstock flicked his eyes toward Braddock, didn't seem to like what he saw there, and turned back toward the sheriff. "We've agreed upon a mutually beneficial price, I'm pleased to say. With Gulf and Standard joining hands, it raised the ante to a point where I would be plumb loco to reject it."

"So, that's it, then?" The sheriff's tone stopped just a fraction short of mockery.

"All parties satisfied," said Haverstock. "The guilty Pinkertons who acted without due authority from their employers will no longer trouble anyone—that is, unless they raise some kind of ruckus down in Hell."

Although he didn't chew tobacco, Ransom took that opportunity to spit before he said, "Well, *I'm* not satisfied. You can be sure of that. And I'm assuming that the U.S. Marshal's Service won't be satisfied by any backroom deal."

"In fact, we had our conversation in my dining room," said Haverstock. "Both Mr. Jamison and Mr. Baker have assured me that the Pinkertons were acting on their own volition, without orders from the companies they were assigned to protect. Maybe they hoped to curry favor with the oilmen, possibly their bosses in Chicago. Who can say?"

"Now that they're dead, you mean," Ransom replied.

"Which was their sad, misguided choice, invading private property. May I assume the raiders who went after you last night are also being boxed up as we speak?"

"You may *assume* that I'll be looking deeper into this," said Ransom. "In the meantime, I'll require whatever you removed from last night's bodies that will help identify them for Chicago and their next of kin."

"Of course. I'll have it fetched straight out to you. And Mr. Braddock, I believe there's still the matter of your pay."

"That's right," Braddock agreed. "It spends the same, I guess, no matter how dirty it is."

The rancher took a roll of bills from his hip pocket, tossed it up to Braddock without bothering to count them out. "That should be more than ample," he allowed.

"With something extra from the Gulf and Standard boys?" Braddock inquired.

"I'm sure I don't know what you mean."

"One thing you might consider that I'm guessing may have slipped your mind," Braddock replied.

"Which is . . .?" asked Haverstock.

"The Pinkertons," Braddock reminded him.

"They should be satisfied with final payments on their contracts."

"I was thinking of the bad publicity they'll get from this, on top of all the other grief they've taken during recent years. I've never met old Allan's sons," said Braddock, "but I hear they don't forget and never figured out how to forgive."

"In which case, they can take it up with Gulf and Standard," Haverstock replied, sounding cocksure.

"They might do that," Braddock allowed. "Or they might want a pound of flesh from whoever allowed those companies to wriggle off the hook."

It made Braddock smile to see the rancher gaping at

him as he turned to Noah Ransom, asking, "Are we done here, Sheriff?"

"For the moment," Random answered. Then, to Haverstock, "But don't think that you've seen the last of me."

Braddock started to turn the dun, then paused to look again at Haverstock, who glared at him.

"You have any more trouble . . . call on somebody else for help," Braddock said.

Then he rode away, eager to get back to some place where the air smelled cleaner.

TAKE A LOOK AT VOLUME FOUR

BY JAMES REASONER

New York Times bestselling author James Reasoner returns with another gritty, fast-moving tale of the Outlaw Ranger.

Lured by the Mexican government's bounty for Native American scalps, a ruthless gang led by serial killer John Grafton roams both sides of the Tex-Mex border, killing hapless travelers and raiding isolated villages, slaying anyone—Native, Hispanic, even dark-haired whites—whose scalps may be translated into cash across the Rio Grande. G.W. Braddock, at loose ends between paying jobs at the moment, teams with a survivor of one massacre to track the killers down and bring them to rough justice, dodging *federales* and rogue tribesmen in the process.

From one adventure to the next, Braddock soon becomes involved in the Chamizal dispute between Mexico and the U.S.. Unclaimed land on the border led to a 385-acre Cordova Island, described as a *"haven of crime"* and smuggling which remained lawless through the years of U.S. Prohibition, and now Braddock is needed to avenge a crime.

Outlaw Ranger, Volume 4 includes: Scalp Hunters and Six-Gun Island.

COMING DECEMBER 2021

ABOUT THE AUTHOR

James Reasoner has been telling tales and spinning yarns as far back as he can remember. He's been doing it professionally for more than 40 years, and during that time, under his own name and dozens of pseudonyms, he's written almost 400 novels and more than 100 shorter pieces of fiction. His books have appeared on the *New York Times*, *USA Today*, and *Publishers Weekly* bestseller lists. He has written Westerns, mysteries, historical sagas, war novels, science fiction and fantasy, and horror fiction.

Growing up in the late Fifties and early Sixties when every other series on television was a Western made him into a lifelong fan of the genre. The Lone Ranger, Roy Rogers, Hopalong Cassidy, Matt Dillon, and John Wayne made quite an impression on him. At the age of 10, he discovered Western novels when he checked out *Single Jack* by Max Brand and *Hopalong Cassidy* (there's that name again!) by Clarence E. Mulford from the library bookmobile that came out every Saturday to the small town in Texas where he lived. He's been reading Westerns ever since, long before he started writing them, and always will.

James Reasoner has also written numerous articles, essays, and book introductions on a variety of topics related to popular culture, including vintage paperbacks and the publishing industry, pulp magazines, comics, movies, and TV. He writes the popular blog *Rough*

Edges and is the founder and moderator of an email group devoted to Western pulp magazines.

He lives in the same small town in Texas where he grew up and is married to the popular mystery novelist Livia J. Washburn, who has also written Westerns under the name L.J. Washburn.